Indestructible

Book One of
The Sanguine Sky Chronicles

Aislin Keeley

Cover design by ©Sarah Hansen, Okay Creations
Chapter heading from Tattoo Designs
Interior design by Aislin Keeley

This book is a work of fiction. Names, characters, places, and incidents either are products of the author's imagination or are used fictitiously. Any resemblance to actual persons, living or dead, events, or locales is entirely coincidental.

Aislin Keeley
Visit my website at www.aislinkeeley.weebly.com

Printed in the United States of America

ISBN: 978-0-9908015-0-4

To Charlene Ansley

You were the first person who made me realize I had stories to tell.

Without your encouragement, none of this would be possible.

CHAPTER 1

"Hey, Alice! When's the last time you got laid?"

Alice Roarke winced at the question. She began to pick up a few items on her desk as heat spread across her cheeks. "And a happy Wednesday to you too, Tina."

"If that's all it takes to make it a happy morning, then Sunday was great as well." Tina sat on the edge of Alice's desk and placed her hand on top of the papers. "I'm serious. Do you remember when you had awesome 'slam-your-headboard-against-the-wall' sex?"

"You think you can say it any louder? I'm sure the third graders down the hall didn't hear you."

"Well, I wanted to get your attention."

"A simple hello works just fine."

"And you're avoiding the question."

"Why do you want to know?" Alice finally made eye contact with her friend. "Or are you just being nosy?"

"A little of both. But since you won't answer me, it must've been a long time ago." Tina waved her hand, a huge smile on her face. "But I'm going to fix that for you. We're going out and I'm going to help you find a man."

Oh no. Tina was a wonderful coworker and had good intentions, but her taste in men was very questionable.

"And it's not even my birthday." Alice stood, hoping that

humor would prevent the situation from turning into a nightmare. "As much as I find you attractive, I don't date women."

"The way you are with your private life, I wouldn't be surprised."

"When have I ever shown an interest in women?"

"When have you even shown more than a passing interest in men?" Tina's smile was tender. "Besides the speed dating dinner I dragged you to four months ago, and the boyfriend you had before that, you really haven't put yourself out there. Can you remember the last time you put on a sexy outfit and had a night out with the girls? Just relaxing and enjoying yourself?"

"I hope there's a point coming up soon," Alice said in an attempt to avoid the potential train wreck coming her way. "My students should be coming back from their chorus class any minute."

"You're coming out with me and Kara this Saturday night. No arguments and no exceptions." She held up a hand as Alice opened her mouth to protest. "We're going out and I'm making it my personal mission that you meet someone."

"I'm fine by myself."

"Hon, all you do is work and sit at home. You're far too great of a person to be by yourself." Tina sighed. "You're a good girl and you should have someone in your life."

"All good girls deserve something nice. But you are a bad girl and need to be punished."

Alice stiffened for a moment and her heart slammed against her ribs. She turned her head toward the window, not wanting Tina to see the panic in her green eyes.

It was all inside her head. He wasn't here. She was at work, safe from the man who abducted her two years ago.

You thought you were safe at work before. That's where he found you, she reminded herself. *What makes this time any different?*

Because he was in jail. She made sure the bastard got life for what he did to her and the two women he murdered.

Could she go just one day without thinking of him?

The computer monitor flashed on and jolted Alice out of her memories. She fumbled with the button and glanced back at Tina. "I don't chalk a man up with the things I deserve."

"Then let's try this," Tina said. "How about you're a good person who's entitled to have a little fun every once in a while? And now is the time for it to be that while?"

What she deserved was a night without being haunted by "him", but she wouldn't let Tina know what happened to her. No one here knew the horror that happened to her two years ago and she wanted to keep it that way. That's why she moved to Ravenna, Georgia, in the first place, instead of staying in Atlanta. She could get a fresh start in a new town and ignore the first twenty-eight years of her life.

"I'm a homebody," Alice muttered, brushing a dark tendril behind her ear, "you know that."

"I know. But there's another reason I'm asking you to come with me." Tina leaned forward. "You know how Kara's dating that new guy, Sam? Well, there's something wrong."

"What do you mean?"

Tina traced the grain of the wood with her fingernail. "I saw the bruises on her arms. She tried to cover it up, but they were there. Again."

She sucked in a breath. Kara Andrews was one of the kindest people Alice had ever met. For someone to put their hands on such a great person? It made Alice's blood boil. She knew all too well what it was like be mistreated by an animal. No one deserved to be abused. No one.

"There's strength in numbers, right?" Tina smiled encouragingly. "I need your help with this. I need to show her that there are guys out there who would appreciate her for the woman she is. Please don't say no."

Alice bit her lip. The last thing she wanted to do this weekend was sit in a bar and meet men, but how could she sit back and not help out a friend?

God would definitely count this as her good deed for the week.

"All right. I'll go."

"You're an angel!" Tina hugged Alice just as a couple of students entered the room. "I'll call you later."

Alice watched the class file into the room. She focused on their chatter from the chorus class instead of the voice in her own head.

They sat on the floor, ready for story time. She plucked a book off the table and looked at the twenty-three second graders staring at her expectantly as she took a seat in her chair.

"The last time we left off, Elsie and Randall were heading through the woods, looking for their lost puppy," Alice said and opened the book. "Let's see if they can find their puppy today."

"Will you do the voices again, Miss Roarke?" a tiny voice piped up.

"Yeah! We love the voices! It makes the story better," a boy added.

Alice grinned at their simple request. "I think I can do a voice or two, but only if you're quiet."

The kids all cheered. How she envied the innocence and joy in their eyes. They knew nothing of the horrors of the world. Nightmares and monsters were things that only occurred in their dreams. Her students had no idea that they existed in real life.

This was all she needed. The light in a child's face with such a simple request as doing voices from a book.

The rest of the day passed quickly and she found herself waving goodbye to the kids as they got on their bus. After setting up her class for the next day and cleaning her room, she headed to her car; the October wind chilled her to the bone.

She put her key in the ignition and started the car. She'd go out with her friends, for the sole reason of helping Kara. A couple of hours of idle chat and drinking. That was doable.

Besides, anything could happen between now and Saturday. She could end up in traction. Or a swarm of locusts could infiltrate every single bar in the city.

Alice sighed as she pulled out of the parking lot. Catching the flu never sounded so good.

~ * ~

"Have I mentioned how much I hate seeing those goddamn Sisters?" Jaden Payne growled as he stormed out of the lobby of the high-rise condominiums.

Salvatore Renato laughed. "Only with every breath you have."

Jaden clenched his hand inside his leather jacket, his palm tightening on the holster holding one of his nine millimeter Glocks. He wanted to stroll back into the Sisters' penthouse and have them retell the prophecy while the women stared into the barrel of his gun. Maybe then he'd get a straight answer from them and they'd think twice before they screwed with his head again.

The two females were powerful vampires even though Jaden had a good seventy pounds of muscle on them. Hell, they had survived close to seven thousand years with humans on this godforsaken planet and could easily fry his ass on the spot. If he was going to die, he'd do it on his own terms.

"I'd have better luck with an Ouija board. At least those give a yes or no answer."

"When you ask a 'yes or no' question." Salvatore chuckled. "Come on. They weren't too bad this time."

"I'd like to know what Liam was thinking when he told me to see them. He knows I'd rather have my fingernails ripped off than see those two." Jaden ran a hand through his black hair, doing his best not to yank a chunk out in frustration. "But he gets off on making me miserable. What did I ever do to him?"

"You're the best warrior he has, not to mention his closest living blood relative. Why else would he send you?"

"Just to piss me off."

Salvatore grinned. "Oh, then I can give you plenty of reasons. For one, you stole his motorcycle."

"He took my car!" he protested. "How else was I supposed to get my target? And it's not my fault that it got wrecked, either."

"You also got caught screwing the female he wanted for the night. In his bed."

Jaden's ice blue eyes flashed at his friend. "Do you want me to shoot you? I already have an itchy trigger finger and you're begging for it right now."

"I remember the last time you shot me." Salvatore held up his pale hands, a contrast to the dark jeans and sweater he wore. "I'm not willing to go through that again."

"That was an accident."

"So you say."

Jaden bared his fangs. "Next time, I'll make sure to shoot you while taking down the target. That way, I kill the Shadow and watch you bleed."

"You'll have to catch me first," Salvatore said, "and the scary vampire fang look doesn't work on me."

"One of these days, I will kill you."

"Who would you talk to? Varrik? That's trading down."

Jaden yanked the door open to his gunmetal gray ZR1 Corvette. Salvatore barely had a chance to get in before Jaden started the car and tore off down the road. Jaden loved driving fast and it alleviated some of his anger, but not by much. He still had the illustrious pleasure of delivering the prophecy to Liam Morgan.

It was going to be a long night.

With his preternatural sight, he focused on the police car three hundred feet ahead of him. If he had any sense at all, he'd slow down. Every college student in Ravenna knew this strip of highway from Atlanta to this city was a favorite of cops. The police loved nothing more than boosting their revenue by catching motorists going five miles over the speed limit.

Jaden didn't slow down. Luckily, there was no traffic on the road which enabled him to speed. He was anxious to get to the compound and relay the prophecy, and two humans would not deter him from his mission.

Two seconds later, he heard the sirens wailing behind him. He tightened his grip on the wheel. Like the cops were going to give him a speeding ticket.

He made a hard left and punched the accelerator. The car leapt forward as it growled its way through the streets. The government issued car was no match for the quarter of a million dollar 'Vette that was designed for speed.

Salvatore leaned his head against the leather seat. "Liam's going to have to change the license plates on the car. Again."

"Not if you short circuit their radios."

Jaden felt the air sizzle as Salvatore went to work on the policemen's radios. Salvatore's particular gift of controlling the elements for short periods of time definitely came in handy on nights like this.

"Done," Salvatore said. "I swear you have a death wish."

Jaden chuckled bitterly. "Like I have anything to live for."

Jaden had no mate, no true home and few warriors he regarded as friends. He didn't need anyone. Rage, vengeance and pain were his true companions. It's what kept him alive for over six hundred years.

And like any warrior, he liked to cheat that prick he called Death as often as he could.

"Feel free to jump out at any time," Jaden replied as he banked down a side street.

The police were no match for Jaden's customized Corvette. Having tampered with the engine and inner workings of the car, he knew the police wouldn't be able to catch him when top speed was 180 mph.

Another car turned on to the road. Jaden cursed and he jerked the wheel to avoid a collision. Jaden swore under his breath. It was one thing to outmaneuver the police. It was quite another to have an innocent human thrown into the mix.

The white car pulled off to the side and into a parking lot, with Jaden right on its heels. He slammed on the brakes and pulled the steering wheel to the right, narrowly missing the sedan.

The police car took the turn too hard and wound up on the other side of the road, the car careening into a UPS drop box. The engine shuddered to a stop and the two cops looked at each other, dazed but unhurt.

Jaden stopped and glanced to Salvatore. "How're you doing

over there? You need me to swing by the store and pick up a pack of Depends?"

"You are such an asshole."

"And you are such a pussy."

Jaden looked into the other car. The woman had her head against the headrest, her breathing rapid and shallow through her full lips, her dark hair creating a curtain for her face. Her hands trembled against the steering wheel as she tried to calm herself down.

She lifted her head and stared straight at Jaden. Which was impossible since the ambient light of the parking lot and the illegally tinted windows obscured a clear view. But those green eyes pierced him in their fury.

"Even though I took care of the radio, the police can still read license plates," Salvatore said dryly. "You want Liam would love to bust you out of jail again?"

"Then go clean their minds and I'll check on her."

Jaden got out of the car and headed toward the woman. He walked slowly, not wanting to spook her. He knew how menacing he could look. At six feet four inches tall and weighing in at two hundred and thirty pounds of solid muscle, he could make grown men wet themselves with a lethal stare. At least he looked somewhat presentable in his black slacks and sweater since he saw the Sisters, but not by much.

Besides, one car chase was enough for the night. He hated the idea of tracking her down and breaking into her home so he could erase himself from her mind.

Those green eyes narrowed as he approached and watched his every move. He held up his hands and stood a few feet away from the door. He didn't want her to feel cornered.

"Are you all right?" he called.

The female lowered the window a crack. "I'd be better if

some jerk didn't run me off the road just now."

"Were you hurt?"

"No."

Man, she smelled good. All humans carried a scent. It was what made them so easy to track. Usually, he hated the collage of smells that assailed him, but this woman's was actually pleasant. She smelled like cinnamon and cloves. Spicy and sweet at the same time.

He shook his head. "Do I need to call anyone for you?"

"I need to get home."

"Are you okay to drive?"

"You always ask so many questions?" she asked.

Jaden smiled, careful to hide his fangs. "Pretty much."

Some of the tension seemed to ease out of her shoulders. "I'm good to go. You think you can try and not drive anyone else off the road?"

"I'll do my best." He took a step back. "Drive safe."

"You too."

Jaden watched as she drove away. He had an irrational urge to follow her home and make sure she arrived safely.

He clenched his jaw. Why the hell should he care about a human female? Just another face in a sea of thousands. A meal. Nothing special at all.

But it didn't explain the sudden concern for her welfare.

"The memories are purged," Salvatore said as he walked up to the car. "Unless you feel like hanging around and making some new ones."

They slid into the Corvette and sped away, arriving at Liam's house twenty minutes later. Liam liked his privacy and preferred a rural area to the lights of a city. It was a smart move to live in the Middle of Nowhere and East Bumble-Fuck since the creatures Jaden hunted would have a hard time finding them in such a quiet locale.

The oak trees created a canopy of darkness as the 'Vette smoothly made its way towards the main house. It was almost impossible to see in the thick night, but with Jaden's advanced sight, he easily saw the curves and dips in the gravel road.

Within a matter of minutes, the eleven thousand square foot house opened up from the trees, a few lights illuminated the otherwise blackened lane. Sitting on forty acres of land, his house kept out all unwelcomed visitors and served as a perfect place for his group to meet.

After all, it's not like vampire warriors protecting their own and the human race was commonplace in Georgia, was it?

Jaden curled his lip as he eyed the massive stone structure. Obviously, Liam missed his native Ireland, because his house looked like he picked it up from the medieval countryside and dropped it in the middle of his substantial acreage.

Jaden shut off the engine and stood next to the car. God, he really didn't want to see his cousin. But Liam's instructions were as followed: see the Sisters, hear the prophecy, haul ass back to the house, and Jaden have his balls busted while Liam tried to decipher the women's gibberish.

All right, the last part was never said, but heavily implied.

He rolled his head from side to side and tried to release the tension out of his neck. Right now, he'd rather patrol the streets for something to kill or screw some woman until she screamed his name. Anything but be at Liam's compound.

"Let's get this over with," Jaden grumbled.

They walked into the house, their footsteps echoed against the hardwood floors. Jaden's muscles rippled with tension as they headed towards Liam's office. Even though he was armed with enough weapons to take on a SWAT team, he still felt naked. Because he knew how pissed Liam would be when he heard the Sisters' news.

Jaden walked into the office first with Salvatore a few steps behind him. He froze in his tracks, the situation going from bad to worse.

Everyone was in Liam's office. All ten of the vampire warriors, the Emain Macha, turned to Jaden expectantly and waited to hear what he had to say.

"Who's the pussy now?" Salvatore whispered.

Jaden glared at him. If looks could kill, there'd be nothing left of Salvatore.

His eyes slid back to the group. So his emasculation would be in front of the warriors who fought with him and feared him. Great. The perfect way to end his night.

"Did you see the Sisters?" Liam asked.

No, dickhead. I went to Starbucks and ordered three espressos while Daniel Powter sang about how he's having a really bad day.

Jaden heard a snicker and saw a dark-haired warrior smiling at him. Damn it. He'd forgotten that Varrik Stolin could read thoughts.

Jaden locked his mind to prevent any other one-liners from escaping. "The Sisters' were very anxious to speak tonight."

"What did they say?"

"Not much, but it was difficult to interpret their message. It's not like we ever get a clear answer from them anyway."

"I didn't ask for your personal opinion, nor do I care. What did they say?" Liam growled.

Let the ball busting begin.

Jaden took a deep breath as he recited the Sisters' prophecy.

The woman you seek, the power she controls
Is desired by vampires, Hosts and Shadows,
A daughter of foster, a son of pain,

She is the heart to make him live again.
The blinding light in the unending dark,
Branded with the animal's mark,
After the storm in a sanguine sky,
Is where the decision will lie.
Their union will take her last breath,
And be the cause of the race's death.

"That's it?" Liam's eyebrows deepened. "What the hell does that mean?"

The silence stretched out and the group looked at each other uneasily, shifting from one foot to the other. Jaden remained motionless. If Liam was about to explode, and there was a good chance of that happening, he would hit the closest body. Jaden didn't feel like nursing any wounds tonight.

Jaden glanced at the open door of the study. Now that he was done with his part, he was ready to get the hell out of there.

"They gave no indication as to who the woman was in the prophecy?" Liam asked, breaking the silence. "Besides that she's human?"

Jaden shook his head. "I asked for clarification, but they gave me a figure-it-out-yourself look."

"She could destroy our race or the Host's?" Liam stared at the group. "Shit, they're talking about a Firebrand. The last known one was four hundred years ago, but the Host got to him first."

Jaden frowned as several murmurs went through the group. A Firebrand was the ultimate tool of destruction, capable of killing any and everything in its path. Hosts, vampires, shadows, and humans...nothing was safe from one of these creatures. Even itself.

This was the first time they could get to one before the Host. An enemy of the Emain Macha, the Host wanted complete control over the humans and to restore the vampires as the true race. Yes, Jaden's kind had been on the planet thousands of years before the genetic mutations of several babies, which then spawned the human race, but that didn't mean they needed to be enslaved.

They were weaker and needed protection. Like the Firebrand.

Now came the insurmountable task of finding her.

Liam's scowl deepened as he stared at Jaden. "One thing's for certain, the Sisters are talking about you."

"Doubtful."

"No one else here has the last name of Payne."

Jaden rolled his eyes. "I'm sure they meant physical pain."

"Which you can also manifest by a simple touch."

Shit.

Liam had him there. His father's gift of manipulating emotions and enhancing them was biting Jaden in the ass right now.

"Until we find this woman, you are out of rotation unless I call for you. Finding the woman in the prophecy is your priority now."

Jaden's jaw dropped. He was no longer allowed to patrol? Oh, there was no way in hell he'd get roped into this. "I don't think so."

"That's not your call."

"I'm making it mine."

Liam walked in front of his desk, his eyes locked on Jaden. "You'd fight me on this?"

"I'm not a babysitter!"

"But you're a Guardian when the need arises."

Jaden clenched his fists so hard the knuckles turned white. He was so getting screwed. And definitely not the way he wanted.

The last time he acted as a Guardian was over four hundred years ago and despite his best efforts, his charge died anyway. That wasn't supposed to happen when you were a Guardian. You protected, not destroyed.

"That was several lifetimes ago," he snarled. "I'm sure there's someone else here more qualified than me."

"Oh, really?" Liam turned to the other warriors in the room. "Besides Jaden and myself, I'd love to know if anyone else here was born of, trained and fed by the original seven Masters of our race. The ones whose undiluted blood made you the most powerful of all vampires. Virtually indestructible and impervious to all wounds."

The other men and one lone woman glanced at each other. Jaden wished he could punch that smirk off Liam's face, but knew it would only lead to more trouble.

"Come on. Don't be shy. Anyone? No one?" Liam's eyes landed on Jaden. "Well, I guess it's just us. Since I rule, that leaves you."

Only because you can't even protect your own pompous ass.

"I went to the Sisters like you asked," Jaden said, nearly spitting out the words. "I came back with the prophecy like you asked. I told you the prophecy, like you asked."

"And you are going to find this woman and protect her like *I* ask." Liam stood in front of Jaden, both six foot four men locking eyes with each other. "I don't care if you want the job or not. This human is an asset to us in our war against the Host. You heard it yourself. Her power will eventually kill the Host." Liam shook his head. "You know he's going to be searching for her, just as we are. You really want him to get to her first?"

"He may already have her. She could be our enemy."

"If that has happened, then you can be the one to kill her," he said. Liam took a step closer, baring his fangs. "You will do this. It's not a request. It's a command."

"Thanks, but find someone else for the job."

"You are such a cocky bastard."

"It's what's kept me alive for almost seven hundred years."

"And it's going to kill you," Liam said. "If you decide not to accept this mission, then I have no choice but to turn you into the new target." He gestured behind him. "They are here as witnesses who will make sure there's nothing left of you but ash."

Fuck, he was serious.

Jaden saw the helplessness in the warriors' faces, except for two. Helene Deaux looked all too eager for him to fail and Varrik appeared bored.

He also saw their determination, even in Salvatore's eyes. Jaden knew they'd hunt and kill him without hesitation. Once Liam issued an order, you followed it, or your life was forfeited.

"It is my supreme honor to be assigned to this target," Jaden ground out.

"I bet it is."

"What do you want me to do with her?"

"Find her and bring her here. Then we can begin her training and use her against the Host."

Jaden lifted his chin. "Despite being beyond pissed, I will not fail you."

He gripped the handle of one of his daggers and slashed his palm as he kept his gaze level with his cousin. The blood dropped on to the floor. The symbolism of this act was not lost on Liam or the other warriors. Jaden's willingness to shed blood and life for this mission was the ultimate sacrifice amongst the warriors.

"I swear to you that I will find this woman and protect her with my life. The Shadows and the Host will not get their hands on her," he vowed, clenching his fist. "But once I bring her here, she's your problem. I want nothing do to with her outside the sparring ring."

There was no way in hell he'd hang around the Firebrand. The other warriors could take care of her once she was at Liam's compound and Jaden would be free to fight his enemy again.

Chapter 2

Alice's bare feet pounded against the asphalt, the uneven road tearing into the tender flesh. Her lungs burned and her heart felt like it would explode out of her chest. She whimpered in pain, but didn't stop. She had to keep going.

The broken handcuffs dangled from her wrists, chunks of metal burned into her skin along with some of the studs of the dog collar around her neck. She didn't care that she was bleeding, bruised and naked. All she knew was that if he caught her, she was dead.

Cars sped down the road and she waved wildly as they came closer. She had no clue who was behind the wheel, but as long as he got her to safety, she'd be okay.

Anything to get away from John-Paul.

"Help! Please stop!"

But the cars whizzed by, the drivers ignoring her screams.

She turned right and veered into a wooded patch, praying the shadows from the trees would deter him from following her. The rocks and pine needles cut into her skin which made her stumble. She picked herself up and ignored the scrapes.

"Bitch, you need to heel!"

A whimper escaped her lips as she heard his voice. Good God, he was so close. How'd he get to her so fast?

He'd kill her for escaping. She pushed herself harder as the panic kicked off another rush of adrenaline. She had no doubt that he'd do to her what he did to those other women.

God, the pain they suffered before they died.

She broke through the other side and froze in horror. She was back at the cabin. How was that possible? She ran away from it. She ran away from him….

"I told you you'd never escape me."

She turned around and came face to face with him. With John-Paul.

"You know what today is? It is Day Three." He grabbed her wrists, grinding the warped metal into her skin. "Now that you've heeled, let's see you beg."

Alice screamed and bolted upright in bed. She clutched the bedspread in her hands, a thin sheen of sweat covered her arms and face. Her eyes focused on the English garden painting in her room as she listened to the clock tick the seconds in the corner.

She was home. She was safe.

She looked at her wrists. There were no cuffs, just the scars from where the metal burned her skin. The same was true with the spot on her neck. A part of the leather and one of the studs had melted into her skin. The doctors couldn't explain it. Neither could she but they were permanent reminders of the abuse she went through.

Alice rubbed her temples, her breathing and heart rate close to normal. Jesus, she hated that dream. But fortunately this time when she had it, she wasn't found wandering eight blocks away from her home.

Her episodes, or at least that's what she called them, were happening with more frequency. She'd had them when she was a child, but those were few and far between. But the past two months, she had one almost every week.

She wasn't right. These episodes had to be the result of some kind of tumor or brain abnormality. The last CAT scan she had showed nothing, but that was two years after the attack.

Something was very wrong with her. There had to be. She'd make an appointment with her doctor on Monday.

But tonight, she was in for a special kind of torture.

Alice glanced at the clock – 6:45 PM.

Time to get ready to go out with the girls.

She tossed the covers aside and headed to the bathroom, turning on the shower. She'd go out with Kara and Tina, enjoy their company and pray that no one noticed her tonight.

~ * ~

Jaden loved autumn. Not only were the days shorter, but his enemies decided to come out and play a lot earlier. He really needed to kick some ass despite Liam's order to only focus on finding the Firebrand.

He and the other warriors were unsuccessful in their attempts to find the human female in the prophecy. It would've been a whole lot easier if the Sisters gave a name, an address, or a "You-Are-Here" map. But no. He had to do all of this investigative shit on his own.

Liam was getting anxious which meant hell for everyone else. With every day that passed, the Host had an opportunity to claim the Firebrand for himself.

And what about the woman? She didn't know her own powers. For all anyone knew, the Firebrand could be dead. The only Firebrands Jaden had heard or seen were vampires and they had control over their powers. They were also males.

The fact that this Firebrand was female made the situation much more dangerous…and interesting. As a human, she'd be volatile, unpredictable and capable of harming others and herself until the power killed her.

Jaden was already running out of time and he wasn't any closer to finding her than he was three days ago. He tried to track her by scent. Firebrands let out a sultry scent, like a smoky musk, but that hadn't worked. Then he checked hospital records nationwide, spanning the past ten years, focusing on women with unexplained headaches, a habit of sleepwalking and temporary loss of eyesight. No one fit into all three categories.

He was planning his next move when he caught sight of one of his enemies.

"Hell yeah," Jaden whispered.

He grinned. His night was about to get a lot better.

The Shadow strolled down the sidewalk on the opposite side of the street. Shadows were a hybrid of human and vampire blood. They possessed some of the characteristics of full-blooded vampires, even if it was a little diluted: speed, strength and an aversion to sunlight. A single drop of blood could turn a human into a devoted blood slave to their master. The only loyalty they pledged allegiance to was the leader they referred to as the Host in the hopes of being turned into a full-fledged vampire. They also relied on blood to survive, but they usually killed their donors whereas true vampires knew when to stop.

Jaden and the warriors had spent the last twenty years trying to learn the identity of the Shadows' Host, but they were unsuccessful. That man was slick and incredibly intelligent although they had tracked him to Ravenna which was why they now resided in Georgia.

Jaden made it his personal mission to take the bastard down. Especially since the Host gave the orders to have Jaden's family murdered in their own home.

Everyone he loved…gone in the blink of an eye. His parents and his fifteen-year-old brother, Ezra, completely destroyed in less than half an hour. The carnage those Shadows caused in such a short time made the bodies almost unrecognizable. The only way to identify Ezra was by his clothing and family's insignia ring on his right pinky.

The Shadow stopped in his tracks for a moment before he turned around and bolted down the street. Jaden grinned and took off after the hybrid. Both men moved so quickly, it was impossible for the human eye to track them. The Shadow might be fast, but Jaden was a purebred vampire and able to move with speed that boggled the mind.

Jaden followed the bastard to the street behind a local strip mall. Ambient light came from the parking lot, but there was plenty of darkness to conceal their fight.

"You know, I like it when you run," Jaden said, bowing slightly to the Shadow. "It just juices me up for the kill."

The Shadow lunged at Jaden, a knife in his hand. Jaden dodged the attack. He could easily unsheathe his own blades, but he wanted to wait to use them. Jaden wanted to show the Shadow just how powerful he was without his weapons.

The male tried to hit from behind, but Jaden ducked and swept the man's legs out from under him. The Shadow fell flat on his back, his skull knocked against the pavement. Jaden stomped on the Shadow's fist and his foot shattered the wrist and fingers in his hand.

The Shadow let out a howl of rage. Jaden took a step back and let his opponent gain his footing. This was the part of the fight Jaden loved. Let the Shadow think he had time to catch his breath. In a few minutes, the Shadow would beg Jaden to kill him.

Another lunge, this time Jaden's attacker led with his

uninjured hand. Jaden caught his arm and twisted it behind his back, the bones splintered in his grip as he rotated the arm.

The Shadow dropped to his knees and Jaden flung him against the building. He sagged against the wall, his head hanging loosely on his neck. One of his feet turned inward, indicating the ankle was broken.

Jaden knelt in front of the Shadow. "That was a little disappointing. Is the Host not training new recruits properly?"

"Blow me."

"Such language!" Jaden tsked at him. "You kiss your mother with that mouth?"

"Feel free to kiss my ass."

He grabbed the Shadow's uninjured leg and twisted his hands in opposite directions from each other, snapping the bone in half. Yeah, he wasn't going anywhere anytime soon.

Jaden plunged the blade into the male's shoulder, pausing at the bone. He adjusted his grip and drew the blade down in one smooth stroke. The Shadow writhed in agony as Jaden pulled the dagger out and worked on the other shoulder.

Sweat rolled down the male's face and his breath came in short gasps. He was in so much pain and Jaden hadn't even used his special talent yet--the one that made grown men beg for death.

Like how his father begged the Shadows not to kill his wife. How they sliced into her skin and choked the life out of her while his father watched.

"Not so chatty now, are you?"

"I won't betray the Host," the Shadow panted.

Jaden smiled coldly. "Did I ask you for any information about the Host?"

"Then if you're not interested in the Host, why don't you just kill me?"

"If I kill you, then I can't make you beg."

The Shadow's jaw went slack. "You're him, aren't you?"

"Him who?"

"The Ice Warrior."

Jaden rolled his eyes at the popular title he received centuries ago. When he discovered his slaughtered family, he had hunted every Shadow down, extracting a pound of flesh for their crimes. It took him ten years to find them all, but find them, he did. And ever since then, the title stuck.

And now as he stood over the Shadow, all Jaden saw was Ezra's innocent face and the life his brother never had the chance to live.

Jaden's phone ringing caught his attention. "Hold that thought." He pulled the phone out and scowled at the screen as he accepted the call. "What is it, Salvatore? I'm kind of busy right now."

"Why aren't you at your house?"

He glanced at his victim. "I'm doing my job."

"Did you find the Firebrand?"

The Shadow's head snapped up. "You're looking for a Firebrand?"

Jaden delivered a swift uppercut which effectively silenced his companion. "Be quiet. This is a private conversation."

"Who the hell is that?"

"A friend."

"You're doing it again, aren't you?" Salvatore groaned. "Jesus. Just kill him and meet me at Siren's Call in fifteen minutes."

"Why? So you can keep an eye on me?"

"Exactly. I'm making sure you don't do something stupid. Just get your ass over there in fifteen minutes."

"Only fifteen minutes? That's not enough time."

There was a pause. "Is he bleeding?"

"He is. But you're taking the fun out of the game."

"I know. I'm such a downer."

Jaden ended the call and slipped the phone in his pocket. "We're going to have to cut our date short."

"Fuck…you."

Jaden knelt back in front of the Shadow, his ice blue eyes shining with hunger. "Now, where were we?"

~ * ~

The Shadow named Markus groaned at the scream in his mind. Someone was slicing and dicing a fellow comrade and there was nothing he could do. If he went to help, he'd be killed himself, and he had lived too long to die by the hand of an ancient vampire.

He winced at the sudden ache in his stomach. Shadows were able to feel the pain of their brethren if they were close, a result of their link to the Host. The Host would only feel anger at this death because one of them was foolish enough to get caught by an Emain Macha.

The pain intensified, a slow burn slicing right across his abdomen. Markus grimaced and clutched his stomach. No doubt the other Shadow was watching his intestines spill onto the street. Only one vampire had the balls to kill a Shadow like this and Markus knew which one it was.

Jaden Payne.

Shadows and vampires knew all about Jaden. A direct descendant of one of the seven Masters, the original creators of the vampire and human race, Jaden was as powerful as he was cruel. He was the one warrior you hoped never caught you. The other warriors might rough you up a little bit before they killed you, but not Jaden. What he did was much worse.

If you were lucky, you died on the street. But if he wanted

to draw out the kill or information on the Host, then he'd take you back to his house. That's where he gave you his "special treatment."

One had escaped Jaden's captivity and told horror stories of how he made the Shadows talk. Of course, Jaden offered everyone an opportunity to give information on the Host, but Shadows were trained to not confess what they knew. When they remained silent, that was when Jaden went to work.

The one thing that chilled Markus the most was when he heard about the look in Jaden's eyes. That vampire's gaze was as cold as those pale blue eyes, devoid of any emotion. Definitely worthy of the title Ice Warrior.

Markus stopped for a moment as the pain disappeared. Finally, some relief. Even if it was short-lived. He would have to report this and the Host was going to be royally pissed off.

Unless Markus followed the warrior.

It was stupid, foolhardy and practically suicidal to tail a one of these vampires. But then he'd be a moron if he went back to the Host with nothing but a dead Shadow.

So he chose the lesser of two evils. Better to die in the field than at the hands of the Host.

Gathering up his courage, Markus turned down the street and tracked his prey.

Chapter 3

"I can't believe we let you walk out of your apartment dressed like that," Tina muttered as they entered the bar.

"What's wrong with it?" Alice asked.

"Can it scream anything other than 'stay away'?"

Alice looked at herself. As far as she knew, she looked pretty decent. She wore a corduroy jacket, black T-shirt, dark jeans and black flats. Completely respectable and appropriate.

So what if she looked like a bartender? At least she was going out.

"You're lucky she didn't put on the blue jean jumper and smiley face shirt she wore for Carnival Day," Kara Andrews said. "That would've been a worse outfit."

Alice lifted her chin. "It's not like I have a massive wardrobe to choose from."

"Neither do I, but I manage to have a couple of outfits for nights such as these," Kara replied.

"You're sending off the typical *no man* signal. You're making my job much harder tonight." Tina leaned forward and grinned. "But that's fine with me. I love a challenge."

Looking at her friends, Alice knew she wasn't getting any attention tonight. She wasn't unattractive, but compared to the two women next to her, she was the ugly duck next to the swans. Both Kara and Tina wore low cut tops and tight pants, accentuating the curves to their advantage. The men would have to be blind and stupid if they chose Alice over her friends.

She shuddered as the bass pumped out of the speakers, the floor vibrated with the heavy rock music. She didn't know how they did it, but people still found the beat as couples locked their bodies together.

At least Tina picked a decent place tonight. Siren's Call held a healthy mix of older college students and younger business people who still enjoyed a night on the town. The cream walls glowed against the ambient light from the candles and the dark floor gleamed from the multicolored lights of the DJ's booth as he picked the next song to play.

Kara and Alice found an empty table while Tina ordered a pitcher of beer from the bar. Alice quickly poured herself a glass and took a sip, but it did little to quell the dread in her stomach. Maybe it had to do with the dream which still lingered in her mind.

Her eyes swept across the room as the hairs rose on the back of her neck. There was something in the room she couldn't quite put her finger on. Like someone was watching her.

What am I doing here?

Alice took a step back, half-hiding behind Kara. She was completely out of her element. Every instinct inside of her screamed for her to bolt, but she was trapped for the time being.

She rubbed her shoulder as the adhesive from the Band-Aid irritated her skin. Fortunately, it was the weekend and she could go home and leave her shoulder bared without anyone asking where she got the weird, paw print scar.

She managed to hide it for two years and planned on to

keep it that way. She never wanted anyone to know how she got it.

"See anything you like?" Tina asked.

Alice shook her head. "Nope. Can we leave now?"

"We just arrived!" Tina said, laughing. "And you're not getting out of here that easily. Give it at least a couple of hours. If you're not having fun, then I'll take you home."

She stared at Tina. At least a couple of hours? Someone was enjoying a very cruel joke at her expense.

Alice saw movement from the corner of her eye. Three men slowly approached their table. Tina and Kara straightened. Their faces lit up with expectant smiles while Alice cringed. A blond with a crew cut and two shaggy brunettes stood on either side of the table.

"Hello ladies," Crew Cut drawled.

Tina sucked in a quick breath, pushing her breasts out. "Hello yourself."

Crew Cut looked her over and his eyes lingered on the deep vee of her red sweater. "You must be new to the area. This is the first time I've seen you three here."

"How do you know we haven't been here before?" Tina asked.

"I'd remember beautiful women such as yourselves. You must be the angels that fell from heaven itself."

Alice nearly gagged on her beer while Tina's brown eyes sparkled at the compliment. "I'm Tina. This is Kara and Alice."

"I'm Brad. And these two behind me are Hunter and Dylan."

Dear God. Deliver me from lame pickup lines and the Abercrombie trio.

Kara leaned over Tina. "Would you like to join us?"

Alice inwardly groaned. Who knew the front doors to Siren's Call was the portal to Hell? And according to her calculations, she was in the fourth circle. If any of the guys turned their attention to Alice, she'd officially enter the ninth.

Her friends began chatting away with their newest boy toys while Alice sipped her beer. Her eyes darted around the club, hoping to find a way out of this situation. As soon as Kara and Tina went to dance with these losers, she was gone. She absently scratched her shoulder again and froze when she noticed two thuggish looking men eyeing her appreciatively.

Not me. Look at someone else. Not me.

Tina and her date slid on to the dance floor, evidently as a way to size each other up. Kara continued to talk to her men, but she kept glancing over to another table. Alice crossed her fingers and hoped Kara was about to follow Tina's lead and take the two guys with her. Then Alice could slip out unnoticed.

Kara paused in front of her dates and turned to Alice. "I think your luck is changing," she whispered.

Did a vortex just open up so that it would dump her back in her quiet bedroom? It seemed too much to hope for, but she was open to any options at the moment.

"Why do you say that?" Alice asked.

Kara angled her head. "Look two tables over. There's a guy over there staring at you."

No one looked at Alice. Ever. Except for those two bikers just now.

And John-Paul.

She shuddered. John-Paul hadn't even seen her as a person. He saw her as something much worse. A bitch that needed proper training on how to obey its master.

Alice rubbed her shoulder and pushed any thoughts of him

from her mind. She wasn't going there tonight. Not when she was already so miserable.

"I'm sure he's looking at you," she muttered.

"Trust me. He's not. See for yourself if you don't believe me."

Alice lifted her eyes and looked over her friend's shoulder, just to prove Kara wrong. She scanned the crowd until she saw him. The heat spread throughout her body, her cheeks reddening as those eyes locked onto her.

"Wow," she breathed.

~ * ~

Jaden knocked back a shot of tequila and motioned to the bartender for another one. There was no way he was going to get wasted since vampire blood filtered out all pollutants rather quickly, but he could try and get some kind of buzz that would last for half an hour. Anything to take his mind off the jacked-up role of Guardian.

Jaden was a killer, a slayer and a damn good soldier. Not the kind protector Liam believed him to be. The last two people he guarded didn't work out so well. One was his brother, Ezra, who died the same day his of his parents' murders.

And the other was his wife, Catherine.

He had tried to reason with her, but she wouldn't listen to him. His love wasn't enough for her. She'd accused him of turning her into a demon, a bloodthirsty monster who had to abandon her human life.

Jaden took another shot and motioned to the waitress for a refill. In the end, when she turned his love for her against him, he had to kill her in order to save himself. The so-called love his life dead by his hands.

Salvatore shook his head. "You're just wasting your money."

"Correction. I'm wasting Liam's money. I made sure the waitress put all my drinks on his tab."

"Well, you're wasting my time."

"You're the one who wanted to come here. Why are we here if I'm wasting your time?"

"So you could find a female for the night." Salvatore folded his arms across his chest. "If you're not going to get laid, can we at least get out of here? Look for a fight? We have Shadows to kill."

"*You* have Shadows to kill. I'm supposed to sit back and find a needle in a haystack."

"The Sisters love giving us a challenge, don't they?"

"Do not mention them to me right now. I'm still pissed off."

Jaden's eyes darted around the room as the waitress brought him a fresh glass. Most of the patrons were human although he caught a couple of civilian vampires on the dance floor, enticing their partners for a quick feed and fuck.

"Play nice," he growled.

The civilians stared at Jaden in wonderment and fear, but this reaction was typical whenever the warriors were out and about. Because not only did they protect their own kind, they watched over humans as well. They caught the warning despite the noise of the club and nodded hurriedly, arm in arm with their donor for the night.

"Can you believe humans actually thrive considering how weak their bodies are?" Jaden asked. "I'd like to know how we became the minority when we were the master race and they were the mutation."

"I think it is called evolution."

Jaden looked at Salvatore in disgust. "They hunt us to extinction and now we're the only thing that can protect them from the Host and the Shadows." He knocked back his shot of tequila and laughed humorlessly. "Life is full of irony, isn't it?"

"They still need protection," Salvatore pointed out. "They are weaker than us and our food source in case you forgot."

"Figures you'd take their side when I'm so pissed off," Jaden muttered. "And your theory of evolution is completely fucked up."

"You weren't raised by humans only to find out you're really a vampire."

"I wouldn't call what they did raising you. More like animal testing, right?"

Salvatore clenched his fist. "It was a different time. Then again, I'm also not the Ice Warrior who's incapable of feeling anything other than satisfaction when out hunting."

Jaden sighed. Cold Slayer, Ice Warrior, Vengeance were only a few of the epithets attributed to him. Vampire and Shadow alike were terrified of him because of his link to the Masters who were long since dead.

A sudden wave of irritation slammed into Jaden. At first, he thought it came from Salvatore since he was anxious to start his patrol, but it wasn't him. It was too much of a human reaction. He looked past Salvatore, searching for the source of the discomfort amongst the lust and drunken revelry of the crowd.

His eyes landed on a brunette two tables from where he stood. He frowned slightly. She looked familiar, but he couldn't place her. Nothing compared to the teased hair, short-skirted, silicone-injected human females who were looking for a quick fuck. But hers was a simple beauty.

Jaden leaned forward slightly as his eyes drank her in from head to toe. What was someone like her doing in a place like this? Her slutty friends belonged here, but not her. She was the kind of person who should read books to little children in a library or work in a day care center.

Her eyes darted around the room. She tucked a piece of her dark brown hair behind her ear before moving to her shoulder. She did that a couple of times. Touched her hair, rubbed her shoulder. Probably her way of burning off nervous energy.

She looked in his direction and he nearly dropped his shot glass as her eyes met his.

Are you fucking kidding me?

Now he knew why he recognized her. This was the human he ran off the road the evening he delivered the prophecy to Liam. Just like that night, those green eyes were spotlights, rooting him in place. She looked him over and his body tensed while she took him in from head to toe.

But it's what he saw in her eyes that made him burn. Despite her small frame, her emerald eyes were hard and defiant. Haunted with an ancient sadness. A warrior's eyes. Someone who survived unbelievable hardships and emerged victorious, but scarred.

Her face reddened under his gaze and her pink tongue darted across her lips nervously. Such a subtle movement and one that made his blood simmer. He imagined her tongue snaking into his mouth. Or down the side of his throat and onto his chest...

Salvatore snapped his fingers. "Earth to Jaden. Are you there?"

He ignored Salvatore. He was too preoccupied with the woman fifteen feet away.

She looked away, her face retaining that warm, red glow. It was strange. Most women tried to entice Jaden by thrusting their breasts out or twisting sinuously in his direction. But this woman retreated further into herself, doing her damndest to fade into the background.

Her fingernail traced a pattern on the tabletop, obviously flustered by his attention. He'd love to feel those nails on his back, digging into his skin, as he made her scream his name while she came in his arms.

Great. Now he had a monstrous hard-on.

He shifted in his seat, his erection punching against the fly of his jeans. Goddamn it, he needed to get his head in the game because this was the last thing he needed. Right now, he had to focus on finding the "woman of foster" before the Shadows got their hands on her. Not some random woman in a club where she didn't belong.

Albeit a very attractive, random woman.

The human female stood up, keeping her eyes on her friends. "Hey, I'm going to take off."

He closed his eyes briefly as her voice cut through the din of the club. Soft and husky. He loved the Southern lilt to her voice. God, he wanted to hear her say his name. It'd sound like honey rolling off her tongue.

"Come on, Alice! You can't leave yet," her friend protested.

Jaden smiled. Her name was as simple and lovely as the rest of her.

Alice shook her head and he caught her scent. All humans let off some sort of fragrance. It's what made tracking them so easy. Vampires released no pheromones which made them the stronger predator. How can you find your target if there's no scent?

He took another deep breath. The scent of cinnamon permeated the air, a refreshing breeze cutting through the sweat and lust of the club. God, she smelled so good. It invaded his heightened senses which made his mouth water. Such a sweet and palatable fragrance. How he'd love to bite into her neck and taste how sweet she actually was.

"You and Tina are having a great time. I'm not going to drag you down."

"You haven't given any of these guys a chance!"

The thought of this female showing an interest in another man made Jaden want to punch something which confused him even more. For God's sake, this woman was human. He avoided them at all costs; he was only interested in them for food or a one night stand.

But those warrior eyes made her different.

"I'm not going to find what I want here. But tell Tina I said thanks for the thought and I'll see you on Monday."

Jaden frowned. She was leaving by herself?

Jaden looked back at Alice while she said her final goodbyes. Out of the corner of his eye, he saw two men watch Alice head toward the door. Their eyes glowed with lust and anticipation as they slid of their stools and followed her.

A growl rumbled at the base of Jaden's throat. They wouldn't dare touch her. Not if they wanted all of their body parts still intact.

Fingers snapped in front of Jaden's face. "Hey! We need to go," Salvatore said, ignoring Jaden's glare. "Ryder just called and he's tracking a group of Shadows. You know when they're out in large numbers, they're up to something. Ryder said that Liam's cleared you to fight tonight since you're already out and we're only four blocks from where they're headed. We can catch up to them pretty quickly."

He slid out of his seat. "You help Ryder. I'll be there as soon as I can."

"Are you serious? You have a chance to kick Shadow ass and you're bailing?" Salvatore asked.

Oh, Jaden was going to kick ass and get a buzz from

something much stronger than alcohol. "I'll meet up with you later."

"Finished with what? Where are you going?"

"Hunting."

Chapter 4

Alice burst out the door and took several deep breaths. The icy air cleansed her lungs from the stale smell of liquor and sweat in the club. She couldn't stand to be in that place for another minute. Even now, she faintly heard the bass thumping against the building. She needed to escape the club, all of its noise and patrons.

But the man across the bar definitely raised her interest.

If tall, dark and handsome needed a poster boy for their campaign, he'd be it. The shadows of the club surrounded him, making him a presence more felt than seen. From what she could see in the dim light, she had enjoyed the view. And he seemed to like what he saw as well.

She blushed, a little surprised steam wasn't coming off her cheeks. For once, she didn't mind someone looking at her. It made her feel attractive. Those pale blue eyes ran over her body. He stared at her with curiosity, like she was a puzzle he wanted to solve.

She shook her head, pushing the image out of her mind. Men like him didn't look at women like her. Women who were just average and forgettable, not the curvy goddess Kara was. He was probably staring at her friend and wondered how to approach through the plain Jane.

Alice walked a few steps, hoping to distance herself from

the club as she tried to catch a taxi. She'd pay a pretty penny for the twenty minute drive to her apartment, but it'd be worth it once she entered her home with nothing but silence greeting her.

"Hey, sweetheart! You need a ride home?"

Alice's blood ran cold. Leaving Siren's Call had provided the relief she needed, but leaving alone was a very bad idea.

She glanced behind her and saw the two thugs from the club were a few feet away. She ignored them as she took a few more steps, hoping the taxi would stop, but it kept going.

She walked half a block to avoid those men, but they herded her to a deserted side street. Three ravens squawked as she approached and perched themselves on the side of the building.

"Come on, baby! There's no need to be shy. I promise to give you the ride of your life."

Their raucous laughter rang in her ears as the panic welled inside of her, but she fought it down. Fear would paralyze her, not help her escape.

The men chuckled again as they stopped three feet in front of her. In this closed space, Alice could smell the whiskey on their breath. She looked around, feeling as if she was in the middle of some horrible Lifetime movie.

She felt the tremor deep inside her bones. The warning sign that the blackout was close behind. She gritted her teeth as she viciously clamped down on the panic. The last one she had was two years ago. She woke up naked and covered in blood.

She'd been lucky that time. It had been her own blood speckled on her body. It wasn't always so.

If she had one now, with these two men in front of her, God only knew what she would do this time. And if she'd live to tell about it.

She straightened her spine. She would face this head on. She wasn't a coward and would never be a victim again.

"Sorry, guys. You're wasting your time with me," Alice said, her voice steady even though she was ready to bolt. "Find someone else tonight."

The tallest one came forward. "We don't think you should be out by yourself."

"I'm a big girl. I can handle myself."

He reached out to touch her face. "A gentleman would escort a lady home."

"Would you mind pointing out that gentleman when he comes by? I sure don't see one in front of me."

The man's face hardened. "Listen, bitch –"

She didn't hear the rest of his words. As soon as he called her a bitch, everything else faded away. All she heard was John-Paul's voice echoing inside her head.

"You'll always be my bitch. I'll never let you go."

Alice's vision blurred for a moment as her fist collided with the man's jaw. His head whipped to the side from the unexpected force of the blow. The raw fury she felt blocked the pain she knew she'd feel in the morning

"I'm no one's bitch," she snapped.

He looked up at her and swung his fist. She ducked, easily avoiding him and delivered a hard kidney shot, grateful she learned something in her self-defense classes. His friend darted in and grabbed her hair, but she elbowed him in the stomach and he let go.

Before she could figure out which way to run, a heavy palm hit her cheek. She was stunned for a moment as a trickle of blood rolled out of the corner of her mouth. That gave her attackers the opportunity to pin her arms behind her back.

The tall one stood in front of her. He backhanded her again

and she bit down on her tongue to keep from screaming. She glared at him as his face was inches from hers.

"You'll be my bitch, tonight. And like all good bitches, you'll know when to beg," he growled.

"Too bad I won't be housebroken."

His knee met her stomach. The air rushed out of her lungs as a fresh wave of pain rolled through her. She gasped for breath, wondering if he cracked a couple of ribs.

Alice fell forward, but those arms held hers and prevented her from hitting the pavement. Still, her knees slammed on to the sidewalk.

"Hold her tighter," he commanded.

Alice struggled, but her arms were held tight behind her, the tendons stretched to their limits. The first one grabbed her hair and yanked her head back. She winced in pain, but kept her mouth closed.

"Not so chatty now, are ya?"

Her heart slammed against her ribs, terror coursing through her veins. She broke free for a moment before the man holding her forced her into the wall.

Stars exploded behind her eyes and she felt herself slipping into that dark void. She heard the flutter of wings overhead as well as the ravens screeching in protest at the scene before them.

There was nothing she could do now. Her vision receded and she closed her eyes, doing the best she could to stay conscious.

It was happening again. In another minute, she'd be totally unconscious. And God help her when she woke up.

~ * ~

Jaden easily picked up Alice's spicy scent. With every step, it grew stronger, more enticing. It overwhelmed him to the point where his gums ached for a taste of her sweet blood.

He tracked Alice's scent until it reached the deserted stretch of pavement. Any thoughts of tasting her disappeared when he found her. His vision went red and it took a couple of seconds for him to hold back his murderous fury. One man held her tightly while the other stood in front of her, his arousal pushing against the front of his pants.

Alice's body shook uncontrollably, her mouth still closed. When she didn't comply, the man slapped her. Hard. But she didn't flinch or whimper. Her eyes were shut, the lids fluttering as if she were dreaming.

"I like it when they make it challenging," he said. "We'll have so much fun with this bitch."

"Dude, she doesn't look so good. We should get out of here." The second one looked down at her. "Christ, is she having a seizure?"

"She'll be still in a few minutes," the first one replied. "And she's too sweet to miss. I'll leave when I'm done."

Jaden smiled. He was the only one who'd have fun tonight.

Moving so fast that they couldn't see him, Jaden pulled the man off of Alice. She fell to the sidewalk, her palms preventing her from landing face first into the pavement. She stopped shaking once she hit the ground, but her eyes remained closed.

"What the fuck!" the tall one roared.

Jaden glanced at Alice. He'd check on her in a minute. He needed to eliminate the threat and get these two alone.

He drew them away from her and pulled them into a side alley. He usually reserved this type of cover for Shadows, but his fury knew no bounds tonight. In his mind, these two pricks were just as bad as the demons he fought.

Jaden didn't need Varrik's power to know this wasn't the first time they had forced themselves on a woman, but it would be their last. They planned to show no mercy on her so Jaden would show no mercy on them.

The friend attacked from behind, but Jaden landed a kick to the man's gut and he dropped to the ground like a sack of potatoes. The dagger found its mark as it sunk into the man's chest. Jaden pulled it out quickly and slit his throat as well, preventing him from screaming.

He shoved the tall one against the wall, the knife pressed against the man's throat. "If I had more time, I'd show you type of games I'd love to play with you. But before I go, I want to hear you beg for your life."

"Go to hell!"

"I don't think so." Jaden grinned, no longer wanting to hide his fangs. The defiance was replaced with sheer terror when the man saw the ivory tips. "Come on. I want to hear you beg."

Jaden sank his fangs into the human's throat. The blood poured into Jaden's mouth and he took deep pulls, satisfying his hunger and the kill. He cradled the man's neck in his hand and intensified the pain with every gulp. He wanted his prey to feel pain. To know there was a stronger predator out there than him.

Jaden pulled back and grinned, licking the man's blood off his mouth. "I know you can still talk. Tell me you want me to stop."

The man panted, his eyes glazed in horror. His mouth opened and closed, but no words came out.

Jaden squeezed his throat, cutting off more of his air. "I said I wanted to hear you beg."

"Please don't," the man pleaded. "Don't kill me. I won't...do it again," the human said quickly.

"Yeah, right. I've heard that one before." Jaden cocked his

head to the side. "What makes you think I'll believe what you say?"

"I'll do whatever you want as long as you let me live."

"This isn't the first woman you've hurt, is it?" He winked at the male. "The truth will set you free."

Tears poured out of the man's eyes, a mixture of fear and pain. "No. It's not."

"Good boy. You learn fast."

"I've l-learned my l-lesson," he blubbered. "I won't do it again."

The blade rested underneath the human's chin. "No, you won't. Because she will be your last."

Jaden sliced the man's throat and moved to the side, watching the blood pump on to the grimy pavement. With all the carnage he caused tonight, there wasn't a drop on him. It took five minutes for him to accomplish his mission.

He ran his tongue across his teeth, eliminating any trace of the man's blood. He quickly wiped his blade clean on the leader's shirt, the silver betraying none of the death it caused tonight. He placed it back in its sheath and hurried out of the alley.

Alice had regained consciousness. She struggled to pull herself up and used the sign post to help with her balance. A fine sheen of sweat covered her brow, her breathing rapid.

What the hell?

His eyes had to be playing tricks on him. She looked brighter, luminescent. Like she was glowing. But humans didn't glow. Not physically, at least.

He glanced up. A street lamp cast its fluorescent light on to her. The sweat from her skin combined with the light gave her that strange radiance.

She lost her grip and Jaden rushed over to her, his arms

outstretched in case she fell. She jerked her head at his sudden movement and pulled her fist back, prepared to strike.

"Back off, asshole!" she shouted, her eyes full of fire. Her eyes softened briefly in recognition. "You were in the club. You were staring at my friend."

Actually, I was staring at you.

But since she was just attacked, he decided to keep that little tidbit to himself. "Are you all right?" he asked.

Alice was flushed and shaky, the adrenaline still pumped through her system. Her lip was cut from where the man hit her, the scent of her blood made his mouth water. For Christ's sake, he just fed, but her cinnamon fragrance made his throat burn.

"I'm fine, thanks."

He swallowed hard and focused on her face rather than her blood. He extended his hand. "You don't look okay. Let me help you."

She recoiled from his hand as if it were a snake about strike. "Are you with them?"

"Of course not."

"Then why are you here?"

"I saw them coming after you when you left the club. I wanted to make sure you were okay."

Alice looked past him, that emerald gaze darting around the street. "Where are they?"

"Gone."

"What?" The blood drained from her face as her gaze slid back to Jaden. "Gone where?"

"They're not coming back to hurt you," Jaden replied.

"They're gone?" She swallowed hard, her eyes wide. "How...how long was I out?"

Jesus, she was terrified. Not because of what could have

happened to her, but of what she might have done while she was unconscious.

It made no sense to him whatsoever.

"You never passed out. You had some sort of seizure, but you stopped shaking when they let you go," Jaden said. "I came around the corner and they tried to fight me. After a few good punches, they ran off."

"That's good." Relief temporarily washed over her, but she seemed to remember she wasn't alone. She pegged him with another hard glare. "What about you? Last man standing gets the prize?"

"It's not like that."

She scowled at him. "How do I know you're not going to make it worse? How do I know you're not saving me for yourself?"

"If I wanted to do anything to you, I'd have done it by now. I want to help." He kept his hand level. "You're hurt."

"I've been hit harder than this and by someone worse than them. It's nothing I can't handle."

Fury coiled in his stomach. She'd been attacked before? He wanted the name of the bastard who hurt her so he could inflict some pain of his own.

Have you completely lost your mind?

He must have. Or the human's blood was spiked. Either way, Jaden was not in his right mind. He didn't know where these protective instincts came from or why they were there. It spelled trouble and he couldn't afford to be distracted right now.

"You also had some sort of seizure so you shouldn't be alone right now. At least let me get you back to the club," he said. "You'll be around more people. You could go back in and be with your friends."

She winced. "No. I'd rather not go back in there."

Now this put him in an awkward situation. He wasn't about to manhandle her back to the club. If she chose to walk away alone, then he'd have to follow her just so he made sure she arrived home safely.

Alice surprised him when she put her free hand in his. He remained motionless as her emotions surged through him. One of his gifts when he came into this life was the ability to know what a person felt and he used that information to his advantage. He could intensify or diminish that feeling. Usually, he made a person's pain worse--even to the point of having them stroke out or have a heart attack.

But something strange happened. He sensed her fear, anger and suspicion. Not surprising given what just happened. There was something else that he felt from her and it almost knocked Jaden flat on his ass.

The fury he felt disappeared and was replaced with a current of fire running up his arm. He'd never felt anything like it. Her touch awakened every nerve in his body, a searing jolt he couldn't ignore.

Jaden cleared his throat as they headed up the street. "How are you getting home?"

"I'll call a cab."

"You could be waiting a while."

"It's no big deal."

To him it was. He didn't want a repeat of what happened in the alley and the best option would be to get her friends out here to take her home. Before he could stop himself, he blurted out the words that changed his life forever.

"Will you let me take you home?"

He needed his head examined. What the hell was he doing? She was the victim of an assault. She didn't know him and had no reason to trust him. For him, it was to see with his own two eyes that she was tucked away from the demons of the outside world.

He cleared his throat. "I'd like to make sure you get home safely."

"I don't even know your name," Alice mumbled.

"Jaden."

She gave a small smile and lightly squeezed his hand. "I'm Alice. Alice Roarke."

Good God that felt good. A little too good. He wondered how her thighs would feel squeezing his hips as he –

Hello, erection! What an inappropriate time to stop by.

Jaden focused on her emotions instead of what was going on in his pants. He stroked the top of her hand with his thumb, the slow caress reducing her anxiety.

"Is there someone I can call for you?" he asked. "Are you sure you don't want me to get your friends inside the club?"

"They're having too much fun and I don't want them to see me like this. I'd never hear the end of it from them for getting myself in trouble."

He let loose another surge of his power, chipping away her resistance. Yes, he was somewhat forcing his will on her, but he'd rather get kneed in the groin than hurt her.

"Then let me take you home."

He watched her wrestle with the decision. For the first time in his life, he wished he had Varrik's ability to read minds. He wanted to know exactly what she was thinking right now.

The tension eased out of her shoulders. "I'd appreciate a ride home," she said wearily. "Thank you."

Jaden swallowed, trying to ignore how his heart fluttered when she said yes. He was immediately grateful he chose to drive his Viper instead of the Corvette. No need to remind her he was the one who drove her off the road a few nights ago.

"I'm going to move my arm to your waist so you can lean against me," he said.

"Thanks for the warning."

"Well, I don't want your fist to collide with my jaw."

She offered a weak smile. "I'd probably break my hand."

His arm snaked around her waist and she leaned against him for support. Oh yeah, this felt so damn good. Didn't matter that the right side of his body was enflamed from the contact and his erection throbbed painfully--he'd endure it just to touch her.

"Alice, I won't hurt you," he promised.

She met his gaze, those emerald pools a balm to the ice in his veins. "I believe you."

~ * ~

Now this was very interesting.

Markus tailed Jaden and the human female. He kept his distance because he knew if he came too close, the vampire would go after him. Jaden should've known the Shadow was following him but he was too preoccupied with the woman on his arm.

Markus tightened his sweaty palm on his gun, anxious in his mission. Really, this was suicide. Many of his brethren, like the one he felt tonight, followed and fought the Ice Warrior, but they eventually met the same fate – death by Jaden's powerful hands. Deadly, selfish and vicious were characteristics attributed to him, acting in no one's self-interest but his own.

But what the Shadow saw right now was neither selfish nor vicious. What Jaden did now was kind and compassionate, two things he was never known to be.

He watched as Jaden opened the door for the woman and slid awkwardly into the car. She was injured. Markus caught the coppery scent of her blood and by the way Jaden moved so rigidly, he smelled it as well. Fresh blood appealed to every vampire and Shadow, but her blood pushed Jaden to the edge. Even from here, Markus saw Jaden struggling to keep his mouth shut and prevent those canines from punching through his lips.

Another interesting development. Jaden wasn't taking her. At least, not yet.

The car peeled down the street. Markus quickly slid into his own car. He wanted to see where Jaden was heading, knowing the Host would be pleased with his findings. He didn't know how the woman would fit into his game, but he was determined to find out because she might be the only one to bring Jaden to his knees.

Chapter 5

"Cell 2124. Lights out!"

"I'll turn the light out when I'm damn good and ready," he muttered.

John-Paul Finch stared up at the gray ceiling, his anger simmering beneath the surface. He hated small spaces, and here he was in this godforsaken cage.

He never let any woman get the best of him. After all, he had eluded police for a year for the rape and murder of the bitches in his town. Hell, his light brown hair, hazel eyes and angelic smile gave him the appearance of an altar boy. Along with his athletic physique and boyish charm, he was the perfect predator hiding behind an innocent mask.

No one would think the man with the boyish charm and Irish Catholic upbringing would ever be capable of such rage and violence. The bodies he left behind were unidentifiable except through DNA and he cleaned up so well behind himself, he was sure he'd never get caught.

Now two years later, he was in a nine by twelve foot cell in a Fulton County prison. All because of Alice Roarke.

He linked his arms behind his head and narrowed his eyes. She managed to break free from the two cuffs on her wrist and the choke collar around her neck. Didn't matter she was naked, bleeding from the brand on her shoulder and her wrists from where he kept her shackled. He was still trying to figure it out where she went when the police slapped the handcuffs on him and hauled his ass to jail.

He should've killed the bitch when he had the chance.

But it wasn't the third day. She escaped on the second. He did everything in threes. He had to. It was why he saved Alice for last. She was the perfect end to his first set of three murders.

How she got out was a mystery to him, but it was right after their last session when he marked her as his. Damn, he still got hard when he thought of that class. It was the only time Alice begged for him to stop. Each plea, each scream, had cranked him higher. Sometimes, it was that memory that made his days bearable in this hellhole.

Even when he gave her his all, Alice never truly broke. And he did his damndest to break her. The other two he had were extremely compliant. No matter what he did, she disobeyed him, fighting him tooth and nail against all the pain he inflicted on her.

Three women. Two murders. One bitch with whom he had unfinished business.

He wiped his hands on his navy jumpsuit, trying to get comfortable, but the bunk didn't accommodate his six foot three frame. No matter. He wouldn't be in here much longer. This cell may have been his home for the past twenty-four months, but he had no intention of staying. He'd planned to escape ever since he was captured. It would happen; it was just a matter of timing.

"Finch!" A sharp bang clanged against the iron bars. "I said lights out, asshole."

He flipped off the guard as he switched off the light in his cell. He glared at the concrete ceiling as his eyes adjusted to the darkness. He wasn't going to spend the rest of his life in this hellhole. His days in here were numbered.

The first order of business when he got out? Find Alice Roarke and make sure that bitch got what was coming to her.

Chapter 6

Oh, girl. What are you doing?

Alice had a concussion. She was sure of it. Those two men gave her a good beating in the alley. Then they must have knocked her head again when she waited for the blackout to pass.

Because if she was coherent, there was no way she just climbed into a car with a complete stranger ten minutes ago--a person who caused two men to disappear.

That should have sent her survival instincts into overdrive, a loud voice shouting *Stranger, danger!* inside her head. However, her internal alarm was quiet. No warning bells, no premonition of harm that may come her way. Her instincts said he was safe even though he looked like a soldier about to go into combat.

She cast a sideway glance at Jaden, getting a better view of him in the dim traffic lights than in the club. His black hair was held back with a leather tie, the ponytail resting at the nape of his neck between his broad shoulders. A strong square jaw with pink lips set in a firm line. His pale blue eyes focused on the road ahead of him yet she was certain he watched her as well.

Not only was the man hot, but he was huge. Jaden was at least two hundred and sixty pounds and she was willing to bet all of it was pure muscle. She saw the curve of his bicep through the black leather jacket which clung perfectly to his skin. She caught the swirls of what looked like a Celtic tattoo circling both wrists. Her eyes traveled down his chest, his rippling six-pack, his stomach and the tops of his massive thighs. There was so much power in his body and he could easily snap her in half without thinking twice.

Yet, she felt safe with Jaden. He said he wouldn't hurt her. Normally she'd scoff at the promise of a total stranger, but she believed him. He saved her from the attack and he touched her as if she were a piece of glass capable of shattering at any moment. That counted for something. Right?

Yeah. Definitely a concussion.

"You okay over there?" he asked, the deep baritone of his voice cutting the silence.

She forced a smile on her face. "Doing fine, thank you."

"You're very quiet."

"I don't have much to say. Just enjoying the ride."

Especially if it didn't end with her body in a ditch.

They reached a stoplight and he turned in his seat to look at her. Alice felt the blood rushing to her cheeks as he stared at her, but she couldn't break away from those eyes. The color of the midday sky, she could lose herself in those eyes, float away from all the horror and pain of her world.

"Interesting," he murmured. His hand touched her skin and it heated up even more. "You really are okay."

"Is that a bad thing? Should I be doing something else?"

He put his hand back on the steering wheel. Damn. She wished he'd kept his hand on her face or moved a little lower to her shoulder. Her breast wouldn't be so bad either.

She shook herself. She usually shied away from sex because of John-Paul's attempted rape. But with Jaden, the idea didn't seem so terrible. In fact, she was open to the possibility.

"Most women would be crying. Or at least in shock."

She agreed with him. But apparently her brain was malfunctioning at the moment.

"I'm not most women."

"Obviously."

She frowned at his tone. It sounded...playful? Not something she'd associate with this guy. Brooding, lethal and animalistic were words she'd use to describe him.

"Do you want me to start freaking out? Would that make you feel better?"

"Would it make you feel better?" He smiled as he turned on to Hooper Road, slowing on the side street as he approached the apartment complex. "Tell me, Alice. How can I make the hurt go away?"

The man nearly purred those words to her. It made her wonder what else he could do with that tongue.

She shifted in her seat. Man, she really needed to crack a window and let some cool air in the car. "I'll be better once I'm home. If I start acting hysterical, I'll feel like an idiot."

"Then just be yourself." He parked in front of her building and turned off the engine. He sat silently for a moment before he turned those piercing eyes on her again. "May I walk you to your door?"

Alice stiffened for a moment. It was one thing to let this guy drive her home. It was something completely different to have him escort her inside her apartment. With everything that happened tonight, she just wanted to climb into bed.

She cleared her throat. "I appreciate it, but I can make it on my own."

"But you were hurt."

"I'll be all right."

"I'd feel better if you let me check your injuries."

She raised her eyebrows. "You're a doctor?"

"No, but I know a lot about injuries from the battles I've been in."

"Were you in the military?"

"Something like that."

"Wow, you could really be useful as a human Magic 8 Ball," Alice said, her voice laden with sarcasm. "You want to try giving me an actual answer?"

He laughed. Jaden wasn't so scary when he laughed or smiled. But at the end of the day, he was still a stranger. A real-life question mark.

Was he one of the good guys? Or a wolf in sheep's clothing?

"I'm not a doctor by trade, but I can assure you I'm highly qualified when it comes to injuries to the human body."

"That's not an answer. Are you a med student? A physician's assistant? Mortician?"

"I've had a lot of experience when it comes to injuries. Let's leave it at that."

She folded her arms across her chest. He was so infuriating! He must work for the government to give her all of those half-answers.

"Why should I believe anything you say?"

He wasn't offended by her suspicion. "You're smart not to. But I won't do anything to make tonight worse for you."

"Maybe you're just waiting for the right moment."

But she didn't believe that. She felt safe with Jaden. More than she should.

Jaden leaned forward, the amusement replaced with a burning sincerity. "Alice, I swear I won't hurt you."

Any irritation she felt melted away instantly. God, those sky blue eyes were hypnotic. She wanted to float away in them, leave her painful world behind and just be free.

"You can trust me."

She bit her lip. Against all common sense and good judgment, she believed him. Absolutely. Without a doubt.

Which was probably going to put the nail in her coffin tonight.

"All right." Alice put her hand on the door handle. "But you're just checking me out and then leaving. Five minutes, tops."

"No problem."

She hardly had a chance to blink when he appeared at her door. How did he move so fast?

He held out his hand and she placed her palm in his. His hand was so warm and smooth, not something she'd expect from someone like him.

She took a deep breath, her stomach fluttering. He smelled delicious, the leather and natural musky scent of his skin made her head swim. Alice had the irrational urge to run her tongue all over his body just so she could savor the taste of his skin.

Good lord, where were these thoughts coming from? Her normal reaction was to fade into the background and pray no one noticed her. She never had thoughts about a man like this.

Then again, she never met a man like Jaden.

Alice opened the door to her ground floor apartment and flipped on the lights. Setting her keys and wallet on the entry table, she stepped into the living room. Her beige sofa and matching recliners had seen better days, but they were comfortable and cozy. Her coffee table held an array of student projects along with a mystery novel she was reading. Her television was on the opposite side of the room with her stereo and assortment of DVDs piled haphazardly in a corner.

Alice looked at him sheepishly. "Sorry for the mess. I don't have guests over too often."

His gaze flitted from one corner of the room to the other like he was assessing possible entry points into her apartment. She very well could believe that he'd been in the military. Nothing escaped this man's gaze.

"It doesn't bother me. It's a nice place."

"I'm sure it's not what you're used to."

His eyes zeroed in on her. "Why would you say that?"

Her heart sped up under his gaze. What was it about this man that made her so hot and bothered?

She took a deep breath to rein in her hormones. "Your car probably costs as much as my apartment. I'm sure you're place is bigger than mine. My home must make you feel claustrophobic."

"You don't know that for certain," he said, "and I know this is a total male statement, but I love my car. So it's quite possible I live in a shoebox and park my car right next to it."

Her chuckle was cut off with a wince as she took off her jacket. Now that the adrenaline had worn off, she felt her bruises in full force. Damn. If she was sore now, she was going to feel awful in the morning.

He moved in front of her, his brows drawn in concern. "Here, let me help you."

He slid his hands in between the soft corduroy and her black shirt and slowly pulled the jacket down her arms. She watched as pale hands grazed the fabric of her shirt before reaching the skin of her forearms. Chills rippled down her spine as his fingertips brushed against her skin. Suddenly, she wished she had more bruises so he could keep touching her.

He draped her jacket on the back of the couch. He took her chin in his hand and cradled her cheek in his palm. His thumb swept across the tender skin and she flinched.

"Sorry. I didn't mean to make it worse," he murmured.

Alice closed her eyes. Who knew such a large man could be so gentle? He caressed her cheek again and she bit her lip to prevent from sighing. His touch was magical and made her ache in all the right places.

All common sense fled as his fingertips moved across her face. She couldn't remember the last time someone had touched her like that. So tender, so loving. She felt herself floating away, his strokes taking her to a place where white-hot energy and pleasure reigned.

"Your cheek's fine. The discoloration should go away in a couple of hours."

The sound of his voice and his touch sent another pulsating wave of heat between her thighs. He cupped her face in one of his palms, his other hand traveling to the scar on her throat. Her thoughts scattered especially with his hand holding her face and his thumb making gentle circles across her cheek.

"Where else did he hurt you?"

Alice's eyes flew open, fear stiffening her spine. Who was he talking about? John-Paul?

"You were holding your side earlier."

Alice relaxed. Oh, the jerks in the alley. That's who he was talking about. The one who hit her.

"The right side. He got me pretty hard in the ribs."

His eyes darkened for a moment. "I'd like to see it. But I understand if you don't want me touching you."

She bit her lip. She didn't care how bad her side hurt as long as he'd keep his hands on her. "It's all right."

He knelt in front of her, his hands at the hem of her shirt. Jaden lifted the fabric with the same care when he inspected her cheek. He held the shirt up with one hand while the other gently probed her ribs.

"Does this hurt?" he asked.

Her chest tightened as his breath blew across her skin. A blast of heat licked over her breasts and settled between her legs. It was the slightest of pressure and it made her knees weak. There was no pain in his touch. Only a surprisingly small amount of pleasure.

"No," she whispered.

Jaden sucked in a breath as his warm palm traveled up her ribcage. He pushed a little harder and she almost moaned. "What about now?"

"Just...a little."

He moved her shirt back in place. "They're a little bruised. No taping necessary." He glanced at her shoulder. "Would you like me to take a look at your shoulder? You were rubbing it earlier in the club."

She took a step away from him. Not a chance. There was no way she'd let him see that scar. "No. It's fine."

"Are you sure? Because I can –"

"No. I'm good."

He raised an eyebrow but didn't comment as he looked around the apartment again. "Are you sure there's no one you can call to be with you right now? It's not good for you to be alone tonight. Especially if you've had a seizure."

"I've been alone most of my life. Really. I'm fine." She waved her hand. "And the seizures are nothing. I'll be okay."

The hell she was okay. She couldn't believe she almost had another episode tonight. God, twice in one day. She needed to make that appointment as soon as possible.

"I'd feel better if you'd let me come by tomorrow night to check on you."

Alice fidgeted in front of him. This very fine man wanted to come back and make sure she was okay. It made her nervous.

And a little hot. She really wanted to see him again.

"Okay. Sure. I don't mind."

"Is eight-thirty too late? Or do you have plans tomorrow?"

"No. Eight-thirty's good for me."

Jaden picked up her hand and kissed the top of it. She sucked in a breath as his lips lingered against her skin, his breath a light tickle. Her skin flared, tingled, and she wanted more of his touch.

"Thank you for the ride home, Jaden." She wiped her hands on her pants and added, "And thank you for...helping me tonight."

"I'm glad I could help." He brushed a strand of hair out of her eyes. "I'll see you tomorrow Alice."

He planted one more kiss on her hand before he let himself out. She heard the car start and roar down the street. Alice stroked the spot on her hand where his lips burned her. Suddenly, tomorrow night seemed a thousand years away.

Jaden parked further down the block, his breathing labored. He closed his eyes and leaned against the leather seat. Her scent lingered against his hand and he brought it to his face. Alice's cinnamon scent inflamed his throat. Spicy. Sultry.

She wanted him. Her body let off the sweet scent of arousal when he checked her ribs. Alice may not have been completely comfortable with it, but her body's response didn't lie. And he was ready to have her. His cock was at full attention and he wanted nothing more than to drive it deep into her body and to be sheathed in that warm, wet heat.

Leaving was the right decision, but God knew he wanted to stay. It would've been so easy to convince her to let him spend the night. One more touch and that would've been it. Reduce tension, increase desire and *voila!* they'd be in bed for the rest of the evening.

But he didn't want to do that to Alice. He wanted her to come to him on her own terms. No tricks. No manipulation.

He glanced back at the row of apartments. He really didn't like the idea of her living on the ground floor. Too many points of entry.

Christ. What was this human female doing to him?

Jaden Payne – warrior, slayer, and vampire – just asked a woman if he could come back and check on her. He *asked*. That was the craziest part. Jaden did what he wanted, who he wanted and when he wanted. For him to get permission from a human woman catapulted him into unfamiliar territory.

He was intrigued by her and her secrets. He didn't miss the cold blast of her fear when he asked about her shoulder. Jaden knew it wasn't from what happened earlier tonight. He watched her fight off her attackers. All she felt then was anger.

When he asked her about her shoulder, it was something much deeper. More primal.

Jaden was surprised by the sudden distance. She wanted him to touch her. She still did. Just not anywhere near her left shoulder.

Why?

He did know one thing. She wasn't the daughter of foster. Her last name was Roarke. After tomorrow night, she was no longer his concern. He'd check on her, make sure she was okay and disappear from her life.

But her hand had felt so good in his and when she leaned into him for support, she tucked into his side perfectly.

The shrill ring of his cell phone jolted him out of his thoughts. He scowled when he recognized the number and pressed the *talk* button. "What do you want Salvatore?"

"You need to come back to Liam's place."

"I don't think so. I really don't want to see that asshole any time soon."

"You don't have a choice." Salvatore's voice was grim. "You are ordered to come back here."

"Why?"

"Ryder was hurt tonight. Almost killed. Several Shadows got the jump on him while on patrol."

Jaden sat up. "How bad are his injuries?"

"Pretty bad, but he'll make it." There was a pause and Jaden knew what was coming next wasn't going to be good news. "And there's been a development."

"About the Shadows going after Ryder?"

"No, it's you. You're the development."

~ * ~

Markus waited a solid fifteen minutes before he approached the human female's building. He wanted to make sure the vampire was far enough away so that Jaden wouldn't come back and confront him.

He watched a couple emerge from the building and he quickly headed for the door before it locked him out. Markus walked over to the mailboxes, looking for any clue as to the woman's identity.

None of the mailboxes listed first names, but one caught his eye. Apartment 2. A. Roarke. He quickly searched the other eight boxes, and none of them had an "A" as the first initial of the tenant.

"Alice," Markus whispered.

He pulled out his cell phone and pressed pound six. After two rings he heard the voice of the Host. The one who'd transform him into a full-fledged vampire once Jaden was dead.

"It's Markus."

"A little late checking in, aren't we?"

He closed his eyes. "I didn't mean to offend you. I'm sorry."

"As you should be. What news do you have for me?"

"We lost Scott tonight. An Emain Macha killed him."

A pause. "Are you sure of this?"

"I felt Scott's death."

"Did you see it happen?"

"No."

"Then how do you know it's a one of the warriors?"

He gripped the phone tighter. "This vampire drew out the kill, and we know only one warrior does that. It was Jaden Payne."

"So you abandoned your brother?"

"He would've killed me as well. Scott was dead before I could get to him."

Markus held his breath as he waited for the Host to speak again. The quiet calm didn't fool him. Markus knew the Host was furious. He only hoped the Host wouldn't punish him for Scott's death.

"You better have some good news for me. Otherwise, I'll take days to kill you for this display of weakness."

Okay. Maybe not.

"I think we've found a way to get to the vampire," Markus said quickly. "He was with a woman tonight."

"So?"

"He dropped her off at her apartment."

The Host chuckled. "A human female? Really? Unless he got her on all fours, he usually avoids them like the plague." The laughter faded away and the voice became harsh. "He not only protects civilian vampires, but also humans. What you've just seen is him doing his job and you've wasted my time."

"He was with her for a while back at her apartment," Markus blurted out. "He was kind to her."

Another long pause. "Now that is interesting. He's never kind to anyone." The voice remained quiet for so long that Markus thought the Host had hung up. "What is her name?"

"Alice Roarke."

He waited several minutes as he heard the Host typing away on a keyboard. A few minutes later, that velvet voice purred in his ear, "Oh, this is good news."

The Shadow listened intently to the Host's findings. When he was sure the Host was finished, he found the courage to speak. "Would you like for me to meet him?"

"The sooner the better," the Host murmured. "You've done well tonight. Despite losing Scott, you have pleased me."

His heart fluttered in his chest at the Host's praise. "I live to serve you."

"And so you shall. Come back home. I want to fully express my gratitude for all your hard work."

The line went dead and Markus's heart pounded in his chest. The Host wasn't going to kill him and he was one step closer to becoming what he desired. He would be a full-fledged vampire.

He'd be a Host himself.

Chapter 7

Jaden had a few minutes to spare before the sun rose over the horizon. He parked the Viper in the garage of his isolated Tudor mansion, punched in the security code and entered through the side door.

Silence greeted him, broken only by the echo of his boots slapping against the hardwood floors. He was grateful for this sanctuary, especially with what happened at the compound tonight.

Damn, he had his balls handed to him by Liam earlier in the night. His cousin screamed at Jaden for about ten minutes for the death of Alice's attackers and not cleaning up properly. Also, he ignored a call from his fellow warrior who was actively tracking a group of Shadows and was nearly killed.

"Where were you tonight?" Liam had shouted.

"Looking for the Firebrand. Isn't that what you want me to do?"

"Really? Does that also include slicing and dicing a Shadow?"

"He got in my way and I took care of it. As Guardian, I am supposed to do everything within my power to locate and keep the Firebrand safe."

"But you haven't found her yet, have you?" Liam had narrowed his eyes. "Why did you leave Salvatore tonight? You two were supposed to stay together and I cleared you to fight."

Yeah. There was no way in hell Jaden was going to tell Liam about Alice. "I told him to leave and take care of Ryder."

"Since when does he follow orders from you?"

"Since I didn't give him a choice," Jaden had snapped. "I was hunting."

"The Firebrand? Shadows? Or a piece of ass? Tell me we didn't lose a potential lead and almost let a warrior die because you were too busy getting a blowjob."

"Isn't that how you got your promotion from the Sisters to rule over all of us?"

Jaden rubbed his jaw as he stopped at the base of the stairs. Still sore from where Liam punched him, but it was well worth it.

He glanced at the portrait hanging above the fireplace. Every morning without fail, Catherine Payne welcomed him home.

He remembered the day she sat for the painting. Hours dragged on, but she never complained as the artist captured her beauty. It truly was a masterpiece and he had brushed every detail on the canvas perfectly from the long blonde hair that fell to the small of her back, high cheekbones, and ivory skin.

The one thing the artist hadn't been able to change was her eyes. At the time, he was displeased with the look in her eyes. Now, it suited her perfectly. Her dark amber gaze stared at him coldly, indifferent to her surroundings. It showed the world the truly frigid bitch she had been.

"I don't know why I keep the damned thing," he muttered.

He should burn it or put it in storage, but she was the painful reminder of why humans and vampires didn't mix in his world--except for food and sex--and how his love ultimately led to Catherine's death.

"Show me how much you love me," she whispered. "Die for me."

He tore his gaze away from the portrait of his dead wife and walked up the black marble staircase toward his room, his boots echoing against the floor. The curtains were drawn tight now, and they'd reopen once it was mid-afternoon. The sunlight wouldn't kill him, at least not outright. The part about vampires bursting into flames was a myth. The truth was much worse.

Prolonged exposure to sunlight turned vampire blood into acid, cooking the body and liquefying the organs. In those four to five hours it took to die, the infected vampire felt every ounce of pain. So before the time of guns and axes, the family would light the vampire on fire, as a way to relieve the fire in the blood and effectively end the life.

He made it to his room and willed the door shut with his mind. Humans only used ten percent of their brains and his race was the same way before they hit puberty. Once their bodies transitioned and matured, a vampire's brain unlocked the other ninety percent. A definite evolutionary advantage.

Jaden sat on the edge of his massive bed, the black wrought iron frame taking up half of the wall. Two candles illuminated the room, the perfect amount of light for his sensitive eyes. He removed his boots, his pants and sweater until he was completely naked.

He crawled in between the silk sheets, his energy fading fast. He needed a clear head and the oblivion of sleep do to that. He didn't need dreams today, especially ones involving a certain brunette with haunting green eyes.

He put his hand to the side, caressing the pillow, wishing it was the soft skin he held in his palm hours before. He hoped Alice was all right. Human bodies were so fragile and even though she put up a tough front, she was hurt last night.

Jaden tightened his grip on the pillow. What if she had another seizure during the day? No one was around to check on her and make sure she was okay. She could easily seize, hit her head on the coffee table and hemorrhage in a matter of minutes.

Goddamn it. Why hadn't he asked for her phone number?

He closed his eyes. He shouldn't be worrying about her. He had other concerns. Like locating that damn Firebrand from the prophecy. She was a female he met last night. Just another human face in a sea of thousands.

But her face was one of the loveliest he'd ever seen. And her skin was so soft. Warm. Her leaning against him set his body on fire. She'd feel so warm with her body under his as she climaxed in his arms, calling his name.

He gritted his teeth at the image. His body was so hard he could hammer a nail with it.

This woman wasn't the one he was searching for, but she was something special. Something he wanted to have even though she was not one of his kind.

He chuckled dryly. Who was he kidding? He didn't need to destroy her life like he destroyed Catherine's. He had no interest in having history repeat itself.

Exhaustion finally took hold and he could feel himself drift into sleep. It was daylight. Alice was safe.

He'd check on her tonight, make sure she was okay and disappear from her life for good.

~ * ~

"You've got to be kidding me!"

Alice jumped when she heard the knock on her door, splashing the warm water from the bowl she was cleaning on her shirt. She glanced at the digital clock on her counter: 8:30

P.M.

Jaden said he'd come back to check on her. How did the time slip away from her, especially since it had been slow up to an hour ago?

She tried to keep herself busy all day and not think about seeing Jaden. She cleaned her apartment from top to bottom-- which took less time than she realized. Then she graded all of her students' art projects while writing out her lessons for the rest of the week. That still left her with almost five hours to kill.

Alice filled that time with watching movies, taking a quick jog around the block and checking e-mail--anything to keep from looking at the clock. Then time accelerated without her knowledge, and Jaden was on the other side of the door.

She quickly dabbed her shirt before heading toward the front door. She hoped to freshen up after dinner, but that was now out of the question.

Alice looked through the peephole and slid back the deadbolt. "Hi, Jaden. Come in."

He walked in and closed the door behind him. She tried not to stare at Jaden, but it was difficult. He wore a black shirt underneath his leather trench which accentuated the rippling muscles of his torso. His huge legs were sheathed in a pair of black jeans and she wished he'd drop the coat so she could get a good look at his ass.

Good grief, he was hot and built for sex.

She looked at herself. She was not.

Because nothing said sexy like a pair of gray yoga pants and a white T-shirt with a huge wet stain on her stomach.

"How are you feeling today?"

"As well as can be expected. A little sore, but nothing too uncomfortable." Alice gave a small smile. "I'm actually surprised I don't feel worse, but I'm not complaining. I'll take any lucky breaks when I get them."

His piercing gaze slowly roamed over her body. She felt her cheeks growing hot from his stare. Like his hands caressed her body instead of his eyes. "What about your side? Did you have any bruising?"

"I'm fine. It's just tender."

"Did you have a relapse last night? Any seizures today?"

"Really, I'm okay. No problems whatsoever." She twisted the hem of her shirt. "You know, you don't have to check on me."

He raised an eyebrow. "Did you call your friends and tell them what happened?"

"Oh, no." She grimaced at the idea of telling Kara and Tina about her attack. "I told you last night that I wasn't going to bother them. Besides, they would have stayed over here and coddle me like I was a baby. I'd rather forget the incident and move on."

"Do you have anyone else who will check on you?" he persisted. "A husband? Boyfriend?"

"No. Nothing like that."

"Then you're stuck with me."

Her body warmed at the thought, a dull ache spreading in all the right places. She actually liked the idea of being with him. A smile crept across his lips, like he knew she was aroused.

She swallowed hard, her mouth bone dry under his intense stare. She knew nothing about him, but whatever he had, she wanted it. And she wanted it now.

"You're quite adorable when you blush. It makes you even more attractive."

Alice giggled and twisted the shirt harder. "You're the only one who thinks so."

"If that's the case, then the men you know are idiots."

"Well, you are the exception. Men don't look at me the way women look at you."

He moved until he was directly in front of her. He cupped Alice's face and his thumb slid across her heated skin. She looked up at him, his eyes burning with a strange hunger. Good God, no one ever looked at her like this. It was the kind of stuff she read in books. A man completely enthralled with her.

"How do they look at me?"

"A handsome guy like you?" She shivered when his breath blew across her ear. "I'm sure the ladies just fall at your feet when you look their way."

"To be honest, I really don't care." He dipped his head so his hot breath caressed her ear. "I'm only interested in how you see me."

Alice eyed his shoulder and bicep, the muscles rippled underneath his shirt. Naked and on top of her was definitely her preference.

He nuzzled her with his nose, his lips brushed against her hair. She closed her eyes as he kissed her forehead. She was on fire. He barely touched her yet her body was hotter than a Georgia summer night.

Her breasts tightened in response. She couldn't help but wonder how it would feel to have his lips glide across her breast, her stomach.

"Scream for me, bitch…you'll never be rid of me."

Alice stiffened at John-Paul's voice inside her head. He was right. She couldn't get rid of him, no matter how hard she tried. She was damaged, ruined. No use to anyone.

"I've upset you." He leaned back, frowning. "I'm sorry."

"You don't need to apologize to me," she said. "You did nothing wrong."

"But I made you uncomfortable."

"No, you didn't. Not really."

"Then why are you so tense?"

She shrugged with a casualness she didn't feel. "I'm not used to getting attention like this."

"Why not?" His thumb stroked her cheek again. "You're a beautiful woman and any man with half a brain would be attracted to you."

"You're attracted to me?"

"Absolutely."

"So according to your theory, you have half a brain."

"I can't argue with your logic," he chuckled. "But you still seemed surprised. Why is it hard to believe I'd be interested in you?"

Alice took a step away from him, breaking contact. She was upset with herself. Upset she couldn't fix what was broken. Angry she couldn't let herself go.

Angry that two years later, John-Paul still haunted her.

"Alice, what's wrong?"

She looked at him. He genuinely seemed concerned about her and it was a welcome change. God, she couldn't remember the last time someone worried whether or not she came back home and how she felt.

But it wouldn't last. This moment was a rarity, a brief respite in her isolated world. He was going to leave in a few minutes and she'd be alone again. Better to distance herself now than to hold on to a dream completely out of her reach.

"Alice?"

"You've already made sure I'm all right so you can check me off your list." She forced a grin. "There's no need for you to stay. I'm sure you have plenty of things to do tonight."

"Do you really want me to leave?"

Her heart said no, but her brain won out. "Yes."

"You're sure about that? Because from the tone of your voice, it sounds like you'd rather I stay."

Great. Even he knew she was lying.

"I'm sure there are plenty of other women who would be just as flattered by your attention as I am."

"But I don't want to be around other women. I want to be with you." He tucked a dark tendril behind her ear. "Why do you think you're not worthy of me?"

"Because I'm not," she said. Was that breathless voice hers?

"I'll be the judge of that."

"That's because you don't know me. You don't know what's happened to me."

Alice cursed under her breath the moment those words flew out of her mouth. She wished she could take them back, but they were out and hung heavy in the air.

Jaden's eyes narrowed. "Last night wasn't your first attack."

"No. It wasn't." She crossed her arms, holding herself. "Bad luck just seems to follow me."

"How long ago?"

"It's been…two years."

"Will you tell me about it? I won't force you, but it might put you at ease to talk to me."

No one here knew what happened to her. Not even Tina and Kara who were her friends. That's why she left her old life behind in Atlanta. Alice couldn't stand to see the pity and revulsion in their eyes day in and day out.

She turned away from him. So what if he did look at her like some poor puppy kicked to the curb? He had no obligation to stay and it'd be easier for her to forget about him.

"I was attacked a couple of years ago."

A muscle ticked in his jaw. "How did it happen?"

"I was coming home from work. It wasn't even that late when I left the school." She braced her palms against the back of the sofa for support. "He followed me home. I didn't even have a chance to set down my purse when he attacked me. He clamped a cloth over my mouth. I smelled alcohol and something sweet." Alice looked down at her scarred wrists. "When I woke up, the first thing I felt was a chill. He stripped me of all my clothes and when my eyes finally adjusted to the darkness, I saw that both of my wrists were cuffed and pulled on either side of me. A dog collar was around my neck, a gag in my mouth."

"Where was your attacker?" Jaden asked.

"He was sitting in a chair next to me, waiting for me to wake up. He stroked my forehead three times. Everything he did was in threes. He even told me my name was divisible by three when you added up all the letters."

"What did he do to you?"

And there it was. The question she hated to answer. Alice took a deep breath as the memories swarmed her. She could tell him a part of the truth. Not all of it. The scars on her neck and wrists she could explain. He didn't need to know about her shoulder.

"He always visited me on the third hour. Three, six, nine, twelve. He brought me two bowls. One was full of water and the other was dog food. I refused to eat the food and I was beaten for my disobedience." She trembled at the memories. "I prayed every time he came that he'd kill me. But all he kept saying was that I was his bitch and he'd never let me go." She swallowed hard. "I wasn't supposed to live through it. He kept telling me Day Three was my special day. I knew that was the day he was going to kill me. Just like the others. That's when he raped and killed the others."

Alice remembered that last session with him, the burns and the absolute horror of what he had done. No, she wouldn't share what happened the last time she was with John-Paul. She'd never let anyone know how John-Paul permanently marked her as his.

"But you escaped," he said.

"I knew I had to get away from him. I wasn't going to die like the animal he thought I was."

"How'd you get away?"

"All of that is kind of hazy. I don't know how I got free, but I did. One minute I was in the cabin and then I was in the woods behind his house. My wrists were bleeding and I was naked, but I ran to a neighbor's house and called the police."

Which was pretty close to the truth. After he burned her, he left, promising something even better when he returned. She blacked out and woke up in the middle of the woods behind the tiny cottage. The metal from the cuffs and the collar melted into her skin. She still didn't understand that herself.

"He's been in jail for the past two years." She looked down at the floor. "But I still dream about it. I dream of him behind me, telling me what a good bitch I am. How I'll always be his."

She knew he was still looking at her, but she couldn't bring herself to look at him. She hoped he'd say some kind of lame goodbye and be on his way. Then she could go back to her normal, boring life.

"Do you regret telling me this?"

Actually, she felt relieved when she told him a part of the story. It was nice to talk about it, but she knew the disgust and pity would arrive shortly.

"No. I just don't like talking about it," she mumbled. "I

moved to Ravenna so people wouldn't look at me with pity."

He leaned forward, his voice gentle in contrast the hard warrior he appeared to be. "You didn't have to say anything, but you did. You chose to tell me what happened to you. Why?"

She had no idea. If she felt uncomfortable with his advances, she could make up some quick excuse or lie to get him to stop. She didn't have to go into her messy history.

But he made her feel…good. And it had been a long time since she'd felt that way about any man. Especially one as visually appealing as Jaden.

"I haven't been close to anyone since that happened. Not that I was ever with a lot of men before. Only two others and one after the attack that ended kind of badly. And that's not where I thought we were headed," she said quickly. "It's just – oh, hell. I just thought you should know. That's all." Alice squeezed her arms around herself tighter. "I'm going to shut up now. I think I've embarrassed myself enough."

Smooth, Alice. Great way to keep a guy interested.

She felt like a total idiot. Her cheeks were so hot she was sure she could roast marshmallows on them. If he was interested in her before, Alice was certain she obliterated any feelings now.

She glanced over at Jaden and frowned at his expression. She wasn't expecting him to look at her like that. Disgust or pity was the common reaction.

But this was unexpected. He looked at her with a mixture of reverence and awe. And desire.

"Why are you looking at me like that?"

"Because I think you're extraordinary."

"I…what?" Alice was at a complete loss of words. Extraordinary? Seriously? "I don't understand why."

"You trusted me with a painful part of your past. Someone who knows nothing about you. I'm betting a lot of people in your life have no clue what happened to you."

"It's not something I broadcast," she muttered. "I don't want anyone to feel sorry for me or look at me as if I'm diseased."

"It's hard to open yourself up like that and not know how a person will react."

"I don't like people lying to me. It's better to be honest." She shook her head. "But your reaction surprises me."

"But that's not the only reason I think you're extraordinary. You fought for your freedom and you've moved on with your life. You're not wallowing in self-pity. You're fighting to overcome what's happened to you." He walked until he was right beside her, his eyes burning with desire. "And it makes me want you even more."

She swallowed hard as he just stared at her. "After all I just told you, you still want me?"

"God, yes."

~ * ~

Well, so much for just checking on her and leaving.

As soon as he caught her scent, he knew he was in trouble. Ever since he arrived, all he wanted was to hold her in his arms and bury himself deep inside of her. It took all of his self-control to not grab her and kiss every inch of her body as it was.

The surprise on her face was precious. Like she half-expected him to bolt once she revealed her secret. But she was tough, a fighter. Courage was such a huge turn-on.

His arm snaked around her waist as she looked up at him with those wide, emerald eyes. With all of his female lovers, there'd been some sort of seduction to get him in bed or coaxing the female to get her on her back. Yet with Alice, there was no calculating gleam, no erotic overtures. Just a simple honesty that was seductive and alluring all on its own.

Jaden couldn't stand it any longer. He had to have a taste, even if it was just of her lips.

He dipped his head and kissed her. Her spicy scent invaded his head as his mouth moved against hers. Dear God, she tasted like heaven. What would her blood taste like against his tongue?

No, he wouldn't take her blood. Not tonight. But he'd have a taste of her just the same.

His tongue ran across her lips and she gasped in surprise. Taking the opportunity, he slid his tongue inside her mouth, gently questing. She gripped his arms and pulled him closer. He groaned in approval, his tongue sliding further into her mouth, a silky penetration he wanted to mimic between her thighs. His erection popped to attention as she returned his kiss.

Hell yeah, he wanted her. In every way possible.

He broke away first, pressing his forehead to hers. "Thank you."

"F-for what?"

"I've wanted to do that since I walked through the door." He brushed a strand of hair out of her eyes. "I'd like to do more, but I won't pressure you."

She took a step back, but he didn't let her go. "I'm really not what you want. Trust me."

A muscle twitched in his jaw. If Alice ever told him that man's name, then God better have mercy on that human male. Jaden would hold the man captive for a couple of days until he was Jaden's bitch.

"It's not pity keeping me here."

"Then what is?"

He grinned. "Apart from being beautiful, you're a fighter. You're sassy, strong, and naturally distrustful."

"Being naturally distrustful is a good thing?" Alice asked.

"It makes you smart and cautious." He tightened his arm around her waist. "I want you, Alice, but I won't force myself on you. I want you to feel comfortable with anything we do."

She touched his mouth, the pad of her thumb running across his lower lip. He kissed the tip, his mouth closing over her succulent skin. He sucked it further into his mouth and felt her pulse kicking against the tip of his tongue.

"Do you trust me, Alice?"

"I do. I don't know why, but I do feel comfortable around you."

"Do you want me to go?"

Fire ran through his veins while she lazily traced his jaw with her free hand. His body ached with need as he forced himself to remain calm. He couldn't remember the last time he felt so strongly about a woman. Not even Catherine had stoked such a desire in him.

He wanted Alice. Tonight.

She looked up at him, bringing his knuckles to her lips. "Don't go," she whispered. "Please stay with me."

Thank you, Jesus.

He dipped his head, his lips inches from hers. He hesitated, giving her one last chance to back out. Alice closed the gap and kissed him. Her lips were soft and silky as they met his. His thirst disappeared as something more carnal took its place. There were so many ways he wanted to please her, but he would let Alice set the pace to tell him what she wanted and when to stop.

Jaden pulled her closer to him. He growled at the contact

with every curve and line molding seamlessly to his body. His tongue ran across the seam of her lips, begging for entrance. Alice moaned as his tongue found hers, sliding in and out of her mouth, making him think of another part of her body he'd soon penetrate.

Jaden could barely contain his excitement. He was a kid at Christmas with the best present waiting to be unwrapped. And like that last gift, he'd take his time with her.

She grabbed on to his arms while he circled his hips, his erection rubbing against her stomach. His hands moved to the hem of her shirt, slipping them underneath the soft cotton as his fingers skirted over the smooth skin of her stomach.

"Will you let me take this off?" he whispered against her mouth.

She lifted her arms above her head. "Yes, please."

He pulled her shirt off and dropped it near her feet. Jaden moved up her torso until he reached the creamy swells of her breasts, the lace tickling his palms.

Shit, they were perfect. Full and heavy, her breasts filled his hands. He caressed her through the lace and her nipples hardened against his fingertips. He couldn't wait to pull those pretty pink tips in his mouth.

Her hand brushed his side, inches away from one of his daggers. He pulled away and she actually whimpered from the separation. He turned off the lights, plunging the room into almost total darkness. The light from a street lamp near her window allowed an ambient glow to penetrate the room, but not much.

Luckily, the corner of the room he needed was completely dark. With lightning speed, he removed his coat and placed it on the oversized chair along with his weapons which he concealed within the folds of his jacket. Alice finding those on him would definitely kill the mood. And she was too beautiful, too delectable to stop now.

"Jaden?"

"I'm right here," he murmured, coming back in her line of vision. "I'm not going anywhere."

He took off his shirt and dropped it on top of hers. His mouth returned to her lips, kissing her with a renewed fervor. Her anxiety disappeared as their tongues danced, a sensuous twirl which conveyed their passion for each other. His hands rested on the small of her back, pushing her hips against his.

She sighed, her breasts flattening against his chest. His groin was on fire from the subtle pressure, demanding he ease the ache. His powers surged, but he clamped them down. He had no intention of manipulating her emotions even though he could make her pleasure more intense. Jaden wanted Alice to come to him all on her own.

He ran his tongue down the column of her throat. Her skin was so sweet, that unique cinnamon scent condensing in his mouth. She shuddered in his arms, a pleasured moan caressing his ear. God, he loved hearing that sound. He pressed the tip of his tongue against a vein, the blood pumping furiously beneath a few layers of skin.

He nipped her throat and another moan bubbled out of her mouth. "What do you want, Alice?"

The tips of his fangs grew past his lips. Just one little pinch and they'd both be in ecstasy. Fuck, he wanted a taste to see if her blood was as sweet as her scent.

But not tonight. Tonight was about her needs. Her desire. He wouldn't take from her like that asshole who almost raped her.

He forced his fangs to recede as he ran his hands down her spine, dragging his tongue against her scented skin. Traced the line of her vein. Nipped the base of her throat. Little torments to heighten her passion.

"Tell me what you want, Alice."

~ * ~

Alice let her head fall back to give him full access to her neck. This incredibly hot, sexy man wanted to please her. And he was doing a damn good job already.

The rational part of her said that getting in bed with a total stranger was a very, very bad idea and she had never done anything like this before. She had no idea who this man was besides that he was incredibly attractive and treated her so gently. It could all be an act.

She didn't care. God help her, she didn't want him to stop. She wanted to remember what it felt like to be loved and cherished for once instead of battered and bruised. He lightly bit her skin, his tongue drawing lazy circles around her collarbone.

"Do you want me to stop?" he asked again. Jaden eased back and stared into her eyes. "Say the word and I will."

She knew he would. No matter how hard he was, he'd stop the moment she felt uncomfortable.

She wanted to answer him, but the words disappeared with every stroke of his tongue. She arched her back, pushing her breasts further into his hands. His thumbs ran across the lace, her pebbled nipples hardening more with each caress. He could do whatever he wanted as long as he kept touching her.

"No," she finally croaked out. "Don't stop."

"Is this all you want? Or do you want more?"

"More," she breathed. "I want more."

Jaden stared hungrily at the bra, her pink nipples peeking out from behind the white lace. He unhooked the clasp and peeled the lace cups away. She groaned as his palms cupped her breasts. The Celtic tattoos on his wrists wound all the way up to his forearms, the scrolls and swirls undulating as if they were alive on his skin. He bowed his head as his tongue circled one of the nipples before he pulled it into his mouth.

Alice gripped the back of his head to keep him in place. Her thoughts scattered as he suckled her breast. God, his tongue was like silk against her body. Circling, stroking and tugging. He moved to her other breast, his slow licks intensifying her arousal.

He moved her until she was leaning against the back of the couch. Jaden knelt in front of her and kissed his way from her sternum to her navel. He hooked his thumbs into the elastic waistband of her pants and slid them down her legs.

Jaden looked up at her. Alice trembled at the raw lust in his eyes. He looked like he wanted to devour her. No man had ever looked at her with such hunger in his gaze.

For a few moments, this exquisite man made her feel whole and she didn't want this feeling to end. And in this moment, she believed she deserved someone like him. Maybe even to keep, no matter how insane the idea was.

"You are so beautiful," he whispered.

"I-I've never felt beautiful before," she said shakily.

"Hmm, I'll have to make sure you remember that." He nipped her skin. "I'll make sure you will not forget it either."

"You're doing a great job so far."

He pressed a kiss against her thigh. His hand moved up further until it was exactly where she wanted him to put his mouth. He stroked her through her white cotton panties.

"You're very wet, Alice."

She closed her eyes as each caress sent a jolt of electricity through her body. She would be lost in another minute. "God, please."

His breath tickled her skin. "Do you want me to stop?"

"I want you to stop talking."

Jaden laughed, the deep rumble vibrating throughout her body. He slid one finger in between the soft cotton and touched the most sensitive part of her. She cried out as his fingertip moved back and forth, an erotic tickle which made her hotter.

"And do what, Alice?" He nipped her hipbone with his teeth as his finger ran up her cleft. "What do you want me to do with my mouth?"

She grabbed the back of the couch. "Kiss me."

He removed his hand and pushed her panties down her legs. Jaden smiled as he lifted each foot and tossed them on top of the discarded gray pants.

"Kiss you where, Alice?" He parted her thighs with his hands, moving his body in between her legs. "Is this where you want my mouth?"

Another rush of warmth pooled between her legs. She was molten, her entire body wickedly hot. His slow, deliberate movements only heightened her pleasure to the point of pain.

"Mmm. You feel so good here, Alice." He licked the inside of her thigh and she shuddered. "But I think you want me somewhere else."

His lips hovered near her sex. The anticipation made her burn as his pale blue eyes looked up at her with the promise of unbridled ecstasy.

She gasped when his mouth pressed against her core, the pleasure nearly splitting her in two. Jaden's growl reverberated through her body when he first tasted her, caressing her intimately with his tongue.

"Oh, Alice. This is exactly where you want me."

He tugged on her secret skin, his breath hot against her

body. Her fingers caught in his hair, locking his head in place. His hair was like silk against her hand. Smooth and soft, it rubbed against her palm as he worked her core.

It was a good thing she was leaning against the couch because she'd be on the floor as her legs gave way. She quickly lost track of hat was his tongue, his lips, and his chin as he tasted her. She looked down at his tanned back. A larger version of the tattoos on his wrists spanned his shoulder blades, her eyes following the serpentine black curves.

Her vision swam as he sucked and teased the most private part of her body. He completely focused on what he was doing while his tongue delved in and out of her. Her orgasm built as his tongue moved faster against her sex.

She cried out his name as her release came hard and furious, a white wave of ecstasy exploding throughout her body. But he didn't stop. He continued to stroke her with his tongue, fingers and lips until she climaxed two more times. Even then, he didn't move until he wrung the last tremor from her body.

Alice sagged against the back of the couch, her legs barely able to hold her weight. Sensing this, he picked her up. He carried her effortlessly as if she weighed nothing more than air and placed her on the cushions, her body still weak and sensitive to his touch.

She stared at him breathlessly as she watched his slow prowl up her body. Her shaky hands moved to the front of his pants, working the button and zipper down to free his erection.

Her eyes widened as he hovered over her, his arousal jutting proudly from his body. Like the rest of him, he was huge. Would he even fit?

Or would he hurt her and only care about his pleasure?

She closed her eyes. John-Paul still haunted her after the trial. Her boyfriend left her because she was too messed up to have sex with him. Not that she blamed him.

She had tried. She really did. But whenever he climbed on top of her, she broke into a cold sweat. And the one time he had entered her, she screamed in such terror that she was surprised the cops didn't show up.

She was broken. Damaged.

John-Paul's bitch.

"Alice?"

She looked up at him. She blinked back the tears as her eyes darted over his face. Desire shimmered in those sky blue eyes, but so did concern.

Tears stung her eyes. It wasn't fair. It wasn't Jaden who was hurting her. It was her memories.

"We don't have to do anything else. I'll stop right now."

"No, it's not that. I – "

"I know." He dipped his head, giving her the sweetest of kisses. "I sense your fear and I get it. What we've done is enough for me."

He started to pull away from her, but she wrapped her arms around him and kissed his shoulder. She'd heard of men like this, but never experienced it. Even though he had no release of his own, he was willing to sacrifice his own pleasure so she wouldn't be hurt.

Alice was through letting John-Paul call the shots from her memory. She wanted Jaden. And she wanted him now.

She placed her hand on his cock. He sucked in a breath as she stroked him slow and steady. He was hard and smooth. Like a column of steel enveloped in soft velvet. Jaden sucked in a breath as she lightly caressed him, her hand cupping his sac.

"It's not enough for me," she whispered.

"You don't have to prove anything to me," he said through

his teeth. "Don't force yourself to do this."

"I'm not." She skimmed the underside of him, his eyes darkening with passion. "I want more."

He braced an arm behind her and lifted one of her legs to circle his waist. He paused for a moment, those piercing blue eyes meeting her gaze. "Are you sure?"

She cupped his face in her hand. His whiskered cheek tickled her as he turned and placed a chaste kiss on her palm. Yes, she was sure about this.

"Love me, Jaden. Just for a little while."

His head probed her core and it made her burn. She forced herself to relax as he surged forward, stretching her inch by deliciously slow inch. There was no pain as he filled her. Just exquisite pleasure.

"Are you okay?" he asked hoarsely.

"Yes," she breathed. "Just…don't stop."

Alice closed her eyes as he rocked himself against her hips, lost in the sensation of all his power. All of him.

She gripped him tightly, her nails digging into the swirls in his shoulders as Jaden thrust in and out of her. Dear God, he felt so good. And it had been so long since anyone had touched her so gently or loved her body so thoroughly.

Alice wrapped her other leg around his hips. She took all of him in, from tip to base, over and over again. Each stroke pounded pleasure into her. She reveled in the hard power of him. She let her desire take her away from the pain of her past to enjoy this one perfect moment with Jaden.

Her nails scored his back as she rode waves of pleasure. When she couldn't take any more, her body exploded in a blast of white heat. Her sex held him tightly and a couple of strokes later, he roared as his release shot into her body. His orgasm poured into her, her core milking him dry as he filled her up with all of his passion.

Jaden buried his face in her neck. She ran her hands across his smooth back, loving the closeness and the warm weight of his body. He was a powerful man, but he treated her with such care and gentleness.

Why couldn't more men be like him?

"That was incredible," she breathed.

"Did I hurt you?"

"Not at all." She ran a finger up his bicep, the muscles trembling from holding his weight. "You made me feel beautiful."

"You are beautiful." He pulled back, hovering above her. "I think you might need a little more convincing."

Her eyes widened as she felt him harden inside of her. How was that possible? From her past experiences, most men needed time to recover. But Jaden was unlike any man she'd ever known.

"I thought you were done."

He grinned devilishly as he rotated his hips and stroked her deep inside. She hissed in satisfaction, her nails digging into his arms. "Not even close."

He picked her up, his hands tight on her rear. She giggled as he kept them joined, wrapping her legs around his waist. "Where are we going?"

"To bed."

Alice giggled. "You plan on tucking me in?"

"Hardly. I'm just getting started."

Chapter 8

A sharp bang rattled the bars. "Finch! You got a visitor."

"Not interested."

"Like I give a shit. Get your ass over here."

John-Paul sat up, staring at the cop from the top bunk. "Only if you say 'please.'"

"Please continue being a prick so I can throw you in solitary for a few days."

John-Paul Finch stood in front of his cell door and glared at the guard. There was a mutual hatred between Officer Ted Olsen and John-Paul. The guard believed himself to be above the lowlifes he watched, but word on the block was he had a penchant for underage hookers. If he wasn't careful, he'd end up in gen pop with a target on his back.

What a sweet day that would be to have Olsen as a bunkmate. He'd make a pretty penny off that bastard. Prisoners loved putting a guard on his knees and shoving whatever they could in his mouth to shut him the hell up.

"I've been locked in this hole for two years, Olsen. Who's visiting me?"

"Does it look like I care what fucked-up person chooses to come visit you? They're here and want to see you." Officer Olsen put the cuffs on and yanked him out the cell. "Let's meet your mystery date."

John-Paul shuffled down the hallway, the guard's sweaty palm clamped on his shoulder. They passed through the common area which housed the majority of the inmates. He let his sandy brown hair fall into his face, which made him able to watch the other prisoners, but they couldn't see his stare.

Rapists weren't too high up on the food chain in prison. John-Paul didn't give a shit what the others thought of him, but that didn't make him stupid. He worked out alone, ate alone and currently had no bunk mate in his cell. The other prisoners made comments every so often, but they usually avoided him and John-Paul preferred it that way. He wasn't interested in being anyone's girlfriend in this place.

If his physique didn't intimidate them, he had a little extra insurance – a three inch shank taped to his thigh which offered some protection from these pricks.

They passed a bank of tables and Olsen shoved him onto a stool in front of a bulletproof window. Two glass partitions were on either side of him, affording him little privacy.

Officer Olsen unhooked one of the cuffs and chained it to the metal bar under the ledge of the partition. "You have fifteen minutes. Realize that any and all uninteresting, dumbass comments you make will be recorded."

John-Paul scowled at the guard with hatred in his hazel-green eyes. When he escaped, he'd make sure Olsen was the first one gutted on his way out.

As soon as the cop was out of sight, his gaze slid to his visitor. John-Paul had never seen this man before in his life. He sat straight in the hard chair, his hands clasped together on the white table. Impeccably dressed in black pants and a navy sweater, he looked like a clean cut, preppy college student.

Yet the more John-Paul studied this person, he knew the outfit was just for show. What made this man stand out was the air of menace that surrounded him. The man's brown eyes narrowed slightly, a cold smile curving his lips.

He picked up the receiver and John-Paul grabbed his. "Hello, John-Paul Finch."

"Who the hell are you?" John-Paul snarled.

"Someone who's going to help you."

"You my new lawyer?"

"No, it's not like that." The man shook his head. "I'm here on behalf of a friend of yours."

"I have no friends."

"You do now."

John-Paul narrowed his eyes. He didn't want whatever bullshit this guy was shoveling. "You better say something interesting in the next five seconds. Otherwise, I'm hanging up."

The cold smile grew wider. "Alice Roarke. Is that interesting enough for you?"

John-Paul sat up straight in his chair. How the hell did this guy know Alice?

"It looks like I have your attention now," he drawled.

"Who are you?"

"I told you. A friend of a friend. As for a name, call me Markus."

John-Paul raised an eyebrow. "That's your real name?"

"Does it really matter?" Markus leaned forward. "But I don't want to talk about me. I'd rather talk about Alice Roarke."

John-Paul shifted in his chair. "I don't know her."

"You're worried about our call being recorded. Don't worry. When they review the tape, all they'll hear is us talking about how we're old high school buddies and how I'll be working on proving your innocence."

John-Paul flinched. This guy could mess with prison tapes? If Markus could mess with the recording, could he get him out of here too? That was a hope John-Paul didn't want to think about, but it was so damn enticing.

"How is that possible?"

"We have our ways."

Damn, this Markus was a slick motherfucker. "Who's *we*?"

"Let's talk about Alice Roarke," Markus replied, dismissing the question. "I know she's the reason you're here. She somehow escaped and made sure you'd be in jail for the rest of your life. She's the only woman to survive your three days of training with your victims. But she didn't make it the third day, did she?"

John-Paul gritted his teeth. God, what he wouldn't give to go back in time and make sure that bitch was secure. If he caught her trying to escape, he'd wrap his hands around her throat until she stopped breathing.

"What if I gave you the opportunity to finish what you started with her?"

He laughed harshly. Now the asshole was jerking him around. "Yeah, like you can do that."

"Tomorrow is November third. At three in the morning, we'd like to release you." Markus chuckled at John-Paul's shock. "Yes. We know about your particular fascination with the number three. We wanted to accommodate your obsession."

John-Paul wasn't laughing now. Freedom this fast? A chance to get back at Alice? This was too good to be true. There had to be one hell of a catch.

"You're not just doing this out of the goodness of your heart." John-Paul leaned in closer and lifted his chin. "What do you want from me?"

"For your release, we need your help with an associate of ours. You see, he has taken a special interest in Ms. Roarke and is spending time with her as we speak." Markus paused as at John-Paul's murderous glare. "Ah, you don't like that, do you?"

He sure as hell didn't. Alice was his bitch and no one else's. He left his mark on her so everyone would know that she belonged to him.

"We need our associate. You need Alice," Markus said. "It's a simple transaction."

John-Paul leaned forward, his eyes alight with interest. "You'd keep the cops off me?"

"Of course. We'd keep you protected until you find Ms. Roarke. Then once we have our associate, you are welcome to do whatever you want with her."

Oh, he already knew what he'd do with her. He never had his third day with Alice and he'd have so much fun with her. He'd start over with her since she needed more training. Then on the third day, he'd gladly choke the life out of that treacherous bitch.

John-Paul opened his eyes and grinned. "All right. I'll do it."

~ * ~

The Host sat in front of the fire, impatiently waiting for Markus's call. Failure was not an option since it meant Markus's death. The Shadow went to the prison as commanded with the explicit instructions to persuade John-Paul Finch to their side by any means necessary. Even if it meant giving the woman to that sadistic bastard.

The Host had no use for John-Paul except to get Jaden Payne away from the other warriors. Once Jaden was contained, Markus would get rid of the human.

The human race was done. They might be able to withstand

the sunlight, but they were a feeble, incompetent species. The Host had grand plans and the Emain Macha was in the way. It would be tricky, but in the end, the Host would be victorious.

Which was why John-Paul was a necessary evil. Jaden had shown an interest in a human woman. Any breach in the Emain Macha's ranks was a liability the Host planned to exploit to the fullest extent possible.

If Jaden Payne was watching over her, then she must be someone important. That bastard cared about no one but himself. Cruel, calculating and lethal, he was what vampires worshipped and what Shadows feared.

And that was the way in to destroy the warriors. Make one weak and they all were vulnerable to an attack.

The phone rang. "Yes?"

"John-Paul Finch has agreed to work with us, but we'll have to get him out of prison."

"When?"

"Later tonight at three in the morning."

"I see." The Host stared into the fire. "Can you handle it?"

"Of course. I have Colin and Zachary with me. We'll take care of everything."

"And bring John-Paul straight to me," the Host murmured.

"Whatever you wish."

"And Markus? This is promising indeed. When you come back with the human, I will show you my gratitude."

The Host snapped the phone shut. How appropriate that the first one to go was Jaden Payne. The warriors' time was up and a new era was about to begin.

Chapter 9

Jaden swept his fingers down Alice's arm and back up again as she slept in his embrace. She'd been out for over an hour and he couldn't stop touching her. With the lightest of caresses, he traced her cheekbone, her jaw line, from the soft arc of her shoulder all the way down to her hips.

They spent the past two hours loving each other until they were both fully spent. He lost count at the number of times she orgasmed as he explored every luscious curve of her body. Once her initial shyness wore off, she offered herself up to him, her lips soft as satin against his throat and chest.

He should be exhausted, but all he could think about was making love to her again. He burned into his brain the subtle nuances of her body. He loved the quivering in her stomach right before she climaxed in his mouth, the burst of pain as she scored her nails on his back and her hot, sweet channel that gripped his shaft like warm, wet silk.

She had as much fun pleasing him as he had her. God, what that woman could to with her tongue. Just remembering how she came in his arms, calling out his name.

Damn. He was hard again and he was willing to bet she'd welcome him with open arms as well.

Alice tightened her arm around his waist, her nipples

rubbing against his chest as she settled into him. She fit so perfectly against him, the warmth of her body seeping into his. He missed this kind of closeness with a woman. In fact, the last time he held a woman in his arms like this was centuries ago. And she cursed him with her very last breath.

Jaden stroked her forearm. His mind was focused on the man who tortured her two years ago. That's the male he wanted to kill.

Where was this bastard? Jaden could get one of the warriors to locate this guy. Then the two could have some fun in his home gym where no one could hear the screams but him. Then Alice wouldn't have that haunted look in her eyes.

His eyes traveled over her face. She looked so small, her strong eyes hidden beneath lids and thick lashes. Alice triggered every protective instinct he had. Jaden wanted to know who it was so he could track the animal down and take his fury out on him. How dare anyone touch his female.

His hand froze on her arm. His female? Where the hell did that come from?

Alice wasn't his. A brief shelter in his tempestuous life, but he could never stay. He didn't belong to anyone, much less a human who knew nothing about him or his world. The only loyalty he had was to his blade and his vow to kill the Host.

He smoothed the hair off her forehead and allowed himself to think of a future with Alice in it for just a moment. Someone to come home to. To share love and be loved in return. A partner who knew everything about him, the good and the bad, and still wanted to wake up next to him every night.

But it was just a dream and Jaden gave those up a long time ago. Although when he looked at Alice, a small part of him wanted to dream again.

His cell phone rang in the other room and he withdrew from her embrace, already missing the warmth of her body. He hurried picked it up on the second ring.

"Yeah?"

"Where the hell are you?" Salvatore barked into the phone.

"Out."

"Looking for the Firebrand, right?"

"Not yet."

"The sun's been down for hours!"

"I've been busy."

"Doing what? Or should I say with what female?" He heard Salvatore's sudden intake of breath when Jaden didn't answer. "Seriously? You've been with a female this whole time?"

"Like I said, I've been busy."

"Well, Helene and I need you. She's tracked two Shadows and they're a little too energized. They're planning something big and we need your skills to make them talk."

"You keep forgetting I'm out of rotation."

"You're not supposed to be banging a female while we have a Firebrand to locate, but I noticed it's not stopping you." Salvatore lowered his voice. "I wouldn't call if it wasn't necessary and you really don't want to piss off Liam any more than he already is. Now's not the time to screw some woman. Ditch her and get over here."

He glanced at the bedroom. Alice wasn't a quick fuck. She was different. Special.

"And how do I explain to Liam that I helped you out with these Shadows?" Jaden asked.

"We'll tell him we ran into each other as you were tracking a lead and I asked for your help."

"That's such a lame-ass excuse. Liam will smell the bullshit for what it is."

"It's the best I can come up with right now." There was a slight pause. "So are you going to meet us or what?"

Jaden gritted his teeth. Despite his strange feelings towards Alice, he owed his loyalty to his fellow comrades. He needed to get his head in the game and out of Alice's body.

"Tell me where you are and I'll meet you in ten minutes."

Salvatore relayed the information and Jaden hung up. He put on his clothes, strapping his weapons to his chest and thigh. He hated to leave, but he needed to do his job.

Jaden put his hand on the doorknob, but he looked back at the bedroom. He could hear Alice's soft breathing, her heartbeat steady and calm. Should he leave a note? Wake her up? Or just disappear?

His chest tightened at leaving her so callously which meant the third option was definitely out. It'd be better for him to leave a note, but he wanted to hear her voice again. See the warmth in her eyes before he went back to his empty house.

Jaden walked back into the room. The scent of cinnamon and sex still hung heavy in the air. He wanted the image of her, sleepy, content – and naked – branded into his mind. His cock stirred in his pants as he drank her in.

Yeah, he really needed to get the hell out of here. Otherwise, he'd spend the rest of the night with her.

He leaned down and kissed Alice's shoulder just above the band-aid. Each time he came close to the bandage, she stiffened and moved his hand or shifted away. He wondered what she was hiding from him.

His fingers hovered above her skin. Just one peek. She'd never know.

Her eyes opened slowly, the haze of sleep clouding her green eyes. He moved his hand toward her head, his fingers threading through the silky strands of her hair.

"Hey," she mumbled. "Please tell me it isn't seven a.m."

"No. You still have a few hours to go."

Alice nodded and propped herself on her arms. The blanket shifted down her back and he caught the curve of her breast. Jaden kissed her shoulder, gently nipping her skin. Saying goodbye like this was definitely the better option.

"I hate to leave you like this, but I have to go to work."

"An emergency case at one in the morning." Alice cocked an eyebrow. "So I'm guessing you're a medical examiner?"

"Yeah."

It wasn't a complete lie. He would have bodies to take care of by the end of the evening and it was a line he used before when he had to leave in a hurry with no time to scrub a female's memory.

So why did he feel a stab of guilt by lying to her?

"It's an important case and they need someone with my expertise."

One hand reached for his, squeezing tightly. The heat from her hand spread all over him and the tightness in his chest worsened. Salvatore and Helene better have left him some Shadow ass to kick. Otherwise, he was going to kick theirs for making him leave such a beautiful woman in bed.

"Thank you for tonight." Alice smiled up at him. "You were amazing."

"You were pretty fantastic yourself."

"I appreciate a chance to say goodbye and thank you for being with me."

He frowned. "What do you mean?"

"You're not the kind of guy that goes for a woman like me. And it's okay," she said before he could protest. "You gave me a part of my life back tonight. I won't forget it."

"Is that what you want? Just one night?"

She blushed. "I'll take what I can get."

God, that stain on her cheeks looked so damn good. Her scent flared as his gaze traveled over her body. That spicy fragrance made him salivate.

Walk away from her.

He looked into those wide green eyes. They were tender as she smiled up at him. The heat from her hand seared him, easing the chill in his bones. For a moment in time, he felt something other than rage and ice in his veins. He felt...warm.

He didn't want to walk away. He wanted to feel warm again and if that made him a selfish bastard, then so be it. Despite the amazing sex, he enjoyed her company. Certainly after all these years, he deserved a little happiness himself.

He took a deep breath. There was no going back.

"What if I do want a woman like you? Would you give me a chance to prove it around seven tomorrow night?"

"As in a date? In which we'd talk about ourselves and share our likes and dislikes?" She quirked an eyebrow in amusement. "Maybe you'll tell me your last name."

"I'll tell you more than that. I'd love to get to know you, Alice."

Her eyes darkened as she shifted under the covers. "I think you got to know me pretty well tonight."

He closed his eyes for a second, his erection pushing against the fly in his pants. He seriously hated Salvatore and Helene right now.

"But not well enough. Think about it."

"I don't need to think about it." Alice sat up and tucked the beige sheet around her supple curves. "I'd love to see you tomorrow."

He spotted a pen and a scrap piece of paper on her nightstand. "Here's my number. I work odd hours so feel free to call me any time you want. And I do mean that. It's never too late or too early to call me."

"Wait. Let me give you mine too." She tore the paper in half and took back the pen. She scribbled her number on it and pressed it into his hand. "You can reach me anytime, except between the hours of eight and three. I'm teaching then."

He leaned down and he nuzzled her neck. Even though he fed last night and should be good for a few weeks, his mouth watered at her scent. God, she smelled so good. Her blood would be even better.

She turned her head, giving him full access to her throat, his tongue tracing circles on her skin. A low moan vibrated in her chest as he nipped the hollow curve at the base of her neck. Gentle scrapes, never piercing the skin.

He pulled back, his breath caressing her ear. He didn't want to feed from her like this.

But he did want to give her one piece of himself before he left. "Payne," he whispered in her ear.

"What?"

"My last name. You said you wanted to know what it was. It's Payne."

She laughed softly. "I bet a lot of people have fun with that."

"They're usually right when they call me a pain in the ass." He caressed her cheek. "Anything else you want to discover about me before I go?"

"I think anything else will take too long." Her eyes raked him from head to toe. "But I wouldn't mind if you stayed and told me a bedtime story or two."

Jesus, this was too cruel. He kissed her soundly, relishing the little moan as his tongue pushed against hers. He wanted to strip off his clothes and climb back into bed with her, but

Salvatore and Helene were waiting for him and he needed to help them.

He kissed her again before he strolled out the door and into the night.

~ * ~

"We can't wait for him much longer," Helene groused as she walked up and down the sidewalk.

"Jaden will be here. Wait five minutes," Salvatore said.

"They could be gone in five minutes!"

"They won't poof into thin air like you."

"Jaden certainly has." Helene stared at the abandoned boutique, itching to get inside. "He's jerking us off right now."

"I doubt that."

In fact, Salvatore was certain Jaden already got off several times tonight, but not by his own hand. He didn't say where he was, but his answers indicated he was definitely not alone. The Ice Warrior never hid his sexual conquests before, even though it had been a long time since he'd taken a lover. Why was he doing it now?

Salvatore felt Jaden's presence a couple of minutes before he appeared. Jaden rounded the corner, his predatory gait slow and deliberate. His "don't-fuck-with-me" attitude radiated from every pore in his body. His dark clothing and black hair made him seem as if he belonged to the night except for those pale blue eyes. Those eyes were cold and lethal, which made most people look away in fear. They took in every movement and promised death to anyone who crossed his path.

"Oh, so you did decide to grace us with your presence," Helene said. "Where were you?"

"Doing something important."

Doing someone important is more like it, Salvatore thought.

"Care to elaborate?"

"You're not my mother, which makes it none of your damn business." Jaden stopped next to her and nodded to Salvatore. "I'm not surprised you needed backup tonight. It's obvious you have to send a man to do the job right."

"Let me know when one shows up," she replied sweetly.

"I see you're still your normal, bitchy self. Why don't you poof back to the compound and wait on Liam?"

Helene shook her head. "I heard you were with a woman tonight. She must not have been very good if you're this pissed off."

"Can we focus here?" Salvatore stepped in between the two, hoping that Jaden wouldn't hit him. "I wouldn't have called you if we didn't need your particular talents tonight."

"You're timing is perfect as always," Jaden said. "And by perfect, I mean completely inconvenient."

"Did you clean her mind before you came?" Salvatore asked.

"I didn't have time because someone called and told me to get my ass over here." Jaden glanced his way. "I'll have to go back tomorrow and do it."

"And get in a couple more lays while you're at it?"

"Drop it, Salvatore."

He's getting attached, Salvatore thought. Not good for the human female or for the other warriors. If their heads weren't in the game, it could cost them their lives.

"It's apparent Helene can't add either," Jaden said, pointing at the building. "There are more than the two Shadows in there."

Helene glared at him. "I said I was tracking two Shadows, asshole. The two I needed joined the other five in that building."

"You up to it?" Salvatore asked.

Jaden scowled at him. "What kind of question is that?"

"You seem tense, my man."

"I'd be more concerned about where you put the twins tonight," Jaden said. "Those little hooks do a lot of damage and I don't want my ass getting filleted."

Helene pulled her Beretta from the folds of her coat. "He always has that constipated look on his face. Why is tonight any different than normal?"

"Let's get going," Jaden growled. "Otherwise, I'm going to kick her ass instead."

The trio moved quickly in the night, their footsteps nothing more than a whisper against the pavement. They entered the building quietly, keeping themselves hidden against the walls. Jaden palmed a knife in his hand, his muscles tensed to strike.

They were lucky Shadows only had strength and speed on their side. Enough to make them a tough opponent to destroy, but they lacked other skills which proved to be as effective and deadly.

Vampires had heightened senses which alerted Jaden there were two Shadows approaching the side door at the end of the hallway. They also had the ability to manipulate matter and slide the locks in place once the enemy walked through the door, barring their escape.

Jaden grabbed the first one and shoved him against the wall. The Shadow was stunned for a moment which was all Jaden needed. The dagger ran across the Shadow's throat before he had a chance to scream. He slumped to the ground, the wound killing him in a matter of moments.

The second one saw his comrade fall and reached into his jacket. Jaden caught the metallic glint of the semiautomatic gun and dove as a spray of bullets came his way. Helene caught the bastard from behind and twisted his head until it completely faced the wrong way.

Feet pounded overhead along with the unmistakable clicks of safeties coming off the guns.

"Think they know we're here now?" Helene asked.

"I'd hate to be rude," Salvatore said. "Let's say hello."

Jaden sheathed his dagger and pulled out his Glock. They made their way towards the back of the building where the other five were waiting. Jaden and Salvatore had no trouble taking on the three of the mindless hybrids as Helene battled the other two she tracked.

Jaden loved hand to hand combat. He preferred to look his enemy in the eye when he killed them. He glanced to the side and saw Salvatore fighting the other two. Specially made for him, Salvatore wielded the twin hooks with lethal precision. He hooked one of the curved blades around the neck of one of the Shadows and with a quick downward thrust, decapitated the creature. After a few minutes, both Shadows Helene fought were unconscious on the dirty floor with the other three lay dead.

Salvatore wiped the blood off his blades on the headless Shadow's shirt before he strapped them to his back. He took out a pair of cuffs and snapped them on the wrists of the two that were still alive. Three times the thickness of regular handcuffs, they'd keep the Shadows restrained until they arrived at Jaden's house.

"That's it?" Jaden wrinkled his nose in disgust. "This is what we came for?"

"What's the problem?" Helene asked.

Jaden tapped one of them with the tip of his boot. "It's hardly a fair fight. I feel like I'm playing checkers with a five-year-old. Ten moves and I win."

"And like five-year-olds, young Shadows are stubborn little

jerks," she said. "You'll have a lot of fun breaking them."

Salvatore dragged the bodies into a pile. "Get them to your place, Jaden. I'll take care of cleanup."

Jaden slung a Shadow over his shoulder and she grabbed the other. "Ladies first."

They hurried to the van Salvatore used to transport Shadows and threw the unconscious men inside. Jaden watched as she pulled a bag from the passenger seat and took out two syringes. She made sure there was no air in the tip before she stabbed each Shadow in the leg.

Once the syringe was empty, she tossed them back into the bag. "What did you give them?"

"A sedative," she said. "It works quickly, but I gave them double the dose so they'll stay knocked out until we get back to your place."

"You sure you didn't kill them?"

"I'm not an idiot. I know my drug combinations. I didn't forget my former life as a nurse." She climbed into the driver's side. "They'll be out long enough to get them shackled at your place. Then you can get the answers we need."

"What makes these two so important?"

"Something big is going down tonight. These two were on the phone with someone named Markus earlier. All I caught was that it was going to happen at three o'clock."

He glanced at his watch. He had about an hour and a half. "Did they say where?"

"Nope."

"And if I can't get them to talk by three?"

"Then you keep at it until they break."

Jaden looked down at his hands. Less than thirty minutes ago, he'd held Alice in his arms, stroking her tenderly, pleasing her body and himself. Now he'd use his hands for pain, to torture the men to levels beyond their imagination. That's why they called him. Because where regular interrogation techniques failed, his were foolproof. It was only a matter of time until they talked.

What would Alice think if she knew what he could do with a simple touch? Would she fear him? Shun him like some of the others? God, he never wanted to find out.

He shook his head. He had to let her go. Despite what he said tonight, he'd have to find some way to remove himself from her life. He couldn't just clean her mind. She had too many memories attached to him. He'd have to bow out of her life.

Shit, it hurt just thinking about it. But she deserved something better than him. She experienced enough demons in this life. She didn't need another one.

What she needed was a male who would give her a peaceful life, free of the horrors and darkness of his world. A male who would give his very life so she could live. That would be the best thing for her.

So why did it feel like someone was peeling off his skin?

"Are you ready to get the party started?" Helene asked.

Jaden glanced at the bodies on the floor. "I'm surprised we're still sitting here," he muttered. "Let's go."

Chapter 10

John-Paul was too anxious to sleep. How could he? The guards just completed their last round twenty-five minutes ago and he'd been keeping time ever since. It was November third and he wanted to see if the man named Markus would hold up his end of the bargain. If he was legit, then John-Paul was out of this cage in five minutes.

If not, then he was seriously going to find some way to pay the fucker back for jerking him around.

Five minutes 'til three. Five minutes 'til three. Five minutes 'till three.

His eyes flickered to the wall outside his cell. It was eerily quiet on his block tonight. Usually, there was some activity – a rustling of sheets, a strangled cry from a nightmare, or a whispered plan of smuggling in some sort of contraband past the guards.

Tonight, there was nothing. Except for the dull thud of the guard's feet making another round.

John-Paul perked up as the sound grew louder. He gritted teeth when he recognized those heavy, slapping footsteps. Olsen's fat ass must have been assigned the night shift. Just fucking great.

He closed his eyes, feigning sleep. He frowned as the feet stopped at his cell door. Why would the guard stop? There was no reason for him to get him up in the middle of the night.

Unless Olsen wanted a piece of him.

His hand went to the shank concealed against his thigh. Olsen better not think of pulling some kind of shit on him while he was asleep. John-Paul didn't care if he got extra time for assaulting a cop. It'd be worth laying Olsen on his pompous ass.

He heard the key in the door and his eyes flew open. He tensed, waiting for Olsen to drag him out of bed.

"Mr. Finch? Are you ready?"

"Markus?" John-Paul sat up at the familiar voice. "You're really here?"

"You're not dreaming. I can promise you that." Markus came into his line of view. "We don't have much time. But if you prefer your current accommodations, I can simply disappear."

Like he was going to turn down a chance of getting out of this place? John-Paul hopped off the top bunk and looked into Markus's cold, brown eyes. "How are we getting out of here?"

Markus grinned. "The same way I came in."

John-Paul's eyes flickered to the floor of his cell where Olsen lay unconscious. "Is he dead?"

"No, but he'll be in quite a bit of trouble for letting you escape. And the weak-minded are easier to control."

"Can I kill him anyway?"

"I'd save your energy for Ms. Roarke. That's who you really want, isn't it?"

John-Paul curled his lip. Yeah, she's the bitch he wanted.

He cast one look at the knocked out pig before he followed Markus. They silently moved through the corridors, their footsteps light against the concrete. John-Paul glanced up at the security cameras. He felt exposed and naked, certain that one of the guards would jump out of nowhere and take him down.

It never happened. And as he passed another camera, he noticed none of the red lights were blinking.

What the hell? Was this Markus's doing too?

"All they will see is static," Markus said as they went down a stairwell.

"I see you plan prison breaks often," John-Paul scoffed.

"We're very good at making ourselves disappear."

He knew he should question Markus more about who was really pulling the strings. But at this point, John-Paul didn't care how they escaped as long as they got out. Then he could kill the bastard and go after Alice.

John-Paul's heart raced with every passing second. Every second brought him closer to freedom. His lungs burned as he pushed himself to run faster. A few minutes later, cold air stung his cheeks. They ran through the yard, past the basketball court until they reached a gaping hole in the fence. Markus grabbed his arm and steered him to a black sedan idling near a bank of sparsely planted trees.

John-Paul slid into the backseat and Markus stood outside of the car for just a moment. John-Paul couldn't see what the man was doing, but he wanted to get out of this place ASAP. Any moment, the sirens would go off and they'd haul his ass back to jail.

A door opened and Markus jumped in the car. "Drive," he commanded.

The black sedan eased effortlessly out of the visitor's parking lot. John-Paul glanced back at the fence. His eyes widened in disbelief. It looked as if the fence was intact, but that couldn't be right. Could it?

No, it was the adrenaline in his system playing tricks on

him. Really, what the hell did he care about the fence? It didn't matter what they did to it as long as he got out.

It wasn't until they were safely cruising down the highway at 80 mph that he let out a sigh of relief. Then a laugh. And he couldn't stop. He knew he sounded hysterical, but he didn't care.

He was free. After two years of being trapped in a nine by twelve cage, he was finally free.

"I told you we'd escape."

John-Paul wiped the tears from his eyes. At that moment, he wanted to kiss Markus. "I can't believe you did it. You are one crazy bastard."

"I'll take that as a compliment."

John-Paul looked out the window. "So where are we going?"

"A place where the police won't think to look."

John-Paul rubbed his hands together. Payback was going to be a huge bitch. "When can I get Alice?"

"Soon. First, you're going to meet your benefactor. When we talk to the Host, we'll both get what we want."

"Which is?"

"You get Alice when we get Jaden." Markus grinned at his companion, although the smile didn't reach his eyes. "Relax, John-Paul. It's going to take a couple of hours before we're at our destination."

He wanted to know more about this Jaden guy and his relationship with Alice, but decided against it. These guys could change their mind and dump his ass at a police station. Best to stay quiet until he met this Host person.

A couple of hours later, the car veered off the highway. After passing a couple of gas stations, the road stretched on endlessly before them, trees and an occasional pasture opening on either side of him.

Now that the adrenaline had disappeared, the hairs on the back of his neck stood up. They were going deep into the country. No people. No cell reception. No witnesses. A perfect setup to get rid of him.

Had he been tricked?

John-Paul had received more than his fair share of hate mail while in prison. Women's rights groups, those for the death penalty and other victims of rape. Was he so desperate for his freedom that he signed up with some weird radical group who actually wanted him dead?

They turned on to an unpaved road littered with oak trees. He could only imagine the kind of canopy it provided for this Host person when spring came around.

The trees opened up to a two story colonial. Strange such a small house sat on a large amount of land. Except for two lights burning in the downstairs window, the place was completely dark.

John-Paul's stomach churned uneasily as he got out of the car. Besides the doors slamming, the area was quiet. Completely silent. No wind blowing, no animals scurrying in the dark. Nothing at all.

Something was really off. He was grateful to this Host person for getting him out of jail, but what was he supposed to do in return? Become a drug mule? Pledge eternal allegiance to protect this guy's ass?

His deeper instincts told him to run. To get as far away from this place as possible. But where would he go? He was in the middle of nowhere.

The wooden handle of the shank pressed against his thigh. John-Paul still had a weapon if he needed to use it. He may not be able to escape, but he would make sure he took down as many people as he could.

"The Host is waiting," Markus said, gesturing to the house. "Shall we?"

Like he had a choice?

John-Paul walked through white doors with Markus next to his side and two other men behind him. He was trapped between the men with no chance to get away. His anxiety spiked as his footsteps echoed against the weathered hardwood floor, each step taking him towards the elusive benefactor. He walked into a study. There were floor to ceiling bookcases that took up an entire wall with a roaring blaze illuminating the mahogany wood.

Markus led him to a sofa and forced him to sit down. "Keep your eyes on the fire. The Host will be here shortly."

The words had just left Markus's lips when two men came around and grabbed John-Paul's arms. "What the fuck is this?" he yelled.

They pinned him, their grip immobilizing him completely. A blindfold came across his eyes and blocked out the light. Fear coursed through his veins, but he refused to let these pricks see him afraid.

"Is this him?" a low voice asked. "The one who will bring us Jaden?"

John-Paul turned his head in the direction of the voice, unable to tell if it was a man or a woman.

"This is him," Markus said quietly.

"You made it just in time. You only had about twenty minutes to spare before the sun rose."

John-Paul heard the soft footsteps move around the couch. The entire time, he felt someone's stare raking him from head to toe.

"He's a strong one. I am very pleased."

"I had hoped you would be," Markus said, his voice dripped with pleasure.

A cold hand brushed his cheek and he jerked from the contact. The Host laughed softly. "He has a fighting spirit. I think he'll be an asset to us after all."

Fingers ran down his throat. John-Paul froze as a finger ran up and down the vein of his neck. It was a tender caress which made him all the more terrified.

"Are you scared?" the voice whispered in his ear.

"No," John-Paul ground out.

"You should be."

Razors tore into his flesh and he cried out from the pain. A mouth clamped on his throat and took deep pulls from the wound.

"Goddamn it! Let me go," he shrieked.

Stop moving. When I'm ready, I'll let you go.

He heard the voice in his head, although it was impossible for the Host to speak with that mouth latched on to his skin. He wanted to thrash against the hands that held him tightly, but the mental command to stay still immobilized him. His heart hammered in his chest as his blood was ripped from his body by the Host's greedy lips.

Why did they free him just to kill him?

The mouth moved away for a moment. "We're not going to kill you," the Host murmured. "We're making you stronger."

Another bite to his neck as pain penetrated every nerve in his body. Dear Jesus, what the hell was going on here? Meetings at night, super strength, bloodletting...

This wasn't happening. It wasn't even possible! These things didn't exist in the real world. The real world didn't have –

"Vampires," Markus finished the thought. "Welcome to our world."

Chapter 11

"You know, this whole process would move a lot faster if you just talked to me." Jaden pulled the screwdriver out of the Shadow's thigh. "Oh, don't get me wrong. The screams don't bother me since it means I'm doing something right. But you're going to crack. I just wish you'd do it sooner than later."

The two creatures hung by their arms as they knelt on the floor, their legs refusing to hold their weight. One passed out from the pain hours ago while the other was barely conscious.

He hadn't exactly lied when he told Alice he was a medic. He knew every inch of the human body, where to hit them with the most amount of pain, but draw the least amount of blood.

Helene stayed with him close to dawn. She miscalculated the dosage and the Shadows didn't wake up until five in the morning. She had to get to her quarters before the sun rose and left him with the Shadows. She was hesitant in leaving him alone, but he assured her he wasn't the one in danger.

Jaden lifted one of the Shadow's tattered shirts and inspected the bloodied gashes across the stomach. The interrogation was entering its twelfth hour. Despite being newly created, they remained silent about their mission as well as the name of the Host. And it pissed Jaden off.

The only thing he heard from them was their screams as he

used various instruments to get them to talk. Knives, blunt probes, needles under the fingernails...it didn't matter what he used as long as he got them to talk. The added bonus was that the room had soundproof walls. The bastards could yell as loud as they wanted and no one would come running.

It was a dirty job, but he had no choice with this task. He had firsthand experience on the subject of torture which made him invaluable in the eyes of the Sisters and Liam. Even though he no longer bore the scars, he remembered the relentless pain of his captivity. For four days, he endured every puncture, every broken bone by the hand of the woman he once loved.

"You once said you'd bleed for me," Catherine said. The blade sliced across his chest. "Let's see how much I can get out of you."

In the first two days, he continued to profess his love for her, but his words incensed Catherine even more. She became desperate to hurt him, to feel the anger and pain he caused her by changing her into a vampire. He was young and foolish and in love. He believed Catherine wanted him, but as he was brutalized by her, he realized she loved his looks and his status even more. He never had her heart, just her body to ease her sexual cravings.

In the end, it was his primal instinct to live that freed him and killed her. That fateful night was a turning point in his life, his heart turning into a lump of ice when he left Catherine's body exposed to the sun.

He glanced at his watch. He had less than an hour before he met up with Alice. Her cinnamon scent lingered faintly on his skin, despite the blood, grime and other fluids from his guests.

He closed his eyes for a moment, remembering the best part of his night. Her arms were so soft and gentle, a soothing balm in his violent life. She looked so beautiful when he made love to her, tasting her slick passion on his tongue as she came over and over again in his mouth, her creamy thighs clutching his waist while he climaxed in her arms.

He rubbed the back of his neck. Best to stop that train of thought right now. And it was why he had to sever ties with Alice. She didn't need to be caught up in his world, just as he couldn't allow himself to get close to her.

But he could allow himself one more night with her.

He turned back to the two males. They needed to talk within the next twenty minutes or he'd start cutting off body parts.

Jaden pulled out a curved knife with a hook at the tip. Definitely painful for the person on the receiving end of this blade. He heard a sharp intake of breath and he grinned at his guest.

"Come on. I know you want to talk to me."

The Shadow lifted his head. "Bite me."

"Sorry, you're not my taste." Jaden stood in front of the Shadow. "Do you really think the Host is going to keep you alive after this?"

"Will you?"

"Not a chance," Jaden said. "But I can make your last few hours very unpleasant."

The Shadow gasped for breath, the uninjured eye staring at him coldly. "What you do to me is nothing compared to what the Host has in store for you."

"Someone's been watching too many horror movies. Should I wait for the maniacal laughter and wringing of hands to reinforce that empty threat?"

"Fuck off."

"That's the plan for tonight, but not with you." Jaden cocked an eyebrow. "Right now, I want you to talk."

"Yeah, right. You've stabbed, punched and cut holes into me. What else can you possibly do?"

Fine. Twenty minutes was too long anyway.

Jaden gently placed his hand where the screwdriver left a hole in the flesh. The Shadow screamed in agony, the sound reverberating off the walls. Music to Jaden's ears.

His ability to intensify and reduce a person's mental and physical state was incredibly powerful because it worked on humans, Shadows and vampires alike. Some of the other warriors were unable to use their gifts on other vampires, but Jaden was a lucky one. Being a direct descendant of a Master did have its perks.

Jaden concentrated on the wound as the Shadow thrashed even harder against the chains. His high-pitched shrieks shook the lights in their fixtures. Damn, he liked the sound. It meant answers were on the way.

"That's just a preview," Jaden said as the last of the screams faded. "Start talking and I promise you your death will be less painful. You said the Host knows me. How does he know me so well?"

"The Host knows all of the Emain Machas," the male panted. "You're just the one the Host is focusing on right now."

"I'm the object of the Host's affections? How sweet." Jaden put the knife in his belt. "That certainly gives me the warm fuzzies, but you put me at a disadvantage. The Host knows me, but I don't know him."

"The Host knows more than you think. Does the name Alice ring a bell?"

Oh, shit. How did he already know about her? This was going to go bad very fast.

"Isn't she the one who met up with the Mad Hatter and the

March Hare for a tea party in Wonderland?" Jaden asked, masking the dread he felt. "Other than that, I don't know anyone named Alice."

"Really?" He began rattling off facts. "Alice Roarke. Female. Dark brown hair, green eyes, five foot seven, weight approximately 140 pounds. Lives in Apartment 2 on the ground floor on the corner of Hooper Road and Highway 28." He paused, his mouth curving into a grin. "Did I miss anything?"

Jaden's stomach tightened at her name, but he remained stoic. "I know a lot of women. They all look the same when I'm grabbing something to eat. How should I remember them all?"

The Shadow spat on the ground and the grin widened. "Two years ago, she was abducted by John-Paul Finch. She was his third victim. Handcuffed by her wrists and a choke collar around her throat, beaten repeatedly within the course of two days. Escaped before he could kill her on the third day. He always said he regretted letting her go."

Raw fury coiled in Jaden's chest. He may not have found out the identity of the Host, but he now knew the bastard who attacked Alice. When he was done with the Shadows, he'd pay John-Paul Finch a visit.

"I'm impressed. I thought all you guys did all day was visit the Dracula message boards and leave children-of-the-night speeches," Jaden said. "It's amazing what you can find on the Internet, isn't it? Tell me, what else did you dig up in your little research project?"

"It wouldn't be on the Internet that John-Paul Finch escaped from prison at three o'clock this morning and his current whereabouts are unknown," the Shadow replied.

Was it true? There was no television or radio to alert either of them of the day's events in this room. If that maniac had escaped, then Alice was alone and unprotected.

"Have you heard from her today?" the Shadow asked. "Do you know if Alice is still at home? Maybe she's getting reacquainted with John-Paul."

Oh, he was going to hurt the bastard.

Jaden grabbed the man by his hair and let his power flow into the Shadow's body. Another scream ripped through him. "I swear to God if she's hurt, I will take days to kill you."

"It's already set in motion," the Shadow said between breaths. "Can you get to her before 6:33?"

"Why?" Jaden yanked his head back. "What's happening?"

"Go find out. If he hasn't found her already."

The Shadow's chuckle was cut off with a flick of Jaden's wrist. He couldn't laugh with his throat slit ear to ear. Jaden stabbed the unconscious one in the chest, effectively ending the interrogation.

He checked his watch. He had forty-two minutes left.

Jaden picked up his phone and called Salvatore. "I need you over here. Now."

"Did they talk?"

"I'll tell you once I get back."

"Get back?" Salvatore echoed. "Where are you going?"

"I don't have time to talk about it! Just get over here now!"

He hung up the phone and unlocked the third cabinet, revealing his cache of weapons. When he typically went out, he had one gun, and his two onyx handled daggers. Tonight, he took two Glocks, the blades across his chest, another one concealed on his thigh and a length of chain in one coat pocket.

Alice had to be safe. She had started to heal and this asshole was about to come back into her life. Jaden would do whatever it took to keep her from John-Paul. If what the Shadow said was true, then the Host turned John-Paul into one of his servants. Which meant Jaden was honor-bound to protect his race and Alice.

Where the hell was Salvatore? Jaden needed the warrior to take care of the mess he made. There was no reason for Alice to see what he did when he brought her back here. And that's what Jaden needed to do. He could make sure she was all right if she hid here for a few days.

Is that the only reason you want her here?

I have to keep her safe, he argued with himself.

Liar.

He may not be able to have a relationship with her, but he would make damn sure John-Paul Finch didn't get her.

Jaden paced in the foyer, ready to jump out of his skin when Salvatore walked inside. The other male raised his eyebrows at the bodies hanging from the chains.

"You really worked them out," Salvatore commented.

Now he was down to twenty-two minutes. "Stay here. I'll be back soon."

"Where are you going?"

Jaden strode past him. "Checking out a lead."

"By yourself? I don't think so."

"I'll be fine."

Salvatore caught up in a couple of strides. "You probably didn't get any sleep today and you're way too juiced," he said. "You need back up especially if you're going after the Host. I'm going with you."

"I'm not going after the Host. I need you to take care of the bodies."

"I can do that once we get back."

Jaden shook his head. "I don't want to bring her back to

this."

"Her? Who are you talking about?"

They stopped in the garage and Jaden yanked open the door to his Viper. "I need to get to her before the Shadows do."

"Did you find the Firebrand? Did they tell you who the woman of Foster is?"

I found someone better.

Jaden started the car, the engine roaring to life. "Just wait for me. I'll explain when I come back."

The door opened and Jaden peeled out of the driveway, praying he wasn't already too late.

Alice balanced the groceries in her arm as she opened the door to her apartment. She could hardly wait to get home from work since Jaden would arrive soon. She wasn't sure if they were going out or staying in and she wanted to make sure she had enough food in the house.

Personally, she hoped they stayed in. She wouldn't mind an encore of last night which kept the silly grin on her face for most of the day.

Tina had just encouraged the smile when Alice met her in the break room at her school. Alice knew her friend was irritated when she left Saturday night, but the frustration disappeared when Tina saw Alice's face.

"I know that satisfied look anywhere! Girl, you got laid!"

"I'm not one to kiss and tell."

"Oh, you did a lot more than kissing. Your face says it all!" Tina exclaimed. *"When did it happen? How long was he at your house?"*

"He stayed for a couple of hours last night."

"You little hussy. I want details! Now!"

Alice remained elusive about her time with Jaden. Sure, Tina pulled some details out of her and Alice was flustered by some of the very personal questions, but she managed to keep most of it private.

She glanced at the couch and blushed. Those were a good two hours on the sofa.

On the floor.

In the bed.

She hoped Jaden stayed longer tonight. The sex had been fantastic, but it was something in those odd blue eyes which captivated her. He didn't run from her or look at her with pity when she told him of her abduction. He was angry on her behalf, something she never saw from anyone who knew about it.

She smiled to herself. Someone cared about her well-being. Even if it was just for a few hours, it was nice to have that feeling. And that feeling coming from Jaden warmed her even more.

As Alice placed the milk and cheese in the refrigerator, she couldn't help feeling something was wrong. No, more than wrong. She felt anxious and exposed. At first, she chalked up her nerves as excitement about seeing Jaden again. Now she wasn't so sure.

If she didn't know any better, she'd say she was afraid. But there was nothing to fear. John-Paul was locked up, she had a good life and Jaden seemed like a nice guy. Things were going right for a change.

Still, it didn't prevent her internal alarm system from warning her of an impending attack.

Her cell phone rang and she jumped at the shrill sound. Alice recognized Jaden's number. "Hey, Jaden."

"Where are you?" he asked.

"I'm home."

"How long ago have you been there?"

"I just got in about five minutes ago."

"Are you all right?"

Her nerves sizzled at his tone. He sounded as uptight as she felt. "I'm fine. Why?" She heard the roar of an engine accelerating. "Where are you?"

"I'm on my way to your apartment."

"It sounds like you're breaking all sorts of traffic laws to get to me." She glanced at her watch. He was a good thirty minutes early and she hadn't had the time to change out of her clothes. "It'll take a few minutes for me to get ready. Is everything okay?"

"I'll be better once I see you."

Alice frowned. He sounded so uneasy. "Jaden, what's wrong?"

"I'll explain when I get there. Meanwhile, stay on the phone with me."

Before she could ask why, a series of raps echoed on her front door. She looked through the peephole. "Huh. There's a man with flowers on my front step. Looks like he's from the boutique a couple of blocks over."

He muttered a vile curse. "Alice, I'm almost there. Don't open it."

If it isn't Jaden, leave it closed! He'll be here in a few minutes.
Get a grip, Alice.

She was being irrational and acting foolish. There was nothing to be scared of. She survived for two years without a man and she wasn't going to rely on one now.

"Hang on a sec. They're probably at the wrong place." Alice pressed the phone against her shoulder and opened the door. "Can I help you?"

"Good evening. I have a delivery for an Alice Roarke," he said pleasantly.

"That's me."

The man held out a clipboard. "Sign here, please." She signed for the flowers and he handed her the bouquet. "Have a lovely evening."

She closed the door with her foot. Three long stemmed red roses linked together with a silver ribbon. A card was taped to the front of the bouquet.

"Alice? Are you still there?"

"Yes. I'm here."

"What did you get?"

She hesitated for a moment. "Red roses. There's a card with it."

"Open it."

"Wouldn't you rather tell me what it says?"

"I didn't send you any flowers."

The hairs on the back of her neck stood on end as her heart thundered in her chest. No one else would have sent her flowers.

She balanced the roses on the back of the sofa. She swallowed hard and pulled out the card. The color drained from her face as she read the message twice.

"Oh...my...God," she whispered.

"Alice, what is it? What does the card say?"

She didn't hear his words because she dropped the phone. She backed away from the flowers as if they were poisonous.

I've missed you.
J.P.F.

Time took her back two years ago to another night where she received three red roses. That was Day One. John-Paul brought her flowers and a dog bone as a way of owning her.

The dog bone was a preview of the abuse. The flowers would be placed on her body once he killed her. That was the first time he beat her.

"Day One," she choked out. "Oh, God. He's come back for me."

This was what she'd been scared of all day. Her eyes were glued to the three, tiny words scrawled on the thin card, a dog bone drawn in the corner.

John-Paul knew where she was and there was no way she'd let him get her again. She had to get out of here. She had to –

"He's waiting for you," a voice said behind her. "Are you ready to see him?"

Chapter 12

Jaden turned off the engine a second before he heard Alice's scream. Adrenaline kicked into overdrive at her terror, ready to tear apart whoever was in that apartment. He wasted no time kicking in the door as it hit the opposite wall.

Alice was against the wall while two Shadows loomed over her. One of them held her by her wrist as she tried to jerk free. Jaden unsheathed his blade. He was going to enjoy cutting off that hand.

Time froze for a moment as everyone turned towards Jaden. The Shadows glared at him, but for the moment, all he saw was Alice and her wild eyes. She was all right. Horrified, but not injured.

"I know you weren't just leaving with my girl. It would really piss me off," he said. "And since you have your hands on her, I'm definitely going to have to kill you."

That sent the Shadows and Alice into action. She kneed the closest one in the groin. He went down, howling in pain and let go of her wrist. She jumped past him while the other one grabbed her around the waist.

A third Shadow burst out of the bedroom wearing a florist's uniform and charged at them both. Jaden pinned the half-human easily and jabbed the knife into the heart. He sprang up as the other one hurtled towards him and collided with the wall.

Jaden's gaze flickered to Alice. The Shadow who held her was at least sixty pounds heavier than her and twice as strong. But she blocked his punches and even got in a few of her own as he attempted to restrain her. It was obvious the command was to bring her in unharmed. Still, there was nothing sexier than a woman who could defend herself.

Yeah, this was definitely the wrong time to get turned on.

"Just so you know, when John-Paul's done with her, we're gonna have some fun too," the Shadow whispered in Jaden's ear.

Blind fury overcame him and he shoved the Shadow against the wall. If any of those cocksuckers went near Alice, he was going to castrate them. Then again, he wasn't going to give them the chance.

His fangs punched out of his gums and bit into the man's neck, ripping open the jugular. Blood flowed into his mouth and he swallowed reflexively. Shadows had a bitter taste because of the mixed blood in their veins, but he didn't care. He wanted to make the bastard bleed out.

Jaden grabbed the man's shoulders and let his powers loose, magnifying the pain. The Shadow screamed, his heart sputtering in his chest. The loss of blood and Jaden's power was too much as he started thrashing against the wall. Jaden felt the man's heart stop and he dropped the body to the floor.

He focused his attention on the kitchen. Alice wrenched herself free which left the last one vulnerable to an attack. That was all the time he needed.

Jaden flicked his wrist and the dagger sunk deep into the Shadow's chest. He dropped to the floor, his mouth open in a silent scream. Jaden snapped the neck of the one he held and let go, the body hitting the carpet with a soft thud.

He stood back, assessing the situation. They entered while the one in the florist uniform distracted Alice with the bouquet. One stabbed, one jugular torn open, one neck snapped. When they didn't check in, more would come.

Her apartment was compromised. She was no longer safe in her own home.

Time was of the essence. If they stayed too much longer, more Shadows would come. Without backup, they could easily take Alice while he fought them. Jaden had to get her out of here, but he could tell she wasn't going to go anywhere with him. Not unless he dragged her out of here.

His eyes flipped to her and his heart sank into his chest. Eyes wide, ashen cheeks, her breathing rapid and shallow. She was terrified.

Things just got more complicated.

~ * ~

Alice pressed her back to the wall, her heart ready to explode from her chest. Good God, three men were dead in her living room. By Jaden's hands.

Alice couldn't stop staring at him. The features were the same: the jet black hair was pulled into a ponytail, pale blue eyes taking in every subtle movement, the strength flowing through the muscles in his body.

But this man was a stranger to her. He looked nothing like the man she made love to last night. The lines on his face made him look harsh, cruel and lethal. Rage and power kept him on edge, ready to strike at anyone or anything.

Her eyes darted to the bodies on her floor and back to him. There wasn't a drop of blood on him anywhere. Not even a smear on those long, tapered fingers or those palms although they caused so much death. Those hands which had touched her so lovingly and held her as she slept caused this.

And what about his teeth? They reminded her of a tiger's fangs, ivory nails tearing deep into the soft tissue. They were normal now, but they slipped out of his mouth and tore into the guy's neck.

Vampire.

Her mind reeled. Jaden wasn't a vampire. He couldn't be. Those things didn't exist except in horror stories and movies.

But no person could move that fast or deadly. Nothing human.

What in God's name was happening here?

"Alice."

She jerked against the wall at the sound of his voice. She didn't bother hiding her fear as she met his gaze. Her eyes widened as he slowly walked over to her. His face was set, his eyes grim.

He was going to kill her. There was no way he'd leave her alive after what she'd just seen. And he was too fast, too strong for her to even put up a fight.

Her vision began to dim, but she quickly shook her head. She wasn't going to give in to her fear. No way she'd lose consciousness with a murderer in her home.

Her heart raced as his face came back into focus. "Alice, we need to go."

"Go where?" she whispered.

"Somewhere safe."

Safe? With him? He had to be joking. The safest place for her was in her car as she drove out of town.

He extended his hand. Cautiously. Slowly. Treating her as if she was a wild animal about to bolt. Alice recoiled from his hand, knowing how fast they could strike and deliver death. If she went with him, who knows what he'd do to her.

But how was she going to get away from him?

"I-I won't tell anyone what happened," she stammered.

"That's not the problem."

"You're right. There is no problem," she said quickly. "I swear I won't say anything. I'll forget everything that happened tonight."

"No, you won't. It's too late for that."

"Really, I won't tell anyone. I mean, no one would believe that you took down those guys. I can't believe you did that. You moved so fast that I could hardly tell it was you." She rubbed her sweaty palms on her pants. "People could say I did it. The roses sent me over the edge. It was public knowledge at the trial that John-Paul gave them to all of his victims. I just lost it and attacked those men." She nodded her head. "Yeah, people would believe that story. Post traumatic stress. That's what I'd tell them. You'd have nothing to do with it. Nothing whatsoever."

Okay, she was babbling, but she couldn't stop herself. If she kept talking, then maybe he wouldn't kill her. Maybe he'd think she was losing her mind and he'd let her live. No one would listen to a raving lunatic.

"That's not an option."

He took a step toward her. He was going to do it right now. She was going to die. After all that happened, she hoped to enjoy her second chance at life after John-Paul tortured her. But she was going to die at the hands of a beautiful killer.

"I'll forget you even exist. Just please, don't kill me." God, she hated how her voice sounded so small. She swallowed hard, trying to keep her voice level. "Jaden, please. Don't do this."

He stood in front of her, all two hundred and sixty pounds of muscle pinning her against the wall. She lowered her eyes so he wouldn't see her tears.

This was so cruel and so unfair.

The fear fell away and helpless resignation took its place. There was no way she could fight him and win. She wouldn't beg anymore because it meant nothing to him. She *was* nothing to him. That's what hurt the most.

But she would make one last request.

"I don't care what you do with my body," she mumbled, "but make it quick. Like you did with those men. They look like they didn't suffer too much. Please don't make me suffer."

His heavy palms landed on her arms. She sucked in a breath and tried not to tremble, but it was difficult knowing she'd be dead in a matter of seconds.

His arms snaked around her, locking her into his body. He dropped his head and buried his face in the crook of her neck.

Alice waited for him to kill her, to break her spine or choke the breath out of her body. Maybe he'd tear her throat out. Literally. But he just stood there with her in the silence.

He lifted his head, his lips inches from her ear. "Did they hurt you?"

Well, that was the last thing she expected to hear from him. "Ah…no. They scared me, but I'm not hurt."

He nodded and put his head back on her shoulder.

She stood there and just let him hold her. The way he held her was tender, gentle. Almost as if he was reassuring himself she was all right. A lover's embrace.

As the seconds ticked by, she had a feeling that he wasn't going to kill her. Not unless he was going to do it by hugging her to death.

A flicker of hope burned in her heart. She still had a chance to make it out of this nightmare alive and get out of town.

Hesitantly, she moved her hands, not wanting to spook him.

God knew he could crush her if she scared him. She couldn't risk startling him. She only had one chance to push him away and bolt for the door.

She placed her palm against the back of his head, her fingers entwining in the silken strands of his black ponytail. He sighed and leaned into her. She stroked him lightly as her other hand wrapped around his shoulders.

There was so much power in him, but he ceded it when it came to her. The club, the night he checked over her injuries, the way he touched her. He let her be in control.

Push him away, she thought. *Do it now.*

Alice counted down in her head. Three…two…

One.

And still she stood there.

She needed to get out of the apartment, but her feet were glued to the floor. She ran one hand down his back and he jerked, his hips moving away from her body. She immediately yanked her hands away, the fear coming back in full force.

"I'm sorry," she blurted out. "I shouldn't have done that. It was completely inappropriate."

"There's no reason for you to apologize." He took a step away from her. "And don't ever beg for anything from me. I'm not going to hurt you, Alice."

Those were the same words he said to her the night she was attacked in the alley. He hadn't hurt her that night. Or last night. God knew he had plenty of opportunities. She wanted to believe him, but he took down three men twice her size in a matter of minutes.

"Who are they?" she asked.

"No one of importance."

She stared him in the eye. "Who are you?"

"I'll tell you everything once we get out of here." His gaze went to the bodies and his eyes hardened. "We can't stay here much longer. More of them will come."

There were more of those men? They said they wanted to take her to John-Paul. What if he showed up and actually got her?

She couldn't go through that again.

"We have to go." He held out his hand to her. "Trust me, Alice."

Alice stared at his palm for a long moment. Knowing she was ten different kinds of stupid, she tentatively placed her palm on top of his. The warmth of his hand traveled throughout her body and she felt some of her fear slipping away. A sense of ease enveloped her like a blanket. She had nothing to fear from Jaden. Not when his hands were as soft as his caress, his kiss.

Yeah. She so wasn't going there right now.

"He sent me flowers," she said, focusing on something other than the lethal killer holding her hand.

"Who sent you flowers?"

"John-Paul. He...he's the one who attacked me two years ago." She looked at the roses which had fallen on the couch. "How could he send them to me from prison?"

"He's not in prison. He escaped last night."

Bile rose in her throat. He was roaming the streets? A wanted man focused on nothing but claiming her again. She trembled at the thought of John-Paul getting his hands on her. He'd have his Day Three. The day he missed with her.

"He's coming after me," she whispered.

"I'm not going to let him get to you. I swear it."

Alice grabbed her purse as he retrieved the knife from the dead man's chest. She'd rather take her chances with Jaden than with John-Paul. Alice watched him as he picked up the card where she dropped it and he slid it in his pocket.

Why would he care about that?

He took her hand and led her into the hallway. He stayed in front of her, his massive body hiding her from any potential threats. His free hand rested inside his coat pocket.

Probably has a gun, she thought. How many weapons was he carrying?

They exited the building, running towards the car. Before she had a chance to belt herself in, he was in the driver's seat, gunning the engine and tearing down the street. She looked out the window and was greeted with darkness. The windows were heavily tinted and she was amazed Jaden could see anything.

She took a deep breath to steel her nerves. She had no clue where she was going or what would happen to her once they reached their destination. Might as well find out the answers to her questions now. She couldn't ask them if she was dead.

"What about the men in my apartment?" She turned toward him. "The police are going to look for me if they find three dead bodies and I've disappeared."

"The police won't question anyone," he said.

"Yeah. Because three dead bodies raise no questions whatsoever," she muttered. "My neighbors will just tell them I'm using a new air freshener called Eau de Corpse."

The corner of his lip twitched as he pressed a number on his cell phone. "At least your sense of humor's intact."

"It's either that or start screaming hysterically because I'm in a car with a murderer."

"I'm not going to hurt you," he repeated.

"It's still a little hard to take you on your word with what I just saw."

Jaden's eyes flickered to her and she caught the sadness in

his eyes before they became impassive again. "Hey, it's me. I need Helene and Varrik to clean house."

Alice bit her lip. Clean house? Must be code for lots of Hefty bags. If they were smart, they'd get the ones with odor lock and extra stretch. They could fit more body parts in the bag without worrying about the smell.

She put her head in her hands. Yeah, she was totally losing it.

"I babysat two for her last night. I don't care what she says. Helene better not give me any shit about doing this. This is the least she could do." He frowned as the person talked on the other end. "What? Apartment 2. Corner building of Hooper Road and 28…No. There were no witnesses." He glanced at Alice. "She was home. We hauled ass out of there so she's only wearing what's on her. She'll need some clothes." His eyes raked down her body and she felt a slight blush creep over her cheeks from his thorough once over. "I'd say a medium. A small would be too tight. Okay. See you at the house."

She leaned her head back and wondered when it would stop spinning. It had been an ordinary day twelve hours ago. She woke up, ate breakfast, went to work and thought about seeing Jaden again.

And in the span of fifteen minutes, her world turned upside down. She was in a car with a man of sorts, three dead bodies in her apartment and an obsessive compulsive rapist hell-bent on finding her.

"Why were those men after me?" she asked. "And how did you know they were coming for me?"

"They weren't after you. They were after me."

That made no sense. Those men wanted to take her to John-Paul. They even said it. Why would they go after him?

"They are what I hunt and what I protect people like you

from," he added.

"Hunt," she echoed flatly. "You hunt people?"

"They're not people, Alice. They're Shadows."

"Shadows? What are they?"

He tightened his grip on the steering wheel. "You really want to have this conversation now?"

"You said you'd explain things to me when we were safe. I think I'm as safe as I'm going to get."

They sat quietly for a few minutes. She believed Jaden wasn't going to answer her question, but he surprised her. "Shadows are a hybrid mix of humans and my kind."

"What is your kind?"

He rolled his eyes. "Speed, strength, long canines and you've only seen me at night. Take a wild guess."

Alice stared at him for a long moment. Somehow, she just bypassed reality and hopped on board the crazy train because he had to be kidding. What he talked about was bordering on insanity.

"No, it's not possible! Vampires don't exist."

"You have a better explanation for what I am?"

"Delusional."

Jaden laughed, his deep voice filling the small space. "Seems that way, doesn't it?"

"I don't know what I can trust. Or who."

The laughter died away and his face became grave again. "Look, I know you've had a hard night and what I'm telling you sounds crazy, but it is the truth."

Alice rubbed her temples. No freaking way vampires existed. He had to be crazy.

But the way Jaden killed those men was unnatural. How he took in every movement without looking at her. Moved so fast she couldn't even track him.

Was it really possible?

"Where are you from?" Alice asked.

"Theologically speaking or geographically?"

Irritation welled inside of her. He was playing with her and she didn't like it one bit. Normally she'd tell him to cut the crap, but since her life was in his hands, she held back the insult.

"I'll let you pick," she snapped.

"London. And let me tell you England in the mid-14th century was not exactly a pleasant place to live. I prefer the States to that archaic country."

She flinched in her seat. He'd been alive since the Middle Ages? Talk about living history.

As insane as his answers were, the curiosity got the better of her. "What was it like?"

"Dirty. Crowded," he said, changing lanes. "People lived so close together and in such unsanitary conditions. You had to be careful when walking because there was a good chance a chamber pot would be emptied on your head."

"How old are you?"

His pale blue eyes narrowed as he switched lanes. "Thirty. At least that's what it says on my driver's license."

"How old are you really?" she demanded.

"Six hundred and ninety-two," he said. "I began my warrior training in the year 1348 at the height of the Black Death in England. Carrying bodies helps with upper body strength."

He was almost seven hundred years old? He looked damn good for his age. Especially in that black sweater and jeans which showed off every muscle in his body although she knew firsthand how built he was.

She almost slapped herself as her cheeks grew hot. What was she thinking? Sex should be the last thing on her mind.

Staying alive was her first priority.

"Were you infected with the plague?"

His face became grim. "No, but I saw a lot of humans die from it."

"How did you become a…" God, she actually had to say it? "…vampire?"

"It wasn't a choice. I was born this way."

Her jaw dropped open. Vampires were a different race?

"You're kidding me."

"You really think I'd screw with your head right now?" He shook his head. "We are a separate species from humans."

"Like the freaks in a circus sideshow."

"That would be your species, sweetheart. Humans are a genetic mutation we didn't see coming. Weak and yet able to tolerate sunlight. Not fucking fair if you ask me." He scowled into the darkness. "How they survived is beyond me."

"You obviously don't think highly of the human race."

"They've persecuted my kind for centuries. Stakes through the heart, setting us on fire and chopping our heads off are all methods they've used to kill the members of my race. We left them alone and let them live in peace, but they came after us and called us the spawn of Satan. So yeah, I'm not crazy about them."

"You know I belong to the weaker species," she said. "If you don't care about humans, then why are you helping me?"

"Because I don't hate you."

Were the surprises never going to end tonight?

Alice cleared her throat. "You don't just bite humans and they become vampires?"

"The gene is dormant in humans, but it can be tapped into." He veered off the highway amidst the angry honks and obscenities he received from other drivers as he cut them off.

"A human can become one of us. It's very rare when it happens and it's not something that is done lightly."

Now that was definitely a sore spot. Don't ask the testy vampire about changing a human until he was in a better mood.

"Are there many of your kind?" she asked.

"No. We live among humans in most major cities or college towns. It's easier for us to hide in places where there's a large population of people." He turned onto a side road. "But in several major cities, you have vampires like me. Sworn to protect those who try to live peacefully and make sure they keep our identity a secret."

"Are there older vampires than you?"

"Not many," he admitted. "The strongest of us live in Ravenna because there's a bigger threat to the safety of my race. And don't ask who that is because it's a question I won't answer."

She leaned her head against the window, closing her eyes for a moment. Good grief. Instead of being whisked to Oz, she was still in the same city, but with an alternate reality. Vampires, Shadows and humans.

We are definitely not in Kansas anymore, she thought.

"Do you believe any of it yet?" Jaden asked.

"I'm having a hard time processing any rational thoughts right now."

"Most humans do when they learn what I am."

And she was with an immortal fighter who hid from the sunlight and had razor-sharp fangs.

Her eyes flew open. Vampires viewed humans as a food source, right? He drank from the Shadow, but she didn't know how many pints he needed to knock back before he was satisfied.

That's why he took her from the apartment. He'd leave no witnesses and take care of his hunger too. A two for one deal. Drink her blood and it'd kill her.

"Will it hurt?" she whispered.

He frowned. "Will what hurt?"

"When you drink my blood." She swallowed hard. "That's how you'll kill me, right? I just want to know if it'll hurt."

Jaden took a deep breath and counted to ten before he responded. "How many times do I have to say it? You're safe with me."

"You're not the human who could be your midnight snack," she pointed out. "I am."

"Your faith in me is overwhelming," he muttered.

"How would you feel if you were in my position?"

"Come on, Alice. You know me better than that."

"I don't know you at all," she said. "One night of sex doesn't mean I know who you are."

Even if it was really amazing, hot sex.

"I won't feed from you without your consent. No matter how tempting I find your blood." His eyes ran over her quickly, piercing her with a searing gaze. "Or your body."

She trembled in her seat, but it wasn't just fear that made her shiver.

They sped through the side streets until they hit a gated community. Jaden punched in the code and drove his car through the gates. She focused on the houses which easily fit into the multimillion dollar category.

He turned his car down a gravel path shrouded with evergreens. The darkness, the expansive grove of trees, screamed loneliness. It seemed as if the driveway stretched for miles before he slowed in front of a sprawling estate. Alice's eyes bulged when she saw how huge the house was. The four-sided Tudor brick structure sat impassively in the darkness with a few pinpricks of light coming from the multi-paned windows. A thin layer of frost clung to the ground and some of the scrollwork on the sloped roof. The moonlight caught the ice, casting an eerie, iridescent glow to the house.

Jaden punched in another code and the garage door opened. He pulled the car inside and turned off the engine. Alice got out of the car, her eyes darting around the garage. In addition to the Viper, two motorcycles, a white van, and a silver Corvette gleamed in the fluorescent light.

Her eyes lingered on the Corvette. It reminded her of the asshole who ran her off the road and the one from her dream. It certainly looked like the same car.

She frowned at him. "You have quite a collection."

"They get me around."

"Does it help you to outrun cops in Ravenna?"

Guilt flickered in his eyes before they became impassive again. "All my cars can outrun the cops whether I'm in Ravenna or Atlanta. They're specifically built for speed."

"And hard to come by in Georgia, I'm sure."

"There aren't many of them."

Wasn't this ironic? So Jaden was the one who ran her off the road. The bastard.

He punched in another code before he opened the door. She followed behind him, clutching her purse to her, the only familiar thing in her chaotic world.

"Why do you have so much security?" she asked.

"In case a dumbass Shadow thinks he can break into my house and kill me while I sleep," he said as they walked through the kitchen.

"Can they?"

"Hasn't happened yet. I like being prepared."

Well, that certainly made her feel a whole lot better. Who wouldn't feel secure with that kind of paranoid optimism?

She rubbed her shoulder as she passed through the kitchen. The outside of the house may have looked Old World, but the inside was outfitted with the latest technology. Top of the line stainless steel appliances, a brick oven and a marble island seemed so out of place for someone who didn't eat human food.

Her eyes lingered on the two refrigerators flanking either side of the stove. She shuddered to think was actually inside them. Hopefully, it wasn't body parts or blood in case he needed a midnight snack. Like the heart. Tastes better with a little chill.

Oh yeah. She was totally losing it.

"You have a beautiful home," Alice said, distracting herself from the fridges.

"This is where I live," he corrected. "A home indicates you have someone you can come back to. I don't have that. When I get tired of living here, I'll move somewhere else."

A sudden wave of sadness washed over her. She knew exactly what he meant. Her little apartment was a place for her to rest her head. No one waited for her to come home. She had some good friends, but they didn't know her all that well. In reality, she had no one.

"Just a roof over your head," she murmured. "I get it."

She paused in the middle of the foyer. The man was filthy rich. Then again, being almost seven hundred years old gives one quite a bit of time to acquire such wealth. The dimmed lights from the crystal chandelier bathed the room in an incandescent glow. Near the steps was an ebony desk where he tossed his keys on top of a pile of papers. An oil painting of a woman with amber eyes and long blonde hair stared at them coldly, as if the woman was insulted by Alice's very presence.

To her right, a black marble staircase curved to the second floor, the railing inlaid with gold filigree. The windows were decorated with heavy, black drapes which blocked out any light from the outside.

"I'm assuming you'll burst into flames without these curtains," Alice said.

"That's a myth. Vampires don't incinerate once the sun hits our skin. The sun does something much worse," he said. "It changes the composition of our blood into acid. Basically, we liquefy from the inside out."

She grimaced. "Sounds painful."

"It is. We have fifteen minutes to get inside. Otherwise, we're as good as dead. Usually, it takes three to four hours before we die. The bursting into flame theory came from the way we execute those who betray us." He glanced at the painting before looking back at her. "We leave them with enough wood and gas to create their own pyre. They can die slowly and let the sun disintegrate the body or light themselves on fire to make it quicker. Most take the fire route."

She gaped at him. Cooking from the inside out? "Your world is so…" her voice trailed off.

"Horrific? Violent? Terrifying?" He turned away from her and walked up the stairs. "It's no different than yours. Except that mine isn't broadcasted on the evening news."

Alice followed behind him, their footsteps echoing in the otherwise silent house. "Does anyone else live here with you?"

"I have guests who stay over from time to time."

"Are 'guests' code for blood donors?" She gestured toward the kitchen. "Is that why you have two refrigerators? You need a place to store the blood?"

His lips twitched and for a moment, she thought he was

going to smile. "I guess you could say my comrades stay over."

"You mean vampires. And they're just like you."

"Didn't think you had so many vampires living among you?"

She nodded, but she also noticed he hadn't answered her question about what was in the fridge. "So it's just you in this big house."

"I have a cleaning crew that comes in twice a week. They'll be here tomorrow morning and can get you whatever you want."

"Do they know what you are?"

"They think I'm an eccentric millionaire with night owl tendencies." He shrugged his shoulders. "I don't like being around others. I prefer living alone."

She nodded even though she felt a little twinge of pain. Weird, since she met Jaden just two days ago. Before she discovered he was a vampire.

Why would it matter to her if he didn't want people in his life? It shouldn't matter to her at all. Yet, it did.

He stopped in front of a room and opened the door for her. Alice walked in, her eyes wide. The room was the size of her living room and kitchen combined. Candles illuminated the room, making it sensual and inviting. Heavy sapphire drapes hung over the floor to ceiling window. An ivory chaise lounge was near a full length mirror, next to an oak armoire.

She peeked inside and saw a bathroom with a double vanity, walk-in shower and Jacuzzi tub. Alice hoped she'd have the chance to get in that tub. It seemed to beg her to climb in and soak her weary bones.

She turned and walked over to the bed. The black wrought-iron beauty took up half of one wall. A sapphire duvet contrasted wonderfully with the silky ivory sheets and pillows.

She touched the comforter. She wasn't used to such nice opulence. In foster care, she was lucky if she had a new, clean blanket on her bed. As an adult, she prided herself on being able to afford her little apartment on her modest salary.

Alice sat on the edge of the bed. "It's a beautiful room."

"I'm glad you like it."

Alice lifted her head, her heart hammered against her ribs. The lustful look on his face said it all.

He wanted her.

Wasn't this the perfect end to her night? With everything going on, learning about his true identity and being chased by John-Paul, she couldn't believe her body was getting hot from under his stare.

God help her, she wanted him.

~ * ~

Jaden's erection was harder than granite as those wide, green eyes locked on his face. And she wasn't doing anything remotely sexy except for sitting on the bed.

She turned toward him. He smelled her arousal, a sweet fragrance permeating the air. Her hands were where he wanted to go, where he wanted to bury his tongue and cock.

His skin felt like shrink wrap. He had to get out of the room before he did something stupid. Like mount her while she was still coming to terms with everything that happened tonight.

"Make yourself as comfortable as you can. Feel free to move around the house, but stay inside."

"Am I the only one on this hallway? Where's your room?"

His fingernails dug into the doorway. There was no sexual undertone to that question, but his body responded as if she asked if she could lick him from head to toe.

"I don't mean to pry. I really don't," she said. "I just don't want to stumble on you while you're sleeping and accidentally give you a case of UV poisoning."

Jaden cleared his throat. "Second room on the left. But since I lock it during the day, you wouldn't be able to get in."

Why the hell did he say it like that? The last thing he wanted to do was lock her out of his room. He'd rather she be locked in it with his mouth on her sex, tasting her as she came calling his name.

He took a step out of the room, needing to put some distance between them. "I'm going to leave you to get settled in. Is there anything you need right now?"

"No, I'm fine."

"There's a robe in the bathroom along with several shirts if you want to change into something else."

God, the thought of her wearing his clothes was absolutely divine. And slipping beneath the covers, those silken sheets caressing her legs and thighs.

Great. Now he was jealous of bedding.

"I might take you up on that. I'd hate to sleep in my work clothes," Alice said quietly. "Thank you, Jaden."

"For what? Not killing you?"

"Well, there's that. But I'm thank you for not letting the Shadows take me," she said. Alice lowered her eyes and absently traced the seam of the duvet. "I can only imagine what they had in mind for me."

He nodded, but they both knew what the Shadows' plans were for her. "You're safe, tonight. If you want, you can lock the door."

"I find it hard to imagine that a lock will keep you out of this room."

"But it would make you feel more secure," he said, placing a hand on his heart. "I swear on my life that I will not take yours or harm you in any way."

Alice looked at him, her green eyes warming a little. "I don't need to lock the door to feel safe. I trust you."

He didn't speak as he closed the door to her room. He cherished the sincerity in her voice. Many innocents thanked him, whether from a Shadow attack or a vampire on a killing spree. It never affected him before because he just accepted it as part of his job. But hearing Alice thank him made him feel proud, especially after the insanity that occurred tonight in her apartment.

His mind screamed at him to go back in there and embrace her, but he continued down the stairs and headed toward his gym. Jaden gave Salvatore credit for cleaning up so thoroughly. The room looked exactly how it had been before the interrogation. No evidence to show they were ever there.

"I saw the human you brought in." Salvatore sat on one of the recumbent bikes, his brown eyes burning with curiosity. "She's cute and she must be special if you're bringing her here to spend the night."

"Back off, Salvatore."

"Should I leave and give you two some privacy? Then you could take your time and see how special she really is."

"I'm fine."

"Really?" Salvatore smirked. "You're strung tighter than a steel cable. I think you need to unwind. I'm sure she could give you the release you need."

"I'd rather talk about what happened tonight. Three Shadows attacked her in her apartment," Jaden said. "I brought her here so she'd be safe."

"You could've taken her to a hotel or to Liam's, but you brought her here. You wanted to keep an eye on her." He laughed. "And your hands. I'm sure there are a couple of other body parts I'm forgetting."

"I'm not in the mood, Salvatore."

"Not for me. For her? Absolutely."

Jaden glared at his friend. "Is there a reason why you're still here besides busting my balls?"

"You told me you'd inform me of what the Shadows said when you came back. So I've been waiting like a good little boy," he said. "What did they tell you?"

"The Host is after us, but specifically me."

"No kidding? I'd think that someone other than the Host is after you." Salvatore counted on his fingers. "Shadows, most humans, Liam, Varrik, Helene. I could go on, but we'd be here a while," he said. "Besides, the Host hates us all.

"Why would that bastard release a sexual predator from prison and go after someone I barely know?"

Salvatore nodded to the ceiling. "Is she the one you were with a couple of nights ago?"

"You're an annoying little fucker tonight." Jaden glared at him. "What the hell does that have to do with anything?"

"Maybe nothing. Maybe something. It's a simple question."

"And one that's irrelevant."

"Is it? You're not shy when it comes to the females you screw." Salvatore eyes held a hint of mischief. "Are you ashamed of this one? Or did you have performance issues and couldn't finish the job?"

"I am not ashamed of Alice."

He leaned back, a satisfied grin on his face. "I guess I have my answer, don't I?"

"Yes, Alice is the one I was with last night," Jaden snapped. "Happy now?"

"And you brought her here."

"She was attacked in her own home. I wanted to make sure she was safe. Didn't we just cover this?"

"You want her," Salvatore said. "That's why the Host is after you. This isn't some random female you met in a bar, screwed and forgot about the next day. For any woman to hold your attention for more than a couple of hours is someone special. And you haven't focused on one like this since Catherine's death."

Jaden walked over to one of the cabinets and put his weapons away. Alice was special to him. She was a fighter, a survivor. But there was a quiet vulnerability about her he wanted to protect. He saw that when she trembled before him, begging for her life. He never wanted her to do that again.

Damn it, he hated when Salvatore was right. Not like he'd admit it to his fellow warrior.

"Alice isn't like other humans," Jaden muttered. "I can't explain it, but I know I can't let her go right now."

"Is she the Firebrand?"

"No. Her last name is Roarke."

"What about her parents? Any of them named Foster?"

He frowned. He hadn't considered the possibility of a Foster in her bloodline. "I'll have to ask her that. From my understanding, her parents are not in the picture."

"Then why don't you give me the detailed version with the Shadows tonight so you can go back to her."

Jaden recounted the attack on Alice. Salvatore said nothing, remaining grim. Jaden gave the other vampire the card he picked up from the flowers.

"This is a good starting point," Jaden said. "Maybe we can talk to one of the florists and find out who purchased them."

"I'll go talk to Liam about this." Salvatore glanced at the ceiling again. "Are you going to keep her here?"

"Until I'm certain she's safe."

"All right. I'll be in touch." He picked up a bag and handed it to Jaden. "Helene brought these over. She pulled some from her closet and thinks they should fit your girl."

"She's not my girl."

"Yeah. Keep telling yourself that."

Jaden took the bag and waited until the warrior left before he went to Alice's room. He knocked on the door, but there was no response. Ever so softly, he cracked it open.

Big mistake.

Her hair was wet, the mahogany tendrils cascading past her shoulders. She was wearing one of his shirts and it looked so fucking good on her. He saw the outline of her breasts, the tips of her nipples rising against the fabric. He remembered how soft her breasts were in his hands, against his tongue.

Her cinnamon fragrance hung heavy in the air from her bath, burning his throat. Jaden tore his eyes away from her chest and landed on her legs. Her creamy skin was tinged pink from her bath, one leg hanging from the bed.

He was back at full attention, his cock hard as bone, his balls tight. Images swamped him from the last time he and Alice were together. He wanted to feel those silken thighs wrapped around him again as he made love to her in her bed.

Okay. He needed to think of something else. Now.

But she looked so damn good, and she felt even better.

The wood creaked slightly and Alice turned her head at the noise. "Jaden?"

His body rippled with electricity when she said his name. It took every ounce of self-control to not run in there and throw himself on top of her. The only thing that kept his passion at bay was the note of fear in her voice.

He didn't have to touch her to know what she felt. Exhausted, scared and overwhelmed. He didn't need to make her any worse than she was.

"Yeah, it's me," he said, his voice as dry as sandpaper. "I wanted to make sure you were all right."

"Oh, I'm fine. Just a little tired."

"Is there anything you need before I turn in?"

"No, but I do have one question," she said. "I hope you don't think I'm being too nosey, but I've got to ask you something before I go to sleep."

Just one? If he were in her place, he'd have a thousand. "What is it?"

She hesitated, her fingertips rubbing her shoulder. The silence was killing him. Several questions ran through his mind. Did she want to know how many more of his kind was out there? His special abilities? His preferred blood type?

He hoped it wasn't the last one. The answer would be hers.

Alice finally looked up at him. "Do you eat food?"

Okay. Not what he was expecting. "It's not necessary for me to eat it, but I can. Why?"

"Because I was wondering what's in the refrigerator."

He stared at her for a moment, stunned. Why would she worry about that? There was nothing unusual in there. Did she think that's where he stored blood?

The tense look on her face answered that question. And she made a comment before they came upstairs about it too.

Jaden started laughing. "There is nothing in there except for food. Help yourself."

"There's food I can actually eat? Not your version of food?"

"Check it out yourself. I promise it's all completely edible and not what I need."

"I thought those cabinets were just for show." She raised an eyebrow. "And you just told me you don't need to eat food."

"If they're pretending to be human they do. I can stomach small amounts of food, but it's mostly red meat," he said.

"Besides, my cleaning crew has to eat. I let them help themselves to what's in there and they restock it for me."

Some of the tension left her shoulders. "That makes me feel a little better."

"But if there's something in particular you need, leave a note for them and they'll get it."

"I'm sure you'll have everything I need. I'm not picky."

"Do you remember where the kitchen is?"

"Down the stairs and to my left," she said. "I won't get lost. I'll even take my cell phone with me." Alice smiled at him. "That way, I'll just call and ask for directions, in case I can't find my way back to the room."

She shifted on the bed and he caught the curve of her ass. His erection kicked in his pants, clearly wanting out now. Just looking at her made him want to come. A direct hit to the groin with a tire iron would be less painful than what he felt right now.

"I have some clothes for you. If they don't fit, let me know and I'll see what else I can get you."

"You didn't have to do anything special for me."

"It's no big deal. Just thought you'd want something better than an oversized shirt."

They looked at each other uneasily for a few minutes. After everything that happened tonight, the silence made them both nervous.

"I'm sure you're tired," he said, breaking the silence. "Get some rest."

Alice nodded. "Good night, Jaden. And thanks again for keeping me safe."

He left the bag at her door and all but ran to his room. A good night's sleep was what he needed to clear his head. That and an ice cold shower.

Chapter 13

John-Paul struggled to open his eyes although they felt like they weighed a hundred pounds. He wondered how long he'd been unconscious and if Alice was here. Once he finished scrawling out the three words on his note to her, all of his strength disappeared and he had to be carried to his room like a baby.

Man, he wished he could've been there when they dropped off the flowers. He was certain it scared the shit out of her and that's how he wanted her. Fear caused people to make mistakes.

He pushed himself up, his spine cracking from the movement. John-Paul wasn't used to a bed that cushioned his aching back or the tray of food which seemed to be specifically for him. A concrete slab and government issued meals was what he had experienced for the past two years.

He touched the side of his neck. The Host had taken quite a bit of blood from him and a painful exchange at that. He wouldn't have fought so much if they had told him what was going to happen and how strong he'd become once he became a Shadow.

The bite wound was still sore, but it was a pleasant kind of pain. The Host could bleed him like that any time as long as he stayed out of prison. And he had Alice. Markus promised he'd bring her to him tonight.

John-Paul stood, the rubbery sensation dissipating with every step. He was about to open the door when he heard angry voices in the hallway. One was Markus. The other belonged to the Host.

"We failed to get her," Markus murmured.

"Failed is an understatement," the Host said, the icy voice chilling John-Paul's bones. "One human woman was our target. You sent three of our best men to bring her back and now they're dead. Tell me how I can see this as anything other than a total disaster and why I should keep you alive."

Alice wasn't here? Now John-Paul was sore and royally pissed off.

"The human is terrified of John-Paul," Markus answered in a rush. "I've seen the taped deposition from the trial. She put on a brave face, but she was scared to death of him. We can use this to our advantage. If Jaden is attached to the human, then he'll try and come after us. His judgment will be clouded and he's more likely to make a mistake."

The Host was silent for a moment. "This is true. Yet we still lost three of our own tonight."

"We're still trying to figure out how that happened."

"It's not that hard to figure out, Markus. That woman didn't kill them. I'm sure it was an Emain Macha who showed up. Most likely Jaden Payne." A few heartbeats of silence passed before the Host spoke again. "You said there was no trace of the bodies?"

"None whatsoever."

"We've been on the defense too long," the Host said. "Now it's time to change tactics."

"What would you like for me to do?"

"Smoke them out."

"How?"

"Start with the human's friends," the Host replied. "When they start disappearing, she'll come out of hiding. Jaden will be with her. I have no doubt about that."

"What about our guest?"

Another pause. John-Paul could just imagine the calculating smile on the Host's face. "I think it's time for our guest to pay his debt."

"He's not strong enough yet."

"We'll have to fix that, won't we?"

John-Paul backed away from the door. The Host sounded way too happy about fixing his weakness. And he had a feeling whatever they were going to do was going to hurt like a bitch.

Markus, two other Shadows and the Host walked into his room. John-Paul scrambled for the bed as they approached. Only this time, they held a couple of needles, a tourniquet and a clear IV bag.

Yeah, this was going to hurt.

Chapter 14

Alice flopped around in the bed, trying to go back to sleep, although it was impossible. She had the dream again and nearly had a full-blown episode. She didn't recognize her surroundings when she woke up with a scream lodged in her throat. It had taken her a good five minutes to calm down and she only relaxed when her vision went back to normal.

She picked up her cell phone and dialed Tina's number. Thank goodness today was a school-wide holiday. It'd be hard to find a substitute this late in the morning.

"Hey, darlin'! I wasn't expecting to hear from you this morning," Tina said warmly. "Enjoying your day off so far?"

"I wouldn't say I'm enjoying it."

"Why? Did that fine man not show up last night?"

"He showed up alright." Alice swallowed the hysterical giggle in her throat. "I-I'm actually at his place right now."

"Damn, girl! Then why are you on the phone with me if you're with the hottie?"

"I need your help with something."

"Sure, hon. What is it?"

"I...need you to find a sub for my class this week. I need some time to myself."

"Got it. I'll tell Denise that you've got the flu."

"Oh, I don't want you to lie for me." Because Alice was

doing a good enough job of lying already. "I just want to take a couple of personal days."

"I'll make sure you're covered for the rest of the week. You need those mental health days every once in a while." Tina laughed knowingly. "Besides, have that man of yours help you out. I'm sure he can make you feel all better."

"Thanks, Tina. I owe you one."

Alice ended the call and stared at the phone. Yeah, she could tell people she was sick. If you called your murderous vampire lover the flu, then she had a raging case of it.

She slid out of the bed and rummaged through the bag of clothes Jaden brought her. Alice pulled out a pair of workout pants, a gray tank top and slipped on her tennis shoes.

She glanced at herself in the mirror. The clothes were a little tighter than what she normally wore, but she knew a part of it was in her mind. She turned to the side and took a good look at herself. Her butt actually looked curvy in the soft cotton along with the fabric clinging in all the right places.

Alice never liked showing off her body so she purposefully wore clothes to hide her figure. It was either walk around in Jaden's shirt or go naked. But she had to admit, she didn't look half-bad in the borrowed top and pants.

She closed the door and glanced down the hallway, her eyes adjusting to the small amount of light coming from the lamps illuminating the narrow space. Two doors away was Jaden's room. She knew he locked himself in as soon as the sun came up a couple of hours ago and she had no intention of disturbing him. He had a rough night and needed his rest too.

Although she had the sneaking suspicion something else bothered him. He practically ran out of her room when he saw her dressed in his shirt. Maybe he liked what he saw. She didn't hide her attraction to him last night. Even though her head was spinning, she wanted him to hold her, to kiss away her fears and reassure her.

She shook her head. He probably was hungry and thought it'd be impolite to snack on her.

She walked down the stairs and headed toward the kitchen. She wasn't particularly hungry, but she needed to do something rather than toss and turn in the bed.

All the drapes were drawn tight and without the glow from a couple of lamps, it'd be impossible for her to find her way in the house. She was certain Jaden wouldn't miss a movement in the almost total darkness. She'd be lucky if she didn't break her neck.

She paused at the bottom of the stairs and spied a beam of fluorescent light spilling out of a room to her right. Curiosity got the better of her hunger so she headed towards the light. At the end of her destination was a huge home gym. Her eyes widened at the assortment of workout equipment from treadmills, weight stations, punching bags and even a separate boxing ring. It was the kind of room most athletes would kill to train in.

She noticed three stainless steel cabinets along the wall. Odd that he'd keep such huge cabinets in here, but she shrugged. Probably lined with more exercise gear or towels after a brutal workout.

Alice went over to one of the punching bags and fingered the worn canvas. She remembered all the instructions and advice from the classes she took after the attack. Get to safety. Scream. Aim for the sensitive parts on an attacker's body: throat, groin, eyes.

She never thought she'd be a victim again. Yet here she was in a strange man's home, a vampire no less and completely at his mercy. Because the alternative left her with John-Paul.

Alice stood in front of the bag, going into a boxer's stance. She should wear gloves. There was even a pair on the floor underneath the punching bag, but she left them alone.

The Shadows' attack, John-Paul's escape from prison and learning about Jaden's true identity was all too much to handle. She had to get it out.

She let all of her fear and anger flow into her fists. She hit the bag, the sting of the canvas abrasive against her skin. She ignored the pain and kept swinging. With the amount of anger and hurt she had inside of her, she'd punch until her hands bled.

"Jab, cross. Jab, cross," she muttered as her fists connected with the canvas.

The chains rattled with each punch. She remembered how they rattled from her training sessions with John-Paul. Every three hours like clockwork, he visited her. The pleading for him to stop. His odd fixation on her. His bitch.

Goosebumps flared over her skin. She punched harder, her eyes filling with tears. "I'm not an animal," she whispered.

But it didn't stop his voice from filling her head.

"Tell me how much you like this," John-Paul said. *"I want to hear it."*

"Go to hell."

"Maybe later. I'm in heaven right now." His lips brushed her shoulder. *"You are mine."*

"I don't belong to you."

"Really? I'll have to change that."

The dam burst and tears poured down her cheeks. She kicked the bag and continued her relentless assault. As if her fists and feet could prevent what happened next, to stop her from remembering the pain.

"That's why I love you, Alice. You're so feisty. And you need more

training than the others."

His hands ran up her thighs, over her stomach, up toward her breasts. He rolled his hips against her and she felt his erection pressing into her skin through his jeans. She swallowed her cry as she looked down and saw the paw print ring on his forefinger. She knew every groove of that ring since it collided with her face every time she refused to obey John-Paul.

She wouldn't give him any more power than he had. No matter how much it hurt.

"I will make you mine, Alice. Everyone will know you're my bitch."

"No one will ever know. It's not like you're going to keep me alive," she said hoarsely.

"True, but it's not the third day. Not yet." His hands left her body and he backed away from her. "But I can make sure people know you were mine well after you're dead."

She heard the snap of a lighter. Terror rippled through her as she felt the heat coming closer to her skin.

"Don't do this. Please."

"I like it when you beg. Do it again."

The metal pressed against her flesh, searing her skin. She couldn't keep this scream in as she felt the ring burning a hole in her shoulder. And she kept screaming. She couldn't stop herself from breaking. After two days, he finally made her crack.

"Oh, fuck yeah."

She could do nothing as she prayed for him to stop. Prayed for death.

"Scream for me, bitch."

Alice drove her fists harder into the bag. Her knuckles were raw and left little red droplets on the canvas. Alice didn't care. She'd stop when she had nothing left.

~ * ~

Hunger twisted his gut as the scent of cinnamon woke Jaden from his sleep. He shouldn't have to feed for another week or two since he drank from the Shadow last night or if he became injured. But this was Alice and his thirst would not be quenched until he had a taste.

He inhaled deeply and another wave of that delicious spice filling his head. Damn, Alice smelled so good. And the scent was strong. Fresh.

Wait a second.

He shot up, his eyes narrowing. There was only one way she'd smell that strong. Alice was bleeding. How did she hurt herself?

Jaden got out of the bed and pulled on a pair of jeans. He left his room, pausing in front of her door. He saw the mussed sheets on the bed and his shirt on top of the covers. Her scent lingered, but it wasn't coming from this room. It was coming from downstairs.

He hurried down the stairs and followed the trail until he was a few feet from his gym. Christ, he hoped she hadn't found any of his interrogation tools. That would really make things awkward.

He stopped in the doorway. She hadn't found his treasure trove, but he was equally shocked at what he saw.

Alice had her back to him. And she was beating the shit out of the punching bag in front of her.

He watched as her bare fists collided with the canvas. It had to hurt, the rough canvas rubbing against her raw skin, but she didn't stop. With each punch, she left a tiny spatter of blood on the bag, a burst of cinnamon filling the air. Why wasn't she wearing gloves?

She delivered harsh blows to the bag, even scissor-kicking it with her feet. Every time she made contact, she whimpered. Damn, it had to hurt, but she said nothing. At the rate she was going, she'd end up breaking her knuckles.

He sensed her emotional pain. He didn't have to touch her

to know how agonizing it was. It festered inside of her, growing and redoubling until it manifested itself on her bloody hands.

"Alice?" he called.

She didn't hear him. Or she chose to ignore him.

He took a step closer and frowned. Her skin had the same slight reddish glow when he first saw her in the alley. Humans didn't have luminescent skin like that. How did she do it?

"I am not an animal."

Her voice snapped him to attention. Her words were strangled as she worked to keep the sobs inside.

So much pain.

A surge went through her and she punched the bag with more force and aggression. "I am me. I belong to me."

Jaden walked into the room. He was halfway across when he saw her left shoulder. The spot she usually kept covered with a bandage moved in rhythm to her punches. Never before had he seen this patch of skin which she kept hidden from else. The source of shame and fear she concealed from the world.

The scar of a paw print.

The rough edges and uneven flesh suggested it wasn't a birthmark. How did it get there?

Unless…

"I was his bitch. He said he'd never let me go."

That familiar dark and deadly rage spread through his veins. Jaden didn't want to guess how it got there although he probably knew the answer. But he wanted to hear it from her lips.

He stood next to her. "Alice?"

Alice gasped and whirled around, intending to strike. Jaden caught her fist inches from his face. Her eyes were crazed and unfocused, her cheeks red from the remnants of the tears splattered on her skin.

He held her wrist gently as he waited for her to recognize him. Her chest heaved from exertion, the sweat clung to her hair, and she trembled in front of him. But there was no glow now, no eerie illumination.

He sucked in a breath as her pain latched on to him, her emotions becoming his. It was such a brutal, raw ache--a bottomless pit of agony.

Jaden stroked the uneven skin and tried to take away some of her sorrow. For once, he was glad he could use his gift for something other than torture. He tried to bring her closer to him, but she tensed as if she were afraid of being trapped so he kept his distance, his thumb drawing circles on her inner wrist.

Eventually the wildness disappeared and her eyes became haunted. Anguished. He tried to minimize the pain, but he couldn't get rid of it. There was just too much.

"Are you okay?"

"I – what?" She blinked rapidly, stunned to see him there. "Um…yes. I'm fine."

The hell she was. And her obvious lie did nothing to quell his fury at John-Paul. "No, you're not."

"Did I wake you?" she asked. "I didn't mean to. I thought I was being quiet."

"This woke me up." Jaden turned her wrist in his hand, glancing at the scraped knuckles. He swallowed hard when a fresh wave of her scent made his fangs throb in his mouth. "What happened?"

Her cheeks darkened in embarrassment. "Oh, I'm sorry about that. You'd think I'd remember I was in a house where the owner drinks blood. Not smart, Alice. Not smart at all." She glanced at the stains on the bag. "I'll get some cleaner and do the best I can with the bag."

He dropped her wrist. "Leave it alone."

"But if the blood sets in, it'll be ruined. If I can't get it out, then I'll pay for a new one."

"Alice, I don't care about the goddamn bag!" Her shoulders sagged at his tone and he immediately forced the irritation out of his voice. He didn't want to make her feel worse. "What I do care about is why you're bleeding and ignoring my questions. Tell me what happened."

"It's not important."

"It is to me."

"I was feeling a little restless. I needed to burn off some energy."

"You can get in a good workout and not rip off your skin in the process," he ground out. "Why would you deliberately hurt yourself?"

"I didn't deliberately hurt myself. I was in the zone and I didn't feel it."

"Then why are you crying?" When Alice didn't answer, he pressed on. "Does it have anything to do with the scar on your shoulder?"

"Oh, no. I-I thought I covered it." The blood drained from her face as her fingertips swept across her shoulder. She put her trembling fingers over the scar. "I forgot to put a bandage on it. I never wanted you to see it."

"He gave it to you, didn't he? That bastard John-Paul carved it into your skin." He took a deep breath. "I can understand why you'd want to hide it from people. What I don't understand is why you'd hide it from me."

~ * ~

This was bad. Really, really bad.

Alice held her shoulder tightly, covering the scar. She made such a stupid mistake. She hadn't planned on him waking up. That was the only reason why she didn't cover it.

"Why did you hide it from me?"

She looked away from him. Because she was ashamed. Because she hated when people looked at her as less than human. Because for once, she wanted someone to see her and not a victim.

Maybe Jaden would be different. Hell, he was an entirely different species. Maybe he'd see her as a person. And he still made love to her after he found out about her attack.

Will the truth push him away? Alice thought.

That was the problem. She liked Jaden. A lot. Even the whole vampire thing didn't bother her so much. It had been a long time since she connected with someone and she didn't want to lose that feeling.

She kept her eyes on the floor. Jaden made her feel special. Wanted. No one had ever treated her with the care and kindness he showed her.

She thought of the night they spent together. She trusted him enough to touch her. She might be able to trust him now.

"Branded," she corrected. "He branded me. He said carving was too messy on the others. The brand was much easier."

"Did he ever tell you why he did it?"

"To remind me that I was his bitch. Like I could forget. Like I could forget how he beat me over and over again for two days." She closed her eyes. "I smelled my own skin burning. It worked the first time, but he did it two more times. Three times the amount of pain and humiliation." She shuddered as she rubbed her shoulder. "I screamed so much then. That was the worst training session for me."

"Training sessions?"

"If I'm a bitch, I need to learn obedience." She recited the words dully. "Along with responding to commands quickly and with respect. Submissive to any and all demands my master gives me." Alice saw the slight tremors in her hands and she held them together. "When I wasn't obedient, I was beaten. Usually after a couple of hard blows, I learned to control my responses, but not my anger. He always saw the anger as a challenge. He said the rage I felt was because I was in heat and he needed to respond to that urge inside of me. But he wouldn't breed with me until the third day."

"When did he mark you?" he growled.

"The second day at twelve o'clock. He came to me again at three and six, repeating the branding. I escaped shortly after the last visit." She choked on a sob when she remembered the florist. "It must've been around 6:30. Why else would he pick that time to send me those flowers?"

"Jesus, Alice. I had no idea."

"Now you know why I hide the scar. I don't like telling anyone what happened to me because they look at me like I'm some kind of freak," she said. "They avoid me like I can give them some kind of disease or because I'm too dirty to be near them. That's why I transferred schools and moved to Ravenna because people didn't want to be near me. Or the ones who did looked at me with pity." She bit her lip. "And it's also why I told you about my attack the night we were together. Men usually don't want someone who's been so broken."

Alice finally looked up at him and saw the fury burning in his eyes. A muscle twitched in his jaw, his hands shaking with a subtle tremor. He looked like he wanted to tear someone apart. She hoped it wasn't her.

Although she was a little scared of him right now, there was a glimmer of hope. Maybe that anger wasn't because he slept with her. Maybe it was because he felt angry on her behalf. She prayed that was it.

Please don't walk away from me, she prayed fervently. *See me for who I am and not as John-Paul's bitch.*

But he turned away from her and walked across the room, stopping in front of one of the large metal cabinets. He kept his back to her, his hands pressing against the steel doors, the muscles of his shoulders tense.

Alice's heart sank as tears filled her eyes. She hoped Jaden would understand. She foolishly believed if she opened herself up to him and bared the most vulnerable part of her soul, he'd accept her, but she knew the truth.

He saw the same filth on her that everyone else did.

When would she ever learn?

"I'm not dirty," she whispered. "I'm just trying to fix what John-Paul broke."

Who was she trying to convince: Jaden or herself? Either way, it didn't matter. Jaden's body language spoke volumes. Tense shoulders, face turned away, putting as much distance between them. He was disgusted with her.

The hurt faded and was left with nothing in her heart. She knew that hollow, cold feeling well. The emptiness embraced her, welcoming her into its icy arms once again. Only this time, she didn't have the strength to fight it off.

Alice wrapped her arms around herself, trying to prevent the warmth from fading away, but the chills shook her body until her bones felt frozen. She wished Jaden would hold her, but wishes and dreams were for people who had something to hope for. The only thing she hoped for now was that the night would come quickly so she could leave.

She walked to the doorway and willed herself to stop crying. Tears were useless. They wouldn't change the past or the present.

"Once I've taken care of my hands, I'll come back and clean up the mess," she said roughly, staring at the Celtic tattoo spanning his shoulder blades. "I'm sorry I woke you and I'll stay out of your way. I won't disturb you again."

Alice trudged up the stairs and back to her room, not bothering to close the door. She went to the bathroom and washed her hands. The soap stung her raw skin, but she ignored the pain. The cupboard in front of her had no bandages so Alice did the best she could to stop the bleeding.

Alice glanced at her reflection in the mirror. Her cheeks were splotchy from the tears, lips swollen. The eyes empty, hollow. Like her heart.

She turned her shoulder and saw the faded skin, but the scar was still visible. A harsh reminder of the dirt on her.

She grabbed her jacket off the floor and put it on, covering the marks on her shoulder and wrists. She walked toward the bed and stripped it of the expensive sheets. He said there was a cleaning crew that came in, but she wouldn't wait for them. She'd wash the sheets herself so the invisible stain she carried wouldn't taint his bed.

Alice picked up a pillow. She couldn't stay here any longer. Once night fell, she'd leave and do her best to forget what happened here. She knew her apartment wasn't safe. She had some money in her emergency fund, which she would empty. She'd purchase a one way ticket out of town and out of harm's way. She could start her life over again and pray John-Paul never found her.

But Jaden was an entirely different story. Time wouldn't let her forget about how he had worshipped her body. How for once in her life she felt wanted and desired.

She'd go back to her life. She'd find the strength to keep going no matter how many times she wanted to give up. And like when she was in foster care, after the abduction, after the trial and every day for the rest of her life, she'd take care of herself and heal as best she could. Alone.

Chapter 15

Jaden knew rage and vengeance well. It gave him strength and purpose, protecting his species and ridding the world of Shadow scum. But he never felt it on a level like this. He wanted to hunt with a hatred he hadn't felt in centuries. It surged through his veins and buried itself deep inside his bones. He took a breath in an attempt to calm himself, but all he felt was the overwhelming urge to kill on Alice's behalf.

When she described what happened to her, all Jaden could think about was getting that animal in this room and slowly gutting the bastard. But he had no outlet because the goddamned sun was still high in the sky.

John-Paul Finch was a dead man. As soon as the sun set, he was going to find that piece of shit and peel the skin off his bones. Hell, he had the tools to do it. He'd make that fucker beg for his life and enjoy every second of it.

He had to focus on something else. Otherwise, he'd destroy the house just to alleviate his fury.

"I'm not dirty. I'm just trying to fix what John-Paul broke."

That stopped him cold. She had whispered the words, but she might as well have shouted it from the rooftop. She was so small and timid when she spoke to him, not the strong, defiant tone he found incredibly sexy.

How could she think of herself as damaged? She was the purest, most beautiful thing in his life. No matter what that bastard did to her, Alice was a treasure Jaden was lucky enough to touch.

His chest tightened. This woman who broke for no one, whose spine of steel bent only when she willed it, disappeared. Today, he saw a woman who craved a little comfort, a little hope that someone would be worthy of her love. This was Alice in her barest form, stripped of all the armor she kept around herself.

She exposed the most painful part of her life to him and trusted him with that knowledge. Only three people knew his darkest secrets.

He had no doubt he was the only person she confessed this secret. The courage it took her to trust him, he'd never known anything like it.

He was the one who unworthy of her.

Jaden ran up the stairs. All he wanted to do was hold and convince Alice how much he wanted her. Unless she asked him to leave, he wouldn't leave her alone.

He was glad that he lived alone because if Salvatore or Varrik or Liam saw him now, they'd shit a brick. The Ice Warrior, who killed without mercy or compassion, wanted to console a human woman. A woman who made him warm again. Someone that made him feel something other than ice and hate. He wanted to be different for her.

Shit, he *was* different when it came to her.

Jaden barged into her room. Alice looked up in surprise, a pillow in one hand, the satin case in the other.

He scowled at the sheets on the floor. She was stripping the bed. Removing her scent. Because she thought he didn't want to touch her.

"What are you doing?"

She bit her lip and dropped the pillow case. "I'm sorry. I didn't hear you come in."

"Just so you know, I didn't walk away from you because you're dirty or damaged," Jaden said. "I walked away because I didn't want you to see how angry I was."

"I didn't think you'd hear that." She swallowed hard. "Do you want me to go now?"

"God, no. Why would you think that?"

"You're mad at me."

"I'm not angry at you, Alice. I'm angry because of what happened to you and because you're still hurting from it," he said, keeping his voice even. "No one should ever be violated like you were."

"I wish you hadn't seen that. The scar. The crying. I usually have better control over my emotions." She took a deep breath. "I won't go to pieces again. I promise."

Christ, it was like getting stabbed in the heart with a dull blade. "Everyone has moments of weakness."

"But it doesn't change what happened," she said, rubbing her eyes. "Crying and wishing things were different doesn't do me any good. It just gives me a headache."

"You don't always have to be so strong."

"I can't afford to be weak. Not now."

"You're not a weak woman."

"No, I'm worse than that. I'm a woman who let an animal brutalize her over and over again." She scooped up the sheets in her arms, heading for the door. "Where's the laundry room? I'll have to come back and do the fitted sheet, but I can wash all of this in one load."

He stood in front of her. "I don't want you to do anything, but look at me."

Alice lowered her eyes. Suddenly, she looked very small and vulnerable. "They need to be cleaned."

"They were cleaned last week and you're the only person who's slept on them since then."

"But they're dirty." She tried to side step him, but he moved with her. She tightened her grip on the sheets. "Please. Let me do this. You don't need any of me left behind."

Goddamn it, could his chest hurt any worse? "Alice, look at me."

"No, I need to do this," she whispered. "I-I'm not clean enough for you."

Jaden wanted to laugh at the irony of it. He was a slayer, a bloodthirsty monster. He killed Shadows, humans and other vampires with no remorse. And she still didn't see herself worthy of him.

Jaden stroked her cheek. He was the one who was unworthy of her. He had no right to touch her, even now. "You're hiding from me."

"I don't want to see the disgust in your eyes. I saw it enough on my friends' faces during the trial, my coworkers afterwards when I went back to work." She leaned her cheek into his palm, her shoulders falling as if they were weighted down. "I want to remember you looking at me the way when we were together the other night. If I look at you now, I'll know exactly how you see me."

"What do you think you'll see?"

Alice trembled slightly. "I don't want to say it. It makes it all too real and I can't let myself get hurt again. I won't let myself get hurt."

"Then if you won't say it, then I will," he said. "I will tell you what I see. That way you know how I see you and you don't have to imagine it."

"I don't want to hear it."

"I want to tell you anyway."

She stiffened and let the bundle fall to the floor. She crossed her arms, bracing herself for his response. "Okay."

"I don't see anyone dirty or unclean. Far from it." He cupped her face in his hands, forcing her to look at him. "I see a warrior in front of me. You went through hell and survived. I have nothing but respect and admiration for you."

"I'm not a fighter, Jaden. Not the way you think."

"You obviously have a distorted view of yourself. You fought those two assholes when I first met you. Then you fought off a Shadow in your apartment." He caressed her tear-stained cheeks, his voice tender. "But what's the most impressive thing to me is that you fight every day to overcome what's happened to you. Every day you wake up and make something of yourself is a battle won."

Alice lifted her wrists. "This is a battle won? The scars?"

"War wounds." He captured one of her wrists in his hand and reverently kissed the marred tissue. "You should look at them with pride."

"Pride," she echoed. "This isn't something that makes me feel good. They remind me of the torture I went through."

"It's a bittersweet victory. How many women did he attack and leave alive?"

She closed her eyes for a moment. "I'm the only one. And he never intended to let me live."

"You survived, Alice. You're alive when the others died." He let her wrist go and peeled the jacket off her shoulders. He stood behind her, staring at the paw print on her shoulder. She flinched as his fingers lightly ran across the brand. "If you can't be proud of them, then I will. Because it means you're with me."

"You're really not disgusted with me?"

Disgust was the last thing he felt for her right now. Her scent and her body caused his blood to seethe with desire. A slow burn ready to ignite at any moment.

His arms encircled her waist pulling her closer to him. "Why don't you tell me how I feel?"

His lips brushed against the brand. He moved to the spot on her neck where the collar cut in to her skin, his tongue stroking the scar. A sigh escaped Alice's lips as he nipped her throat with his teeth. She arched her back against him, her hips pressing into his groin. He groaned at the sensation as his cock hardened from the subtle pressure. He wouldn't last long if she kept this up.

His fangs ached as he sucked on her skin. Her pulse throbbed underneath his lips, a mere inch separating him from what he craved. God, he wanted a taste. But he didn't want to feed from her, not when she still felt so vulnerable.

Alice pressed her hand against his scalp, keeping his head in place. The amount of trust she placed in him, knowing he could bite her and drain her dry both shocked and amazed him. No one had done that to him. Not even after Catherine's transition. His wife never trusted him like this. She only let him drink from her wrist because he'd have too much control at her throat.

He ran his tongue up the smooth column, his teeth nipping at her jaw. "Tell me how I feel, Alice."

"Good," she sighed. "You feel really, really good."

"I feel honored that you let me touch you," he whispered. "To let your guard down and trust something like me to hold you. You know what I am and how vicious I can be." He ran his hand down her side and her body arched under his gentle caress. He lightly gripped her hips as he pulled her closer to him. "For you to be with me like this, knowing what I am amazes me." He licked the nape of her neck. "You are extraordinary, Alice Roarke. And I am humbled you would let me hold you in my arms."

She turned in his arms and captured his face in her hands. Alice stared at him for a long time, looking for some hint of revulsion. Anything that would show he was lying.

But those icy blue eyes were open and clear. She couldn't see the lie when spoke the truth.

"Let me touch you." Jaden turned his head and kissed her palm, his tongue stroking her skin. "Let me show you how much I want you."

"But I –"

He silenced her protest with his lips. He ran his tongue over her lower lip, delighting in the moan deep in her throat. Jesus, she tasted so good. A quiet haven in his endless nights of violence.

How could he stay away from this?

"I want you, Alice. Every part of you," he murumred against her mouth.

She responded by pressing herself against him, the supple curves molding to every inch of his body. His blood ignited, a slow burn threatening to consume him alive.

Her lips moved urgently against his, her fingertips digging into his shoulders as she brought him closer. He smiled at her impatience. Gone was the pain, the self-loathing. All he sensed now was her desire for him.

And he intended to answer her call. He planned to show her how much he loved touching her. He had the rest of the morning to explore every luscious inch of her body.

Her mouth parted slightly and his tongue slid into her mouth. Alice moaned as she met his tongue stroke for stroke, a silky penetration of what he wanted his tongue and fingers to do between her thighs.

Lust seized Jaden as he yanked off her shirt, his hands just as demanding as her lips. She fell on the bed and he slid the pants off her long creamy legs.

"Fuck. You aren't wearing any underwear," he groaned.

Jaden prowled up her body as Alice moved further back on the bed. He held himself above her, gazing down at her beautiful body. Her dark brown hair fanned across the pillow, her lips reddened from the force of their kiss. Her skin was flushed from his touch.

But those eyes held him captive. He wanted to fall into those emerald green pools, bathe in the warm waters and remove the chill from his body. His heart.

Sweat bloomed on his forehead. His skin was hypersensitive, his muscles burned and it only happened when he was with her. How did this one woman stir so much passion within him when Catherine never had?

The sensations in his body were overwhelming. Intense. He'd never wanted a woman like this before. It made a mockery of what he once felt for his wife.

Alice brought her hand up to his cheek. "Are you okay?"

Jaden turned and kissed her palm. He was better than okay. For the first time in a long time, he felt happy.

"If you want to stop, I understand. I won't think –"

He silenced her with his mouth again and kissed her with a renewed fervor. She moaned as his tongue danced with hers, delving and exploring inside her mouth.

"I feel wonderful. And you need to stop thinking," he murmured. "I only want you to feel me. Feel us together."

His lips slid to her jaw, his tongue stroking the column of her throat as his hands glided down her arms. His mouth paused on the scar on her neck, his tongue massaging the darkened skin.

Alice writhed on the bed, her breasts against the hard muscles of chest. He kissed his way to the crevice between her shoulder and throat, dragging his fangs along her skin. He unhooked the lacy bra from its clasp and her nipples tightened from the rush of cold air. He dropped the silky fabric next to the bed as his eyes devoured her flushed skin.

He caught her nipples and rolled them between his thumb and forefinger. The buds tightened in his grip and she gasped when he pinched them again. Her breasts were full and heavy in his hands, begging to be suckled. His tongue circled and flicked the nipple before he took one into his mouth. He worked her breast, tugging and pulling, before he moved to the other one.

She undulated on the bed, pushing her breast further into his mouth as he suckled. She tasted so damn sweet. But he knew of another spot where she tasted even better.

He kissed her way down her stomach, nibbling on her hipbone as he stopped at her thighs. His hand moved between her legs, his fingers coated by her arousal. The scent of her arousal hit him at full force, invading his head, making him burn.

"You are perfect," Jaden said hoarsely, his finger stroking her cleft. "I'm dying to taste you again."

Alice looked down at him as he continued to touch her. He nibbled her inner thigh while he slipped two fingers inside of her, the heat of her sex stinging his hand. She dropped her head back as she rode his fingers.

She arched her back as he sank his fingers deeper into her. She moaned as he moved in and out of her, writhing on the bed as pleasure slammed into her. His body shook with need, but he held back. He wanted to make sure she never doubted how much she made him burn.

"You feel so good. I am exactly where I want to be." He stroked her again, her wetness coating his fingers. "Well, almost exactly."

Alice grinned and he felt the last bit of tension fall away from her body. She opened her legs even wider. "Then don't let me stop you."

He bent down, her legs going over his shoulders. He kissed the inside of her thigh before he put his mouth on her sex. He groaned at the taste of her. Fuck, she was better the second time around. He could stay here all day, worshipping her core.

He licked and teased with his tongue, his fangs. She palmed the back of his head, locking him in place. As if he wanted to be anywhere else. He moved his thumb to stroke her cleft, the sounds of her pleasured cries mixed in with the sound of his mouth kissing her swollen lips. Her hips moved in rhythm with his thrusts, his tongue swirling faster, delving deeper.

He felt the muscles quivering in her thighs right before she came. He growled at the rush of sweetness in his mouth, but he didn't stop. He needed more of her.

Jaden continued his relentless assault as Alice rode out the waves of her orgasm, probing her with his fingers, chin and mouth until she came again and again.

When God knew how many times she orgasmed, he looked up at her as her body stilled. She was holding on to the iron frame, her breath coming in gasps. He licked his glossy lips, savoring the taste of her body.

He pulled back long enough to tear off his pants. He rose to his knees, his erection heavy and hard between their bodies. She ran her hands along his shoulders, lifting her hips to meet him.

He slid into her slowly, gently stretching her. Alice wrapped her legs around his waist and pulled him deeper into her. He hissed at the slickness of her sex sheathing him like hot, wet silk. His hips bucked against hers, his release poised in his shaft. But he wasn't ready yet. He wanted to draw it out and replace any bad memories with one they were creating tonight.

Jaden leaned down to kiss her while his hips moved in a slow, torturous rhythm. He wanted to move faster, harder, so she'd feel the wildness of his passion for her. But he didn't want her to push him away. He needed her just as much as she needed him.

He gritted his teeth when her nails dug into his back. He wasn't going to last much longer like this. Every stroke warmed his flesh, the ice melting away from his bones and his heart.

He looked down at Alice. Her cheeks were red, her emerald eyes glowing with passion. A whimper escaped her reddened lips with each stroke. Every line, every curve molded seamlessly to him. To him, she was perfection.

"More," she whispered.

Her hands clutched his ass and a shot of pleasure ran through him as her nails pierced his skin. A shot of his release pumped into her before he regained control.

"Harder," she said, her thighs squeezing his hips. "I want more."

"Are you sure?" He looked down at her and kissed the tip of her nose. "I don't want to hurt you."

"You won't." Alice raised her hips, matching his thrusts. "Please, Jaden. I want this."

He surged forward and let all of his passion, all of himself, into her. His hips slapped against hers as she met him stroke for stroke, her body welcomed him with every hard thrust.

He put one arm behind her head, his hips bucking, pushing as deep as he could go. She took him in from base to tip, her body accepting all of his power, relishing it. She reached up and buried her face in his shoulder, her teeth biting into his collarbone.

He threw his head back, roaring when he felt her teeth on his skin, nearly coming as the pleasant pain ripped through him. A crazy thought ran through his mind before it disappeared. He wanted her to drink from him, to have a part of him in her.

His thrusts grew more urgent. Frantic. He needed her like the air he breathed and the blood he drank.

She cried out his name as she climaxed. Her molten core clenched his shaft, the satiny walls stroking him, pulling him into her. She tightened her thighs around him, biting him again, harder than before, almost breaking the skin.

It was more than he could take. He shouted as he orgasmed, surrounded by white heat and blinding ecstasy. He shuddered as her core milked his cock dry, clutching and pulling him until he thought he'd die from the pleasure of it.

When he finished, all he heard was the desperate sound of their breathing. He rolled onto his side and pulling her with him. Jaden stayed inside of Alice, not wanting to let her go of her warmth.

He traced her lips with his thumb. "You're so beautiful."

He nuzzled her throat, luxuriating in her fragrance. He sighed as she traced the tattoos along his back and biceps, her fingernails lightly caressing the swirls.

His skin suddenly burned as she continued to run her finger along his biceps. He looked at his wrists. The tattoos rippled on his skin, the intricate knots slithering like snakes towards Alice's arms, heading toward her wrists.

For a moment, he was too stunned to move, but there was no mistaking what was happening. His body wanted to mark and make her his mate.

He closed his eyes and focused on making the tattoos resume their original shape. Once the burning sensation subsided, he looked at his wrists. The tattoos and patterns were in place.

He stared at Alice. Her fingers swept across his forehead, brushing several strands of his hair out of his eyes.

She smiled up at him, pressing her cheek against his palm. She hadn't noticed the tattoos stretching towards her and he was thankful for that. It'd be hard to explain how his body wanted to claim Alice as his.

But his heart had already done that, hadn't it?

The Ice Warrior was in love.

Chapter 16

John-Paul felt like shit, but it was an improvement from the near-death experience he had three hours ago when the Host had finished "strengthening" him. A direct transfusion from the Host's body into his, the vampire promised John-Paul would feel better in a couple of hours while Markus and two other bastards held him down.

He sure as hell didn't feel strong at the moment. Nauseous and disoriented was more like it. That blood better be worth all this hassle so he could get to Alice. Otherwise, he'd find a way to kick that vampire's ass.

John-Paul sat up in his bed, a wave of dizziness threatening to knock him out again. He gripped the side of the mattress and willed himself to stay conscious. He took several deep breaths and after a few minutes, the room stopped spinning.

Thank God for small favors.

He lifted his head and gasped. He could see the subtle flickering of the light bulb in the lamp, the variations in the wood of his nightstand. It's like his vision magnified while he was out.

And his hearing? Shit, he could hear the insects scurrying in the walls, not to mention the hushed voices of other Shadows a couple of doors down.

Metal cut into his hand and he looked down at the bed frame. His eyes widened as he knelt on the floor. He saw the curve of his fingers in the frame. The metal had warped under his grip. A few drops of blood smeared against the bed and splattered on the floor. He looked at his hand and froze.

"No. Fucking. Way."

His hand was completely healed. No gash, no scab, no nothing.

John-Paul laughed. This was better than any high he'd ever known. Too bad he couldn't bottle this shit. He could make a fortune off it. Retire to some nice little country with all the bitches he could ever ask for.

But in order to get to them, he had to move.

He stood up, his legs wobbling slightly. Every sensation was more intense, right down to the very marrow of his bones. If this was what he felt now, what would sex be like?

He always had control of the women he trained, but this new power took his sessions to a whole new level. Finally, he could break Alice. Not just her body, but her spirit too.

He was tired of being on his ass. He could take on anyone and anything. They sprang him from jail and now he was ready to fulfill his end of the bargain. He wanted Alice. Now.

Markus opened the door, grinning at John-Paul. "It's a good thing the Host didn't kill you. That would have ruined our plans."

"It's going to take a lot more than one vampire to kill me."

"I don't doubt it. How are you feeling?"

"Ready to take on the fucking world."

"Let's focus on one thing at a time." Markus handed John-Paul a jacket. "So you're up for a little ride?"

"Where are we going?"

"Alice Roarke's apartment."

John-Paul shoved his arms inside it, his hazel eyes glimmering with malice. He was finally going to bring his bitch home. "I call shotgun."

Chapter 17

Alice woke to Jaden's body pressing into hers. Usually she hated it when people were behind her. It reminded her too much of John-Paul being at her back, helpless against his beatings.

It was hard to hate Jaden with the way he held her right now. He cradled her against him, his arm around her waist, his hand resting on her inner thigh. She ran a hand up his arm, the smooth muscles relaxed for a change. She smiled at the involuntary twitch of his fingers on her skin, like he was making sure she was still there.

She turned to face him. He sighed and tightened his grip around her waist, pulling her closer. A flush crept over her cheeks as her eyes moved down his magnificent body. From the muscular chest, the washboard stomach to the hard length of him pressing into her hip.

She lost count the number of times they made love. He definitely enjoyed pleasuring her, taking half the morning to explore every dip and curve. There wasn't a spot on her that escaped his hands or his tongue. Every inch of her still craved his touch even though she was a little sore. But she was ready to let him do it all again.

She stared at him as he slept. He looked so peaceful, the frown lines nonexistent. He looked so lethal when he was awake. For a moment, she imagined this is must have how he looked as a young man before he became the hardened warrior she knew.

She caught a lock of his hair and let her fingers slide between the silken strands. Jaden stirred something inside of her that was more than sexual. He made her feel like she mattered. That she could belong to a man who would do anything to see her happy. She wanted Jaden to be that man.

Alice was falling in love with him. Like any leap once it's made, she couldn't stop it. She tried to fight it and shut him out, but it was useless. He saw all of her flaws and imperfections and he still wanted to touch her. He wanted to make love to her and hold her close.

She sighed. It was stupid for her to think like that. He was a warrior, a vampire warrior at that. Someone strong, virile. Someone who would never die.

Alice would die one day. She was human and therefore very breakable. She had no place in his world or in his heart.

She glanced at the clock. Less than an hour until sunset.

She needed to get her things together. As much as she wanted to stay, she had to think about herself and where to go. She had some money in savings. Maybe she could skip town and lay low until John-Paul was caught. Then she could come back and pick up the pieces of her life. Or start fresh in a new town.

Alice moved to get out of bed when Jaden's arm locked her in place. His fingers rubbed circles on the small of her back as his lips pressed against her throat. He stretched, his body, pushing into hers. He was definitely awake.

In more ways than one.

"Good evening." Her smile widened as he opened those sky blue eyes. "I was wondering when you'd wake up, sleepyhead."

Jaden kissed her and any thoughts of leaving scattered. God, she loved his kisses. It was like getting hit with lightning bolts every time. Lazy drags of his lips and tongue. Exploring. Invading.

"It's definitely starting off to be a promising night." His tongue ran up her throat. "I usually don't wake up in bed with a beautiful woman."

"Funny, I don't usually wake up with a handsome man in my bed."

"Good. I want to be the only male you think of when you're in bed." Jaden kissed the tip of her nose. "How are you feeling?"

"Very satisfied." She traced his jaw with her fingertip. "What about you?"

"Better when you do that."

Alice brushed over his six-pack abs and palmed his heavy cock in her hand. She wasn't sure where this boldness came from, but she liked touching him.

What were a few more minutes in bed anyway?

He growled low in his throat as she skimmed the underside of his shaft. He ground himself into her hands, his hips moving in tandem with her strokes.

"And now?"

He sucked in a breath. "Fuck, Alice."

She licked the side of his neck, her tongue tracing the bulging vein in his throat. He rolled her over so she was on her back. He covered her with his body, his mouth hard against hers. Demanding. As if he wanted to devour her.

He spread her thighs wide and plunged himself deep inside. They both groaned at the sensation, but he didn't pause for long. His pumping was feverish, like he was trying to leave a piece of himself in her body.

Alice closed her eyes, losing herself in the sex. She loved the feel of him, the raw power, and the unrestrained passion. A man only hungry for her. It was unlike anything she experienced. And she wanted to remember him exactly like this.

Her orgasm slammed into her, rendering her breathless as a million sparks of heat shot throughout her body. And before she could catch her breath, she felt his release pouring into her, his hot seed filling her up, heightening her passion until she thought she'd explode from it.

They both lay sweaty and panting in each other's arms. She brushed a tendril of inky hair out his eyes. How she wished she could stay here forever.

But they both had their own worlds to get back to and she wouldn't keep him any longer.

"You'll need to get going soon," she murmured.

"No, I don't." He buried his face in her throat. "I am perfectly happy where I am."

"I'm sure you don't plan on lying here all night."

"If you're here, then I have no reason to leave."

She sighed as he trailed a row of kisses up her throat. He said all the right things. And it made her hurt all the more knowing she had to go.

"You can't stay with me all night," she said as he nipped her jaw. "You have things to do, battles to fight."

"I'm calling in sick." He traced the curve of her earlobe with his tongue. "I have all sorts of aches and pains only you can fix."

"Jaden, be serious."

"I am." He brought her hand to his hardening cock again. "This is where I hurt the most. You have the touch that makes the pain go away." He surged forward, stroking himself with her hand while he kissed her. "And this is even better."

She took a deep breath and his tongue snaked into her mouth. She was going to forget her argument if he kept doing what he was doing. But he felt so good like this. All of her thought scattered whenever this male touched her so lovingly.

Alice turned her head to the side, breaking the kiss. "Jaden, I can't stay here. I have to go."

That got his attention.

He pulled back, looking into her eyes. "I need to make sure you're safe. If you're here, then I know you're alive and well. And that bastard doesn't have his hands on you."

"I've taken care of myself for a long time."

"I don't doubt it."

"I can't stay here," she repeated.

He propped himself up on his side. "Why not?"

She traced the intricate swirls tattooed on his wrist. "Because you need to get back to your life and I need to get back to mine."

"You're not going anywhere until I settle this John-Paul matter. Until he's dead, you're staying here."

"And if it takes weeks? Months? That's not a burden I'll put on anyone, no matter who's after me." She ignored his growl of protest. "I'll be fine on my own. Really. I'll move to another town. I've done it before."

"There's no need for you to do it again. That asshole won't get you as long as you're here."

"Leaving is the best way to make sure he doesn't get me." She held up her hands. "Look, I've always done what I've had to in order to survive. Even when I was in foster care, I had to look out for myself. Some homes were worse than others, but I depended on no one to –"

Jaden shot up, his eyes pinning her. "What did you say?"

"What? That I've been able to take care of myself?"

He shook his head impatiently. "Before that. Where did you live when you were a child?"

"I lived in different foster homes," she said. "I never knew my father and my mother died of a heroin overdose when I was two. I was a ward of the state until I was eighteen."

"You were in foster care until you were eighteen," he said slowly.

"Yeah. Why?"

He turned away from her and put his head in his hands. His body was tense, the muscles in his biceps flexing with each breath.

Alice scowled at him. Why would it matter if she'd been in the system? No one really cared about stuff like that.

She sat up next to him. "What's wrong with me being in foster homes? You got a problem with those kinds of kids?"

"Not at all."

"Then why do you look like I just hit you with a sledgehammer?"

He moved his hands from his face. Alice's frown disappeared and she became a little concerned. Jaden was downright angry by what she said.

"Nothing. I'm fine."

"Are you sure? You don't look right."

"Really. I'm okay." He kissed her forehead. "Look, I'm going to take a shower. And you're going to stay. No arguments."

"A few minutes ago you didn't want to leave. Now staying here seems like the last thing you want to do."

Jaden slid out of the bed and grabbed his pants off the floor. "Like you said, I've got battles to fight and I need to get ready. I'll see you before I go."

He kissed her quickly and bolted out of the room, closing the door behind him.

Alice sat up after he left, confused at his sudden dismissal. After all he knew about her, he was freaked out because she'd been in foster care?

What was going on?

~ * ~

Jaden stood under the shower and let the hot spray sting his shoulders, but it did little to relieve his tension and anger. He wanted to kill the Sisters. How the hell could they do this to him? Now that he found someone he truly connected with, he had to let her go. Because being a part of her life would cause her death.

It was Catherine all over again.

Well, not exactly. Catherine had no clue he was a vampire. Alice knew what he was and still wanted him. At least she knew some things about his life. There were still some things he kept from her, but it was for her own safety.

He curled his hands into fists. He wanted to punch something because all he heard was the Sisters' prophecy in his mind.

The woman you seek, the power she controls
Is desired by vampires, Hosts and Shadows,
A daughter of foster, a son of pain,
She is the heart to make him live again.
The blinding light in the unending dark,
Branded with the animal's mark,
After the storm in a sanguine sky,
Is where the decision will lie.
Their union will take her last breath,
And be the cause of the race's death.

"A daughter of foster," he muttered bitterly.

Jaden always knew he was a part of the prophecy. He never would have guessed that Alice Roarke was the woman the Sisters' referred to as well.

Alice was the Firebrand.

It all fit into place. The red glow to her skin. The blackouts. She said she wasn't sure how she escaped from John-Paul, but Jaden knew. She said she found herself in the woods behind his house once the fear for her safety had worn off. When she became threatened or there was an imminent danger to her life, her true form broke through.

Her power manifested itself in those blackouts. Being human, she couldn't control that power and it made her weak which would inevitably kill her.

And if the Host got her, he'd use her to kill him and the other warriors and probably mark Alice as his. It'd be a cold day in hell before Jaden let the bastard get her. The thought of the Host getting his hands on Alice made Jaden want to punch something.

Her face flashed in his mind. She was beautiful through and through, from those mahogany tresses, emerald eyes, full mouth and supple curves. There wasn't a part of her body he didn't want to touch.

But it was more than physical. She was kind, clever and strong. Her sass kept him on his toes. And she was survivor from the abuse she suffered by the hands of that animal, John-Paul. He admired her strength and cherished her quiet vulnerability when she let her guard down. But most of all, she thawed his icy heart.

He closed his eyes and lifted his face to the spray. Jaden used to scoff at his father's bullshit about falling in love with his mother so quickly. His father mated his mother just two days after they met and were together for over a thousand years before they both were killed. Hell, his father shielded his mother with his own body to prevent the Shadows from killing her.

Jaden now understood his father's actions because he'd do the same thing. He would give up his life for Alice and not just because she was the Firebrand. He'd do it so he wouldn't have to spend a day without her.

He stepped out of the shower and quickly dressed in his usual fighting clothes of black jeans, a sweater and boots. He went into the fireproof cabinet in his room which contained some of his favorite weapons. He strapped his two blades to his back, another knife on his thigh, one of his Glocks and a few throwing stars for good measure.

He shrugged into his leather trench which concealed his arsenal of weaponry. He headed out of his room and knocked on Alice's door, his stomach churning. He could torture a man a thousand different ways, the blood and gore never once making him queasy.

Yet telling Alice he loved her was enough to make him throw up. Like the teenage nerd asking the beauty queen to the prom.

When she didn't respond, he peeked inside, surprised to find the room was empty. The hairs on the back of his neck rose as he sensed someone other than Alice in his home. They came suddenly which meant Helene was here. No doubt Salvatore came with them. But there was someone else.

"A guest of Jaden's?" a voice purred. "Jaden doesn't have humans stay overnight. Not unless he intends to let us play with his food."

Varrik.

Great. A vampire who screwed any breathing female who

came across his path.

"Fine. Then a friend of Jaden's."

"Jaden doesn't have any friends."

"I guess there's a first time for everything," she said.

Jaden tore down the steps, slowing once he reached the kitchen. Jaden saw Varrik's massive form towering over Alice. He was a good foot taller than her and Alice stared at him as if he were nothing more than a fly to be swatted.

"Varrik, I'd back off if I were you," Salvatore said.

"He's been all over you." Varrik ignored the warning and leaned down, breathing deeply. His blue-black hair brushed against Alice's cheeks. "I'm surprised he hasn't taken a bite of you yet. You smell delicious."

"Gee, thanks." Alice glared at the six foot eight vampire. "You know, I was concerned my scent wasn't appetizing enough for Jaden's buddies. Good to know I smell as wonderful as I look."

"I really like you. Sassy and sexy. It's an irresistible combination." Varrik tilted his head, his black eyes devouring her. "I bet your blood is just as spicy as your scent. Mind if I have a taste?"

"I sure as hell do," Jaden snarled and moved in front of Alice. He would take the bastard down in a heartbeat if Varrik got too close again. "If you want to walk out of here with all your limbs attached, I suggest you walk away from Alice right now."

Varrik smirked at Jaden. "Pity you're keeping this one to yourself. You know, sharing is caring." He raked Alice with a searing gaze. "She's a saucy little kitten. I'm sure Jaden's got the claw marks to prove it. When you're done, can I have a ride?"

Jaden's fist flew so fast no one could track it. He punched

Varrik so hard that it knocked the vampire into the island. Jaden grabbed Varrik's throat and dug his fingers in deep.

He glanced at Alice whose eyes were wide with shock. "You'll have to forgive Varrik. He isn't as civilized as some others of my kind."

"You certainly fit into that category," Varrik muttered, spitting on the polished floor.

Apologize to Alice. Jaden nearly shoved the words into the male's head. *Or I'll cut off the part of your anatomy you use more often than your goddamn brain.*

"Oh, lover boy here wants me to play nice. Obviously she prefers slug to stud." He chuckled and looked over Jaden's shoulder. "I'm sorry if I offended you, female."

Jaden let go of Varrik and turned his attention to Salvatore. "You want to tell me why you brought this asshole to my house?"

"For her protection," Salvatore answered. "I talked to Liam earlier today. He was very interested in your particular attraction to her."

"She is pretty hot," Varrik added. "Tell me, Jaden. Does she feel as hot as she looks?"

Jaden curled his hands into fists. God, he wanted to wipe the sneer of that fucker's face. "So he sent Laverne and Shirley to watch her? That's the best Liam can do?"

"You said I was safe here," Alice said. "And who are these sisters you're talking about?"

"It's nothing you have to worry about."

"That's not what your friend says."

Salvatore cleared his throat. "We really need to get going."

"Why?"

"The...target's on the move." Salvatore glanced at Alice before he looked back at Jaden. "And we have a good feeling he's going back to her place. I asked Liam if you could come with us and he said just tonight. After that, you're job is to watch her."

Jaden took one of her hands in his. "I'll be back later. Helene's going to keep you company while I'm out."

"What?" both females said.

He'd rather stay with her himself, but if she needed to get out quick, then Helene could teleport them to a safe location in a matter of seconds. Leaving Varrik with her wasn't an option. Not only could he read thoughts, he could project his ideas into their minds, convincing them to do things they wouldn't normally do. And he'd have to kill him if he touched Alice.

Jaden kissed Alice's forehead and hugged her tightly. He felt the stares of his fellow warriors on his back, but he didn't care. All that mattered was keeping Alice safe and out of the Host's hands.

"I'll see you when I get back," he whispered.

"Jaden, we talked about this. I need to –"

"Stay here for one more night," he finished for her. "When I come home, we can talk about your options." Alice opened her mouth to argue, but he placed a quick kiss on her lips. "Another night won't hurt you and it would be nice to come home to you instead of an empty house."

"Come on, Jaden!" She narrowed her eyes. "That's not playing fair and you know it."

"I know, but I don't want you to leave yet." He kissed her knuckles. "Please, Alice. Just one more night."

There was a cough and Jaden glanced at Salvatore. His jaw was open in shock. Varrik raised an eyebrow and Helene seemed frozen in place.

He understood their disbelief. Jaden never asked anyone for

anything. "Please" was not a part of his vocabulary.

Unless it was Alice.

"Fine. I'll stay," Alice muttered. "Even though you're manipulating me into it."

With words? Yes. But not his power. He wanted to know how she genuinely felt, without any emotional blackmail.

"Thank you." Jaden pinned Helene with a hard glare. "You two play nice while I'm gone."

"Oh sure. We'll paint each others' toenails and gossip about the newest issue of *Tiger Beat* magazine."

Alice looked horrified. "Please tell me she's joking."

"Yes, she is joking. Helene, stop being such a pain in the ass," Jaden said.

Alice pulled him out of the kitchen and into the hallway. Obviously she wanted some privacy, but he knew the others would be able to hear their conversation.

"I'm only going to stay on two conditions." Alice stood in front of him and locked her eyes on his. "The first one is you're going to tell me what the hell is going on when you come back. Especially why you're so upset about my being a foster child."

"It has nothing to do with you being in foster care. I could care less about that."

"But it still bothered you. It's why you bolted from my room when you found out."

"Because it reminded me of something else." His thumb stroked her cheek. "I'm sorry if I gave you the impression I was upset. It caught me off-guard."

"Will you tell me why?"

"When I come back," he promised. "What's the second condition?"

Those emerald pools softened as she squeezed his hands.

"Please be safe. I want you to come home in one piece."

His heart stopped for a moment and then sped back up. No one ever said those words to him. Hell, no one ever cared what happened to him, whether he was going into battle or simply doing his nightly rounds.

Except Alice. She cared if he made it home alive.

His mind screamed for him to tell her how he felt. He wanted her to know that the only reason why he would be careful was because of her. But he wasn't going to say it with an audience.

He pulled her in his arms, hugging her tightly. "I'll be careful out there."

"You better. I want you to come back breathing and all body parts attached."

He chuckled. "Absolutely."

Jaden walked back into the kitchen and motioned for Salvatore and Varrik to follow. The three men walked out of the house and piled into Salvatore's black SRX Crossover. They tore out of the driveway and Jaden glanced back one more time. Alice was safe. The Shadows wouldn't get to his home. But he'd feel a hell of lot better knowing Alice was all right by seeing her with his own two eyes.

"What the fuck is wrong with you?" Salvatore demanded as they hit the highway.

"Can I answer for him? My list is extensive," Varrik said from the backseat. "I might get punched again, but it'll be worth it."

Jaden ignored Varrik. "What are you talking about? I'm fine."

"Are you serious? I heard you say 'please,' 'thank you' and 'I'm sorry' to a human female all in one night!"

"Her name's Alice. And I'm worried about leaving her

behind."

"You're worried about her?" Salvatore almost drove off the road and jerked the steering wheel. "All right. Who are you and what have you done with Jaden Payne? The brooding prick who loves nothing more than to kick Shadow ass?"

Jaden rolled his eyes. "Look, the sooner we take care of the Host, the safer everyone will be."

"And what about Alice?"

"I haven't worked that out yet."

Salvatore looked over at Jaden. "What's to work out? You've obviously had sex with her. Her scent's all over you. How many more times are you going to screw her and not get caught?"

"I really don't want to beat the shit out of you, but you are treading on thin ice," Jaden said. "Alice is not just a screw that I can send home. It's not that simple anymore."

"You want to keep her?" Salvatore shouted. "Have you lost your mind?"

"I think so," Varrik quipped.

"She could possibly be the Firebrand, for Christ's sake! Do you know how dangerous that makes her? All it takes is for her to get pissed and you're a pile of ash."

"She won't hurt me," Jaden murmured.

"And if Liam found out you fucked her? He'd snap off your balls and wear them as earrings." Salvatore shook his head. "You're supposed to protect her. Not keep her."

Jaden pressed his fingers to his temples. He wasn't about to tell them how hopeless the situation really was. He was so in love with Alice that the thought of her leaving made him sick.

He suspected Alice cared for him on some level, but he didn't know how deeply those feelings went. He could find out, use his power to reveal her emotions, but it was an invasion of her privacy. Not only that, what if it wasn't the answer he wanted to hear?

Whether or not she loved him, she was a part of his life now. He had to figure out a way to be in her life without endangering it. And Alice wasn't safe with that monster John-Paul waiting to capture her again.

"Last time you fell for a human, it didn't work out so well. You remember what Catherine did to you, right?" Salvatore demanded. "You really want to go back there?"

"Catherine didn't know what I am," Jaden said. "Alice does."

"You haven't marked her. The tattoos are on your wrists."

He looked down at the serpentine swirls. He remembered the burning sensation of the ink lifting on his skin, inching towards Alice's hands. Marking her as his. An unbreakable bond which would mate them for life. If a human bonded herself to a vampire, a blood exchange would take place, which would awaken the dormant gene to turn her into a female of his kind.

Jaden wanted that with Alice. He wanted everyone to know she belonged to him and he was hers. The thought of her being with him forever made him crave her to the point of madness. She was what he was looking for. A place to finally call home.

Would she accept him? Or would she shatter his heart completely?

"I haven't marked her yet," Jaden muttered.

"You're actually considering it?"

"Look, I don't want to discuss this anymore. All of this talk has made me edgy and I'm ready to kill something. I'd rather it not be you two."

"Why are we going back to Alice's place?" Varrik asked. "Is

it because one of the Shadows left something behind?"

"They didn't leave anything there," Salvatore said. "I made sure of it."

"What about John-Paul? She might have something in her apartment that would lead us to him."

Jaden scowled at Salvatore. "You want me to drive? At least I can make sure we get there before ten o'clock."

Salvatore slammed his foot on the gas. "On our way."

John-Paul stood in the middle of Alice's living room along with Markus and two other Shadows. Another two were in her bedroom, looking for any sign as to Alice's whereabouts. All of her clothes and personal items were still there. Plus, her car was parked in the complex's lot which meant she was in the area.

John-Paul loved his newfound power. He'd been strong before, but he was now three times more powerful than a professional bodybuilder. He moved with the agility and speed of a panther, a deadly predator in the night.

He took a deep breath. Cinnamon. John-Paul could smell the bitch's scent. It was faint, indicating she hadn't been back. He wished he were stronger to try and track it. Maybe another visit from the Host would juice him up even more.

What better way to use that power than on Alice and her friends?

There was no way she disappeared without a trace. The Emain Machas – now that sounded like a rip off of a *Xena: Warrior Princess* episode – had her. That would make finding her a little more difficult. Markus told him their headquarters was unknown and any Shadow that met them never lived to tell about it.

John-Paul didn't like knowing another man had his pet. In

fact, it pissed him off. If the warrior Jaden put his hands on Alice, he was going to gut the bastard in front of her.

"Did you find anything?" Markus demanded to the Shadow who came out of the bedroom.

The Shadow handed Markus a small, leather-bound book. Markus flipped it open, his frown turning into a slow grin. "John-Paul, you might want to see this."

He peered over Markus's shoulder. Inside were newspaper clippings of John-Paul's arrest, trial and sentencing.

"Where did you find this?" John-Paul asked.

"Inside her nightstand."

"So she kept a diary of our time together, did she?" John-Paul said.

She must've thought about him every day. With the scar and the book, how could she not?

God, he couldn't wait to see her again.

"This may help us as well." Another Shadow came over to him. "Here's a phone list of the people she works with. She's circled a couple of the names. More than likely they're friends of hers."

John-Paul glanced at the stapled papers. He didn't care if he had to go through every fucking person on that list. One of them would eventually bring Alice to him.

"Good work," Markus said. "The Host will be pleased with this discovery."

John-Paul felt a shiver ripple through him and he looked towards the door. Something felt a little off. The two men cleaning the living room went about their business as if nothing was wrong. But when John-Paul met Markus's eyes, he knew the other man caught it too.

"You two stay here and leave everything as it was. Call us when you're done. John-Paul and I are going to meet some of

Ms. Roarke's friends."

"You want us to come with you?"

Markus turned to the two Shadows next to him. "No, you two stay as well. The quicker you finish up, the sooner you can join us."

They exited the apartment and got into the Celica at the back of the building. Markus started the car and punched the gas, the tires squealing as they peeled off down the road.

John-Paul glared at Markus. "Why are we leaving them behind? What's going on?"

"What did you feel back there?"

"Almost like something bad was coming our way," he said.

Markus nodded. "And we're staying out of the way."

"Why didn't the others feel it?"

"I'm sure your incarceration helped honed your instincts when trouble came your way," Markus replied. "And I felt it because like you, I'm stronger than them. When you feed from the Host multiple times, your power increases. They are weak."

"So we're just gonna leave them? That's pretty shitty, Markus."

"You want to meet an early death? Feel free to stay."

"Hell, no. I'm just saying it's pretty shitty."

But it kept him on guard. He had no doubt the Host and Markus would sacrifice him. He just needed to make sure that he'd take both of them down if they tried.

"It sucks to be them."

"They're our exit plan." Markus glanced at him, grinning. "Now why don't you take out the directory and see which of Alice's friends we'll visit tonight.

Chapter 18

Salvatore, Jaden and Varrik crept towards the apartment complex, leaving the Crossover parked in front of a bank of stores half a block away. All three of them caught the malevolent presence in the air. As they moved closer, the hairs on the back of Jaden's neck stood on end. Shadows were in Alice's home.

It pissed him off that they were going through her stuff, destroying her possessions in order to find her. He'd gladly rip their hands off for touching her things.

Salvatore nodded towards the building. "What's going on in there, Varrik?"

Varrik closed his eyes. "There are a couple of kids in there wondering if they should watch Jimmy Neutron or SpongeBob Squarepants, an elderly couple looking over the bills, a teenager talking about her lame mother. OMG, I can't believe she – "

"Quit being an asshole and tell us what's going on," Salvatore barked.

"All I hear is that they need to get out of there and meet up with John-Paul. Something about picking up some friends." Varrik looked at Jaden. "I'm assuming they're not looking for Ringo and George to round out their Beatles cover band?"

A muscle ticked in Jaden's jaw. "John-Paul's the name of the man who attacked Alice two years ago."

"And he's in the Host's hands. This is not good." Salvatore nodded to the two other warriors. "How do you want to handle this?"

"I think we need to have a talk with our wannabe friends." Jaden palmed a blade as the four Shadows appeared on the sidewalk. "Then let's send the Host a clear message about fucking with us."

The trio walked across the street and as a unit, the Shadows turned to look at them. "Good evening, ladies," Varrik called out pleasantly. "Can we give you a lift somewhere?"

No sooner had the words left his lips than the Shadows bolted. Jaden and his crew gave chase, not giving them a chance to escape. They caught up with the Shadows a few streets over where they paused in an alley.

Two lunged at him and all hell broke loose. Jaden fought them without the assistance of the other warriors. He could handle them just as Varrik and Salvatore could be on their own.

The bastards were cocky enough to think he'd go down easily. Jaden dodged their punches, their movements slow and uncoordinated in his vampire eyes. One of them pulled out a gun, but a flick of Jaden's wrist made the man drop the weapon, the wrist slit all the way down to the tendon.

The Shadow fell to his knees and Jaden drew the blade across the throat. He now focused his attention on the other one who had his own weapon. The six inch steel kept missing its crucial marks and Jaden felt the irritation welling up inside his sparring partner. Jaden swept the legs from underneath the Shadow which caused the bastard to fall on his back.

Jaden stood over him. "This is all you've got? It's like fighting a child. Hardly a fair match."

The Shadow grinned as it glanced behind the warrior. "And

like children, we don't fight fairly."

Jaden heard a gun cocking on his left and the bullet discharged a moment later. He twisted his torso to avoid a direct hit and received a wound in the shoulder. Jaden glanced to see Varrik taking the bastard down while the Shadow at Jaden's knees slashed his thigh.

Now he was really pissed off.

Howling in fury, Jaden tackled his prey. The knife forgotten, Jaden used his fists to teach the Shadow who was the stronger fighter. Knuckle collided with bone, shattering the cheek.

A pair of hands pulled Jaden off the Shadow. Varrik threw the hybrid against the wall while Salvatore grabbed Jaden.

"We can't get answers from him if you beat him into a bloody pulp!" Salvatore yelled.

Jaden wrenched himself out of Salvatore's grip. "The bastard ruined my pants! That alone is a good enough reason for a severe ass-whipping."

Salvatore frowned. "I thought you had three other pairs just like it."

"Not only are my pants ruined, but so is my shirt. Because I was fucking shot!" Jaden shouted. He shoved the torn fabric coated with his blood in front of Salvatore. "You think a moth chewed a hole through this?"

"The bullet went through the wound cleanly and you're not bleeding out from your thigh," Salvatore pointed out. "At least you're going to live."

"And the sound of your voice soothes my weary soul," Varrik said. "Quit your bitching and get over here. If you want to really get back at him, make him talk."

"I'll do more than make him talk." Jaden faced the Shadow. "Want to tell me why you're in that apartment tonight?"

The Shadow spat on Jaden's boot. "Fuck off, asshole."

Jaden looked at his boot and then at Salvatore. "Did he just spit on me?"

"Pretty sure he did," Salvatore said.

Jaden grabbed the man by his throat forcing all of his power into him. "This shithead seriously has a death wish."

The Shadow's eyes rolled into the back of his head. His mouth opened in a silent scream as his body shook uncontrollably. The pain was too intense for him to make a sound.

"Not so tough now are you?" Jaden flipped his gaze to Varrik. "Are you getting anything?"

"No. Nothing." Varrik shook his head. "Ease up a little. He's about to have a heart attack."

Jaden reined in some of his power. The Shadow's legs went out from underneath him and the male slumped against Varrik for support.

"Let's try this again," Jaden said. "Why were you in that apartment?"

"We needed information," he gasped.

"What kind?"

"On Alice," Varrik answered while he probed the man's thoughts. "There were another two Shadows in her apartment."

"Who are they?" Jaden asked.

Varrik closed his eyes while the Shadow struggled against him. Jaden sent another blast of intense pain and that stopped the hybrid's movement. "He keeps saying the name Markus. And there's a list," Varrik said. "Phone numbers and names. I can't read them all."

"Can you see who's on the list?"

"Four names are circled. Tina and Kara are the only two jumping out at me." Varrik opened his eyes. "Do those names mean anything to you?"

"They do to Alice," the Shadow rasped. "Hit your enemies where it hurts the most."

"Good advice." Jaden punched the Shadow in the stomach as well as maximizing the effect of the blow with his power. "Hurt much?"

"He's shut down his mind. We're not going to get anything else out of him," Varrik said.

"Fine. The fortune cookie bullshit pissed me off anyway."

Jaden let loose all of his power on the Shadow and kept the pulsating waves of anguish rolling through him until the heart sputtered and stopped. The Shadow fell to the ground with a wet thud.

The adrenaline rush wore off and Jaden leaned against the wall, his strength fading. He stopped bleeding, but still felt the raw ache of his wounds. The loss of blood and stress on his body was too much. He needed to feed so he could heal.

"Do you have enough strength to go into her apartment and see if there's anything that might lead us to this woman named Tina? Or do you want to call Alice and ask her?" Salvatore asked.

"I'd rather see what I can find on my own. I don't want to upset her unnecessarily." Although he had a feeling he'd have to talk to her about this later. "I'll rummage through her apartment and see if there's anything those pricks missed."

"Varrik, why don't you check in with Liam and let him know what went down tonight?" Salvatore looked at the bodies. "I'll take care of the mess. Meet back here in fifteen minutes."

They went their separate ways and Jaden entered the apartment. Everything was neat and tidy as if he hadn't killed three Shadows in front of Alice twenty-four hours ago.

He closed his eyes for a moment, his fangs punching out of his gums. Her scent was everywhere. In the sofa cushions, a hand towel in the kitchen, a blouse slung over a chair. It wasn't as strong here as it was at his house, but it was enough to make his throat bone dry.

He went to the bedroom first. He checked through her nightstand, a stack of papers, under the bed, any place where he might find a list with the names and numbers Varrik saw. He made quick work of the room, finding nothing that would indicate the list the Shadows had which meant he'd have to ask Alice about it. It wasn't a conversation he was looking forward to having.

He paused in front of the opened closet. She'd probably like the idea of wearing some of her own clothes. And since she was staying with him indefinitely because of her being a weapon of destruction, she'd probably want something familiar.

Jaden pulled a bag from her closet and shoved in a couple pairs of jeans, shirts and sweatshirts into it. He opened another drawer and came across her bras and underwear. Simple, practical, like Alice.

Except for one.

"Well, what do we have here?" he murmured.

He was hungry and wounded, yet his cock became stiff as a bat when he found a green and white polka-dotted bra with matching panties. He wondered what made her keep these items while everything else in there was so sensible. Whatever the reason, he shoved them in the bag. He was fairly certain he could get them on her. And have so much fun taking them off.

Jaden slung the bag over his uninjured shoulder as he made his way out of the apartment, meeting back up with Salvatore. Varrik paused at the entrance of the alley, his eyes locked on something down the street.

He frowned as he read Varrik's emotions. For a moment, Jaden sensed the other vampire's regret and sorrow, those black eyes softening for a moment. Varrik snapped his head towards Jaden, his gaze cold.

"So what's the word from Liam?" Salvatore asked.

"He wants us to see if we can track the Shadow named Markus," Varrik said, pocketing his cell phone.

Jaden glared at the other male. "Did he forget that Shadows don't leave a scent like humans do?"

"They leave enough of one." Varrik grinned contemptuously at Jaden. "I've never had any problems finding them."

Salvatore shuffled a couple of cell phones in his hands, handing one of them to Varrik. "I took these off the bodies. If we're lucky, maybe this Markus guy will call one of them to see where they are."

"And if we're not so fortunate?"

"Then you need to talk to Alice." Salvatore looked up at the sky. "We've got a good five hours until dawn. Varrik and I will start searching."

"What am I supposed to do?" Jaden retorted. "Sit in the apartment and wait for someone to show up?"

"Feed and go home. Your job is to keep the Alice safe. Whether or not she's the Firebrand, she is a target for the Host." Salvatore shot him a hard look. "Make sure whomever you feed from doesn't remember you."

They split up and Jaden went in search of prey. He wanted to help track down those assholes, but Alice's safety was his top priority.

His throat burned, the hunger gnawing in the pit of his stomach. He needed blood to heal and he couldn't go back home like this, even though he desperately wanted to drink from Alice. She'd be so sweet and feeding from her while they made love would be downright explosive. But he'd take too much from her and she needed to be strong. For when he told her she was the Firebrand.

And that he loved her.

Jaden walked a couple of blocks before he entered a local bar not too far from Alice's apartment. He kept to the darkness, hiding his injuries from curious eyes. Luckily, he had stopped bleeding and the bar he was in didn't cater to a well-dressed crowd.

He dropped the bag at his feet and leaned against the wall, watching as several couples grope each other not too far from where he stood.

He thought back to a few days ago when he'd been at another club, knocking back shots of tequila when a pair of haunted green eyes captured his attention. And his heart.

He focused his gaze on a redhead who was eyeing perspective dates from the losers in the crowd. Her gaze landed on him and smiled like a cat that just cornered a mouse. She slid off the bar stool and made her way over to Jaden.

He smiled back, careful to hide his fangs from the woman. His mouth watered as she came closer. It wasn't the scent he wanted, but it would do the job. He just needed enough to heal his wounds and appease his hunger.

"Looks like I've met my handsome stranger," she drawled.

"So you have." He cocked his head, his eyes boring into hers. "What's your name?"

"Paige."

"A beautiful name."

Her grin widened. "I have a lot of beautiful parts to me."

"I can only imagine."

Jaden took her in from head to toe as she thrust her plentiful chest towards him. She was attractive, but she paled in comparison to the strong, sensual woman that waited for him back at his house. The only person who cared if he came back home tonight.

That alone made Alice the most beautiful woman in the world.

"Let me help you with your imagination."

She leaned forward, her lips lightly pressing against his. He forced himself to sample this woman and pretend he was as aroused as she was. He closed his eyes, wishing it was Alice's lips he felt against his mouth, her body pressed against him.

Guilt stabbed his heart. He had to feed if he was going to heal himself and not drink from Alice. This felt so wrong. But what choice did he have?

Paige pulled back, her tongue darting across her lips. "That's just a taste."

"I'd love to nibble some more."

He tightened his grip around Paige's waist and brought her back to him. He heard her contented sigh as his lips traveled her neck. Jaden nipped her skin with his fang, feeling the pulse throb under the tip of his tongue.

He sank his teeth into her throat. The woman surrendered herself to him as waves of pleasure overtook her that made her oblivious to the feeding.

Jaden closed his eyes and blocked out the sounds of the bar, the woman in his arms and thought only of Alice.

~ * ~

Alice resented the fact that she had a babysitter just as much as the female vampire hated being stuck in the house. She understood Jaden's concern over her safety which made her love him even more, but he was being a little overprotective.

She was in the middle of nowhere with no contact to the outside world except for her cell phone.

And her world shifted again with the appearance of Jaden's friends. They were here for her and she didn't understand why. Last time she checked, she wasn't the Chosen One in some cheesy horror movie. They knew something about her and they weren't willing to share their information, which ticked her off even more.

Alice cast a wary eye towards Helene. The female took up the entire sofa in the den adjacent to the kitchen. She twirled a knife in between her fingers as she watched Alice's every move. They hadn't said much in the past few hours as they waited for Jaden and the others to come back and every minute kept Alice on edge.

Was Jaden all right? Did he find John-Paul? Could she go back to her apartment? Would she able to go back to a normal life knowing vampires roamed Ravenna?

So many questions burned inside of her and she had no answers.

"Are you going to pace the floor the entire night?" Helene asked. "I thought it was past your bedtime. Dawn will be here in an hour."

"Isn't it getting close to yours?" Alice said. "If you want to stay here, I can tuck you in and read you a bedtime story. Will that help you go to sleep?"

Helene's gray eyes hardened on Alice. "You'd better watch yourself, human."

"Or what? You're going to use that knife on me?"

"It's tempting to teach you a lesson, but I'm supposed to keep you out of trouble. I don't want to be on the receiving end of Jaden's anger," Helene muttered. "His power hurts like a bitch."

"What do you mean?"

"He didn't tell you?" She raised an eyebrow. "Interesting."

Alice stopped pacing. "Mind telling me what's so interesting? I'd love to be in on the secret."

Helene focused her attention back on the knife. "Every vampire has a special ability. Jaden's particular talent comes in handy when we need to talk to our enemies."

"And that would be?"

"He can manipulate not only emotions, but whatever injury you sustain. Make your pain worse or your pleasure more intense." Helene shook her head. "I've seen grown men cry when he merely brushes his hand against their skin. It's a pretty awesome talent to have."

Alice went cold inside. Manipulate emotions? So that meant every kiss, every touch was a result of his power?

He hugged her so tightly when he left, asking her to stay one more night and she caved. She had to wonder if she made that decision on her own, or if he gave her a little booster.

No. She didn't believe that. The way he looked at her and touched her said he cared for her. She wanted to stay and chose to stay all on her own. Didn't she?

"How does he do it?" Alice asked quietly.

"The same way I teleport from place to place. I just have to concentrate and it happens."

"So I could be standing in a room full of people and all he has to do is concentrate on me and I'll feel pain?"

"Doesn't work that way." Helene put her knife away. "He can sense your emotions, but he can't do anything without physical contact."

Alice thought of all the times he kissed her, his hands stroking every part of her body, the expert way he made love to her. Was everything a lie?

She swallowed the lump in her throat. "Any part of his body can cause a surge in emotions?"

"No. Just his hands."

"How do you know this?"

"Because he's used it on me. I never want to feel pain like that again."

"He did it on purpose?" Alice stared at her, horrified. "Why?"

"Training purposes," Helene replied. "It makes us better fighters and eliminate any weaknesses."

"Does Jaden have any weaknesses?"

Helene laughed, the harsh sound echoing in the room. "Why on earth would I tell you that?" The laughter faded and she pinned Alice with a hard look. "As much as I think Jaden's a frigid bastard, he is my brother-in-arms. We always protect our own. And since you're not one of us, there's no way I'm going to tell you anything that would hurt him."

"I won't hurt him. I want to understand him."

"You want understanding? Let's go."

Helene grabbed Alice's arm and dragged her to the gym. They stopped in front of one of the metal cabinets. Alice yanked her arm out of the vampire's grasp.

Helene opened the doors. Alice's eyes widened as her eyes darted from shelf to shelf. Surgical scalpels of varying lengths, dental tools, rope, handcuffs with inverted spikes to go into the wrist were just a few of the items in the cabinet.

She gulped as she settled on the blades. There was still blood on several of them. He hadn't had time to clean them which meant they had been recently used. Before she came to the house? While she was sleeping upstairs?

"It's quite a collection, but not his best stuff. The ones in here are nothing compared to what he's got in the other two."

Helene touched one of the daggers. "You should see him in action. He can keep a Shadow alive for days and not bleed them out. It's pretty amazing."

Alice's stomach churned at the horror of what Helene said. It was like her time with John-Paul. Beating her for days and taunting her with her imminent death. How was Jaden any different?

"Why are you showing me this?" Alice whispered.

"You want to understand him, don't you? Then you need to know what he really is."

"So you're telling me he's a monster."

"The real monsters are the ones we fight." Helene pinned Alice with a hard stare. "Jaden doesn't do this because he needs to keep himself entertained. It's something he has to do."

"Torture is something he has to do? That's a new one." Alice shook her head. "Everyone has a choice. This isn't right."

"Even if the end justifies the means?" Helene asked. "How do you think he discovered what went down at your place last night?"

Alice took a step back. "What?"

"It took him a while, but he got the truth from them. That's why he got to you before the Shadows took you away. He uses his talent to find out where the Host is before he kills the innocents, whether they're humans or vampires."

"How often does he do this?"

"Whenever it's necessary." Helene closed one of the doors. "I can't blame him for doing these things to the Shadows. They deserve whatever he gives them after what they did to him."

"What did they do?"

"Not my place to tell. But ask him about a woman named Catherine and his parents," she said. "If he tells you about her, then you'll have a better understanding of him than anyone else."

Helene must have heard something because she jumped up, her hand tight on the dagger from the cabinet. Alice followed Helene's gaze. She prayed that it wasn't a Shadow, no matter how improbable it seemed to track her here.

Jaden walked in with a bag slung over one of his shoulders. "Put that damn thing away. It's just me."

"Oh, goody! You're back," Helene exclaimed in mock delight. "Did you boys have fun?"

"Bite me, Helene."

"I don't care for the way you taste."

"Fine. Then get out of my house."

"Well someone's a Mr. Crankypants."

"If you had the night I had, you'd be seriously pissed off too."

"Yeah. Because Alice and I had such an awesome time hanging out," Helene said. "We should really do this again. You know, you big strong men going out and defending us poor, weak women."

Alice let out the breath she was holding, relieved he came back alive. But her relief was short-lived when she saw his gaze flicker to the open cabinets. He stared at the shelves for a long time before he looked at her.

Sadness crept into those pale blue eyes. "Oh, Alice."

"Yeah." She glanced back at the cabinet. "Imagine my surprise when I saw what was in here."

"Are you okay?" Jaden cleared his throat. "That's a stupid question. Did you...ah, did you touch–"

"Touch anything in there? No. I just saw them," she said. "I thought the whole knowing-everything-about-the-human-body was a vampire thing. I didn't know you were so skilled."

"Did you look in the others?"

"Do you want me to? Because to be honest, I think this is enough."

"No. I never wanted you to see them in the first place."

Helene held up her hand. "Actually, I'll take the blame for this one. I showed her what was in there."

Jaden swiveled his head. The pure malice in his eyes made Alice cringe. "You. Did. What?"

"She wanted to know more about you. I was just helping out."

He took a step toward Helene, looking as if he could barely contain his rage. Alice frowned when she noticed him favoring his left leg. His shoulder looked damp, as if he gotten it wet. As he came closer, she saw a tear in the fabric. The rip suggested a stab wound. Maybe even a gunshot. How could he tolerate such pain?

Not only that, how many times had he come home to an empty house with no one to care for him?

"You're hurt," Alice said.

"It's not the first time and it certainly won't be the last." He scowled at Helene, tightening his grip on the strap of the bag. "Dawn will be here in thirty minutes. And trust me, I won't have a problem turning your annoying ass into the sunlight."

She winked at him. "Sleep tight, you two."

Alice blinked and Helene was gone. Completely disappeared.

Jaden turned to her. "Why are you still awake? Did Helene keep you up and she decided to show you what was in the cabinets just for fun?"

She hesitated. The thought of him not coming back to her

made her feel hollow. Cold. Like she lost a part of herself. But she wouldn't admit that to him. Especially since she didn't know what the truth was anymore. Or how he felt about her.

She had so many questions for him. Who was Catherine? What happened to his parents? Why did he not care about himself?

But more importantly, was everything she felt for him really a lie?

"My sleep schedule's a little off right now," she said. "Hanging around vampires tends to alter your sleeping patterns."

He took the bag off his shoulder and handed it to her. "I stopped by your place and picked up some things. I thought you might like to wear something that belongs to you."

The breath rushed out of her lungs. Here was this man, wounded and bleeding, and he was thoughtful enough to bring her something familiar.

But what about Jaden? Was there ever anyone who took a few moments to take care of him?

Her concern for him tipped the scales. No matter what Jaden did to find her and keep her safe, he wasn't the monster she knew John-Paul was. Not when he treated her with such care and gentleness.

"Let's get you cleaned up," she said.

He stared at her as if another head sprouted out of her neck. "What?"

She took the bag and slung it over her shoulder. She could ask her questions while she bandaged his wounds. "You're hurt and I'm awake. Let me help you."

"Aren't you afraid of me?"

"Anyone in their right mind would be afraid of you. I'm not." Alice looked back at the cabinet. "If you wanted to hurt me, you would've done it already. You've had so many chances."

"But why would you want to help me?"

"Because someone should help you out every once in a while." She grabbed his free hand and tugged gently. "I'm not taking 'no' for an answer. We need to clean you up."

Chapter 19

This is my mate.

It was the only thought that came to Jaden's mind as he let this determined female lead him to his room. She was scared and overwhelmed, no doubt from what she saw in the cabinets, but she shoved all her emotional shit aside so she could help him.

She was a warrior like him. She fought to help others despite her fears and her perceived failures. An iron will and stubborn streak that rivaled his. And a sweet haven from the malevolent storm in his dark existence. Why would he want anyone else but her?

He could kill Helene for showing her his interrogation tools. What the fuck was she thinking? Show Alice those weapons would only scare her and remind her of her captivity. He wondered what else Alice and Helene talked about while he was gone.

But none of that mattered right now. Alice's hand felt so good in his. His heart swelled in his chest. Alice deserved someone better than him, but he was too damn selfish to let her go.

Jaden mentally willed a lamp to come on so she could find her way around. A soft glow illuminated the room which would be romantic under other circumstances. Instead, it concealed both of their faces in shadows so that neither one could see the other's expression.

"Thanks," she said. "Sit here. I'll be right back."

He threw the black and gold duvet to the side and sank on to the mattress. She placed her bag near the bed and headed into the bathroom. He loved watching her move. Such a subtle sway of her hips but one that made him crazy with desire.

He shrugged out of his jacket only to have his injured shoulder sizzle in a fresh wave of pain. The blood from the woman in the bar helped some, but not much. He wanted to get back to Alice and hadn't taken all that he should. He'd heal, but slower than normal.

Jaden tried to take off his shirt, but the pain prevented him from getting it over his torso. He sucked in another breath as he prepared himself for another try until Alice's hand rested on top of his arm.

"You're only making it worse," Alice said. She placed several bandages and cloths on the bed. "Sit still. I just need to grab a something else out of the bathroom and then I'll help you take it off."

He swallowed a grin as he sat perfectly still. She disappeared for a moment and returned with a bowl of warm water and scissors. His hands fell into his lap as he watched Alice place the bowl on the nightstand.

"I think it'll be easier to cut the shirt off of you. The less you move the better." She sat next to him, the mattress dipping to accommodate her weight. "Is that okay?"

"Might as well. It's not like I can fix it."

Alice scooted nearer to him and his throat went bone dry. She was so close, the heat of her body seeping into his. He could sit here for eternity with her hand resting tenderly on his side.

The cool metal of the shears rested at the base of his spine before it slowly traveled towards his neck. He clenched his jaw as the metal stroked his flesh, the smoothness of the steel as light as Alice's fingernails scratching his back.

She moved the scissors to the front, starting at his Adam's apple and slowly making its way down his torso. His cock stirred with every tickle of the point against his chest, a surprisingly erotic sensation. He was tempted to throw Alice on the bed and return the sensation, but his wounds reminded him he was in no shape to do anything tonight.

Alice slid the shirt off one arm, but paused when she moved to his injured side. "If I hurt you, tell me to stop, okay?"

Jaden nodded, but he didn't care if his arm was hanging on by a single sliver of muscle. Hell, he wanted to shoot himself so he could keep feeling her soothing caress.

She peeled the shirt off his shoulder slowly, a delicious pain rippling through his body as she worked the blood-soaked fabric off his skin. The rest came off easily enough and Alice placed it on top of the other torn piece.

She squinted in the darkness, trying to see the extent of his injury. "Can you make it any brighter in here?"

"It's not pretty."

"Gunshot wounds rarely are. I'd rather see what I'm doing than hurt you worse." She picked up a washcloth and dipped it in the bowl, wringing the water out of it. "Please let me see it."

Another lamp flickered in the room and she gasped at the wound. He looked down and saw it caked in dried blood. There was a hole clean through his shoulder although the skin was beginning to knit itself together. At least the bullet exited his body because pulling out a lodged round with no anesthetic was a one step short of torture.

"Oh, my...*God*," she whispered. Her green eyes bored into

his. "How can you stand the pain?"

"It looks worse than it actually is. And it only started hurting once the adrenaline wore off about an hour ago."

"How long ago were you shot?"

"Maybe three hours before I came home."

"And you didn't bleed out?"

He shifted on the bed. He didn't want to tell her about the redhead who'd replaced some of that lost blood.

"It sealed up before I had the chance to lose more blood. I was lucky it healed quickly."

She shook her head. "I'd hate to think of what it looked like a few hours ago."

"I know it doesn't look good." He put his hand on the washcloth. "You don't have to stay for this. I can take it from here. I've done it before by myself and I'll do it again."

"I'm not going to faint at the sight of blood. I said I would help and I will." Alice yanked it away from him. "With everything I've seen over the past few days, blood is the last thing that makes me squeamish. Let's see how bad it is once I've cleaned it."

Jaden quirked an eyebrow in amusement, but didn't protest. He watched her as she dabbed his skin with the softest of strokes. She moved slowly to make sure every bit of blood was brushed away before she moved to another patch of skin.

Chills shot through him as her gentle hands cleaned his wound. Here he was shot, stabbed and exhausted, but all he could think about was how much he wanted to kiss her. To have her tongue move as sensuously over his skin as the cloth in her hand.

Alice noticed the shiver and paused on his shoulder. "I'm sorry. You must be cold. Do you want me to turn the heat up?"

He shook his head. The room could be on fire, but it wouldn't do anything to stop the caresses that made his body come to life.

"The chills are nothing. I'm fine."

Especially since his throbbing cock made him forget everything else.

He watched Alice through lowered lids while she wiped the blood off his shoulder. Christ, she was exquisite. He could stare at her for hours and never get tired of those dark brown waves framing her rose-tinted cheeks. Or those haunting eyes filled with tenderness and concern.

His eyes moved lower to the column of her throat to the vee in her t-shirt. He saw the outline of her breasts rising and falling with each breath, her nipples pressing against the thin cotton.

Jaden felt the tattoos shift on his wrist. He burned for this woman. Every part of her melted the ice around his heart and awakened feelings he thought were long since dead. Emotions he believed had been buried the night he killed Catherine.

"Can we talk about what happened earlier tonight?" she asked, breaking the silence.

"You mean my getting shot?"

She shook her head. "No. About me and this Sisters' thing. What's that all about?"

"It's complicated."

"Then give me the uncomplicated version. It's not like I'm going anywhere anytime soon." She pointed a finger at him. "And don't tell me I can't handle it. I'm sitting here with my vampire lover, cleaning his bullet wound after finding his secret stash of weapons. I haven't run for the door yet so I think I can handle it."

He couldn't help but grin. "You're also stubborn."

"And you're avoiding the question. Who am I to these Sister women?"

"No one. I know how harsh that sounds. They're soulless harpies who like to screw with my head."

She raised an eyebrow. "Why listen to them if they're so bad?"

"They're like that parent who you don't want to listen to because you know they're right," he said. "They may be cryptic and infuriating, but they want our race to thrive and they want us to protect the civilian population."

"And vampires," Alice added, "but I still don't understand why they care about me."

"They care about themselves. But you are invaluable to someone else."

"Who?"

Me, Jaden thought.

"To all of us. They saw you coming." He cleared his throat. "You are a target for the Host. We need to keep you safe."

"But how do you know they're talking about me?"

"You're a daughter of foster," he said. "You were in the foster care system."

"There are a lot of women who came from foster care."

"There's something else. The scar on your shoulder sets you apart." He ran a finger across her skin. "'Branded with the animal's mark.' A paw print of a dog. They like to do cryptic shit like that and it's how we know they're talking about you."

"Anything else?"

Yeah, you're going to die for me because my love for you is going to be the nail in your coffin. Oh, and depending who gets a hold of you first, you can destroy the entire vampire or human race. Or both, depending on your mood.

Yeah, that would go over real well.

He shook his head. "Nothing of importance."

Alice narrowed her eyes. She knew he was holding back, but wasn't pressing the issue. "Despite them being soulless harpies, who are these women?"

"The Sisters' are two females who are older than I am by thousands of years. They, along with the Seven Masters, were the first of our race. We can all trace our lineage back to them or one of the Masters. Over the millennia, the lines have been diluted with the mix of human and vampire blood."

"Does that make your race weaker?" she asked.

"Not at all. And there are only a handful of vampires who have a direct link back to the Sisters or the Masters."

"Are you one of them?"

"Yeah. My father was the last living Master of my race." A muscle twitched in his jaw. "He was killed in the late sixteenth century. A group of Shadows infiltrated our compound and slaughtered everyone there. I only survived because I was checking out a false lead. Otherwise, they would've killed me too. I tried to get back to them, but I was already too late."

She picked up a fresh compress and dabbed the blood at his side. "Did you find the bodies?"

"Yeah." He closed his eyes. "He died while trying to protect my mother. I found them together, his body on top of hers. It was obvious he was trying to shield her from the Shadows arrows. He could've left her behind. As a leader of the race, no one would've blamed him for saving his own life. But he loved her too much to let her go. He didn't want to live without her and chose to die by her side."

"So you fight for them?"

"For them and for my brother, Ezra." He swallowed at the lump that rose in his throat. "He was only fifteen when he died. He never had a chance to have a life."

"The Shadows got him that day too?"

"I found him in his room. The Shadows placed him back in his bed, making it look like he was sleeping. When I pulled back the covers, I barely recognized him. Ezra was an innocent male."

Jaden lowered his head. He was the perfect warrior, the one Shadows feared, but he was a failure. He lived with the guilt of his baby brother's death every day he hunted while Ezra was only ash.

"It's his body I see when I fight," he mumbled. "So that no other sibling has to find their brother or sister the way I found mine. If that makes me a monster, then so be it."

Alice stopped cleaning the wound and put the cloth in the bowl. She wrapped her arms around his waist and placed her cheek against his uninjured shoulder.

"I'm so sorry, Jaden," she murmured against his back. "I can't imagine losing your family like that. I wish that I could've been there for you."

He felt something wet against his shoulder blade. He looked down at her and saw the tears on her cheeks.

The pain in his shoulder disappeared as Alice held him in her arms. His throat closed up while he idly stroked the top of her hand. Why couldn't he have met her seven hundred years ago?

He stroked the top of her hand. She was beautiful through and through. Even after her attack with John-Paul, she still found it in her heart to let something like him in.

He looked down at their hands as her fingers interlaced with his. It felt so right and good for her to be here. She made him feel whole. Warm. Loved.

Alice cleared her throat, suddenly embarrassed. "I should finish with your wounds. You don't need to be sitting here in the cold."

She pulled away, the absence of her warmth leaving him cool. He wanted to reach around and bring her back to him. He didn't care about the impossibility of her being human and a Firebrand. He loved her. Period.

Tell her, damn it. Tell her you love her.

"You're right. It's not as bad as I thought," Alice said as she reached for another cloth. "Then again, bullet wounds are never good to begin with."

"You're very good at this."

"Really? This is my first time cleaning a bullet wound. Good thing to know I'm doing it like a pro."

He grinned. "What I mean is how gentle you are. It doesn't hurt so much when you touch me."

"When you have to take care of little kids, you learn to be gentle."

"At your school?"

"There too. But I learned it in one of my foster homes." Alice wiped away another smear of blood. "Most of the homes I lived in were pretty decent, but there was one that was just awful. The Drysons were absent parents who only wanted to collect the money to support whatever habit they had at the time. Sometimes gambling, but most of the time it was alcohol." Her eyes dimmed at the memory. "The house was in really bad shape. Bottles littered everywhere, half-eaten food, even used diapers in some corners. The little kids would have normal scrapes and bruises that come with being a kid, but there was no one there to wipe their tears or make them feel better."

"But you did."

"I did." A sad smile curved her lips. "I was one of the older kids and it broke my heart to see them hurting. They had no one. No mother or father to kiss away their tears. So I'd sit them on the edge of the tub, find some clean scraps or toilet paper and just tell them they'd be okay."

"How old were you?"

"I was ten at the time."

"You were still a child yourself," he pointed out. "You can't be expected to take care of children yourself."

"Growing up in foster care makes you older than you are." She dipped the cloth and wrung the water out. "I've had a lot of things happen to me that make me seem older than I am. Not like the almost seven centuries you have on me, but old enough."

"I'm amazed you're not bitter. Most people would be with what you've gone through."

"Being bitter makes me miserable. And that's not a way to live. I'd rather find some beauty in my life and hold on to happiness as long as I can. I never know when it'll be taken away from me."

"Especially when that happiness is taken by a woman you love."

"Is that what happened to you?" Alice asked.

Fuck. He hadn't meant for that to slip out.

"It was a long time ago," he muttered.

"Helene mentioned a woman named Catherine and that I would understand you better if I know about her."

"Did she?" Jaden scowled. "Helene should learn to keep her damn mouth shut. Just like she shouldn't have shown you what was in those cabinets."

"Helene said she's seen firsthand how you work." She dabbed his shoulder again. "Do you enjoy what you do?"

"You mean keeping my people protected against maniacal assholes bent on enslaving the human race as well as trying to kill me every chance they get? Yeah, I enjoy it."

"That's not what I meant." Her brows drew together, her face pinched with worry. "I mean…like with the two Shadows you and Helene…talked to. Did you enjoy that?"

"Sometimes I do. It means I'm getting the information I want and a killer off the street," he said. "It got me to you last night, right?"

"Isn't that what you are too? A killer?"

He hid his wince. He never wanted Alice to see the demon he was, but there was nothing he could do about it now except to tell her the truth and expose the darker side of him.

"I don't prey on innocent people."

"What about when you have to eat?"

"When I feed, I don't kill. I only take enough to appease the hunger. But when you're talking about Shadows, I don't regret it," Jaden said. "It means you're safe and both races are unharmed. So it may not be right, but it's what I do."

Alice sat back from him, her head turned toward the bowl. He tried to read her, but she was blank. No emotions whatsoever. Like she closed herself off to him.

The silence was deafening and he braced himself for her reaction. What was she going to do? Get up and leave? Curse him? Demand he let her go?

"Thank you."

He flinched. He wasn't expecting to hear that. "For what?"

"For telling me the truth. It's difficult to hear, and I may not like what you do, but I understand it. And if they murdered my parents like they did yours, I might want to give them a taste of their own medicine." Alice paused, her hand resting on his back. "We all have something unpleasant inside ourselves. Sometimes we can see it, like my scars. Other times, we are able to hide it from everyone else."

He placed his hand on her knee. He needed to touch her right now. Feel her warm skin underneath his palm to let him know he wasn't dreaming.

She could easily go back to her room and put distance between them. But she chose to stay, to face his demons head-on and not run away. God, he loved her strength and spirit.

"But I am curious about something else."

"Catherine," he guessed.

"I'm guessing she's the woman in the painting downstairs. She's beautiful."

"So are you."

Alice blushed and looked down at his shoulder. Her shyness was so endearing and it made him want to gather in his arms.

She was so much different than Catherine. He couldn't remember a time when her eyes gazed at him with tenderness or warmth. She'd given him her body and her blood, but never her heart. No matter how much he loved his wife, she never saw him as anything but a monster. The ice in her veins froze her heart until it froze his as well.

That changed when he found Alice. She thawed the ice encasing his heart and made him feel again.

"Helene said if I wanted to understand you better, I should ask you what happened to Catherine." She placed the bloodied cloth in the bowl and began drying his shoulder. "But I understand it's personal. You don't have to tell me about it."

He looked at her. There was no malice, no calculating gleam in her eyes. Just curiosity and a tenderness that burned him. She trusted him with the painful secrets of her past. He needed to return the favor.

Jaden took a deep breath. "Before I came of age and went through my training, I fell in love with a human. Her name was Catherine James and she was a wonderful seamstress. Many women of the court coveted her attention to detail and her stunning work, but she was a part of the working class, not royalty.

"I courted her as any gentleman of the time would. I didn't want anyone to know I was running after a human woman and she didn't want her father to know she was sleeping with an aristocrat.

"Around this time, I went through my transition. Similar to human puberty, changes went through my body that I couldn't control. She noticed something was different about me, but she couldn't figure out what it was. At that point, I hadn't learned to control my thirst. Her blood smelled too good and I couldn't help myself."

"You drank from her?"

"I nearly bled her dry. It hurt her so much. Catherine kept screaming for me to stop, but I couldn't. I just kept drinking." He closed his eyes for a moment. "When I realized she was dying, I forced her to take my vein. She tried not to drink, but it was too powerful for her to resist. Enough of my blood made it into her system and she changed as well."

"How did your parents react to this?" she asked.

"I thought my father was going to kill me," he replied. "He was furious with what I'd done and that I'd change a human."

She frowned. "I thought you said that wasn't unusual."

"As a child of a Master, my blood is extremely powerful. So strong that it can unlock powers inside a human they didn't know they had." He glanced at her. "That's why when we choose a mate, it's for life. He didn't approve of my choice."

"Was Catherine happy being with you?"

"The first few days, she was confused, but that quickly disappeared." His shoulders slumped at the memory. "She said I damned her because of the demonic blood which now flowed through her veins. Despite her newfound strength, she said a demon was in her soul and I was that demon. I tried to tell her that I loved her too much to let her die and that's why I changed her. She didn't care. She still hated me for it."

Alice went back to cleaning the wound, her touch soothing his weary heart. "Where did you two go?"

"We went to live in a compound with Liam. His father was also a Master which makes Liam a cousin of mine. He gave us shelter while helping us to learn how to control our thirst. That's when I discovered my ability to affect people's emotions with my hands."

"Did Catherine have any special talents? I mean, she was human."

"But my blood activated that dormant gene and made her pretty damn powerful."

"What could she do?"

"Mind control," he mumbled as he rubbed his eyes. "We all have some way to erase ourselves from a human's memory, but hers went beyond that. She could make you do whatever she wanted. It made sense because she captivated me the very first time I met her."

"Did she do that to you?"

"I remember her leaning over me with a dagger," he said. "Catherine wanted me to hurt for taking her away from the human world and she did a damn good job of it. She tortured me for a good four days, slicing into my body, asking me to bleed for her as I made her bleed for me."

"She held you captive?" she asked. "Like me?"

"Yeah," he echoed. "Like you."

"What did you do?"

"When I felt her power straining, I used what energy I had left and broke the mind spell. I lunged for her, ripping the blade out of her hand. Even though I was weak, she never stood a chance against me." His voice faltered at the memory. "I only wanted to immobilize her. I-I didn't want...to kill her. But I didn't want to die, either. I stabbed her in the chest and she just stared at me, like she couldn't believe I had the balls to do what I did." He cleared his throat again. "She lost too much blood and there wasn't a pulse. I carried her body outside and let the sun turn whatever blood she had left into acid." He met her gaze. "This is why my brothers call me the Ice Warrior because I killed Catherine and left her body to the sun. Only an animal can do that to someone they care about."

"Do the others know what she did to you?"

"Only Salvatore and Liam know the full of extent of what she did. Varrik has some idea because he can read minds, but he doesn't know much. The other warriors believe I became tired of her and wanted her out of the way," he replied. "I never contradicted them. The lie was better than the truth."

"You changed her because you loved her and she made you hurt yourself so she could feel better," she said. "You killed her so you wouldn't die. That doesn't make you cold."

He looked away from her. "It makes me stupid."

"If you could change things, would you do anything differently?"

"I would have let old age take her. I never would've turned her into a monster."

Gentle hands cupped his face and his eyes met Alice's. Her green eyes were full of sympathy. For him.

"You're not a monster, Jaden," Alice said.

"I'm a killer and a damn good one at that. You've seen me in action." He flashed his fangs at her. "And these aren't cosmetically enhanced because I have a Dracula complex. How can I be anything but a monster?"

"Now who's the one with the distorted opinion of himself?" Alice shook her head. "Because you feel remorse for your wife's death. A monster would boast about the killing, not burden themselves with guilt." She stroked his cheek with her thumb. "I've seen monsters in reality and in my dreams. I'm hunted by one now. But you? How can you think of yourself that way? You hold me like I am about to shatter in your arms. And you kiss me so passionately that you make me feel like I'm the most beautiful woman in the world." She kissed his lips. "You're not a monster to me, Jaden. If anything, you're my guardian angel. My saving grace. You made me whole again."

Shock rendered him speechless. Everyone feared him, afraid of his anger and his power. Even Salvatore, the closest thing he had to a friend, kept his distance.

Alice didn't see the evil or horror that others saw in him. Where others condemned him, she consoled him. She saw something good and honorable in him when others turned away.

She scooted over on the mattress and put some space between them. "Sorry. I didn't mean to make you uncomfortable. That's twice in one night. I must be trying to set a record here."

"You didn't make me uncomfortable," he said roughly. "You surprised me."

She finished bandaging the wound and stood up. "It's getting close to dawn and I'm sure you're tired." She reached for her bag next to the bed. "I promise not to wake you up this time. Just remember that I'm right down the hall if you need me."

Jaden grabbed her hand. He wanted to feel the warmth of her touch a little while longer. He didn't want sex. He just wanted to hold her.

"Please don't go."

"But you need your rest," she protested.

"I'll sleep better with you next to me."

"Men are all the same no matter the species." Alice raised an eyebrow. "Is that all you have on your mind?"

"I like how you think, but I need to regain my strength," he chuckled. "There'll be plenty of time to play later."

"If you don't want to have sex with me, then why do you want me to stay?"

"Is that how you see us together?" The laughter faded. "You really think the only reason I'd want you to stay is for a quick fuck?"

She shifted uncomfortably and gnawed on her lower lip. "It sounds so bad when you say it like that."

"Then make me understand what you're saying."

"No one's ever wanted me like you do. And I'm not saying that to have your pity. It's the truth," Alice said. "My mother died giving birth to me. I know that one can't be helped. My father never made the effort to find me. I was shuffled from home to home, school to school. I never belonged to any place." She bit her lip. "The only person who ever wanted me was John-Paul."

"I want you."

"Why?"

Because I love you.

He clamped down on his jaw. He wanted to confess his feelings for her. To know that relationship meant more to him than the physical aspect. She somehow burrowed herself in his heart and he couldn't get her out.

And even if he had the power to get rid of her, he wouldn't. He never wanted her to leave.

But no matter how much he loved her, he couldn't have history repeat itself. He never wanted Alice to stare at him with contempt or hate him.

So he said the three words that he never said to anyone else in his life.

"I need you."

"You need me? The human I-might-need-to-store-her-blood-in-the-refrigerator-later me?"

"I'd rather store the blood in the cooler in the gym. I always like to knock back a pint after a good workout." He stroked the inside of her wrist with his thumb. "I don't want to be alone tonight. Please stay with me."

She stared at his thumb for a long moment before she met his gaze. "All right. I'll stay. But I need to change out of these clothes first." She glanced back down at their hands. "You're going to let me go so I can come right back?"

He reluctantly let go of her hand and watched her fine ass as she bent down to grab her bag. She walked into the bathroom, shutting the door for privacy and gave Jaden the opportunity to change out of his soiled clothes. The wound on his thigh was completely healed although he was still a little stiff from the injury.

He put on a pair of boxers and slid under the covers. Alice came out a moment later, his heart nearly stopping in his chest.

She pulled her hair out of its braid and it fell in soft waves around her face. She wore a pair of white and blue striped pajama pants and a white T-shirt. She climbed into the bed and smiled at him.

Why did she always look so damn irresistible?

Alice settled next to him. "You're sure you want me to stay?"

"Absolutely."

She placed her hand on his arm, her fingertips stroking his bicep. "You know, sometimes I have really bad nightmares. Well, it's actually one," she confessed. "I dream that John-Paul's coming after me and I can't get away from him. No matter how hard I run, he always catches me."

He kissed her forehead. "I won't let him get you."

"I toss and turn a lot when I dream. I don't mean to, but it happens."

"I do this funny whistling thing with my nose that wakes me up in the middle of the morning," he replied, brushing a tendril of hair out of her eyes. "Why are you telling me this?"

She lightly touched the gauze pad on his shoulder. "What if I hurt you?"

Love swelled in his chest at her tender words. She wasn't concerned about him lashing out at her while she slept or the temptation he had to sink his teeth into her throat whenever she was around. Instead, she was afraid of causing him more pain.

He caressed her cheek, the skin heating his hand. "You won't, Alice."

"But I —"

He silenced her protest with a kiss. "Your leaving would hurt worse. Don't go."

"I won't leave you tonight." She smiled up at him. "I promise I'll be here when you wake up."

Jaden stretched out next to her, listening to her steady heartbeat as she settled further into the bed. He placed his arm around her waist. Alice sighed and scooted closer to him, his body curving to hers.

He watched as her breathing evened out as sleep descended upon her. Without waking her, he trailed his fingertips across her cheeks, her lips, down the column of her throat. He needed to touch her, reassure himself she was still there.

She was so beautiful and fragile in his arms. The closest thing to happiness a creature like him could hope for.

And he dared to hope.

Alice took care of him, but most of all she trusted him. She saw the monster in him and didn't run away. Instead, she let her guard down and allowed him into the most vulnerable part of her. He knew how incredibly hard it was for her to give herself over to him like that.

In return, Jaden gave her his heart.

He had to find some way to keep her in his life and not change her into a demon like him.

Because living without her would kill him.

Chapter 20

"She's a lovely female, isn't she?" Markus asked. "She is an attractive woman and one who would be worthy of your attentions."

They grabbed Tina Hardy from her house nearly an hour ago. They made short work of her date, leaving his body in downtown Ravenna and easily staging it to look like a drug deal gone bad. Then they knocked Tina out and dragged her back to the Host's home.

Tina was still unconscious on the floor, her hands tied behind her back, her mouth gagged.

"I guess." John-Paul leaned against the wall, frowning. "But she's not what I want."

"We are well aware of what you want," Markus said, chuckling. "Have patience, John-Paul."

John-Paul nodded to the Shadow although he was becoming very anxious. He wanted Alice. The more time they wasted, the greater the chance she could escape with that warrior.

Not only that, he was itching to get back in the game. He wanted his third day with Alice. To break his bitch and make her beg for mercy as he slowly choked the life out of her.

"My patience is running thin. You sure this'll work?"

"I doubt Ms. Roarke is the type of person who abandons her friends."

"So what do we do with her all day?" John-Paul growled.

"Keep her alive."

Both men whipped around at the Host's voice. They stood back respectfully as the Host walked over to the human female.

"Where should we keep the woman?" Markus asked. "I can move her to a different room if you'd like."

"Keep her anywhere you want as long as you don't kill her. Remember, she's a means to an end. She's no use to us dead and it's a long time until sunset."

"Can I play with her? I swear I won't leave a mark on her." John-Paul rubbed his hands together. "I want to make sure I'm ready for Alice and I need something to practice on."

The Host shrugged. "Entertain yourself however you want as long as she stays alive."

"And when we get your guy and Alice? What do we do with her then?"

"Drain her dry for all I care." The Host smiled widely. "Tonight, we all get what we want."

Chapter 21

Alice emerged from the haze of sleep to the sensation of a hand gliding down her side and resting on her hip. A gentle rush of air caressed her ear followed by a soft kiss.

A woman could definitely get used to waking up like this.

She sighed and snuggled closer to Jaden, her cheek pressed against his hard, smooth chest. She didn't want to open her eyes just yet. She needed a few more moments of silence like this--where the world didn't exist and it was just the two of them.

His thumb traced the outline of her lips. There was such tenderness in his touch and in his heart. Even if the outside world viewed him as cold and ruthless, he was gentle and kind with her.

She wished she could see into his heart, just as she knew he could read her emotions. He had to know she was madly in love with him. He had wanted to tell her something last night, but he changed his mind at the last minute. Surely he had told her his darkest secret with his killing Catherine. What was worse than killing the love of your life?

Falling in love with a human?

That was highly unlikely. She knew Jaden wouldn't allow that to happen again.

Sure, he cared about her on some level. But she was certain the rest of it was because he was duty bound to protect her. They weren't compatible. Human and vampire. The stuff of fairytales. There was no place in his life once John-Paul was taken care of. She'd go back to her world and Jaden to his.

At least she had these few moments with him.

Alice opened her eyes. "How long have you been up?"

"Maybe ten minutes. Not long."

"How'd you sleep?"

His thumb stroked her cheek. "Great because you stayed."

"Really? I didn't keep you up?"

"No tossing and turning whatsoever." He planted a kiss on her forehead. "You slept like a baby."

"How's your shoulder?"

He shrugged and glanced at the bandage. "It's a little stiff, but more than likely healed. I've definitely had worse wounds than this one."

"Do you mind if I check it?" she asked, sitting up.

He shook his head and Alice reached for the strip. She peeled it back slowly as to not rip his skin and was shocked at what she saw. The hole was completely sealed shut and all that was left was a small, pink scar. Judging by the way the tissue repaired itself, the scar would disappear within the next day or two.

"It's amazing how quickly you heal," she said. She pulled the other one off his back and tossed it into a small wastebasket by the bed. She pointed at his thigh. "Weren't you injured there too?"

"You are full of questions tonight," he said with a grin. "Are you always this chatty when you wake up?"

"Only when someone's suffered a gunshot wound."

"And what about a stabbing?"

"I can't help it if Salvatore or Varrik took a bite out of you because they wanted a quick snack. You're on your own there."

He laughed, the deep rumble filling the room. She couldn't help but smile at the sound. She had a feeling she was one of only a few people who ever saw this side of him. The harsh lines melted away and revealed the gentle male behind the warrior.

"I probably deserved the bite." He kissed her nose. "My thigh's just fine. It was only a flesh wound."

She pulled back the covers and removed the bandage. No scar or hint that there had been a stab wound. "You sure you're okay?"

"I'm just a little sore. Nothing a shower won't fix."

"If you're sore, then a shower won't do it. You should soak in the tub for a little while."

"I'm not one for taking baths. I don't have the patience to just sit there." Jaden's eyes glimmered mischievously. "Unless I have company. Will you take one with me?"

"Your body needs to heal itself," she scolded him.

"But I seem to heal much faster when you're around." He took her hand and pressed it against his hard cock. She gently gripped him as he pushed himself against her palm. "See? I feel better already."

"I can tell." An idea sparked in her head. "I'll be right back."

"Why do you want to leave this nice, warm bed?"

He nuzzled her throat. She shivered as his hot breath glided across her skin, his tongue tracing a vein. His hand moved to the small of her back, pressing her closer to him. She felt his head probing her through his pants and a rush of wetness hit between her legs. She let out a little moan as he lightly bit her throat. If he kept this up, she wasn't going to move from the bed.

"I'd rather you stay here with me," he murmured. "Although the only change I'd make is that we're both naked."

"I promise I'll make it worth your while." She kissed his lips. "Wait here."

Alice slid out of his embrace and headed for the bathroom. She turned on the water in the tub. She thought the one in her room was pretty luxurious, but his could easily hold four people in it with room to spare.

She winked at him before she closed the door. Thankfully, her duffel bag of clothes was in the bathroom with her. She pulled out the green and white and polka dotted bra with the matching panties.

She found it in the bag last night. She expected him to toss in some jeans, sweatshirts and loungewear. But these two pieces, which were so obviously feminine, shocked her when she saw them on top of her pajama pants and shirt.

She remembered when she purchased them, right after John-Paul's conviction. A little celebration for getting some of her pride back and knowing she'd put him in jail. When she came home that night and put them on, she felt silly. Wearing the garments for herself didn't do anything for her. She wanted to wear them for a man who would enjoy seeing her in them. Sure, she had gone on a couple of dates, but none of them panned out. Two years passed and they sat in the back of her drawer until today.

She smiled as she slipped on the silky undergarment and fingered the little ivory satin bow below her belly button. It seemed right that she wore it now even if she was a little anxious. Jaden had made love to her a number of times, climaxed more time than she could count, but the thought of putting on something so sexy made her nervous.

It gave her a slight thrill knowing Jaden had touched her clothes. His fingers tracing the satin lining of the bra, the wedge of cotton resting against the most private part of her.

Alice quickly tested the temperature of the water and turned off the faucet. She put on his black robe. Like any present, she needed to be wrapped up good and tight. She pulled her hair into a loose bun, a few tendrils brushing against her flushed skin.

She took a deep breath and opened the door. He looked so delectable in the bed, but he'd be even sexier in the tub. She heard a low growl at the base of his throat and those icy blue eyes smoldered with lust.

She bowed slightly and gestured inside the bathroom. "Your bath is ready, my lord."

Jaden got out of the bed and walked over to her like a hungry lion sizing up its prey. He stood next to the tub, his eyes never leaving her face. She closed the door and dimmed the lights. Not only did it help his sensitive eyes, it made her feel more comfortable with what she was about to do.

"You've done so much for me." Alice turned back to him and captured his face in her hands. "You've kept me safe and protected me when you didn't need to. I don't know how I'll ever be able to thank you for that."

"I'd do the same thing again." He placed his hands on top of hers. "And not because of any prophecy. It's because I care about you." He kissed her knuckles. "I can't bear the thought of you getting hurt again."

Her heart skipped a beat at his confession. She kissed him deeply, her blood sizzling at the contact. She wished for more, but knew this was the best she would get.

"And that's why this is all for you," she said against his lips.

She stepped back from him, her heart slamming against her ribs as her hands on the knotted belt of the robe. She took a small breath and undid the belt and slid her fingers down the length of one of the ties. She shrugged one shoulder, then another, until just her bra was exposed. His eyes darkened and his breathing accelerated while he stared at her breasts. She let the robe fall into a black pool at her feet.

The look of pure rapture on Jaden's face, as he gazed at the little scraps of cloth covering the most feminine parts of her, made her more relaxed. And desirable.

He took a step closer, his eyes burning with the promise of unbridled ecstasy. "God, you're beautiful," he said roughly.

A blast of heat licked over her breasts and between her legs. Jaden grinned as if he knew she was excited, his blue eyes shimmering in anticipation.

"Nope." She stepped away from his outstretched hand. "I don't want you to touch me."

"What?" His grin faded. "Why not?"

"I know your talent lies in your hands," Alice said. "Helene told me that you can magnify feelings or reduce them."

"Helene has a big mouth," he swore under his breath. "She should've never told you that."

"Are you ashamed of what you can do? Or you just never wanted me to know?"

"I didn't want you to know because of the look on your face right now. I wouldn't mess with you like that."

"But you've done it before, haven't you?" She nodded to herself when she saw the guilt on his face. "How many times have you done it to me?"

He hesitated for a moment. "Twice."

Alice's stomach twisted into knots. That would be the two nights they spent together, but she needed to hear the truth, no matter how unpleasant it was.

"When did you do it?"

"When I first found you outside the club and when the Shadows attacked you in your apartment," he said. "I wanted to ease your fears and let you know you could trust me. I tried to take away some of your pain when I found you in the gym, but I couldn't. Those were the only times I used my power on you."

It was her turn to frown. "But you never intensified my feelings when we slept together? Not even the first time?"

"I didn't want to force myself on you. I wanted you to be with me because it's what you desired. Without any tricks or deception." Those blue eyes pierced her with his sincerity. "No woman deserves to be tricked into something they don't want to do."

Alice just stared at him. He never used those powers in bed with her? After Helene had confessed Jaden's ability, Alice was certain he had used his talent on her. Sex wasn't supposed to be that amazing.

But she saw the truth in his eyes. He never manipulated her feelings. Knowing it had been their bodies own natural response to each other just made her want him more.

Alice stood behind him and traced one of the swirls of his the tattoo on his uninjured shoulder with her tongue. She smiled as he hissed in pleasure.

"Like I said, this isn't about me. This is about you and I don't want you to touch me." She nipped his shoulder as she placed her fingers inside the elastic waistband of his boxers. "But I can touch you as much as I want."

She pulled the boxers down his legs, her fingertips caressed his thighs and calves before she tossed them on top of the robe. Her nails raked over the taut muscles while she trailed kisses as she worked her way up. His skin was so smooth, her tongue roamed over his hip and the curve of his ass. She ran her tongue along his spine in one long lick as she stood behind him.

Alice pressed herself against his back, her hands roamed across his chest. He sucked in a breath as she nipped his throat. His heart pounded against her hand, his breathing ragged and barely controlled. She loved it. It meant he was as hungry for her as she was for him.

She looked down and saw his cock proudly jutting out of his body. He was huge and already straining to keep himself in control. She wrapped her hand around his shaft, gently skimming her fingers up and down his hard length. She desperately wanted him inside of her, but this wasn't about her needs. It was about Jaden and how much she loved him.

"I'd hate for you to get cold," Alice whispered in his ear. "Won't you get in the tub?"

His hips flexed, pushing his erection further against her palm. "I don't know. I'm feeling pretty good right now."

"But that's doing nothing for your sore muscles."

"Your hand is easing one very sore muscle right now."

"Then I'd better quit fooling around." He actually groaned when she removed her hand. "I'd really like to bathe you."

"Are you getting in with me?" Jaden asked. "I think you should. We need to conserve our resources especially since we're losing quite a bit of our fresh water. And I'd hate to think we'd cause any more damage to our environment by not bathing together."

"Whether or not I get in depends on you and if you can keep your hands to yourself."

He nodded. "I can do that."

Her nails flicked his nipples and he clenched his hands at

his sides. "I was serious when I said you couldn't touch me. That includes all body parts."

"Now that isn't fair."

"I promise I'll make it worth your while. But if you touch me, all you'll get is a cold shower. Then you'll really be wasting resources." She smiled at him wickedly. "Now are you getting in by yourself or do I have to drag you in?"

Jaden chuckled at her threat and slowly lowered himself into the water, his arms resting on the both edges. "Your turn."

"Not yet," she said.

She sat on the edge of the tub, her foot brushing against his thigh. She skimmed her toes against his leg, the muscles jerked in anticipation. His hand was inches from the center of her body and she smiled at his trembling fingers. He wanted to touch her, but kept his hand to himself.

Alice picked up a washcloth and reached behind his head. He clenched his jaw as her breasts pressed against his cheek. Alice stayed there for a long moment, arching her back as she purposefully lost her grip on the soap. His whiskered chin tickled her breasts and it made her ache in all the right places. He turned his head so his lips brushed against the top of the lacy cups.

She bit her lip to prevent a moan from escaping. He opened his mouth and let his teeth accidentally scrape against her breasts. His hot breath made her nipples tighten to the point of pain. So he found a way to taste her without technically touching her. Smart bastard.

"Sorry about that." Alice leaned back and looked at him innocently. "The soap was very slippery."

"Not a problem. I don't mind if you lose your grip again." He glanced at her hands. "Only next time, drop it on my cock."

Alice giggled as she worked up a good lather. The rest of her nervousness faded away and in its place was a deep need to have him inside her. How could she feel anxious when he looked at her with such desire in his eyes?

She ran the washcloth around his neck and shoulders, moving carefully around the scar. She leaned in and kissed his throat as she washed his chest. He turned his head, giving her full access as she ran her lips over the corded muscles. She lightly bit his skin, but not hard enough to break it, before her tongue stroked the bite.

Her hand traveled down his collarbone, his chest, her nails lightly raking across his chest, abs and stomach. He shifted in the tub as her hand moved lower, his cock hardening even more when she gently ran the washcloth over his thighs.

She wasn't sure where this boldness came from, but she reveled in it. She didn't see herself as damaged goods when she was with him. She was sexy. Desirable. Beautiful.

She smiled at the way he let out his breath when she touched him as if staying in control was the hardest thing he ever had to do, his hands slipping as he clenched the side of the tub. But she especially loved the groans when she brushed her fingers against his erection.

"You're killing me here," he growled, his eyes hooded with pleasure.

He wasn't the only one in pain. She was killing them both.

Alice placed the cloth on the edge of the tub and stood up. She grinned down at him as she placed her hand on the bra strap. His eyes widened in anticipation, his breath coming faster when she ran the thin satin between her fingertips.

"Then how about some relief?"

~ * ~

"Oh, fuck yeah."

Jaden watched her hungrily as she unhooked the front clasp of the bra, her eyes on his face. Alice peeled the lace off her full breasts, the air tightening her pink nipples. She turned to the side and slid her panties down her long legs. She stood there, gloriously naked, waiting for his response. He sat in the tub while locking his body down so he wouldn't pounce on top of her.

Damn, she was good.

She didn't know it, but she had already completed a part of the bonding. When a female took a male vampire as her mate, she cleansed him. A way of purifying his love for her and making him ready to take all of himself into her. It didn't matter if it was through tears, a walk in the rain, or a bath--as long as she did it of her own free will. What followed was a declaration of love and a blood exchange in which she'd become like him and the marking where a part of the warrior tattoo on his skin would be a part of hers.

The marking would be the hardest part because he'd mark her skin, just as John-Paul had scarred her. He didn't know how she'd react to that or when he declared his love for her.

And God, did he love Alice.

Not reaching for Alice, as her gentle hands bathed him, was torture. He thought for sure he was going to come several times, but he managed to keep it under control. Barely.

"Do you need help getting in?" he asked. "I'd like to offer you my hand, but you said I couldn't touch you."

She placed her hand on his arm. "I think I can manage on my own."

She stepped into the tub, her knees on either side of him. She placed her hands on his shoulders and leaned into him, her nipples brushing against his chest. She tucked an ebony lock of his hair behind his ear and her tongue followed her fingers.

She took his earlobe between her teeth and playfully nipped the tender skin.

Jaden arched his back and pushed himself against her, her breasts flattening against the muscles of his chest. He didn't know where this confidence came from, but he loved it. Loved that she dropped all her defenses to be with him in this moment. He wanted to pull her to him and kiss her senseless, but he promised not to touch her in any way.

She ran her tongue along his jaw before she sat back. She smiled, her emerald eyes glowed with ecstasy as she caressed his cheek.

Hands off. Hands off.

Jaden kept telling himself that as she picked up the washcloth from the edge of the tub. She ran it through the soapy water and placed it on top her chest. She wrung it out over her body, the frothy suds trickling down her breasts, her stomach, to the dark hairs at the juncture of her thighs.

Goddamn it, she was killing him.

He growled low in his throat and she met his hooded eyes. Alice placed her foot next to his knee, her leg bent as she took her slick hands and ran them from her ankle all the way up to her inner thigh. She did this several times as the rivulets of water caressed her intimately.

Her fingers trailed across her stomach before they slipped lower to the curls at the center of her body. She inched her them further down, slowly, staring at Jaden the entire time as she –

Jaden groaned as she gave him one hell of a show. If he thought he was being tortured before, then this was absolute and total slaughter.

Alice stroked her cleft, a pleasured sigh escaping her lips. Her mouth parted and her breath came in gasps as she caressed herself. He clenched his hands so tightly the knuckles turned white.

"It sounds like you're about to jump on top of me."

"I'd love to right now," he said hoarsely.

Alice opened her eyes. "But then that breaks my no touching rule."

Her free hand cupped one of her breasts, catching the nipple between her forefinger and thumb. She bit her lip as she squeezed, the pearled tip begging to be suckled.

"Do that again, Alice."

She smiled and pinched herself again, murmuring his name. He nearly came all over her thighs--he wasn't going to last much longer if she kept doing this. His cock was hard as steel and screaming for release. He was tempted to grab her hips and impale her on his shaft.

But this was the sweetest agony he'd ever known and he didn't want her to stop.

She slowly moved to her other breast and Jaden closed his eyes. "Christ, Alice. It's painful to watch what you're doing right now."

"And you're still suffering from a gunshot wound. That's very inconsiderate of me," she murmured. "I'll have to fix that."

He opened his eyes as she moved closer to him. Her hot, wet body slid against him in a most delicious way. The water lapped against him, the simplest movements cranking him even higher.

She sat on his stomach and he groaned as her thighs gently squeezed his sides. She was so hot, her wet core scalding his skin.

She leaned forward and kissed him, her full lips molding to his. Her scent filled his nostrils, down this throat, until every part of him was coated with that heavenly fragrance. He groaned and her tongue slid into his mouth. A slick penetration that left him wanting more.

Thank God he could kiss her back. He returned her kiss forcefully, using his mouth alone to convey how badly he needed her.

How much he loved her.

"Mmm. That felt good." Alice pulled back, her emerald eyes dark and scorching. "I wonder where else can I go."

"Anywhere you want."

She traced his lip with her fingertip and he gently nipped her skin. "Remember. No touching."

Alice went down his throat, her lips gliding across his collarbone. She sucked on his nipples, her tongue flicking and tugging. Waves of stinging heat attacked every nerve in his body. She kissed a trail down his washboard stomach, nibbled his sensitive hipbone.

She lifted his hips out of the water, her mouth inches from his erection. He rested his weight on his knees. Just seeing her so close to his shaft made him want to come.

"I think this is where you are hurting the most," she said.

A single tear welled from the tip and she licked it away. Her gaze locked on Jaden as she teased the head with her tongue.

"Oh, yes." She nodded her head in approval. "That's definitely a sore spot. Let me make it better."

His eyes rolled into the back of his head as her lips wrapped around him, her mouth hot and welcoming. Tendrils of her hair fell over his stomach and thighs, the tips dragging over his skin-- a delicious, erotic tickle which made him even more aware of what she was doing to his arousal. She took more of him as she found a slow, steady rhythm. He clenched his hands into fists as her mouth worked against his sensitive skin.

Jaden laid his head against the back of the tub as white hot bolts of pleasure coursed through his veins. He was never so thankful then at that moment for the builders installing the colossal Jacuzzi tub in his master suite.

She had the sweetest lips, the warm suction of her mouth spiraling him into oblivion where only pleasure and heat existed. She tongued him from tip to base and back again, her hand caressing his soft sac.

The head popped from her mouth with a soft smack. "Feel good?" she asked.

"You have no idea." His throat was all gravel, his pleasure robbing him of his voice. "You are exquisite."

She smiled and then went back to making him growl. He flexed his hips, pushing more of himself down her throat and she didn't complain. She needed to stop before he released, but the words wouldn't come out of his mouth.

He moved his hand and froze. Goddamn it, he couldn't touch her! She'd stop and he wanted to see what was next.

"Alice," Jaden moaned.

She gave him one long lick before she pulled away. "Still hurting?" she asked innocently.

"Yes," he breathed.

"And here I thought I was easing your aches and pains. Maybe this will help."

Alice climbed up his body so that her thighs were spread wide over his cock. Her breasts slammed against his chest, the tight nipples brushing against his pecs.

And he thought his torture with Catherine was bad? Shit, Alice could give Catherine lessons.

He moaned at the sight of her wet, swollen core poised over his shaft. She placed her hands on either side of his head on the tub as she sat on him, sheathing him in one smooth stroke.

Jaden threw his head back as she rocked against him. Her sex gripped him like a vise, the hot, wet walls enveloping him tightly. It took all of his self-control not to come. Without pausing, she slid up, almost breaking the connection before she sat on him again.

She captured his lips with hers, her tongue penetrating his mouth as she rode him slow and hard. How had he ever lived without her? And once the John-Paul problem was solved, how was he going to keep her alive? He refused to have the Sisters' prophecy come true. She wouldn't die because of him.

Jaden pushed those thoughts to the side as she quickened her strokes and he lifted his hips to match her pace. Fuck the Sisters' prophecy. Fuck the fact she was the Firebrand. He loved her. And if she'd have him, he was going to keep her.

They were both so close to the edge, his balls cinching tight as his orgasm coiled in his belly. She broke away and trailed her lips down the corded muscles in his neck. She opened her mouth and bit him.

He roared as he exploded inside of her, coming so forcefully he almost passed out from the sheer pleasure of it. A few strokes later, she called out his name as her climax ripped through her. He filled her up as her core milked his cock dry-- his orgasm going on and on until the last tremor left his body.

Jaden was still fully erect inside of her as the last pulse faded. She collapsed on top of him, her head on his shoulder. They were both breathing hard, her heart pounding against his chest.

Alice placed a sweet kiss on his throat. "Do you feel better now?"

"Much better," Jaden said, his voice rough. "Can I hold you now?"

She nodded and his arms shot around her. He loved the

little gasp she made as he pressed himself against her and gave her one luscious stroke deep inside her body.

She smiled down at him. "I'm glad I have that magic touch that makes you all better."

"You did a pretty good job, but I'm not quite there yet. I'm ninety-eight percent better."

"What?" The smile disappeared. "Why not one hundred percent? I was pretty good, thank you very much."

"You were incredible. But sometimes, it's better to receive than to give." Jaden nipped the side of her neck and the shudder that followed traveled straight to his body, making him harder. He clamped his hands on her hips and leaned her against the back of the tub. "And right now, Alice Roarke, I want to give you something no female has ever had from me."

He delivered hard, quick thrusts, sliding in and out, pounding pleasure into her. The water acted as a conductor, a thousand fingers sliding against their skin. She made the most wonderful cries with every stroke he made, her hips matching his intense pace.

He gritted his jaw as his own release almost barreled into her body. But his orgasm would wait just a little while longer. This was too sweet to stop any time soon, and he wanted her to know where his true talents lie.

Because he was about to make her head spin.

Jaden let his powers loose and he knew exactly when she felt the surge. Alice arched her back, pulling him deeper inside of her. She hooked her ankles around his back as concentrated pleasure ravaged her body. She closed her eyes as Jaden watched her succumb to her passion and to him.

He slid his hand between where they were joined and touched her. He stroked her cleft in time to his thrusts. He dipped his head and pulled her nipple into his mouth. Her mouth parted, gasping for breath. Her nails scored his back and he drove her harder, intensifying his own passion as well.

She threw her head back as her orgasm tackled her, her core stroking his shaft as ecstasy traveled to every nerve in her body. The sound of her screaming his name pushed him over the edge. He finally let himself go, his shout mingling with her pleasured moan.

Alice sagged against the back of the tub, her body deliciously hot and limp and her labored breaths mingled with his. He ran his hands up and down her back. He could hold her like this forever.

"I've never experienced anything like that." She cradled his face in the palm of her hand. "Was it that intense for you?"

He brushed away a few damp strands of her hair. "Absolutely."

"Does it hurt you when you use your power?"

"It doesn't make me weaker if that's what you mean."

She raised an eyebrow. "Why do I sense a 'but' in there?"

"But I can't magnify the pleasure for myself. I can only do it for you."

"You said it was intense for you too," Alice said.

"It was. More than you can imagine."

"But if you can't do it for yourself, then –"

He cut her off. "I wanted to do that to you."

She frowned. "Why?"

Jaden kissed the tip of her nose. "Because I never felt connected to anyone the way I feel with you."

"I feel the same way with you."

He got out of the tub, but she didn't move. He raised his eyebrows in amusement. "You need some help?"

"I'm not sure my legs are working right anymore." Alice brought her knees up. "Okay. I can move them so that's good.

I just don't know if I can put weight on them."

"You can't stay in there much longer. The water's going to get cold."

"True, but then you'd have a whole lot of fun warming me up again," she giggled.

Jaden chuckled and helped her out. He set her on her feet, reaching for a towel. He dried himself quickly and used his towel on her. He paid extra attention to her breasts, her hard nipples teasing him as he cupped her through the fabric.

Alice leaned against him while he moved the towel in between her thighs, his fingers stroking her cleft. He dropped the towel and ran his fingers along her still swollen lips. He buried his face in her neck as he slipped a finger inside her.

She let out a soft moan and his cock hardened instantly. So what if he just had two intense orgasms? He couldn't get enough of her and doubted he ever would.

"Jaden," she sighed. "You're not drying me."

"You're right. I'm making you wet again." Jaden dropped to his knees. "Give me a few minutes and it won't be a problem."

"Down, boy."

"Already am." His teeth nipped her sensitive hipbone. "Now if you let me go lower, I'll be in business."

Alice backed away from him and quickly threw on the robe. "You have a job to do and I don't think your leader will be very happy if you stay with me all night."

"I'll be very happy if I stay with you all night."

"You can do that?"

He caught the scent of her arousal and he grinned. "You wouldn't mind that, would you? Me staying the whole night?" He moved behind her, brushing the damp hair off her throat. "I'll keep a very close eye on you."

"Just your eyes?"

"And whatever else you'll let me put on you."

A sharp trill rang throughout the room and Jaden bared his fangs. She laughed at his impatience. "Saved by the bell."

"Leave it."

"It's Tina," she said, recognizing the ringtone.

"You told her you were fine, right? She doesn't know you're here."

"No, but she's probably checking to see if I'm all right." She grinned sheepishly. "She's the one who told my coworkers that I have the flu."

"And you should have plenty of fluids and bed rest," he said. He pressed against the nape of her neck. "In fact, I think we should go there right now. You were a little flushed earlier in the tub. You probably need to lie down and let me take extra special care of you."

"Just give me a couple of minutes and then you can take me to bed." She gasped when one of his hands slid inside the robe, cupping her breast. "What are you doing?"

He toyed with her nipple and licked the side of her throat. "Giving you an incentive to talk faster."

"You're terrible."

"Then I definitely need to take you to bed and show you how great I can be."

Alice flipped open her phone. "Hey, Tina. How're you doing?"

"She's been a lot better. I, for one, am so happy to hear your voice, my pet."

Chapter 22

Bile rose in Alice's throat as her legs went weak. She was surprised she was still standing, but Jaden's strong arm prevented her from collapsing on the floor.

"Are you there? I hope you didn't hang up on me. Tina would be very upset to know you were the one who left her in my care."

"No, I'm here." She tightened her grip on the phone. "I'm still here, John-Paul."

"I'm happy you didn't hang up, Alice. I would've taken my anger out on your friend. We both know what happens when you disobey me."

She heard Jaden hiss, but she paid no attention to him. John-Paul had Tina. That monster had one of her friends.

Alice's mind worked quickly. How long had Tina been with him? Two days ago, maybe. At least a day. She'd be scared and confused, but she'd be safe the first day. Day Two was when the games started.

He wouldn't have killed Tina yet. His compulsion of threes would forbid him from changing his pattern. Wouldn't it?

Unless he killed her on a third hour. He could justify that.

Alice moved out of Jaden's embrace and sat on the edge of the tub. "How do I know she isn't already dead?"

"I've always loved hearing your voice." His voice dropped

lower. "Do you remember our last time together? You talked the most then. And when you screamed, it made me want you even more."

Alice swallowed hard. She couldn't let him get to her like this. She had to keep herself level-headed so she could find out whether friend was still alive or dead.

Let Tina be okay. Please don't let her die because of me.

Jaden snatched the phone out of her hand and hit the speakerphone button. "Where the hell is she?"

"Alice? Where did you go?" John-Paul's voice quickly went from gentle to irritated. "Who the fuck is this?"

"Someone who doesn't need to degrade women to get off. Or the male who's going to put your ass in the ground," he snarled. "Take your pick."

"Ah, so you're the one who has my pet. You must be Jaden. The Host mentioned you'd be with Alice."

"Did the Host mention how many times I was with her? I can assure you I've lost count."

"She's such a sweet little thing, isn't she? Especially on all fours." John-Paul chuckled meaningfully. "I'm sure you found her very trainable. It took a while, but I was able to break the bitch."

Alice cringed at the look on Jaden's face. Gone was the tender man who made love to her so passionately a few minutes ago. Now she saw the murderous vampire his fellow warriors feared. The person who made grown men afraid of the night.

If John-Paul was right in front of them, she knew Jaden would have him in his gym with all three cabinets open.

"I prefer her on top. It's so much better when she rides me and I can watch her get off," Jaden said. "At least I know I'm doing something right when she's screaming my name."

"Maybe you need the reassurance," John-Paul said.

"Please tell me this just isn't a social call and you're letting us know where you're staying. I know you're dying to meet me."

"I'm more interested in seeing Alice."

"I bet you are," Jaden said. "Let me tell you before you called, I saw quite a bit of her in the tub. Felt a lot of her too."

That pissed off John-Paul even more. "I know I had a lot of fun making her beg like the good bitch she is."

"Ah, but here's the difference. She was begging you to stop. She was begging me to never stop."

Raw fury radiated from every pore in Jaden's body. He gripped the phone so tightly Alice was surprised it didn't shatter in his hand. She walked over to him and saw the hurt in his eyes. She cupped his cheek and he closed his eyes for a moment. Some of the tension eased out of his body and he wrapped his free arm around her waist, tucking her into his side.

"I asked you a question earlier, asshole," Jaden said. "I'd hate to repeat myself."

"Oh, you mean Tina? She's right here with me. In fact, I know she wants to talk to Alice." A door opened and closed. Alice heard muffled breaths. "Go ahead. Say hello."

Silence. Then, "Alice? Is that you?"

Tears sprang into Alice's eyes at her friend's terrified voice. "Tina! Are you all right? Are you hurt?"

"No. I-I'm okay," Tina said. "I'm so scared."

"Don't be scared. We'll get you out of this. I promise."

"Okay. Please, come soon. I –"

A sharp cry cut Tina off and Alice grabbed Jaden's arm. "Tina! Are you there? What's happened?"

"I'm so glad to hear your voice again, Alice." John-Paul

came on the line. "If I had to talk to your friend for another minute, I'd have to hurt something. Tina would be a fine choice."

"What do you want?"

"You."

Alice buried her face in Jaden's shoulder. No, he didn't just want her. John-Paul wanted Day Three with her.

"You can't have her," Jaden snapped.

"Then I'll have to use Tina until Alice gives me what I want," John-Paul said. "And when I finish with Tina, I'll move on to Kara. She's much easier on the eyes and I'm sure I can train her fairly quickly."

Her eyes flew open. Jaden's gunshot wound, Tina's abduction, Kara's safety threatened was all because of her. She wouldn't let the people she loved pay for her sins. It ended with her.

She'd go to him. If John-Paul wanted her, then he was going to get her. Even if it meant she'd have to die to keep everyone safe. No one else would get hurt because of her.

"Where should I meet you?"

"What the hell are you doing?" Jaden whispered.

"Our place at six thirty," John-Paul said. "You come tonight and I'll free your friend."

"You'll bring her alive?" Alice asked. "She'll be okay?"

"I only want you. As soon as I have you, Tina's free to go."

Alice looked at her watch. She had a little less than an hour to get ready and meet him. "All right. I'll meet you there."

"I can't wait." The lust and excitement in his voice made her skin crawl. "I'll be waiting for you."

Alice stared at the phone for a long time after John-Paul hung up. God, she was actually going to do this. Her stomach twisted in knots as to what waited for her, but she tucked it away. No one else would get hurt because of her.

And her top priorities were to get her friends out of harm's way and keep Jaden safe.

"Where does he want to meet you?" Jaden demanded. "I can get the others here in a few minutes and we can go hunt."

He was livid and ready to kill. But she heard John-Paul say that the Host, whoever he was, knew about Jaden. And the Host controlled the Shadows and he was shot by them. Jaden was lucky he hadn't been killed. She wouldn't take that chance again. She loved Jaden too much for him to die for her.

She stepped to the side, but he moved in front of her. "You need to tell me where I can find this animal so he'll never bother you again."

"No."

"No?" He put his hands on her shoulders. "What the hell are you thinking?"

"Nothing," she said.

"Where does he want you to go?"

"Some place that isn't here."

"Goddamn it, Alice! This isn't a game!"

"I'm not playing one."

"The hell you're not!" he roared. "You're hiding this from me and I can't understand why." He let go of her shoulders. "Not only am I a fighter, I am also a Guardian. My job is to keep you safe and protected. Let me do it and tell me where to find him."

"I'm sorry, but I can't." Alice knelt in front of the bag, pulling out a pair of jeans. "I need to get ready."

He stormed out of the room, slamming the door behind him. She heard him rummaging around in his closet, yanking clothes off the hangers. A few minutes later, his thunderous footsteps echoed down the hallway.

She stared at the door for a long time, tears rolling down her cheeks. She was uncoordinated and sluggish as she removed the robe and drew on her jeans and a blue sweater. Her mind screamed at her to stop but it didn't stop her from putting on her socks and tennis shoes. She looked down at herself. She was ready.

At least physically.

Alice knew what she was walking into. A full twenty-four hours of torture until John-Paul got tired and killed her. She'd spend her last day on earth being brutalized and torn in two instead of safe and warm in Jaden's arms.

She wiped another tear away. In less than a week, she'd fallen in love with Jaden. He repaired the damage to her body and her heart with his touch and his kiss. His determination to protect her only made her love him more.

And that's why she had to do this. She refused to let him get hurt again or killed because of her. She wouldn't sacrifice anyone else to the monsters that haunted her. She'd face them herself. Now she had to figure a way to get out of the house without Jaden following her.

Alice walked out of the bathroom. Each step made her feel like she was shedding her skin. She focused on the floor, but she caught the edge of the duvet. She didn't want to look at the bed where she'd slept with Jaden. Otherwise, she'd just burrow herself under the covers and wait for him to come back to her.

She closed the door to his room, but paused for a moment in front of hers. She stared at the sapphire drapes, the chaise lounge, and the dark blue and ivory bed. He'd made love to her for hours in that bed, worshipping her body with his hands, tongue and mouth. She remembered feeling beautiful and desired in his arms.

She headed toward the stairs, her footsteps light against the hardwood floor. With every stair, a piece of her soul died. She'd leave her heart and happiness here with Jaden. He would need a few pleasant memories after tonight.

For John-Paul? She'd give him nothing. There'd be no tears, no pleading with him to stop. Because the moment she left this house, she was dead. She only hoped there'd be enough of her remains behind for a proper burial and she'd still be recognizable after John-Paul finished with her body.

She stopped at the bottom of the stairs. Jaden was there with reinforcements.

Jaden stood to her right with Varrik right next to him. Helene and Salvatore were on the opposite side. Alice could convince one of them to get her out of there. She only had one shot and she needed to make it count.

Alice looked from one vampire to the other, ignoring Jaden. "So which one of you is giving me a ride tonight?"

"No one since you're not leaving this house," Jaden barked.

"You can't keep me here. I'm not your prisoner."

"And I am not letting you go to him."

Alice sighed. "Do you really think you can stop me?"

"I know I will just as I know you will tell us where he's going."

"If I don't?"

"I'm not the only one who can get information out of people." Jaden nodded to Varrik. "Varrik has some special abilities himself. He can read your thoughts as if you said them out loud as well as project thoughts into your head. If he concentrates hard enough, he can actually see your thoughts and memories. So as soon as you think of where you need to go, he'll tell us."

Alice turned her gaze to Varrik. "I'm thinking of a number

between one and ten. Can you tell me what it is?"

"I don't feel like doing parlor tricks with you," Varrik said.

"Can't read my mind, can you?"

He gave her a droll stare. "Eight."

"Impressive." She narrowed her eyes. "What about now?"

"Thirteen…wait. Twelve…oh, Jaden's getting pissed even though I'm having fun. Although what we did in the tub was much more fun." Varrik grimaced as if in pain. "Jesus, I don't need the image of Jaden naked and getting off in my head. You want me to keep going?"

Fine, she shot to him mentally. *I need your help.*

"Why?" Varrik asked out loud.

Because I need to get out of here. I need to get to John-Paul before Jaden does.

"So do we," he replied. "But you haven't given me a good reason."

"What is she saying?" Jaden demanded.

Varrik ignored Jaden. "Why aren't you telling us what we need to know?"

I don't want Jaden to know where I'm going.

Varrik raised an eyebrow. "Why?"

Alice looked Varrik in the eye. *Because I love him.*

Seriously? She heard his voice in her head. *You never struck me as the type who liked brooding assholes. If you want some real fun, try me. I can really give Jaden a run for his money.*

Alice glared at him. *I'm trying to protect him.*

Self-sacrifice is always the easy way out.

John-Paul said something about the Host knowing Jaden. I can't risk him getting hurt because of me. Or any of you. Do you really want this person to take out one of your race?

Varrik's eyes widened. *You'd sacrifice yourself for him? For us?*

She nodded once. *I'm one person out of millions. Better to let me go to save the lives of others.*

Jaden won't see it that way. You're special to him and to us.

You need him more than you need me, she pleaded. *Make him understand.*

And disobeying a direct order to keep you safe? Varrik asked. *You want me to go against that?*

I'm not the person you're looking for. And if I am, I can save you and my friends at the same time.

He narrowed his eyes. *You have a plan to get out of here?*

Alice let the thoughts loose in her mind, including where she was meeting John-Paul, and what she planned to do when she met him again. Varrik took all of the information, no emotion registering on his face.

When she finished, Varrik studied her for a moment. *You've got a set of balls on you, Alice. I hope you know what you're doing.*

Varrik glanced at Helene whose eyes narrowed. He then turned to Jaden. "I know where she's going."

"Care to tell us?" Jaden asked.

"I will after I do this."

Varrik's fist collided with Jaden's jaw. The blow momentarily stunned Jaden which was all the time Varrik needed to wrap his arms around the other vampire, holding him in place.

"Have you lost your mind?" Salvatore shouted.

Varrik glared at Salvatore, no doubt the two males were communicating silently. Alice saw Salvatore's eyes harden as he came around and helped Varrik restrain Jaden.

"What the fuck are you two doing!" Jaden shouted.

"Keeping you safe," Salvatore said, "although I think this is the worst idea I've ever heard.

Alice grabbed Helene's hand, her eyes on Jaden. He was furious and about to throw the other two vampires off him.

"I need you to get me out of here," Alice whispered.

Jaden looked up and saw Alice holding Helene's hand. "Alice, whatever you're thinking, don't do it."

"I'm so sorry," Alice said. "But I'm not going to let you get killed because of me. Your race needs you. You're worth more alive than I am."

"I'm not going to get killed because of you."

"I know. That's why I'm going to him."

"We can't hold him much longer," Varrik said. He glanced at Alice, his dark eyes softening for a moment. "You should tell him before you go."

"Tell me what? You can't do this!" Jaden fought against the hands clamped on him. "I am her Guardian and I have to protect her at all costs! That's straight from Liam."

"Please don't be mad at them because they're only doing something I asked them to do." Her eyes roamed over his face, her heart squeezing painfully in her chest. "So many others depend on you to keep them safe. Help them, not me."

"Jesus Christ, Alice! You don't know what you're doing!"

"I'm protecting someone I love."

Jaden froze at her words. "You're what?"

"I love you, Jaden Payne." A tear slipped out of the corner of her eye. "Even though you may hate me for this, I want you to know that you are the best thing that ever happened to me. You fixed what was broken and I'm so grateful you were in my life." She smiled sadly. "I just wish you could've been in it longer."

~ * ~

"Alice! No!"

Jaden kept staring at where Alice and Helene just vanished, his mind spinning. Alice loved him. Something as vile and despicable as him had someone beautiful like her loving him.

But she was gone. Completely and totally gone and he had no clue where she was.

Varrik let Jaden go and stood a few feet away from him. "That actually worked better than I thought."

"Where did Helene take her?" Jaden demanded.

"I can't tell you that."

"Don't fuck with me, Varrik! I need to know where she is!"

"Alice doesn't want you to know."

"She doesn't know she's doing!"

"I was inside her head. I know exactly what she's doing."

"I have to get to her. Liam will lose his shit when he finds out what happened here tonight!"

"She's just one human," Varrik said quietly.

He glared at Varrik. "She's not one human to me."

"You love her, don't you?"

Jaden took a deep breath. "Yeah, I love her."

"Then let her go."

"Fuck that!" He grabbed Varrik by the throat and pressed him against the railing. "You don't want to mess with me on this. Tell me where she is and I won't hurt you that much."

Varrik bared his fangs. "I'm not afraid of you."

"You should be. Remember, I can make you relive the worst day of your life."

"You want to rethink that one? We're not sparring here." Jaden caught the flicker of fear in Varrik's eyes before they became hard again. "You know it is death to torture or kill one of us."

"And she is the Firebrand. As Guardian, I'm supposed to kill anyone and anything that gets in the way of protecting her, including you. You know that."

"And she's doing her job by protecting all of us. That is what the Firebrand is supposed to do. Let her go."

"Let me say this slowly so you can understand this." His face was inches from Varrik's. "I. Love. Her. She is worth the risk and worth more than your life."

"You should tell him what she was thinking," Salvatore said.

Varrik glanced at Salvatore. "I doubt it'll make a difference."

"Tell him anyway."

Varrik sighed. "She didn't want you to die because of her."

"Like you give a shit what happens to me," Jaden snarled, the fury flashing in his eyes. "There's something else."

Varrik looked away from him, suddenly uncomfortable. "She said whatever happens to her didn't matter because you have the most valuable part of her. You have her heart."

Every molecule in his body screamed for Alice. The woman was his female, his mate. They may not have completed the mating, but he was hers. She bathed him, taken care of his injuries, said she loved him. All that was left was the communion of their blood and skin.

Now he wouldn't have the chance to be with her because she was making the ultimate sacrifice. Giving up her life for his. There was no way in hell he'd let Alice do this. Living without her was not an option.

"Tell me where she is." Jaden squeezed tighter. "I'm not going to ask you again."

"It doesn't matter."

"Because the Host will already have her?"

"No. She'll already be dead."

"What the fuck are you talking about?"

"I've seen how this all plays out, and it's not the happy ending you're looking for," Varrik said quietly. "She won't let John-Paul do anything to her. Once they free the human, Alice is going to kill herself.

Chapter 23

It took a moment for the dizziness to pass before Alice realized she and Helene had escaped. She was certain Jaden would break free of Salvatore and Varrik, but they managed to hold him back. She'd never seen him so angry before. She could only imagine what he'd do to her and the others when he was freed.

The bitter air stung her cheeks and brought her back to reality. A storm had passed through and the setting sun and storm clouds gave the sky a red-orange glow. A crow perched on top a branch, its mournful call a funeral song for her. Another one answered its mate in the same sorrowful tone.

She looked straight ahead and saw the tiny cabin nestled amongst the trees. A small four room home with a patch of evergreen bushes growing on either side of the steps. A porch swing moved slightly to and fro in the breeze. Such a quiet, unassuming place as were most of the homes in this remote part of the county.

But this was John-Paul and he wanted to finish the game.

This was the house of horrors she remembered. It's where he had his fun with all of his victims. The screams, the pain, the branding of her skin. No one ever came by and the closest neighbor was half a mile away. It was completely secluded from the outside world, giving John-Paul the privacy he needed for his training classes.

She never thought she'd come here again. Yet, here she was. The sacrificial lamb for Jaden and his brethren.

"This place gives me the creeps. And that's saying something," Helene said.

"I know. Hard to imagine something so quaint could be so frightening." Alice turned to her. "Thank you for getting me here. You don't have to stay any longer."

"Are you sure about this? It's not too late. We don't have to go through with this crazy idea." Helene looked around uneasily. "I can get you back to the house and make sure you're protected. The rest of us can take care of John-Paul and the Host."

"You won't have enough time. This is where I need to be," Alice said. "I have to get Tina out of here and make sure Jaden's safe from all of this."

"She's just one human."

"She's someone important to me."

"And Jaden? He's not special enough for you?"

"I'm doing this for him." She glanced back at the cabin. "I'd rather him remember me the way I was an hour ago. I don't want him to know that this place exists or what will happen."

"He's going to avenge your death. You know that, right?"

"There's nothing to avenge. I'm here of my own free will."

"He won't see it that way," Helene argued. "He will come after the Host with a renewed vengeance until the bastard's dead."

"But he'll still be alive and he won't have to worry about protecting me," Alice said. "If he comes here tonight, I have no doubt he'll die."

"So you're going to die in his place?"

"You all need him. Your race needs him."

"He needs you more."

Alice swallowed hard. "He'll find someone else eventually."

"Are you kidding me? It took him almost seven hundred years to find you," Helene pointed out. "You're irreplaceable in his eyes."

Her heart tightened in her chest. Helene was saying all the right things, making it harder for Alice to follow through with her plan. But they were just words, and she wouldn't allow herself to be swayed.

Alice held out her hand. "I need your gun."

"You know your human friend is probably dead. They're just luring you here so you can tell them where Jaden is. That's who they're really after."

"And they won't get him either."

"We can protect the both of you," she repeated.

Alice shook her head. "My mind's made up. Stop trying to convince me to leave."

"No wonder you and Jaden get along so well. You're just as stubborn as he is." Helene put the Beretta in Alice's hand. "All you have to do is release the safety. Once that's done, you pull the trigger."

Alice stared at the gun. So small and capable of so much damage. She never thought this was the way she was going to die. But better to die for someone you loved than for no reason at all.

"You better go. I don't want you to get hurt because of me." She shoved the gun in the waistband of her jeans and took a step towards the house. "Thanks for getting me here, Helene."

Alice only walked a few feet before Helene voice cut

through the night. "It's you."

"What?"

"Jaden's weakness. It's you."

Alice turned her head. "You're wrong. Jaden has no weaknesses."

"Am I?" Helene moved in front of her. "He's willing to lay his life down for you. For a human he met a few days ago. You don't do that for someone you have a passing fling with."

"He was only protecting me."

"You don't have sex with the one you're protecting. A Guardian would never touch his charge."

"He didn't know that I was the one in the prophecy which still makes no sense to me."

"That didn't stop him, did it? He couldn't stay away from you." Helene chuckled humorlessly. "Face it, Alice. You're the one for him."

"Why are you telling me this now? Is it because I won't live to tell about it?"

"You're dying for him. I just think you should know that your love isn't one-sided. Jaden loves you too, Alice." Helene shook her head. "Did you not see the way he acted tonight? I've known him all my life and in that time, he's never reacted that way to anyone. Hell, he even said 'please' to you the first night we met. That is the one and only time I've ever heard that word come out of his mouth."

"But he's never said he loves me."

"He doesn't have to say it. It's obvious to me and everyone else. His whole face changes when he's around you, or even when he thinks of you. You've made him a better male and you're the only one who's done that in hundreds of years." Helene looked around once more. "Are you sure you don't want to get out of here? I can take you back to him."

That would be the smart thing to do. Run like hell away from this place and straight into Jaden's arms. But John-Paul would always be waiting for her, stalking her until he claimed her once again.

No one else would get hurt because of her.

"I'm sure," Alice whispered.

"Good luck to you."

Helene's face was grim as she disappeared. Alice stared at the spot for a few minutes, ignoring the cold, November wind. She was now alone.

Alice turned back to the house. She wanted to run. She wanted to bolt from this place and never look back. She had to do this for her friends. For Jaden.

Her feet carried her up the six wooden steps to the front door. Although she didn't remember it, these had to be the same ones she ran down two years ago. When she awoke from the branding and wore nothing but the collar around her neck, she ran through the woods to the neighbor's house. Alice had been too stunned to do anything while the woman called the police. It was after the woman draped a blanket across her shoulders that she was still naked and bleeding.

A lump rose up her throat when she paused in front of the door. The wind shook the pine branches, the evergreen limbs voicing the wails within her soul. She saw the two crows sitting grimly, the silent witnesses to this private battle.

She turned the knob, not surprised to find it unlocked. If John-Paul wasn't inside, he'd soon be here.

A blast of cold air hit her as she walked across the threshold. The police left everything in its place. The ratty brown and orange upholstered sofa ran along the length of one wall, the recliner in front of an antiquated television with the floor lamp near the coffee table.

The bedroom door was open. She didn't go in, but from where she stood, she saw everything. A candle flickered in the room, creating an illusion of romance.

"This is our special place, Alice. Cry, scream and beg all you want. It'll make my memories all the sweeter."

The police took the bed and the restraints when they arrested John-Paul. It was cataloged as evidence in his trial. But there was a new mattress, a new set of chains hanging from the bedposts. And a new dog collar.

It was as if time stood still. Nothing had changed.

She patted her stomach, the cool steel of the gun pressing into her skin. John-Paul wouldn't touch or break her again. She'd kill herself before he even had the chance.

"You're still as beautiful as ever."

Fear shot through her at that smooth voice from her nightmares. But she used her terror to steel her spine. She'd give him no power, no satisfaction with her body.

Alice slowly turned around. John-Paul Finch stood in the living room, ten feet of air separating them. Two other men – Shadows – stood to the left of him. They watched her carefully as they kept their distance.

Tina was nowhere in sight.

Dread turned her stomach to lead. "Where's Tina?"

"We'll get to her later."

"We'll get to her now."

"God, you haven't changed." John-Paul's eyes ran over her body. "I've missed you so much. There were so many nights I dreamed of you. My hand was the only thing I could use to relieve myself when I was hard."

God, he truly made her sick. "You said if I came to you, you'd free Tina," she said through her teeth.

"And that was my intention, but Tina had an unfortunate

accident on the way over here. Vampires. What can you do?" John-Paul grinned. "They drank her like she was a cherry slushie."

Tears stung her eyes. Her vivacious, beautiful friend dead for the sole reason they knew her. Everyone she ever loved was hurt because of her.

But she wouldn't fail Jaden. Her death would keep him safe.

"She did a lot of screaming for you," he added. "Why you abandoned her and left her to die."

Alice clenched her hands into fists and nodded to the Shadows. "I see you brought friends. Tag teaming this time?"

"It's soon just going to be us once you tell us where your current boy toy is."

"He's not here," Alice said flatly.

"We can see that," one of the Shadows snapped. "Care to tell us where he is?"

"He's not with me. And since I don't have him fitted with a GPS chip, I couldn't tell you where he is."

"Still defiant as ever." John-Paul grinned as he reached for her. "I can see I need to retrain you."

A hand clamped down on John-Paul's arm, pulling him back. "You're not supposed to touch her."

"You better move your hand before I do it for you." John-Paul glared at the Shadow. "Come on, Markus. I fulfilled my part of the bargain."

"You don't get her until the Host gets Jaden."

"Well, tell the parasite to hold his breath because Jaden's not coming," Alice said.

The Shadow named Markus turned his angry gaze to her. "Don't you dare show any disrespect to the Host, human."

"Like I care what that tick thinks of me. Really, can't he think of a better name than 'The Host'? It makes him sound like he should belong on some cheesy game show. Or at least carry around a banner with a leech on it."

"You have courage," a voice floated from the doorway. "No wonder Jaden's so enamored with you."

Alice turned her head as the three men looked at the figure respectfully. The Host walked into the room watching Alice. No wonder the vampire could control the Shadows so easily.

The Host was a woman.

Alice took in the slender female. A warning bell went off in her head as she stared at the Host. She looked vaguely familiar. Her blonde hair was pulled into a braid that fell to the small of her back, her calculating eyes raking Alice from head to toe.

She could tell the Host had once been a beautiful woman, but scars ran down the right side of her face, uneven rough patches puckering the once smooth skin. Spider web-like scars radiated from the right side of her face down her throat. Both hands contained the same pattern.

But those eyes were what bothered Alice. A dark, cherry amber gaze which took in every movement. They took Alice in calmly, but burned brightly, as if her presence infuriated the Host.

Those same eyes glaring at her from a picture frame.

Alice's eyes popped wide open as the truth slammed into her. No wonder the Host knew all about Jaden and the other warriors. She'd been married to one.

She now knew where she'd seen this woman before. In the portrait over the fireplace in Jaden's home. Alice knew the woman in the picture and in the flesh were one in the same.

"Catherine," she whispered.

The Host flinched as if she'd been slapped. "What did you call me?"

"You're Catherine Payne. Jaden's wife."

"Don't you ever link my name with that bastard again," Catherine hissed. "He is not my husband and I am certainly not his wife."

Alice's head was spinning. Jaden's wife was alive. How was that possible?

"I thought you were dead," Alice said. "Jaden said he killed you."

"Oh, he certainly tried. He almost succeeded. Twice," Catherine said. "Just because I was too weak to manipulate his mind didn't mean I was dead."

"He left you exposed to the sun. I can't believe you survived that."

"Where do you think the scars came from?" Catherine sneered. "Do you know how painful it is to have your blood turn into acid? Not to mention the fun task of slicing open your veins so you can let it run out of you." She touched her face. "And these never healed. My other wounds closed up and disappeared, but God chose to leave these scars, to show others the monster I never wanted to become." The cool mask disappeared and her face twisted into one of pure malice. "I hate Jaden. I should've killed him when I had the chance."

"But he loved you so much."

"Infatuated with me was more like it," she scoffed.

"Did you ever love him?" Alice asked.

"Can't say I did. I certainly loved his status and wealth. And he was one of the most incredible lovers I ever had. But love him as a wife loves her husband?" Catherine curled her lip in disgust. "He's a stain on this Earth that needs to be snuffed out. A genetic mutation that took me away from my family and made me an abomination like him. How could I ever love such a thing?"

"He didn't want to live his life without you."

"But I could've lived my life without him. I've done that ever since he changed me."

"You tortured him," Alice retorted. "You made him bleed."

"Which time?" Catherine's mouth curved into a cold smile. "I had him for four days. There's a lot you can accomplish when you're angry enough. And he loved me enough to let me break his body many times."

Alice trembled in fury. Her beautiful warrior ravaged by the woman he once loved. No wonder Jaden couldn't trust her or anyone else with his heart. How could anyone recover from such a wound?

John-Paul and Catherine were perfectly suited for each other. They both were monsters.

"Love makes you weak. Hate makes you strong," Catherine said. "It's what healed me and gave me my life's purpose. I may be damned, but I will make sure to use that time to wipe out the entire Emain Macha clan and begin anew."

"You bitch."

The smile vanished. "You'd better think twice before you address me so rudely."

"Or what?"

"You'll know not to cross me again. John-Paul will be the least of your problems."

Alice chuckled, the hollow sound echoing in her ears. "Threats are for people who have something to live for. Me? I'm already dead."

"Really?" Catherine moved towards her. "Why is that?"

"I have nothing to live for."

"Not even Jaden?"

Alice glared at the woman. "I'd rather bleed for him than let you have him."

"I'd love to see a dead woman bleed," Catherine smiled

pleasantly. "Let's see how what we can get out of you."

She was about to tell Catherine to shove it when an odd sensation thrummed in her body. Like someone was trying to push her from the inside out. Alice frowned as the strange vibration traveled to her head. She felt some pressure as invisible fingers pressed against her skull.

She looked at John-Paul. Her left leg wobbled as if someone was pulling her leg forward.

Walk to John-Paul.

Hell, no. That was the last thing she wanted to do.

Walk. To. Him.

A dull throb pulsated behind her eyes. She didn't want to that, but the command was hard to ignore. It was insistent, angry, and demanding. Her body lurched forward but she caught herself before she took another step. Alice wouldn't willingly move towards that bastard. Why was she doing it now?

Because Catherine was using her power on Alice.

Alice pushed back, forcing herself to remain in control, even though it gave her a headache. She knew she couldn't win against Catherine, but she could make it hard for the bitch.

"You're a tough one," Catherine said. "Humans usually break quite easily with me. I'll have so much fun with you."

"Excuse me?"

Catherine glanced at John-Paul. "Don't worry. I'll make sure there's enough of her left over."

"This is not part of the deal," John-Paul snapped. "You promised her to me."

"Watch your tone with me, Shadow," Catherine said in a low voice. "I only said you could have her when you delivered Jaden to us." She gestured around the cabin. "Do you see a six foot four, two hundred and sixty pound male demon in here? I sure don't. So that means you failed. Miserably."

John-Paul narrowed his eyes. "I can't control what this bitch does. I couldn't know that she didn't tell the asshole she's fucking where we are. I want to know when I can get my hands on her."

"You touch her and you'll be missing more than your hands."

Alice jerked her head towards the door. Jaden's massive body took up most of the doorway, the rage blazing in his eyes. He palmed his daggers, ready to deliver death blows to anyone who got in his way.

Her heart leaped in her chest. She didn't want him to find her here, but a part of her couldn't help but be glad he found her.

Catherine smiled at Alice. She heard the Host's voice in her head, a soft whisper at first then an insistent command. Alice pressed her fingertips to her temples as sharp pains pierced her head. She knew the pain would only get worse, because she wouldn't follow through with Catherine's command.

You know how to stop the pain, Catherine whispered in Alice's mind. *End your suffering and do what I say.*

No, she couldn't do it. She wouldn't give in to the Host. But it hurt and she didn't know how much longer she could stand the pain. She had to resist the command.

Do it, Alice. Kill him. Kill Jaden.

Chapter 24

Jaden thought he had seen it all. There wasn't much that could surprise him, but seeing his dead wife standing over his true mate shocked him to no end.

Catherine was the Host. The fucking Host. How the hell did she survive?

The initial part of his plan, beating the shit out of Varrik started out pretty well. While Varrik bled all over the hardwood floors, Jaden followed through on his promise and made the vampire relive the worst day of his life. Varrik screamed on the floor, trapped in the past and in the pain at the loss of his family.

Jaden then turned on Helene to get him here. No one dared to argue with him after what he did Varrik. The fury terrified her and Jaden vowed to kill them if they tried to stop him.

He didn't know how much time he had before Helene came back with reinforcements, but he needed to get to Alice. So if that made him the biggest moron on the planet by going in with no backup, then it was fine with him.

The two women he ever loved stared at him, but there was only one he wanted. There was no competition. He didn't know how Catherine survived, but he was going to make sure the bitch didn't rise from the dead again.

Catherine clasped her hands together in mock delight. "Oh, dearest husband! How fare thee these last few centuries?"

"I fared very well. Not seeing your face every day has made life so much easier."

"Ouch! That hurts," Catherine pouted. She glanced at Alice. "But I see you've found a new way to occupy your time."

Jaden's gaze flickered to Alice. Thank God she was still alive and unharmed. "I can't believe you're the one we've been searching for all these years."

"I'm just the most recent one you're looking for. There are several of us. The question is can you find us all?"

"I killed you once. I'll do it again."

"Actually, you killed me twice. But really, who's counting?"

"Hard to rise again if your head's detached from your body. But enough with the chit chat," Jaden said. "So why are you here? Is it just to piss me off?"

"That's just a bonus. I want you to hurt."

"You're doing a great job. I hurt just by looking at you."

"But not enough. I thought killing your parents would destroy you, knowing how close you all were." Catherine shook her head. "That one backfired on me. It just angered you more."

Jaden's knuckles turned white from gripping the dagger so hard. "You sent the Shadows to kill my family?"

"And let me tell you how pleased I was with them. I was able to successfully send them out and kill the last Master of your race." Catherine clapped her hands with glee. "A novice demon taking down one of the biggest vampires of all! How great is that?"

His mind struggled to come to terms with this knowledge. Catherine sent the execution order on his family. His parents and Ezra suffered because of Jaden's mistake of letting this bitch into his life. But he wouldn't let Alice suffer. He may not have saved his family, but he had a chance to save her.

"I may have killed many creatures, but I never once killed a child. Only an evil, heartless bitch could do that."

"You made me that way." Her dark amber eyes sparkled with malice. "Didn't expect that one, huh? Just as your human won't expect this."

Alice cried out and clamped her hands on the side of her head. Even though he wasn't touching her, he felt the pain coursing through her body from the bond that started to form when she bathed him. She was resisting whatever Catherine was commanding.

Jaden lunged at Catherine, but two Shadows tackled him from behind. He let his anger loose, letting these pricks know who the more powerful creature. He took them down easily. His dagger hit home as it went all the way to the hilt in the Shadow's chest. He wrapped his hands around the face of the other one, the snapping of the neck bones echoing in the cabin.

Jaden crouched, ready to strike when he saw Alice in one of the Shadow's arms. Tears rolled down her eyes as she gasped for breath. She was in so much pain from resisting Catherine's request, but it wouldn't be long before she succumbed.

"Let her go. This is between us," Jaden barked.

"You made it about her once you helped her outside that club." Catherine turned to John-Paul. "Wait for Alice in the bedroom. I'll send her to you when we're done."

John-Paul looked as if he was going to argue, but his face changed underneath Catherine's cold eyes. He dutifully went into the bedroom and shut the door.

Jaden was going to enjoy killing that bastard. But his first priority was getting Alice out of here alive.

His heart clenched in his chest. God, Alice was in agony. Her dark hair clung to her forehead, her teeth clenched so tightly he was surprised they didn't shatter.

"Leave me," Alice ground out. "Get out of here."

"Not without you," he said.

"No, Jaden." She moaned as another wave of pain slammed into her. "Won't let…you get hurt…because of me."

Blood trickled out of Alice's nose, the scent of cinnamon flooding the air. Her brain was shutting down. The same thing happened to him when he resisted Catherine. The pain was unbearable, but at least he was able to heal because of his vampire blood. Alice was still human and wouldn't survive.

The fucking prophecy was coming true. He was watching the woman he loved die right before his eyes. He had to stop it. But how?

"Mistress? Something is wrong with the female," the Shadow said.

All eyes focused on Alice. Her skin flared, that red iridescent glow radiating off her body. She slumped against the Shadow as a white blast came out of her body.

Jaden turned his head away, his eyes seared by the light. Once they adjusted, he turned back to Alice. Her skin glowed, a pulsating wave of energy sizzling around her. Her green eyes were electric and focused on the floor.

Jaden followed her gaze. The Shadow who held her was gone. A pile of ash was all that was left behind. But there was still a body on the floor. It was Alice's.

The other Shadow in the room backed away from the glowing apparition. She fixated her eerie stare on to Catherine as she held Alice's body in her arms. Those sizzling green eyes turned to Jaden. They softened in recognition as her gaze met his.

"Jaden. I need your help."

He was mesmerized. They all were. A live Firebrand in front of them and she was still human. To separate from her body like that was unheard of. How powerful was she?

"With what?" he whispered.

Those ghostly arms wrapped tighter around Alice's body. "I'm not strong enough."

"Strong enough for what?"

"To survive. I won't last much longer like this," she said. "Don't let me go. Don't let me die here."

The figure exploded in a flash of light and Alice opened her eyes. She curled on her side, one hand at her temple.

"Jaden, you naughty boy. Why didn't you tell me she was the Firebrand?"

"It must have slipped my mind."

Catherine eyed Alice with a renewed respect. "She's a destroyer. Whoever has her has the ultimate power. She can obliterate the human race if we get her first." Her eyes flickered to Jaden. "But if the Emain Macha gets her, you will use her against us. So I either take her or kill her."

Jaden shifted, ready to take the bitch down. "Hate to break it to you, but I don't see that happening. It'll be a cold day in hell when you get your hands on her."

"Then in the meantime, I'll clean house." Catherine wrinkled her nose. "This human loves you so much, it's sickening. Why she does is beyond me."

"Loving someone other than your own spoiled ass must be an alien concept for you. Don't think too hard. I'd hate for your brain to explode." He raised his eyebrows. "Actually, I take that back. Think all you want. I'll even clean up the mess."

"My head won't be the mess you'll clean up," she giggled. "In a few minutes, her brain will be splattered all over the carpet."

Alice screamed and writhed in agony, desperate to escape the pain. Jaden knew she wouldn't last much longer. And when Alice died, his heart would die as well.

How could he save them both?

"You know why she's hurting like this? Because she won't kill you." She pointed at Alice's waist. "She has a gun. I noticed it when I first walked in the door. I merely suggested that she shoot you, but she keeps ignoring me. It takes a lot of strength to resist that command."

Jaden glanced at both women. He had a clear shot of Catherine. He could kill her and the world would be rid of one less Host. But she'd anticipate his attack and kill Alice before he took her down.

His training told him what needed to be done. Let the human die to save the lives of many. One death to prevent thousands of others.

But was Alice's life worth sacrificing even if she belonged to the Host?

He knew what he had to do.

He unholstered his gun and slid it across the floor to Alice. "You are not going to die because of me."

"Oh, this is good," Catherine murmured. She nodded toward the Shadow. "Check on the others, Markus. Make sure they are ready to go at my command."

Jaden ignored the Shadow as he left the room. Jaden didn't give a rat's ass where that fucker went because what he wanted was still in the room.

Alice knelt on the floor, her palm resting near the gun. She looked up at him, her eyes swimming with tears. "I won't kill you."

"And I will not let you die because of me," he said softly.

"I…I can't do it."

"Yes, you can." Jaden opened his arms, spreading his chest for her. "All you have to do is pick it up and pull the trigger."

Tears poured out of her eyes, her hand trembling as she palmed the cool steel. She grimaced and moved her hands to the sides of her head, her body trembling.

His tone was desperate as her breaths became labored, her eyes glazing over. "Alice, I can't let you die. My life for yours. You don't deserve to die because you got mixed up in my world."

Her knuckles turned white as she pressed her hands tighter against her skull. "No…life…without…you."

Alice wasn't going to do it. She'd resist until Catherine killed her.

Jaden looked at Catherine. "You want me dead?"

"More than anything," she said.

There was only one option left. He looked at the dagger in his hand. Fine. If Alice wouldn't kill him, he'd kill himself.

Before he could raise his knife to his throat, Jaden felt the hairs on the back of his neck stand up. At the same time, Catherine looked out the window. The Shadow named Markus burst into the room, his brown eyes wild in panic.

"We have to go now."

"Where are the others?" she demanded.

"Dead," Markus said. "The last ones standing will be dead soon. I need to get you out of here."

Jaden smiled. Backup had arrived. He counted Salvatore, Helene and Ryder among the Shadows. Varrik was not with them. No doubt recuperating from the wounds he received because of Jaden.

Catherine swore at the timing. It was either she stay and die or escape to fight another day. She looked at Alice and Jaden again before she stepped over to the Shadow, placing her hand in his.

"I want her dead," Catherine hissed.

"I doubt she'll survive. Look at what you did to her." The Shadow nodded toward the bedroom. "What about John-Paul?"

"He is of no use to us anymore and he'll help us get away." Catherine turned her hateful eyes to Jaden. "The warriors' time is over. I will enjoy killing all of you."

"And I swear to hunt you down," Jaden promised. "And I will take great pleasure in burning your body before the sun does."

When Catherine had successfully escaped, Alice cried out and fell to the floor, finally released from the mind spell. Jaden rushed forward and cradled her in his arms.

Her body contorted in his arms, her eyes rolling into the back of her head. She was seizing, her heart beating erratically in her chest. Jesus, this was worse than anything he ever felt. The pain seeped into his skin, and he absorbed it all without complaint. Anything to take away her agony.

The seizures soon stopped and she let out a long breath. Blind panic seized him as he held Alice's limp body. Her heart rate slowed, her chest rising slowly with each shallow breath. He brushed away her damp hair, the swirling tattoo flexing at his wrist.

His blood could save her. This wasn't the way he wanted to finish the bonding ceremony, but he needed her in his life. He wouldn't spend one second of it without her. All he had to do was bite himself and bring his blood to her lips. She'd live, be his partner for eternity.

But would she hate him? Alice said she loved him, but he wasn't giving her a choice. Just as he never gave Catherine a choice. In the end, he was a selfish bastard. He wouldn't let her go.

"I'm going to make it all better," he whispered. "Trust me.

He only prayed she didn't hate him for this.

Before he had a chance to score his wrist, Helene, Salvatore, and Ryder burst into the cabin.

Helene approached cautiously. "She's not dead, is she?"

"No, and she's not going to die," he said, bringing his wrist to his mouth.

Salvatore clamped his hand on top of Jaden's. "Don't. Not like this."

"Don't fuck with me right now." Jaden bared his fangs. "You saw what I did Varrik. You want to end up like him?"

"If you're going to mate with her, then do it the right way. Not on the floor of some dirty cabin." Salvatore motioned for the male to come forward. "Heal her."

Ryder Wells stepped forward and placed his hand on Alice's brow. He grimaced from the contact. "Jesus. The Host really worked her over."

Fear stabbed Jaden's gut. "You can heal her, right?"

"I don't know. The damage is pretty severe," Ryder said. "It might be better to let her die. You know I can only do so much. I can make it quick and painless."

"Dying is not an option." Jaden came face to face with Ryder. "You hurt her in any way and I will come after you."

Ryder narrowed his gray eyes. "You can't attack us. Not without consequences."

"You don't want to see what he did to Varrik," Helene muttered. "Don't mess with him when it comes to this female."

"I'm not crazy enough to get between a mate and his female." Ryder nodded to Jaden. "I will do my best to heal her."

"Helene, take them to my house now."

"Varrik's still there," she said.

"He's not getting up any time soon. And on the chance he's actually moving around after the hurt I put him in, remind him it'll be ten times worse when I get back."

Jaden touched Alice's cheek. God, she was so cold. Where was that warmth, the fire that made him burn? She couldn't die like this. She couldn't leave him behind.

"Alice, listen to me. I need you to stay with me. I need you to fight a little longer so you can hear how I feel about you." He kissed her forehead and looked at Ryder helplessly. "Please don't let her die."

"I'll treat her like she's one of us," Ryder said, cradling Alice's body against his. "I'll do what I can to make her whole."

Helene held on to Ryder and Alice and disappeared.

She's going to be okay, Jaden told himself. *She's too damn stubborn die. She'll be all right.*

He stood and looked around the cabin. This was where Alice lost so much of herself to that animal in the other room. He was certain she never wanted him to know of this place. Why else would she keep it a secret from him? Yet she willingly came back here to keep him safe.

He caught John-Paul's irritation and fear from the other room. Jaden wanted him to be afraid. Because he couldn't wait to get his hands on the bastard.

Salvatore looked around the room. "So what do you want to do here?"

"I want this hellhole burned to the ground. I don't want anything left but scorched earth."

"And what about its current tenant?"

They both heard glass shatter in the bedroom. John-Paul was trying to escape? Yeah, like the fucker was going to get far.

"You want some help?" Salvatore asked.

Jaden laughed darkly. "No, this one's all mine."

He ran from the room and jumped out of the shattered window, grabbing the collar and chains on the way out. He caught John-Paul heading for the woods and tackled his prey about thirty feet from the house. He might have let Catherine go, but there was no way he was going to let this cocksucker hurt Alice again.

"Now where do you think you're going?" Jaden whispered in his ear. "We have some unfinished business."

He pulled John-Paul to his feet and slammed him against an oak tree. He was going to make this Shadow bleed and love every minute of it.

Jaden grinned, baring his fangs. "Not so tough without your friends, are you?"

"Like you scare me," John-Paul scoffed. "They'll come back for me."

"Keep dreaming, dickhead. If Catherine wanted to save you, she'd have taken you with her."

Jaden quickly disarmed himself, tossing his weapons and the chains and dog collar on top of his coat. The blades, gun and throwing stars kept him at a distance. And this fight was very personal.

He stepped back and let John-Paul gain his footing. It wouldn't be fair if he just beat the shit out of him. He wanted to let John-Paul try to get in a few hits before Jaden took him down.

John-Paul attacked. As a Shadow, he had quite a bit of power and speed, but only a fraction of Jaden's strength. Plus, Jaden had his rage over Catherine's escape and Alice's torture to fuel this fight.

Jaden blocked all of John-Paul's punches, even though the bastard was fighting hard. Jaden's fist landed squarely on the Shadow's cheek, the force shattering the jaw. Blood spurted from the wound, as the flesh sagged inward from the crushed bones.

He howled as he lunged for Jaden again. Jaden seized John-Paul's arm, twisting at an awkward angle until it broke. The screams, the cracking of bones was a soothing balm to Jaden's fury. He kneed John-Paul in the ribs and the Shadow went down.

"This is all I'm going to get from you? I'm actually a little disappointed." Jaden knelt beside the Shadow and grabbed a chunk of his hair. "It's amazing you survived in prison."

"Let me go, and you'll see what I've got."

Jaden obliged. Far be it from him to deny a Shadow its last request. If the bastard wanted to keep bleeding, then Jaden would keep punching.

John-Paul pulled out a knife. Jaden didn't even bother reaching for his. With a broken arm and busted cheek, the Shadow wouldn't last long.

Jaden easily sidestepped the blows and grabbed John-Paul's wrist, twisting it until he dropped the knife. He elbowed the Shadow in between the shoulder blades and John-Paul kissed the ground. Jaden flicked his wrist and the knife embedded itself in the tree.

Jaden grabbed the dog collar and chains from his coat. John-Paul tried to get up, but a heavy black boot forced him to the ground. With his foot pinning the Shadow, Jaden snapped the collar around John-Paul's neck. He linked the chains around each of the wrists and hooked the chain into the round peg at the back of collar. He yanked on it, bringing the head and upper torso off the ground.

"Glad to see all of your weight training classes in prison really worked out," Jaden said. "With your nonexistent skills, you must've been somebody's bitch."

"Like anyone messed with me in prison," John-Paul chuckled. "But speaking of bitches, how was Alice? Was she any good? Did you have as much fun with her as I did?"

"A gentleman doesn't kiss and tell."

He looked up and grinned. "That was a sweet one right there. I bet she is. I loved her on all fours, ass in the air, just begging for me."

Jaden grabbed the back of John-Paul's head, his rage flowing directly into the Shadow. He didn't hold back. He wanted this son of a bitch to feel the full force of his power. John-Paul's grin disappeared as his mouth opened in a silent scream. His body spasmed, the tremors so hard his teeth chattered.

"I'm sorry. I didn't hear that last part. Could you repeat it for me?" He leaned in next to John-Paul's mouth. All Jaden heard was grunts of pain. "No? I guess you decided to shut the fuck up. Smart move."

"You really think killing me will help her?" John-Paul gasped.

"I know it will. And it'll make me feel a lot better."

"You can't kill me."

"You think those leaks from your face are watering the lawn? I've been told that if it bleeds, it can die." Jaden chuckled. "I'm so going to enjoy watching you die."

"I own a piece of her!" John-Paul shouted. "Whenever Alice looks in the mirror and sees the scars, she'll always think of me. When you two are fucking, she'll remember me and everything I did to her. I am with her forever."

"In a few months, you won't even be a memory."

"Keep telling yourself that. It may help you sleep at night."

"Speaking of sleep, it's time for me to put you to bed. Nighty night, asshole."

Jaden wrapped his hands around John-Paul's face and twisted his head until it faced the opposite direction. He let go of John-Paul and stared into his glassy eyes, almost daring the fucker to get up.

He reattached all of his holsters and dragged the body towards the house. Jaden barged through the door and saw Salvatore standing next to the sofa, picking dirt from underneath his nails. He carelessly yanked John-Paul into the room, a trail of blood and dirt staining the wooden floors.

"I wondered when you'd stop playing with him," Salvatore said dryly.

"I wish I had days with him." Jaden scowled at the corpse as blood trickled out of his nose and mouth. "It was too quick."

"It won't take me long to burn this place." Salvatore tugged on Jaden's arm. "I know you want to get home to Alice."

His anger immediately vanished and was replaced with anxiety. Did Ryder heal her? Or was the damage too much?

Those thoughts were with Jaden as they walked out of the house. Salvatore took a deep breath and closed his eyes. The wind, once a soft whisper in the trees, snarled in the night. It pushed against the wall, angry at the foundation for holding strong.

A rumble of thunder sounded in the distance. Out of nowhere, two lightning bolts fell from the clear sky on to the cabin. Salvatore opened his eyes. No longer hazel, his eyes glowed silver as the flames raced to the attic.

They quickly spread throughout the house, incinerating any

and everything in its path. The sickly smell of burning flesh filled the night air. Good. The flames had found something even better to feed upon. Jaden smiled and hoped the bastard was already roasting in hell.

More bolts fell from the sky, the house desperately trying to withstand the assault. But the small space was no match for the fire's fury or Salvatore's determination. It fell like a house of cards, the beams quickly turning into a pile of ash.

"Almost finished," Salvatore ground out.

The wind whipped around them, a massive gale which picked up the ash, bits of bone, and metal and spread it throughout the woods. The only thing left where the house once stood was an uneven patch of burnt grass. Never again would a woman be subjected to John-Paul's sick games. The cops would come and check to see if they could find clues to his whereabouts, but there were none.

Jaden frowned. He thought the cops would've already had this place under surveillance.

"Did you come across any police officers out here?"

"There's a car with three bodies. Two of them were cops and one of them was a human female."

Jaden nodded. Alice's friend was good as dead when the Shadows first put their hands on her.

"Thank you for destroying this place."

"I've got your Corvette just down the road because someone needed to drive here." They ran to where the car was parked. Jaden grabbed the keys out of Salvatore's hand and the engine roared to life. He punched the accelerator, speeding down the pitch black roads. As the pavement passed underneath them, Jaden prayed he would be returning to her arms and not preparing for the funeral rites of a warrior's fallen mate.

She had to live through this. He promised to not let her go and he would keep that promise.

He thought of his parents, their arms around each other as death finally took them. The ache in his chest when he found them was nothing compared to the hole in his heart right now. This must be what his father felt as he tried to protect his mate. A life without his love was no life at all.

Jaden tightened his grip on the wheel. He'd do whatever was in his power to make sure Alice lived. If she died, then he would expose himself at dawn's first light. The physical pain wouldn't matter. Because the pain in his heart would kill him.

Chapter 25

Catherine stood in front of the fire, her mind a million miles away. Tonight was a failure and a massive one at that. Not only was she unsuccessful in her attempts to kill Jaden, but she allowed Alice Roarke to slip through her fingers as well.

Who would've thought the human female was the Firebrand? She was a destroyer, a harbinger of death and the one being that could restore her damned race to its former glory.

But Jaden had the Firebrand and there was no way in hell the warrior would give her up. Especially since he loved her.

Catherine curled her hands into fists. She was still paying the ultimate price for Jaden's "love." All because she spread her legs to let him have what he wanted and what she thought she needed.

He never watched his family grow old and leave him behind. Never saw his parents cry over the loss of their child, praying that her soul made it to heaven. She had to watch it all. Parents, brothers, nieces, nephews. Everyone she loved died and turned to dust. Alone in an ever-changing world.

And that's why she killed Jaden's family. She wanted him to suffer and know he was alone in the world. But then he dedicated his life to protecting those weaker than himself.

Civilians. Humans.

Alice was only weak because she wasn't in a vampire form, but Catherine knew this Firebrand was stronger than the other two she had encountered. The woman changed forms while she was still human. The others Catherine met were both males and already vampires. Neither of them had the power Alice had.

All Alice had to do was blink and an entire city block would be wiped out. She was the ultimate tool of destruction. One Catherine needed.

But how was she going to get to Alice now? The warriors were going to guard her tighter than codes to a nuclear warhead. They would all lay down their lives to keep her safe so she couldn't attack her enemy from the front.

But all other angles were open.

"Mistress?"

Catherine snapped her head around. "What did I tell you about disturbing me?"

"I'm sorry, but there's someone here to see you."

Catherine scowled at Markus. She drew on her power, ready to use it on him. "I don't care who it is. I'm not receiving anyone tonight."

"But it's him."

"Him who?"

I'm only giving you two minutes to invite me in, Catherine. Then if you still say no, I'll blow the goddamn doors off their hinges.

Catherine froze in place. She hoped she had at least until the next evening to report what happened. But for him to be here tonight meant he knew about what happened and was pissed off.

As soon as Catherine discovered what Alice Roarke was, she should've taken the woman and brought her back here.

Her vengeance for Jaden had clouded her judgment. Now she'd have to pay the price for her failure.

She looked at Markus. He certainly looked worried in front of her, but she could tell that he was a little satisfied at the situation. She didn't trust the Shadow and although he obeyed her, she knew he had his own agenda. She'd have to keep a closer eye on him so he wouldn't bury a blade in her back.

She straightened, her amber eyes hard as steel. Showing fear to her guest was like throwing a bloody steak at a lion. He'd relish her terror, make her pain much worse.

"Tell him I'm more than happy to see him tonight." She nodded to Markus. "Send him in."

Markus left and she gathered her thoughts. Yes, she failed. She hoped he wouldn't kill her. She'd beg for her life, promise to do better and accept whatever consequences he dealt. No matter how much it hurt.

No matter how much she'd bleed.

Chapter 26

Alice wasn't in heaven. She was sure of it since heaven couldn't hurt so much.

She didn't know how long she'd been unconscious, but it had been silent. Peaceful. She knew her death would save Jaden. Leaving him behind broke her heart, but she knew it was for the best. So many others would be saved because of him and that's what mattered to her.

But something prevented Alice from falling into the darkness. Gentle fingers stroked her skin, but the contact made her want to scream. Her head felt as if someone had pounded nails into her skull. She wished she could escape that touch; however, her body lay limp on the bed. And as those fingers caressed her face again, a fresh wave of pain coursed through her, like they were pulling those nails out.

She just wanted to go back to sleep. To go someplace where the pain didn't exist. Where she could sit on a cloud with a gold halo above her head and play the harp.

Where were the white lights, St. Peter and the pearly gates?

Alice tried to lift her hand, but it weighed a thousand pounds. She tried to open her mouth, but it was glued shut.

What was happening to her?

John-Paul, she thought. *He did this to me.*

He had her. Alice passed out from the pain after Catherine had released her mental hold. And he somehow killed Jaden and now had her. He was going to make her go through Day Three.

She whimpered as those fingers caressed her cheek. The gentleness terrified her. Because the pain would be more horrific.

Voices started coming to her through the black fog.

"She's upset," an unfamiliar voice murmured.

"You'd be upset too if you were attacked by an obsessed rapist and murderer. Not to mention the person you love asked you to shoot them." A hand clasped hers. "Alice, this is Helene. You're in your room at Jaden's house. You're going to be just fine."

Even in the hazy state of sleep and suffering, she had a hard time wrapping her mind around that fact. She was alive. They somehow got her out of there and someplace safe. But where was Jaden?

Alice tried to open her eyes, but they remained shut. Did nothing work on her body?

"Alice, don't struggle," Helene said. "You'll heal quicker."

She'd heal a lot faster knowing Jaden was alive. She had to open her eyes. She had to see Jaden for herself.

"Why does she keep moving?" the strange voice asked, the irritation in his tone cutting through the pain.

"She wants Jaden."

At least Helene was smart enough to figure out what Alice couldn't say. She couldn't go to sleep without knowing if Jaden was alive or dead.

"He hasn't come back. It's a good forty-five minute drive from that shack to here."

"Wasn't it just him and the Shadow? Jaden should've been

able to take that bastard down." The male paused. "You don't think anything happened, do you?"

Alice's heart sank. John-Paul had taken her happiness again. Despite her attempts to keep Jaden safe, her love had killed him.

Silent sobs wracked her body. Catherine's version of pain was nothing compared to the huge gaping hole in her chest. Helene and the others had saved her life. Now she wished they'd let her go.

"Ryder, shut up! You're making it worse." Helene's voice was soft in her ear. "Alice, calm down. Everything's going to be okay. You know Jaden's too stubborn to die."

The hell it was. She lost the one person who mattered the most to her and now had to find the strength to live, when the one she loved was dead.

A door opened and closed. Helene's hand disappeared and Alice's fingers twitched at the loss of heat. At least something worked on her.

Strong fingers laced with hers. Alice sucked in a deep breath as fresh tears sprang to her eyes. A single tear escaped and rolled down her cheek.

"Hey, don't cry. Everything's okay," Jaden's voice rumbled in her ear. "I'm right here."

God, she hoped she wasn't hallucinating. She had to see him for herself. She had to open her damn eyes and see he really was there next to her.

Alice's lids fluttered for a moment before she forced them open. The overhead light seared her eyes and she closed them quickly, the illumination making her headache worse. She tried again, the lids slowly peeling back.

This time someone was kind enough to turn off the lamp. A couple of candles flickered instead which was fine with her.

She blinked a couple of times and his face came into view. She really wasn't imagining things. He was right beside her.

Jaden smiled at her as he stroked her cheek. "Hey baby."

Relief rushed through her as more tears fell down her face. John-Paul and Catherine hadn't hurt him. By some miracle, they both made it through this hellish night and survived.

"Hey, let's have none of that," he murmured, kissing away her tears. "I'm fine and you're going to be okay. So there's no reason to cry."

Was he kidding? They were alive and together. She had every reason to cry.

He stroked her cheek and shifted back from her. "You need to sleep."

Raw terror seized her as the warmth of him started to fade. She squeezed his hand tighter. He couldn't leave her alone. Now that he was here, she didn't want to be left alone in the dark.

She opened her mouth, but only a croak came out. She swallowed hard, but her mouth and throat had turned to ash.

"Shh, I'm not going to leave you. I'll come right back." Jaden kissed her cheek. "I promise."

It didn't matter to her if he was gone five seconds. She didn't want him to go.

"Stay," she mumbled. Her tongue was so thick, she was surprised she could speak at all. But she wanted to make sure Jaden would stay with her. "I...don't want...to be...alone."

"You're not alone. Helene and Ryder are here."

"They're not you." She stared into those beautiful blue eyes. "Please, don't go."

"Shh." Jaden put his finger against her lip and smiled. "I'll stay with you. But only if you sleep. Your body needs to heal. Deal?"

"I'll sleep as long as you stay," she whispered.

He climbed in next to her, lying on top of the covers. He settled her into the crook of his arm while she tucked her hand around his waist. Alice latched on to him tighter as the warmth of his body seeped into hers. Now that she had him back, she wouldn't let him go.

This time, she'd hold on to him and hope Helene had told her the truth. That Jaden loved her as much as she loved him.

I love you.

She wasn't sure if she said them out loud, but her exhaustion took hold. She closed her eyes and gratefully fell into darkness.

~ * ~

Jaden brushed a few tendrils of her chocolate brown hair off her forehead. Looking down at the woman he held, he knew he never cared for Catherine the way he loved Alice. Catherine had loved him with conditions. Alice accepted him as he was.

And she wasn't afraid to say it out loud. He and the other warriors heard the whisper as if she had shouted it. He had her love. In return, she owned his heart, body and soul.

The tattoos burned on his wrists, writhing underneath the cuff of his sweater. This was his female. His mate. His body knew it as surely as his heart.

He wanted nothing more than to hold her in his arms, but he had some loose ends to tie up. And deal with Liam. That shit wasn't going to be pretty.

He backed away from the bed and looked at the other warriors. Ryder looked tired from his efforts to heal Alice. Helene remained impassive. Salvatore stood in the hallway, keeping his eyes and ears open for Varrik.

"Will you stay with her for a few more minutes?" Jaden

asked Ryder.

"You're going to come back in one piece? I saw what you did to Varrik." Ryder shook his head. "Liam will kill you for this."

"No, he won't."

"You sound awfully sure about that."

"When he hears what I have to say, he'll have no choice but to keep me alive."

Ryder nodded. "I'll stay with her until you come back."

He and Helene left the room and Salvatore followed close behind. Jaden didn't need an escort in his own home, but he was too tired to argue. He wanted to get this over with so he could be with Alice.

They headed down the stairs silently and banked right, heading for the entry hallway. All three walked into the room, their eyes going straight to Liam and Varrik.

Jaden knew he should feel some remorse for what he did Varrik, but he felt nothing. In his mind, the bastard had it coming. As Guardian, he could use whatever means necessary to keep her safe, even murdering a fellow warrior. Luckily for Varrik, it hadn't come to that.

He was healing quickly, the left eye not nearly as swollen as when Jaden left, the split lip almost mended back together. The arm was still in a sling from where Jaden had broken it. Varrik's breathing was labored, indicating that the fractured ribs hadn't even started to heal.

But that was nothing compared to what he did to Varrik emotionally. Jaden made the male relive the death of his daughter and grandchild. Jaden knew how crazed he looked because Helene and Salvatore were too shocked to intervene. The pain had been unbearable and that's what finally forced Varrik to tell him where Alice was.

Liam turned around from the fireplace. "Is the human still alive?"

"She's resting in my room."

"And yet you traded her life for the Host's," Liam growled. "I'm sure you have an excellent reason because I want to kill you right now."

"The Host won't be leaving the area anytime soon."

"I didn't know you could predict the future."

Jaden met Liam's glare. "The Host is Catherine Payne. You remember her, don't you? A frigid bitch yet very good with her mind?"

"You're shitting me." Liam stared at him for a long moment. "Catherine? As in your supposedly dead wife?"

"The very one."

"How the fuck is she still alive?"

"I didn't have time to ask her that."

"She knows how we operate. Our strengths and weaknesses." He looked at Catherine's portrait hanging over the fireplace. "She is alive and she is working against us. This is a fucking nightmare."

"Yes, she knows about us, but we've changed so much in six hundred years," Jaden said.

"Anything she knows about us is a possible breach of our defenses," Liam snapped.

"I learned that firsthand. She confessed that she was the one who decided to kill off the eldest members of our family."

Liam was quiet for a moment as the truth sank in. "She killed the last Master?"

"She was smiling when she told me."

"And you had the chance to avenge your father's death, but you let her go." He paced back and forth, the rage about to explode. "You let her get away. How the hell could you do that?"

"I had no choice."

"Goddamn it, Jaden! You were thinking with your dick and not your brain," Liam shouted. "I want to know why Catherine isn't dead when you had the chance to kill her again!"

"I was doing the job you told me to do which was to protect the woman in the prophecy." Jaden glanced up at the ceiling. "I swore to keep her alive and so I have. That was what you wanted me to do."

"And Varrik? You're breaking all the rules tonight," Liam said. "You want to tell me why you turned him into a piñata? You know the penalty of attacking one of your own is death."

Jaden glanced at Varrik. Fights were common amongst the warriors as a way to let off steam and frustration. But Jaden launched an all out attack on his fellow warrior and that was a treasonous offense.

Under his law, he should die. The only reason why he was still standing was because of his link to his father and because of his guardianship of Alice.

"He kept me away from Alice. Since you put me in charge of her safety, I used whatever means necessary to keep her alive. I had no choice but to beat some sense into him until he told me where she was." He nodded to Helene and Salvatore. "Ask them if you don't believe me. They were there."

Liam looked at Varrik. "Is this true?"

"She asked me not to disclose her location," Varrik muttered.

"So that would be a yes," Liam said. "Why would you listen to a human?"

"Because she was trying to save me," Jaden answered. "She didn't want any of us, much less me, to get caught up in Catherine's games. She didn't want any of us to die for her."

He met Liam's scowl. "But more importantly, she's the Firebrand we've been looking for."

The silence in the room was deafening. Varrik, Salvatore, Helene, and Liam just stared at him.

"The Firebrand?" Liam repeated. "You're absolutely sure about this?"

"Are you going senile? You told me to protect her."

"I said she might be the woman in the prophecy."

"Alice is the Firebrand. I saw it with my own eyes. The glowing skin, the ability to reduce a body to ash, moving from place to place because of her blackouts."

"And she did all this while still human?" Liam shook his head. "Damn, she's powerful."

"We need her to harness her energy. She could destroy the whole eastern seaboard if we're not careful." Jaden raised his hands. "I can teach her how to control her power. She won't hurt me. She had the chance to do it tonight when she was in her true form and she begged me to help her."

"You're asking a lot of me right now, you know that?"

"You know I'll be able to keep her safe."

"But that's only a part of the reason. You want her as your mate. You think I can't see that?"

"And as her mate, I'll be duty bound to protect her. Isn't that what you want me to do as Guardian? Now I will be able to keep an extra close eye on her."

"Like it's going to be only your eyes on her." Liam rubbed his temples for a few minutes. "The only reason I'm not going to do anything to you is because you followed my orders in making sure the Firebrand stayed alive."

Jaden grinned. "It's killing you to say it, isn't it?"

"Don't push me tonight. I'm about to fucking lose it over here and I don't need you to be such a prick." He shook his head in amazement. "I can't believe we have a Firebrand. We can finally take down that bitch Catherine and all of the Shadows with her."

"Alice is more than just a Firebrand and a tool to be used in our war. She's also my mate."

"You are so screwed. Then again, you might be the right man for the job," Liam said. "You'll have to move back to the compound, you know that? This place isn't completely secure."

Jaden gritted his teeth. He hated living under Liam's thumb, but the vampire was right. Alice would be much safer in the compound than in this house.

"Once she's well, we'll be there."

"I'll inform the Sisters of what happened. They will be pleased to know we were successful in acquiring the Firebrand." He looked at the other warriors. "We'll meet at the camp tomorrow night and discuss our next move. Right now, rest up. I have a feeling we're going to be in for one hell of a fight."

Everyone left, except for Varrik. He stood in front of Jaden, the malice evident in his black eyes.

Jaden closed his mind off to the warrior. There was no way he'd let Varrik read his mind. Especially since he was thinking of Alice and how he just wanted to be with her.

The vampire stared at Jaden with his good eye. "For the record, I hate you."

"I understand your hate and I'd want me dead too if I were you," Jaden said.

"You are such an evil bastard to make me relive that day," Varrik choked out. "Of everything I've done, everything in my life, that one day has haunted me more than you know, and you used it against me. You made me watch them die again. I will never forgive you for that."

"It was wrong, but Alice is alive. I can't apologize for that."

"I can't understand why that human loves you. She knows what an asshole you are and she still wants you."

"I'm not an asshole to her. I'm someone who loves her. Someone who will kill anyone and anything to protect her."

Varrik narrowed his uninjured eye. "Although a part of me wishes I could kill you myself, I'm glad that Liam didn't sentence you to die. I can't collect any favors if you're dead."

"And I will honor whatever request you make of me."

Varrik nodded and limped past him. Whatever favor Varrik had in mind would be huge, but Jaden would do it. It was the least he could do after Jaden reminded him of the death of Varrik's family.

He looked at the portrait of Catherine again. That woman was no longer his wife, no longer someone he cared about. Alice was the wife he wanted. A woman who was his equal, his partner, and loved him with her whole heart.

He grabbed the portrait and yanked it off the wall. He tossed the whole thing, frame and canvas, into the massive fireplace and watched it burned. Catherine was the past and he needed no reminders of her in his life. Alice was the present and future.

Jaden ran up the steps and checked on her. Ryder held her hand, his eyes closed in concentration. Jealousy coursed through Jaden as Ryder stroked her rosy skin. Yes, he was healing her, but it didn't stop the possessive instinct to rip Ryder's hands from Alice's body.

He shifted his eyes to her face. Her breathing was even, her lips parted slightly as she dreamed. Her head lolled to the side and faced him. Even asleep, she knew where he was.

Jaden left them to quickly shower and change. He barely

finished wiping the water off his body before he threw on a pair of loose black pants, anxious to get back to his Alice.

The fireproof cabinet was still open from where he grabbed his weapons earlier. He secured his guns and blades inside the safe. He was about to shut it when he looked at the thin black box against one wall.

He pulled it out, his palms marring the shiny surface. He remembered the day his father gave him this present. It was two weeks after he changed Catherine and the mating was incomplete.

"Use this on your female," his father said. *"A symbol of trust. Let her hold it in her hand as you lay there. Whether to plunge it into your heart or take from you vein, be at her mercy. Show her the depths of your love and of your trust."*

Jaden had never placed that trust in Catherine. He'd done that tonight with Alice when he gave her his gun. No resistance, no flinching. He waited for her to kill him so she could live.

He would do it again. Alice was his world. And he'd do whatever it took to keep her in it.

He tucked the box under his arm and headed to Alice's room. She looked so small and pale on the bed. Ryder sat next to her. He didn't look so great either. With the exception of Jaden, Liam, and Salvatore, vampires that used their powers for an extended period of time became weak themselves.

"How is she?" Jaden asked as he stopped at the bed.

"She'll make it," Ryder said, opening his eyes. "She's a fighter."

"Yes, she is. And stubborn as hell too."

"She's a good woman and she'll make an excellent warrior," he said, standing up. "She deserves a happy life. I think you can give her that."

"Dawn will be here soon," Jaden reminded him. "I don't want you staying the whole day. My female and I need to be alone. Understood?"

"Loud and clear." Ryder grabbed his jacket off the chair. "Glad to see she hasn't completely changed you. You're still a surly bastard."

"Goodbye, Ryder. And thanks for what you did tonight."

"Just watching out for a fellow warrior." Ryder grinned. "She's one of us now. Or soon will be. I'll see you at Liam's later."

Jaden made sure all the locks were in place and activated the security system before he slipped into bed with Alice. He tucked Alice in the crook of his arm, her head resting on his chest.

She stirred against him. "Jaden?"

"I'm right here," he said, stroking her cheek. "Go back to sleep, baby."

She shifted, burrowing further in his embrace. Her hair fanned over his chest and he leaned down, inhaling deeply to let himself fall into that heavenly cinnamon scent.

She tightened her arm around his waist, falling back asleep. He eyed the box on the table as he stroked her hair. He only hoped that once she woke up, she wouldn't plunge the dagger into his heart.

Chapter 27

Varrik slid the lock on the door to his spacious basement apartment as the inky darkness shielded him from dawn's first light. He didn't have enough time to make it to his rooms back at Liam's place so he had no choice but to come to his city hideaway.

He heard several humans refer to his three room apartment as a bachelor pad--with the sixty inch flat screen television, endless collection of DVDs, and a sound system that could blow the roof off his building. But it was all for show. He had everything here for his donors to entertain themselves before he called them back to his bed.

To him, it was his own space where he could feed and fuck as much as he wanted. The soundproof concrete walls muffled the cries of the females who shouted his name when they orgasmed and if needed--a temporary holding cell for Shadows before Jaden interrogated them.

No one knew about this place and he preferred it that way. It was his personal paradise. Or in today's case, his personal hell.

He dragged his weary body through the bedroom, bypassing the bed for the shower. God, he needed the rest, but he wanted to the clean the blood off his body as well. He stood under the shower's spray for a good hour, the heat stinging his skin like needles. He welcomed the sensation, but it didn't quite reach the coldness in his heart.

He wanted to go after Jaden. He wanted the bastard to feel every ounce of pain by hurting Alice, but he kind of liked Alice and it wasn't her fault her mate was a maniacal asshole. Not only that, if he went after Jaden, he would be put to death. Period. He didn't have the purebred lineage or the distinction of being a Guardian to justify his actions.

Jaden owed him. Big time. The best thing to do would be to put the vampire at his mercy and extract whatever pound of flesh he could when the time was right.

Varrik wrapped a towel around his waist and looked at himself in the mirror. In this space, he didn't look like the cavalier man-whore they believed him to be. His blue-black hair was slicked back and his lips were pressed together in a grim line. His onyx eyes were flat and sunken in his skull. The stubble along his jaw lent an added ruggedness to his looks which normally attracted both human and vampire females, but today, he looked tired and rough. Not to mention, the bruises and split lip made him look like he was in the bar fight from hell.

Varrik headed to his bed, falling onto the down comforter. He'd have to feed once the sun set. He could easily convince one of the women who lived a few floors above him to come down, but he was too tired to put forth the effort to get her here.

He turned on his side and opened the nightstand. Rummaging around, he finally found what he was looking for. He pulled the weathered photograph from the drawer. A sepia picture of a woman, her eyes sparkling as she smiled for the picture, her light hair falling to the small of her back. She rested her hand on her stomach swollen with the life she carried inside it, the happiness in her face was a warmth he had not felt or seen for close to one hundred and thirty years.

"Irina. Lucian," he whispered. *"Bucuria mea, lumina mea."*

My joy. My light.

Both of them gone in less than an hour. Sixty minutes separated them from life and death and he lost them both. And Jaden reminded Varrik how powerless he was to prevent their deaths.

He held the photograph to his chest and cried.

Chapter 28

Alice was thoroughly satisfied, surrounded in a cocoon of heat that made her feel whole. Content. And to top it all off, her head had finally stopped hurting, thank God. She was sure one of Jaden's friends had healed her. There was no way she could rebound from Catherine's mind control so quickly or her blackout without a little vampire booster.

She nestled deeper into all that warmth and felt the arm around her waist tighten. A hand caressed her cheek and she turned her face to those gentle fingers. Jaden had stayed with her, his touch soothing her as she slept.

His thumb ran across her lips and she parted her mouth. She sighed and kissed his fingertips. Yeah, she wasn't opening her eyes anytime soon.

"You don't do this in your sleep." She heard Jaden's chuckle rumble in his chest. "I know you're awake."

"If my eyes are closed, then I'm still asleep."

"Reality is better than fantasy."

"I don't know. I'm feeling pretty good right now." His hand glided down her arm and she let out a little moan. "I like where this dream is headed. I might end up naked."

"I'm really here. And if you want to be naked, I can take care of that right now."

She moved her hand across his stomach. Oh, he wasn't wearing a shirt. This was a fantastic dream. Except for the talking. She'd rather have more kissing and touching.

"Open your eyes, Alice."

She shook her head and squeezed them tighter.

"Why won't you look at me?"

"I'm afraid if I open my eyes, you won't be here. I'll be in my apartment or..." Alice shuddered and turned her face into his chest. "Somewhere else. And I don't want you to be gone."

"I swear to you that you're with me at my house." He pulled her across him, her body on top of his. "See? I'm here."

"Of course you're staying with me. It's my dream." She sighed in contentment. "Try telling me something I don't know."

There was a long pause. "I love you."

Alice's eyes flew open. That was something she definitely didn't know. She sat up so fast her head swam. She grabbed on to his biceps to steady herself as his face came back into focus.

"I'm sorry, but I don't think I heard you correctly," she said. "What did you just say?"

"I think you heard me the first time, but I don't mind saying it again." Those pale blue eyes were tender, but serious. "I love you, Alice Roarke."

Alice couldn't wrap her mind around his words. Only her ex-boyfriend had told her that, but it was after the abduction and more of a courtesy. To hear it from someone as powerful and virile as Jaden was unbelievable.

Alice looked away from him. It was too good to be true. It couldn't be real.

"You don't have to say them to me just because I said them to you," she said quietly.

"I wouldn't tell you I love you if I didn't mean it."

"This is the dream, isn't it?" she insisted. "My eyes are open, but I'm still asleep."

He turned her head so he could see her eyes. "Why are you so surprised? Why is it so hard to believe that?"

"Because no one has ever wanted me," she blurted out. "My foster parents, friends, no one. And no man has ever wanted me like you say you do."

"All those other males are assholes. And quite frankly, I'm thrilled they didn't want you. Because I would kill any man who would even think about looking at you with lust in his eyes." He kissed the tip of her nose. "I love your strength, your sass. I love how you take care of me and worry about my safety. But most of all, I love how you make me burn. You don't hide from the darkness inside of me or curse me for it. You make me feel again and I've been empty for so long. I don't want to lose this feeling you stir inside of me." He ran his fingertip across her lips. "Or more importantly – you."

A tear rolled down her cheek. "You love me."

"Enough for you to let you shoot me," he added. "Trust me. There are plenty of people who want to take a shot at me. They'd be so pissed you missed your chance."

"Why doesn't that surprise me?" Alice laughed as she wiped the tears from her eyes. "Besides, I was thinking about shooting you."

"You were?"

"Yeah. I'm still angry you ran me off the road."

"I'll find some way to make it up to you," he said, grinning.

"Hmm. I'm sure I can think of some way to get rid of my anger. You being shirtless is definitely calming my anger."

"I wonder how you'll feel when I'm totally naked."

"Take off the rest of your clothes and you'll find out."

"I don't want to live my life without you." He placed a soft kiss on her lips. "But to me, it doesn't matter where we are as long as you're with me. Because you are home."

She wrapped her arms around him. "I know this is going to sound horrible, but I'm so glad Catherine hates you."

"So am I. If she didn't, then I never would've met you."

"But where does this leave us? How are we going to have any kind of life when I'm different from you?"

The humor left his eyes and it was replaced with concern. "You're different from everyone." He tucked a strand of hair behind her ear. "You know that."

"I've had a lot happen to me."

"Besides that. Your life's never been normal, Alice. You have never been normal."

"Way to sweet talk a girl, Jaden." She thumped his chest. "You sure do know how to lay it on. But I think you might need a little work."

"Your mother died at birth, right? The pregnancy didn't kill her because you used her body the way my kind uses humans as donors. When she gave birth to you, her body could no longer function and she died." He caressed her cheek. "The same thing is happening to you. Your body can't handle the power inside of you. You're human, but you have a vampire's powers. It's what's killing you."

"I'm perfectly healthy."

"No one has blackouts for no reason," he said gently. "You're dying. You just don't know it."

"I'm human. I have a shorter shelf life than you."

"Alice, I saw it firsthand last night. You're not an ordinary human. Technically, you're not human."

"Why?" She leaned away from him. "Because of the blackouts? I've had those since I was a kid. That's all it is."

"When did you have them?" he asked. "Did you have them

all the time, or was there a trigger?"

"They didn't happen all the time. They only…" Her voice trailed off.

"Keep going." He squeezed her hand to continue. "Only when?"

"They only happened when I was terrified."

"Do you remember the first time it happened?"

"I was six," she said absently. "One of the older kids – her name was Debra – threatened to take my favorite stuffed tiger. Debra said she was going to get me later that night and I was so scared to close my eyes. I thought I had fallen asleep, but when I opened my eyes, I was in the hospital."

"What about the other girl?"

"Debra was in the burn unit. She had second and third degree burns on her hands and arms and was there for two weeks. They couldn't figure out why she was on the floor screaming and I was passed out. She told everyone it was my fault she was burned, but no one would believe her." Alice chewed on her lip. "It really was me, wasn't it?"

"It was an accident."

"She has to carry those scars around for the rest of her life." She laughed harshly. "Kind of like me."

"Alice, it wasn't your fault. The blackouts are because you can't control the power inside of you. It's triggered by fear and it controls everything you do. Once you learn to control it, you won't black out again." His blue eyes were warm, tender. "How do you think you escaped from John-Paul? You knew he was going to kill you and the power you have freed you." He stroked her arm. "You are the Firebrand. As a human, you're weak, but if you're like me, you'll have unbelievable powers. Actually, you'll be stronger than me. You will have the ability to destroy our enemies."

She shook her head vehemently. "No. I don't want to be the thing you say I am."

"You can't help who you are."

"I can't be!" Her eyes filled with tears again. "But I don't want hurt anyone. I just want to be with you."

"You have me, Alice. I won't abandon you. I swear it," he said and kissed her forehead. "And you don't have to learn your powers on your own. I'll teach you how to control it. Then you can decide if you ever want to use it."

She chewed on her lip. "I changed last night, didn't I?"

"Yes, you did. You dusted a Shadow in front of my eyes. Completely turned him to ash."

"Did I do anything to you?"

"Nothing at all. You were terrifying, but still beautiful. You were in a whole lot of pain and you asked me to help you." He leaned forward and kissed her. "I trust you not to hurt me. Do you trust me?"

"Of course I do."

"Then I only have one more question for you." His hands fell from her waist and landed on the mattress. "How long do you want me?"

She glanced down at his hands, palms down. He didn't want to touch her. Because he wanted her to make the decision on her own, with no influence on his part.

Love swelled in her chest. She knew in her heart what she wanted as she looked in his pale blue eyes.

"For as long as you'll have me. I love you, Jaden Payne. I don't want to imagine one second of my life without you."

~ * ~

He gripped the covers tightly, his heart pounding in his chest. "You have no idea how long I've waited to hear you say something like this."

"Why?"

"I've never had love until you came into my life. I never thought I'd find you."

Alice straddled his hips, her hands framing his face. "Now that you've found me, what are you planning to do with me?"

"I can think of several things. All of them involve you losing your shirt."

She lifted her arms over her head. "So what are you waiting for?"

She sighed as he removed her shirt, his hands reaching up to cup her breasts. His thumbs flicked her nipples, the buds tightened in his palms. Sitting on his lap in just her black panties made him hunger for her. His sex inflated, a hard staff that wanted in now. She gave him a knowing smile and rolled her hips, grinding against his erection.

He leaned forward and pulled her nipple between his lips. She arched her back, her body warming from his kiss.

"I don't want to lose you," she breathed.

"You won't. I'm not going anywhere."

"Last time I checked, I had an expiration date. With or without this firebrand thing inside of me," she said. "You don't."

"What if I could fix that for you? Would you want it?"

She didn't even hesitate with her answer. "Yes."

He pulled back. "Are you really sure about this? Because once it's done, it can't be undone."

"I'll have to drink blood, right? Troll for humans?"

Jaden chuckled. "That won't be necessary."

"Isn't that what you do? Or will I be knocking over blood banks to score a couple of pints of B positive?"

"If we're mates, you'll only drink from me." He smiled with an edge as he caught the honeyed scent of her arousal. "I take it that doesn't bother you."

"What about you? Will you only drink from me?"

"Yes."

She frowned slightly. "But why drink from humans if you can drink from your own kind?"

"Because it's an exchange of life," he said. "I'm taking a part of you into me, just as you take a part of me into you. We are giving each other what we need in order to survive. With humans, it's one-sided and impersonal. When it's between mates, it's private and very personal."

"I don't have to think about it. My life is with you."

He growled low in his throat. She wanted to be his mate. And there was only one thing left to do.

He reached over and held the black lacquered box in front of her. She hesitantly touched the top, but he nodded told her to continue. She opened the lid and gasped.

Inside was a sapphire-handled dagger. The hilt had intricate scrollwork, similar to Jaden's tattoos. The blade was made of polished obsidian and so clear that she could see her reflection.

She took it out and held it in her hand. "What's this for?"

"For you. You need to cut me."

She flinched. "Cut you? Why?"

"You have to." He turned his head, exposing his throat. "It's a part of the mating."

She glanced down at the knife. "What do we have to do?"

"We've already completed a part of it. Remember when you washed me?

A slight flush crept across her cheeks and he grinned. Oh yeah, they both remembered that bath. As soon as they finished the mating, he was going to pull her back into the tub with him.

"You bathed me and declared your love for me. Now all

that's left is the marking."

"What's that?"

He hesitated. This was the part he was the most concerned about. "A piece of me is marked on you."

"Not your blood?" Alice asked, confused.

"That only changes you internally. It awakens the vampire gene in you, but it doesn't bind us together." His thumb caressed her scarred wrist. "But the tattoos on my wrists do. They tell other males that you are my mate and I belong to you. It's the vampire version of a wedding band."

"Will it hurt?"

"I won't let it hurt you." He kissed her wrists. "I'll take the pain away."

He held his breath for a moment as her eyes locked on the tattoos. A mark to show others that Jaden was her mate. Only this one could be worn with pride and not shame. He hoped she'd see it that way.

"Love me, Jaden," she moaned against his mouth. "Make me yours."

She surged forward and then undulated against his shaft. Jaden nearly came from the sheer pleasure of it, but he needed to hold off a little longer.

He turned his head, exposing his throat. He sucked her skin, scratching her with his fangs. He brought her hand to his throat, lightly pressing the dagger against his neck.

"Cut me," he whispered and stared into her eyes. "Take from me."

She drew the blade down the smooth column of his throat. He groaned at the slice of pain and he gripped her hips, pushing himself into her, the head pushing towards home through the barrier of their clothes.

She leaned closer and caught a rivulet of blood as it ran

down his neck. Her tongue lapped it up and trailed back to the puncture, latching on tightly, taking deep pulls into her mouth.

Jaden's eyes rolled into the back of his head. Now he knew why his people did this naked. The sound of her taking his life into her body was a huge fucking aphrodisiac.

He cradled her head in his hand as she continued to drink. His hand caressed her spine and her breasts rubbed against his chest. Holy shit, she was so hot. Her skin on fire from his blood, her love for him.

She leaned back, her mouth slightly parted and that's when he saw them. Her canines sharpened and he saw the tips of her fangs.

She dropped the knife and repositioned her head. She wasn't through with him yet.

Jaden barked out a curse as she pierced his throat. He hissed in pleasure as she unbuttoned his fly, springing his erection. One hand cradled his throat while the other palmed the hard length of him, his sex kicking in her grip, hot as a flame as she stroked him from base to tip.

Jaden's own fangs punched out of his mouth. He returned the bite and sank his teeth into the smooth skin. She jerked in his arms, pausing for a moment before she went back to pumping him off with her hand. Jaden's mouth clamped down on her throat, his mouth latching on to her vein.

The scent of cinnamon invaded his head, making him dizzy. Thick and warm, her blood was a powerful, rich elixir and he reeled from the flavor. Never had a woman tasted as delicious as Alice. And her blood mingled with his, each giving the other life.

Their blood.

One blood.

Mates.

His wrists burned, the ink undulating on his wrists. She moaned and pulled him closer, her breasts flattened against his hard chest. Jaden locked his hands with hers as she continued to drink. He licked the side of her neck and trailed kisses from the bite to her shoulder. She arched in his grasp, breaking away from his throat. Her tongue glided across the punctures instinctively, sealing the wounds.

He caught his lips with hers and pushed his tongue into her mouth. It was a fevered, desperate twirl, as if she was trying to get inside any way she could.

Alice let Jaden roll her on to her back, his fingers still laced with hers. The serpentine swirls lifted off his wrists and inched closer to Alice's. It was like someone was shaving his skin with a paring knife an inch at a time. The tattoos slowly made their way to Alice's wrists and he saw the skin reddening from the contact.

Jaden turned his attention to Alice, reducing the pain and focusing on her pleasure. He moved past her collarbone, her sternum and kissed the side of her breast. He blew one hot breath across her nipple before he took it into his mouth. She cried out as he suckled her, straining against his wrists, her body screaming for more. He pulled back staring into those vibrant, emerald pools.

"Is it done?" she asked breathlessly.

He glanced at her wrists. The skin was still tender, but the tattoos were in place. He was hers.

"It's over. We are mates, Alice Roarke."

Jaden already sensed the changes in her body. Her muscles quivered and flexed, his blood giving her the strength she needed to survive. He caressed her wrists, igniting her desire.

Alice placed her palms on Jaden's face. Her eyes fell to her wrists and she gasped. On top of the scarred, reddened skin were Jaden's tattoos. The beautiful swirls that she traced on his back and wrists were now on her. A part of her.

"Everyone will know that I am yours," he murmured, "and you are mine."

She caught his hand and saw the raw skin of his wrist. Concern flashed in her eyes. "Does it hurt?"

"I'm fine."

"It has to be tender," she protested.

"I don't care if I have to do this every damn day. It means I have you. That's all that matters and that's all I want."

"I'd hate for you to be hurt because of me." Alice brought his wrist to her mouth, her tongue stroking the skin. "Does this feel any better?"

"That feels amazing." His eyes darkened as the tip of her tongue moved further down his chest, circling his nipple. "Like I said, you have a magic touch that makes the pain go away."

He wrapped himself around her, falling into her warm embrace. He no longer felt cold and empty and like he had no place he belonged. This was what he always wanted and where he wanted to be. In her arms, he finally found a place to call home.

ACKNOWLEDGMENTS

First and foremost, the biggest thanks go to YOU, the reader. Thank you for allowing Jaden, Alice and the Emain Macha to enter your lives.

A shout out to my Sanguine Sirens! Theresa C., Claire W., Wendy H., Jessica J., Ginger W., Bekki C. and Ann C: your support and enthusiasm, especially with the early drafts, kept me going when I felt like giving up. You are all epic people to me!

Thank you to Dare to Dream Editing for your awesome eye and for catching all of my errors as well as Okay Creations for creating a beautiful cover for this book!

Much love to my family, especially my parents, who urged me to write even when my tales bordered on strange, terrifying, and bizarre. You supported my dreams, and it's because of this encouragement that led to the creation of my stories. Thank you for believing in me when I didn't believe in myself.

ABOUT THE AUTHOR

Aislin Keeley was born in New Orleans, Louisiana and eventually transplanted herself in Atlanta, Georgia. She loves nothing more than cool, November days while curling up on her couch with a cup of coffee and a good book. She lives close to her family with her literary kitties Oreo, Shadow, and Peewee to keep her company. When she's not writing, she enjoys reading, listening to symphonic metal, and finding new recipes to bake for her family and friends.

For more information on upcoming releases, blogs and events, visit the following websites below.

- www.aislinkeeley.weebly.com
- www.facebook.com/aislinkeeley

www.ingramcontent.com/pod-product-compliance
Lightning Source LLC
Chambersburg PA
CBHW020225180626
46810CB00006B/2056